HIS WICKED
SEDUCTION

Regency Hearts Redeemed Series

Book Two

Jade Lee

USA Today Bestselling Author

Book design by eBook Prep www.ebookprep.com
Cover by The Killion Group www.thekilliongroupinc.com

October, 2015
ISBN: 978-1-61417-789-0

ePublishing Works!
www.epublishingworks.com

REVIEWS & ACCOLADES

THE
REGENCY HEARTS REDEEMED
SERIES

Her Wicked Surrender
His Wicked Seduction

ALSO BY JADE LEE

The Regency Rags to Riches Series
No Place for a Lady
Devil's Bargain
Almost an Angel
The Dragon Earl

A Lady's Lessons Series
Rules for a Lady
Major Wyclyff's campaign
Miss Woodley's Kissing Experiment

PROLOGUE

One English boy shackled to the mast. That's what Kit Frazier saw as he crept over the side of the slave ship. One boy of about seventeen years, feet tied with rope, arms shackled with iron. There was blood dripping to the deck too, but Kit couldn't see from what wound.

Bloody hell, this was a trap.

He wasn't sure what tipped him off. Everything was silent. The man on watch stood like a statue on the foredeck, not even bothering to whistle. Kit cocked his ear toward the hold. No sobs. No low moans. So, no slaves trapped below either. Just the one English adolescent, his dirty blond hair a mat that obscured his face.

Kit crept around the edge, slipping through shadows. He'd spent years on this boat as a slave, and coming back now made his hands slick with sweat. If he had any sense, he'd turn and run now before it was too late. What did he care that another English aristocrat had been abducted for ransom? But once, long ago, he'd been chained to the mast, waiting for a ransom that never came. He couldn't leave this boy to the same fate.

A flash of yellow teeth caught his attention. Kit froze, peering into the blackness, waiting until he heard a telltale pop of knuckles. That had to be Abdur, the one who like to whip the children. Kit smiled. Suddenly he didn't care if it was a trap so long as he could strike against the nightmare of Venboer's slave ship.

Kit crouched, wiped the sweat from his hands, then struck. After four years as a free man, he was faster than Abdur. And stronger too. The bastard collapsed to the deck. Kit even remembered to cushion his fall so that all was done in silence. Then he looked around. One down, how many more?

Three that he could see, spaced behind barrels set much too obviously along the rail. Perfect spacing from which to attack. Not so good for defense. Kit slipped behind each one, his panic easing now that he was in action. One by one, they fell. Easily done, but it took too much time.

Kit looked around again. The boy had raised his head to listen. Sharp ears that one, but was he smart? Would he know to keep quiet until Kit could effect a rescue? Taking a huge risk, Kit slid Abdur's knife across the deck, wincing at the sound. Not so loud, but not so quiet either. And sadly, no help against the shackles. But at least the boy would be able to defend himself while Kit went in search of the key. Or a heavy axe.

The boy didn't appear to move as the blade settled against his leg. But a blink later, the knife was gone and he was drooping more where he sat, presumably so he could cut the rope at his ankles. So. The kid was smart too.

Kit began to creep toward the forecastle. The slave key was kept…

Three figures stepped out of the shadows, two large men flanking their very large captain. Kit spun around. Two more men stepped behind him, one of them the watchman who had jumped down to join the fray. Five to one with the boy still chained to the mast.

Hell.

Then a miracle happened. The boy stood up, his iron shackles dropping to the deck with a clang. Kit raised his eyebrows in surprise. Apparently, he was rescuing a lockpick. Which narrowed the odds to five against two. Better, though he doubted the boy really knew how to fight. Still, things were definitely looking up. Especially since he could see the boy's wounds now. Swollen face from a beating, jagged cut along his arm, but nothing that would keep him from swimming to safety.

"I knew you would come," Venboer gloated and Kit slid his attention back to the bastard who had destroyed so many lives, Kit's included. "He looks like you, yes?"

Kit shifted into the cocky drawl that he knew irritated Venboer. "We English are a pretty lot."

The bastard released a growl, low in his throat. It took a moment for Kit to realize he was trying to chuckle. "He will do well in the dens, I think. Pretty enough for the women, but strong enough to be used by men."

To the side, the boy stiffened in horror, his jaw clenched tight. Kit too had to repress his visceral response. He'd seen what happened to the pretty ones in the dens. Some things were worse than death, and that was one of them. Meanwhile, Kit tried to appear as if he weren't choosing between death and worse than death. "No one paid the ransom then?"

Venboer shrugged. "Not enough."

"How much? Maybe I'll buy him," Kit drawled as he turned to inspect the boy. It was a ruse. He didn't have near enough to buy a slave, but it gave him an excuse to catch the prisoner's eyes. With a tiny flick of his eyes, he indicated the far rail. That was their best escape, assuming the boy could swim. He took a step forward. "He looks a little sickly—"

Venboer's men attacked. The bastard never had been one for idle chat. Kit had been ready for it but hoping to get in a better position first. No time now as the back two men suddenly lunged. They were trained sailors, well versed in sea fighting, and armed with cutlasses. Kit, on the other hand, had only his daggers, which were light enough for swimming and little use against a large, heavy sword. But at least the boy could escape.

Kit leaped aside, then began the game of feint and dash while simultaneously listening for Venboer's other men behind him. He narrowly missed being gutted, but was being slowly, steadily pushed back into Venboer and his other two men.

Hell. He was running out of time. His two attackers had slowed down, stepping sideways in order to flank him better. It was now or never. Kit abruptly spun around, giving his back to his attackers while he threw.

Venboer's first mate fell to the ground, a knife sticking from his throat. Kit didn't allow himself the time to even smile. Later he would relish the satisfaction that the man who had beaten him nightly for months was finally dead. Right now, while the others were gaping at the first mate, Kit spun back and threw again. The one closest to the boy dropped.

The boy? Bloody hell! The idiot was supposed to be over the side now and swimming for his life. But no, in an admirable show of bravery, the kid was lifting the dead man's cutlass—in the wrong kind of grip—and closing to Kit's side. Damned English honor. Now they were both going to die.

Except they didn't. The fighting closed in tight, with even Venboer lending a hand. Against cutlasses, Kit wouldn't usually have stood a chance, but the boy had a special genius for interfering at just the right time. First it was a rope, kicked beneath one man's feet. That gave Kit time to use his last throwing knife and thin their opponents to two.

Then the boy tossed Kit the cutlass. No small feat given the weight and heft of the blade, but Kit was able to snatch it out of the air in time. Better and better. But two against one was still hard fighting, and Venboer was smart. Kit couldn't hold them off for long.

"Go!" he barked at the boy. "Swim!"

There was a moment's hesitation, then the boy abruptly spun on his heel and ran. A moment later, Kit heard a telltale splash and felt an inner release. If he did nothing else in his misbegotten life, at least he had saved one boy. He grinned at Venboer.

"Your prize has escaped."

The bastard actually grinned. "The boy is nothing. You are the prize."

"That's what I meant," Kit countered with a maniacal laugh. "I'm leaving." It was a bluff. Kit threw himself into a rush of speed and ferocity that would never win him freedom against these two. They were too good and he was too tired, and all three of them knew it. But it was Kit's only hope. With luck, it would force Venboer to kill him. He'd rather die than be enslaved to this bastard again.

Luck was on his side. Venboer hated the sound of joy, especially a slave's. So while the bastard flinched away from Kit's bizarre laughter, Kit was able to press close and slice him across the chest. But he paid dearly for that victory. The other sailor struck before Kit could move aside. A crippling blow to this leg that had him crumpling to one knee. He felt the slick wash of blood and knew the gash was deep. He was done for, but maybe he had one more swing left in him. He took it gleefully.

"For Jeremy!" he bellowed, then stabbed upward. Throwing all his weight behind his thrust, he pierced Venboer like a fish on a stick. The bastard's mouth gaped open, his eyes shot wide, and then he dropped in the slow fall that men take when their heart has been pierced.

Victory! And now…death. In order to make the thrust, Kit had to exposed all of himself to the other man's swing. His neck, his arm, hell, his whole right side was open for gutting. And yet in that moment, a sense of satisfaction entered his soul. He'd saved a boy and ended Venboer's reign of terror. All in all, a good way to die.

Except the blow never came.

Confused, Kit pulled his guard back up, scrambling for footing while trying to figure out why he wasn't dead. His enemy's cutlass was raised for the strike, but his eyes were wide and his back was arching in clear agony. What had happened?

The boy! The damned stupid, honorable, wonderful boy had not swum away! He'd merely pretended to jump overboard, then had grabbed a cutlass from somewhere. He'd used it to cut open the bastard's spine.

They would live! They would both live!

Kit tried to grin. He tried to laugh and dance a jig. Instead, he dropped to all fours, his breath shallow with pain. Looking down, he saw his leg was slick from blood. Not as bad as it could be. He'd live if it could be stitched up and he didn't die of fever. But he was sitting on the deck of Venboer's slave ship with no surgeon in sight. He couldn't swim now, not trailing blood the whole way. Couldn't run far either. And he damn sure couldn't man the slave ship with just himself and the boy.

He quieted his breath a moment, willing his pounding heart to ease. He eased himself to the side then stripped off his shirt to bind his leg. And as he worked, he listened for a human sound. Nothing. No pounding feet. No screams of outrage. Just himself and the boy on the quietly rocking boat. Was it possible? Had Venboer been so confident that he'd put no more than nine men on the ship? Was Kit now in possession of a fully seaworthy galley ship?

Kit suppressed a grin. A dozen things had to line up perfectly for this to work. But he'd just cheated certain death and killed Venboer, the worst of the Barbary pirates. On tonight of all nights, he was feeling lucky. He looked at the boy, who was still standing frozen, his gaze locked on the body at their feet.

"Look at me, boy. What's your name?"

The young complied slowly, his words barely audible. "Alexander Jacques Morgan, sir."

"Well, Alex, can you row? Can you row a boat straight and for a mile?"

The boy blinked then nodded. He was coming back to himself, clarity finally entering his eyes as Kit gave him something new to focus on. "I'm a damned fine rower, sir."

"Good man, Alex, now listen. I can't leave the boat. There's things to be done here."

"But you're hurt." The boy's eyes dropped to where the shirt was already turning red.

"I've had worse," he returned, which was true enough, but he'd never had to stitch himself up while preparing a ship for ocean voyage. "Now see those two lights over there? You're going to row straight over there. Up the beach two yards is a shack that serves the best rum in Africa. There's a man behind the bar who knows English. I named him Puck since he looks just like you'd expect, 'cept he's black. Give him this, and tell him it's time." He yanked a chord off his neck and passed it to the boy, who blinked down at the ugly broach.

"What is it?"

"A peacock, I think, but that doesn't matter. Tell Puck we sail tonight."

"Tonight?" the boy asked, hope sparking in his eyes. "For..." He couldn't even say the word, so deep ran the desire.

"Yes," Kit answered, his own voice cracking on the words. "For England." After seven years, Kit was finally going home.

CHAPTER 1

"You're related to an earl? We're going to visit an *earl?*"

Kit winced as Alex's voice dropped to an awestruck whisper. "He's just a man like any other man, only more arrogant," returned Kit, working hard to keep the bitterness out of his voice.

Far from being impressed by Michael and Lily's elevated position as the Countess and Earl of Thornedale, Kit was feeling anxious about his reaction to the pair. It had been seven years since they had thrown him—against his will—onto a ship bound for the colonies. He'd been about to marry an actress, and they'd decided that wasn't acceptable. It wasn't their fault that the boat had been taken by Barbary pirates and his life became one horror after another. But they were responsible for starting the whole thing in motion.

What did one say to the people responsible for such a thing? He'd spent years despising them with a darkness that consumed him. But he was home now, Venboer was dead, and what was done was done. His anger was gone, but in its place was an emptiness that he couldn't fill. And he sure as hell didn't know what to *say*. Sadly, there wasn't any more time to figure it out. They had arrived at Michael's elite London residence.

Alex tumbled out first, all gangly limbs and uncontrolled movements. The boy was too thin for his large frame, but months at sea had made him strong. A month or two of his mother's good food would see that he filled out nicely, though the scars would last a lifetime.

Kit stepped out second, wincing as his thigh pulled painfully through his back. Sadly, a month, a year, or a decade of good food would do nothing for him. His wound had become infected and he'd spent much of the trip to England in a feverish haze. He'd survived, but his days at sea were at an end. Walking was painful, climbing the rigging was impossible. His leg would no longer lift as it needed to, and Kit had seen enough injuries to know that he would never again use his leg as fully as God intended.

"We should have bought new clothes," Alex said as he tugged at his coarse seaman's shirt.

Kit shrugged. "This is the best we own. He should respect that."

Alex wasn't satisfied but knew better to comment. Instead, the boy grabbed his seamen bag from the cabbie and began walking up the path to Michael's door. Kit followed slowly, carrying his own satchel while using all his senses to find something familiar. He failed. Birds chirped rather than squawked or honked. The air tasted bitter with coal dust but without the smell of fear and sweat. The ground was solid beneath his feet, and that alone made him nervous. But most of all, even in this exclusive neighborhood of the very elite, buildings and trees seemed much too crammed together. There was no ocean expanse and no gentle rock of waves.

He was still struggling to orient to that when the front door opened. Owen stood there, his face craggy with an extra seven years' age, but his uniform and his expression remained as haughty as ever.

"Hello, Owen," Kit said. "Do you remember me?"

The man narrowed his gaze over his pointy nose. His brow furrowed, but there was no mistaking the moment his eyes widened in shock. "Master Kit? Master Kit! It can't be. You're dead!"

Kit quirked his lips. "I'm not a ghost."

Owen stared at him, his eyes watering from emotion. Kit could see his hands twitch as if the man wanted to embrace him but knew it wasn't his place. Kit didn't stand on ceremony, finding a well of emotion he hadn't expected. Owen remembered him. And Owen was the first positive breath of his past he'd felt since returning to England. Stepping forward, he embraced the man, startled to find his own eyes moist with tears.

"Oh, Master Kit, they said you were dead," Owen breathed in his ear. Then he pulled back, wiping his eyes as he gestured inside. "Come inside, come inside."

Kit stepped into the foyer, moving with an odd sort of disassociation. His body stepped into the house and went about the usual routine of stripping off his gloves and handing over his hat. Except he had no gloves or hat and hadn't for seven years. So he stood there awkwardly gripping nothing while he looked at his surroundings. Had it always been this clean? Had the footmen always sneered so clearly, their faces pasty white without so much as a smudge or beard to mar their pale skin? He had seen opulent palaces in the last seven years, displays literally dripping with jewels, but this dark wood that gleamed golden brown even as it absorbed every sound was distinctly English.

Kit rubbed at his dirty face, realizing now how filthy he appeared compared to everything here. Even the butler's clothing was pristine. Perhaps Alex was right and they should have bought new clothes. He'd forgotten how much refinement was possible in fabric and style. Even his shoes appeared a horror against the elegant wood.

"We should have waited," he murmured and was about to turn around when a cascade of feminine laughter flowed from the drawing room. Multiple women, multiple laughs, all musically delightful. His memory conjured up ladies in ball gowns, elegant jewels, the rustle of expensive fabrics. He remembered the laughter, remembered what it had been like to wander among them. He moved toward the sound as a man toward a dream. He had to see women again.

"Sir! Master Kit!"

Kit heard Owen's voice, but only distantly. He needed to walk among English girls again, see their bright colors and laugh at their silly banter. In this way, he would know he was finally home.

He crossed through the long parlor, through the dining area, and into the back patio that overlooked a small manicured garden. And there they were: ladies in beautiful gowns. White skin, winking jewels, ringlets of curls. English ladies all frozen in shock as they stared at him. Were they even real? They all sat so still!

His gaze roved from one to another, memorizing the curve of this one's nose, the color of that one's eyes. She had teeth that were in disarray, and this other one was like an English doll: blond and blue eyed in a beautiful confection of white lace.

One woman moved. She stepped forward, her movements smooth and her lip curled in disgust.

"Owen!" she snapped.

Owen rushed forward. "My apologies, my lady, but it is Master Kit. Kit Frazier, my lady, returned from the dead!"

It took a moment for Kit to place the woman. She was his cousin's wife Lily, her body softened from age. Had she always looked so unhealthy? Pale, powdered, and with grooves on her forehead as she forever lifted her brows above the crowd. He had seen ladies just like her, come for the spectacle of the slave markets. This was Lily?

She stared at him, her brows narrowed in thought. He watched her scan him from head to toe, her mouth pinched tight. He caught himself straightening under her regard, squaring his shoulders and curling his own lips in feral challenge. Silently, he dared her to fight him. Doubt my strength, he projected, and die.

He watched her eyes widen. She swallowed reflexively and backed away. Too late he realized that this type of silent power struggle was not the way of the civilized world. And certainly not with the fairer sex.

Meanwhile another man came rushing in. His steps were heavy and erratic with an extra thump to his bizarre gait. Kit turned automatically to the sound, gripping his bag tighter in his fist as he prepared to wield it as a weapon. The man was older, but his face was the same. Even with the extra weight around the jowls, Kit knew his cousin Michael.

"My God!" the man breathed as he leaned heavily against his cane. "Oh my God!" he said again. Then he threw his arms around Kit. "Oh God!"

Kit froze, his mind stuttered with disconnected thoughts. This was Michael hugging him in a weak embrace. Unlike with Owen, Kit had not chosen this

touch but had been surprised. And with that surprise
came a flood of emotions that he could not sort through.
But his body understood, even if his mind did not. One
of his hands still gripped his bag, holding it ready as a
weapon. His other hand, however, raised of its own
accord, returning Michael's hug without Kit even
realizing what he was doing.

Then Michael released him, stepping back far enough
to look at him. He was still young, Kit realized, but
wealth had made him fat. His eyes watered with unshed
tears. His arm shook slightly as he leaned on his cane
and stared.

"How, Kit? How did you escape?"

Kit swallowed, the words too crowded against his lips
to answer. And in the pause, his mind leaped through
fact and situation to arrive at a conclusion. Michael
asked about his escape. That meant he knew Kit had
been captured.

"You knew," he said. "You knew I was a prisoner."

Michael nodded. "The ransom was outrageous. My
agents negotiated but we couldn't make headway. I
thought if I waited, they would accept less money."

They. Had. Negotiated. While Kit sweated in the
bowels of a pirate ship, Michael had tried to barter.
While Kit daily fought like a beast for food and water,
while he had second by miserable second become an
animal to survive, Michael had bargained and dithered.

"Do you know what I did as a slave?" he asked, his
words flowing without conscious decision. "Do you
know what it means to fight for every breath, every
morsel, and to not know if the next moment will be
your last?"

Michael's brows lifted at Kit's tone. "Well, I'm sure it
was all very terrible, but that's hardly reason to give in

to the heathens."

Kit gaped at his cousin. He felt his hands clench in fury, and yet his mind felt strangely apart. Good God, he thought, the man was an idiot! A bloody moron! How had he not realized that years ago?

He forced himself to take a deep breath, to slow his erratic heartbeat, and to find that place of calm that had served him so well. The past was gone. Kit had survived. He had long ago come to terms with his capture. And now he was a captain with a boat in the harbor and a crew loyal to him alone. So Michael's stupidity was unimportant. Certainly the man was an arrogant ass, but that was Michael. Only a fool would expect anything different. And in this way, Kit wrestled his emotions under control.

But he had forgotten Alex. The boy had trailed along behind him, no doubt as lured by the women as he had been. But whereas Kit had had years to recover from being a slave, Alex's trauma was fresh, the wounds barely healed. And worse, the boy was smart, brilliant even. It took him less than a second to understand Michael's crimes, and just like that, the boy found a target for all of his pain.

With a growl of fury, the boy launched himself at Michael, who went down like the soft dough he was. While Kit was just starting to reach forward, Alex began a rain of blows that sounded like a man pounding a sack of flour. *Thud, thud, thud, thud.* But there was bone underneath, and within a second, Kit heard the telltale sound of ribs snapping like twigs.

Madeline Wilson winced as her cousin's scream. Lady Rose screamed as only a twenty-year-old girl can, and she wasn't the only one. Every other woman at the countess's tea party had gasped, squealed, screamed, or pretended to faint. Really, from the excitement of the reaction, you would think they had never seen men roll around in the dirt before, even if one was an earl and the other a pirate.

"Calm yourself," she said to Rose, as she gently pushed her cousin out of the way of the men. "It will be over in a moment." The footmen were already rushing forward, ready to pull the pirates away. Personally, she thought the boy had ample reason to pummel the earl, though it was hardly a fair fight. The older man obviously was not up to defending himself. It wasn't the gout or the man's age, it was that he clearly didn't know what to do when someone was straddling him and raining down blows to his face and torso.

The older pirate was trying to help. He had one arm wrapped around the boy's shoulder and was hauling him off. He'd have the boy under control in a moment if only the footmen would let him. But men could not resist a brawl, and three idiots were scrambling forward, obviously getting in the way.

"Oh, for heaven's sake!" she snapped. She could see the problem well enough. The two seamen's bags were blocking the path. If they could be pulled backward, then the man would have enough room to haul the boy off the earl, and everything would be set to rights. With a grimace of disgust, Maddy stepped forward to pull the bag out of the way.

Sadly, it turned out that there was a reason the others had hesitated to do this. The moment she grabbed hold of the sturdy canvas, both pirates—boy and man—whirled around to glare at her, teeth bared like dogs. She froze right as she was: half bent over with two hands gripping the bags. The pirates didn't say anything. Neither even moved. Whereas a moment ago everything had been flying fists and blood, now all was completely still and absurdly focused on her. At least the butler had pulled the footmen back and away, but that did nothing to help her.

"Hello, sirs," she said, her voice coming out rather rough. Behind her, Rose released a high-pitched whimper of fear, but Maddy had no time to shoot the girl a be-silent glare. Her mind was completely absorbed by the oddly pale blue color to the older pirate's eyes.

"I know this is your bag," she continued, "but it is rather in the way, don't you think? We should set it over there under the table. That way you can continue, um, with whatever you intend without damaging its contents."

The countess released a puff of disgust at her words. Presumably the woman didn't want her husband bloodied any further, but the goal right then was to bring rational thought back to the men. Just as she'd hoped, the man's expression lightened with humor. Excellent. But it was the boy who was the problem. His eyes were still wild with fury.

"It's an excellent suggestion, don't you think, Alex?" said the man, his voice coming out in a congenial tone. "Getting the bags out of the way and all?"

The boy didn't respond except to raise his fists. Thankfully, the man had him restrained in a kind of head lock, but he didn't have the room to pull the boy off the earl. Which left it to Maddy to try to keep things calm while the boy regained his senses.

"You know," she said, keeping her voice light, "I would think that such a punishing victory over the earl would make one quite thirsty. Would you care for some tea?"

She had meant to appeal to his male pride by emphasizing that he had just won his battle, but it was her last word that threw him. The boy blinked and his mouth lost some of its fury.

"Tea?" he said.

"Yes, tea," agreed the man. He clearly wasn't winded by his efforts, and so the words came out as courtly as if he had just rode in from Hyde Park. "Tea would be capital. Don't you think so, Alex?"

Maddy didn't wait for an answer. "Lovely!" she cried as she reached behind her for Rose's cup. It was the only one at hand, as Maddy had finished hers. "Here. You'll have to tell me if it is how you like it."

She extended the cup toward the boy, but he was still straddling the earl, who was busy moaning and bleeding and thankfully not further inciting the man. His wife, Lily, was not so intelligent. She huffed and stepped forward, ready to snatch the teacup away.

"Of all the ridiculous—"

"My lady!" the butler cried, obviously smart enough to grab his mistress and haul her backward. "Perhaps it would be best to allow Miss Wilson and Master Kit a moment to manage the boy."

"The boy needs to be taken out back and whipped!"

The man—presumably Master Kit—glared at the countess, his hackles rising. Maddy knew it wasn't appropriate to think of a man having hackles, but that was exactly what he looked like. A dog shifting his shoulders before an attack.

"Tea is most soothing, don't you think?" she inserted desperately. "Just the thing after heavy exertion." Then with a sudden lack of sense, she did the one thing she'd been told never, ever to do: get between men as they are pummeling one other. She stepped over the bags and wedged herself between the wall and the large pirate's knee. If he lost control of the younger one, then she would have nowhere to go. Thankfully, one glance at the man's eyes reassured her all the way down to her toes. His eyes were steady, his gaze clear. And with a slight nod, he told her that she was not in any danger.

She couldn't know that, of course. It was irrational to trust either pirate in this situation, but she did. So she smiled her thanks and returned her attention to the boy. "There," she continued as if her heart weren't beating right in her throat. "I have managed to not spill the tea, which is a minor miracle. Please do try it."

She extended the cup and saucer to the boy. And when he still did not move, she actually bent down and brushed his right fist with her hand. As if by magic, his fingers jerked opened and she was able to set the cup and saucer in his palm. Then she turned her attention to his other fist, which was wrapped tightly around the earl's cravat.

"Oh dear," she said, making sure to keep her tone light. "It appears you have gotten some blood on your hand." She pulled a white linen handkerchief from her skirt and held it out to him. "May I clean it off for you? My father was a doctor, so I am quite capable with wounds. Gentle too, even if I do say so myself."

She held out her hand for his and waited with everyone else as he just stared at her. Thankfully, it was time for the older one to play his part.

"I think tea would be most helpful," he said. "I'm going to loosen my hold, Alex, so that you may take a drink. Be polite now. Don't spill it on her dress, what?"

The boy blinked, reason obviously beginning to sink in. He only needed a bracing tone to complete the process.

"Sir," she said, hoping she sounded just like his mother. "I must insist that you stop bleeding on the earl. It really isn't done. Come, come, let go and give me your hand."

Then the boy spoke, his voice rather high given that he was half strangled, but no less clear. "It's not my blood," he said.

The older pirate huffed in disgust. "My leg is beginning to ache, Alex. So release my cousin and drink some of the damned tea." And with that, he slowly, steadily relaxed his grip. He moved gently, but Maddy could see the control he exerted. At the first sign of madness, he would be there to haul the boy back.

Alex didn't move. He did, however, take a deep breath and open his fist. The earl's head dropped back to the ground with a *thunk.*

"That's it, boy," said the older pirate. Then he tried to straighten but flinched at the movement. "Jesus, that hurts."

Maddy risked a glance in the man's direction, noting for the first time the lines of pain etched into his handsome face. She recalled now that he had limped when he first entered the room. It hadn't seemed to slow his efforts to capture the boy, but obviously the strain was beginning to tell.

"Would you, um, like a cup of tea as well?" It was a silly thing to offer, but it was the only thing she could think of right then. And then the most incredible thing happened.

His eyes warmed, his lips softened, and she thought, *He is the most incredible man in the world.* He was standing there, in obvious pain, his arms wrapped around a feral boy, and yet he had the presence of mind to smile at her. In that one moment, she saw kindness, warmth, and something that she could not name. Nobility, perhaps. Or simply a man who matched her ease with the absurd. He had no trouble at all speaking of tea while holding off a child intent on murder.

"I'd rather prefer grog right now," he said, "but I doubt you have any at hand."

"I haven't the tea either," she quipped, "but that didn't stop me from offering it, now did it?"

Then the countess chose that moment to assert herself. Really, the woman had the worst timing. "Grog, tea, good God, Miss Wilson. Tell him to get off Michael!"

Fortunately, the butler was there to soothe his mistress. "In a moment, my lady." Then he snapped his fingers. "Simpson, go fetch the doctor, quick as you can."

"And the guard," inserted another matron.

Both pirates tensed, and Maddy was close enough to see the older one's eyes darken. But the boy was the danger, so she simply leaned forward and touched his hand.

"Is it too cold?" she asked. "Should I get more?"

He blinked at her and she gestured to the teacup. She held his gaze, relieved beyond measure when he finally, slowly lifted the cup to his lips while the older man relaxed his hold. Everyone watched, though she doubted any but the man had the air of taut readiness. If Alex should go wild, he was there to restrain the boy.

Instead, the adolescent abruptly grimaced. "Sweet!" he gasped.

Oh yes, Maddy recalled too late. Rose liked her tea

extra thick with sugar. Enough to make anyone's teeth ache.

"Oh dear. I'm so sorry." She held out her hands. "Shall I get you another?"

The child pulled back as if she were about to take away his favorite toy. "I like sweet," he rasped. Then as if to prove his words, he downed the rest of the drink in one gulp. Then he set his cup down with a click. It was hard enough to break the fine porcelain, and Maddy instinctively winced. So did the man and the boy, for that matter, as all three of them looked worriedly at the cup. How absurd that they worried about a tea set while the earl was beginning to moan.

Fortunately, the china remained intact, and the boy passed it back to her with hands that shook. Maddy took it, her gaze steady on his face. She saw no trace of madness anymore. Even the image of a feral dog was gone. Instead, she saw a haunting pain in his eyes. And fear. Bone-deep fear as he looked from her to the earl then up to the man who was just now straightening to his full height in the tiny space.

"What should I do?" he asked, his voice low, panic trembling just beneath his words.

Mr. Frazier shrugged. "Not much to be done, Alex. Stand up, let the servants do their job, and deal with the rest as it comes."

"But they've called the watch." And just like that, Maddy saw sanity start to drain from his eyes. "I won't be locked up again. I won't!"

"That's just what's going to happen, young man," screeched Lily. "Now *get off my husband!*"

"No!" bellowed the boy, and quick as a flash his fists were raised and he was on the move. In truth, Maddy couldn't tell if he was attacking the countess or just trying to push past her to escape. But it didn't matter. Before anyone could do more than gasp, Mr. Frazier intervened.

He grabbed the boy then wrapped an arm around his neck. Alex flailed, his eyes bulging and his legs thrashing, but his movements were uncoordinated with panic. Mr. Frazier grunted as blow after blow hit his legs and Alex's nails dug into his arms, but he did not relax his grip. Maddy stared transfixed as he gritted his teeth when blood began to run down his forearms, but his eyes remained apologetic. Obviously, he didn't want to do this, but there was no choice. And bit by bit, the boy's struggles slowed. Alex's eyes fluttered, then rolled back in his head. A moment later, Mr. Frazier was pulling him backward to lay him gently on the floor.

"Oh! That was simply masterful!" cried Rose from the side. In truth, Maddy had forgotten the other women in the room, but trust her cousin to remind everyone that they were still there. Indeed, Rose was clapping her hands in applause, clearly oblivious to the regret plain on Mr. Frazier's face.

Meanwhile, Maddy knelt down beside the boy to feel for a pulse. Her eyes told her that he still breathed, but she had never seen someone squeezed to unconsciousness like that.

"He's alive," said Mr. Frazier, his voice thick. "Just asleep for a while."

Maddy looked up and extended her handkerchief to him. Her other hand was pressed against Alex's pulse, feeling it beat strong and steady beneath her fingertips. Meanwhile, Mr. Frazier simply stared uncomprehending at her already bloodstained scrap of linen.

"For your arms," she said softly. "You're bleeding."

He blinked and looked down at himself. "So I am," he said. He took her handkerchief, but it was far from useful. It only smeared the blood already drying across his tan skin.

"I'm sorry—" she began, but her words were cut off as she was roughly shoved aside by the countess as she scrambled for her husband. Maddy stumbled, caught completely off guard. She would have landed in an undignified heap if it weren't for Mr. Frazier again. His hands were quick as they kept her from the floor, then he easily lifted her up, guiding her to stand safely protected between him and the wall.

Meanwhile, the countess was alternately snapping orders and dabbing ineffectively at the earl's cut lip.

"Don't move him," Maddy warned. "His ribs are likely broken and…" Her voice trailed away. No one was listening to her as the footmen worked together to lift and carry the man to his bedchamber. Just as she feared, the earl cried out, turned white as a sheet as he grabbed the nearest footman's ear, then sunk unconscious, much to everyone's relief.

"It's all right," said Mr. Frazier at her gasp. "His ribs are cracked, not broken. Alex isn't that strong, and Michael's got a good deal of padding. But it'll hurt like the very devil when he wakes."

Maddy thought his words were for her alone, but apparently the countess had very sharp ears or perhaps simply a very big temper. He'd barely finished speaking when she abruptly rounded on him, her finger pointing straight at his heart.

"This is all your fault! How dare you come here and bring that…that animal into my home!"

"He's a boy, Lily. *That* is what happens to boys who are taken by Barbary pirates."

"I don't care what happened to him! Get out of my house. Get out now!"

Mr. Frazier's reaction was quiet. A simple flinch, barely noticeable by anyone at all. Except Maddy was right behind him, pressed against the wall. She felt the impact of the countess's words in the way his breathing completely stopped and his body tightened almost unbearably. And then it was gone as he sketched a shallow bow.

"As you wish, Lily."

Maddy doubted the countess heard. The woman had already stomped off after her husband while all around them, the ladies erupted into noise and movement. Like a gaggle of disturbed geese, she thought distractedly, her gaze going to Rose. But she couldn't see her cousin as Mr. Frazier's rather large shoulders blocked her view. And then when she was about to step around him, the butler abruptly appeared before them.

"Best go now, Master Kit," the butler intoned. "The watch has been called. I couldn't stop it. Have you a place to stay?"

Kit shook his head, his gaze dropping to the unconscious boy at his feet. "We just arrived. The ship is barely habitable, but—"

"Come with us," Maddy inserted suddenly.

Butler and pirate both turned to her, their brows raised in surprise. She couldn't blame them. It wasn't at all the thing for an unmarried woman to be inviting pirates to her home. Especially as it wasn't really her home but her uncle Frank's. She was just the poor relation they housed. But there was no help for it now. The invitation had been issued, and Mr. Frazier was looking at her with a gratitude that seemed to warm the air between them.

"I'd be most grateful," he said. "The boy needs to remember what it's like to be in a home, not locked down on a ship. A real bed on dry land will ease his nightmares, but I haven't any English coins as yet for an inn. I was hoping that Michael..." His voice trailed away on a sigh.

Put like that, she couldn't possibly change her mind. "It's settled then," she said briskly, as she turned to the butler. "Would you summon our carriage please? And make sure to bring his bag."

Then she took a deep breath, knowing there was one last thing for her to do, much as she regretted it. It was petty of her, of course, but she had enjoyed being the only woman holding Mr. Frazier's attention. But sadly, her cousin would be traveling in the carriage with them, so she had to make the introduction. Her stunningly gorgeous and titled cousin. The one who had men falling at her feet like raindrops.

But she had to. So she touched his arm, forced a smile, then gestured to the side where Rose was bouncing on her toes beside them, clearly beyond anxious for this moment. "And please, allow me to introduce my cousin Rose."

CHAPTER 2

"A pleasure to make your acquaintance," Kit said, barely looking at the beautiful blonde. He could tell from Owen's frantic expression that time was slipping away fast. If they didn't leave now, they might very well be spending the night in gaol. With that thought in mind, he bent down and hoisted Alex into his arms. Thank God the boy hadn't grown into his adult weight, otherwise Kit's leg would never support the task. As it was, he worried that he wouldn't be able to walk the distance required.

"Oh my," breathed the real beauty, the brown-haired angel with the pretty voice and the kind eyes. "Are you sure you should do that? We could probably fashion of liter of some sort."

Kind and smart. She had correctly guessed his difficulty and made a suggestion without pointing out his damnable leg. But they didn't have time, so he shook his head. "I'll be fine," he said as he began maneuvering his way toward the front door. Owen rushed ahead, pushing the gawkers out of the way. Meanwhile, the blonde chose that moment to hiss to her cousin.

"But we can't take him home with us! He attacked the

earl! The countess will give us the cut direct, and then neither of us will ever marry!"

Kit didn't bother to look as the shrill noise cut through his thoughts. In an odd way, the sound was comforting. It had been nearly a decade since he'd heard a spoiled beauty in hysterics. It brought back his childhood and the vague urge to tease the woman out of her tantrum. But just then Alex began to stir and he had to focus on maneuvering quickly thorough Michael's drawing room.

"Hush, Rose, of course that won't happen," returned the brown-eyed angel.

"You know Father will never allow this. You shouldn't have invited them. It's your country ways. They just don't serve in London!"

Kit made it out the front door, but he didn't know which carriage was theirs. So he paused, watching the women as they moved forward still whispering loudly between them.

"It will be fine, Rose. It's very proper with your father there. And the countess will not cut us. We're helping her husband's cousin."

"But he attacked the earl!"

The angel sighed, her expression clearly exasperated and a little guilty. It had been seven years since he'd last been in polite society, but he did recall that as a rule, unmarried women did not invite men home with them. A gentleman would find a way to stay at a hostelry. Fortunately, it had been a long time since he'd been a gentleman, so he could conveniently ignore the prompting of his conscience. He wanted to stay near the women—both of them—and that whim he could indulge. What he truly wanted with the angel, however, even he wouldn't do. Meanwhile, a carriage pulled up, one with a crest on the side and a footman leaping to assist.

"Your carriage?" he asked, turning slightly toward the women.

"Yes, yes," the angel rushed to say.

Meanwhile Alex was definitely stirring, and he murmured to the boy. "You're safe. You're fine. Just stay quiet a moment more and we'll be away."

"He's not safe!" gasped the girl. "He'll murder us all!"

"Rose!" the angel gasped, clearly at the end of her patience. "Just get in and be quiet." She didn't even wait as the beauty huffed dramatically and stomped into the carriage. Instead, she gestured to the footman. "Thomas! Do you think you could help us please? Perhaps support the boy's head?"

The footman jumped to assist, and Kit gratefully surrendered some of the boy's weight. "Help me lay him on the seat," he said, and together he and the footman maneuvered around the gasping beauty to set the boy down. Then finally, blessedly, he was able to straighten his back and leg.

"Maddy!" squealed the girl inside. "He's waking up!"

"Hush! Don't startle him!" snapped the angel. "Sir, if you would step inside and comfort him. Perhaps help him sit up, then I could sit with Rose."

"And we can be away," he finished for her. Those words were spoken to the driver as much as to the lady. Both nodded their understanding as he ducked inside. Alex was indeed becoming alert, his eyes wide with panic as he pushed himself upright. But one look at Kit and his breath steadied out. "That's it, boy. Just a moment more and we'll be on our way. Mind, we're in the presence of ladies, so be on your best behavior."

The boy nodded, his gaze going to the blonde as he managed a tremulous smile. But it was the brown-haired angel who spoke as she entered the carriage. "I'm so glad you're awake. My name is Miss Madeline Wilson, by the way. And this is my cousin, Lady Rose."

A titled girl, then. And her poor relation, he guessed, given that the angel's clothing was an obvious castoff from the blonde. The color and style were completely wrong for a statuesque brunette and more suited to the doll-like blonde. Add to that the slightly worn state of the crest on the carriage and the fading livery of the footman, and Kit formed a picture of his hostess's family. An earldom, he guessed, well past their prime and probably struggling for every penny.

"A pleasure, of course." Kit did his best to bow in the tight confines of the carriage. Then he gestured to his side. "I am Mr. Frazier as you already know, and this is Master Alexander Morgan, now much recovered from his recent bout of insanity. Right, Alex?"

Alex flushed, obviously embarrassed, but that didn't stop him from staring at the blonde.

"You're quite beautiful," he said, obviously smitten.

"Oh, sir!" she simpered, clearly pleased.

Kit glanced at the angel, expecting to share a look of amused tolerance with her. Instead he found her expression sad more than amused, and resigned more than tolerant. Kit felt his eyebrows raise. Perhaps the angel was unaware of her own appeal and much too used to being passed over in favor of her rather young and obvious cousin. Meanwhile, the blonde was beginning to speak, making sure to punctuate her words with many bright smiles and coquettish looks at them both.

"It's really quite exciting to have you both here with

us, but you know, my cousin doesn't always understand London ways. She's from the country, you know, and not really wise to the ways of town. You understand, of course, that—"

"Actually, Rose, I was thinking that there must be some way for us to turn this to our advantage. After all, Mr. Frazier is the cousin to an earl. Surely you can think of something." She glanced at the men. "Rose is very clever at this sort of thing."

Kit smiled, not in the least bit fooled. Obviously the angel had some skill at manipulating her cousin. Far from being offended, he was rather entertained. He remembered the subtle fencing of words as one might remember a boyhood game. Had he once been counted accomplished at it? He could hardly remember.

Meanwhile, Rose was softening. "I suppose, but you know what Papa will say: One charity case is quite enough."

Unfair! To throw that back at the angel, and in front of male company no less, was the mark of a cruel woman. And given the angel's quiet acceptance of the slight, Kit knew that she was treated to such comments frequently. So he was roused to defend her, though he had to search through his memory for the most appropriate words.

"I am capable of paying," he said softly. "And I would count myself in your debt. Indeed, the charity you extended to us demonstrates a true and good heart. I wonder that you are not buried in suitors. Is all of London blind?"

He spoke to the angel and was gratified to see her eyes widen in surprise. But naturally, the blonde took the words as her due. "Well, as to that, an earl's daughter is not free to marry whomever asks, you know." There was a wistfulness in her tone and an openness of emotion that caught Kit by surprise. She wasn't truly cruel, he realized, just young and very spoiled, as was typical for an earl's daughter. "As for payment, I'm sure you can discuss the details with my father."

He nodded and was about to respond when he saw the angel's eyes on Alex. Her expression was troubled.

"Miss Wilson?"

"I was thinking perhaps that we should call for a doctor." She smiled gently at Alex, and Kit found himself feeling oddly jealous of the boy. "I know the blood was mostly the earl's but perhaps, just to be safe—"

"No doctor is needed," he interrupted, more harshly than intended. "Some simple food and rest on land would do us a world of good."

"As you wish," the angel said as she nodded slowly, her eyes lowered. She looked appropriately demure, but Kit could tell there was a wealth of thought behind her quiet facade.

"Miss Wilson," he began, but again the blonde spoke and everyone had to wait in silence for her to finish.

"Was I to understand, Mr. Frazier, that you were captured by pirates? Barbary pirates? I thought that's what the servant said, but I couldn't be sure, you understand. Such a fantastical tale! And you escaped, no less! Oh please, you must tell us how you did it! And were you, Mr. Morgan, equally enslaved? My goodness, how horrible!"

"It was, Lady Rose. It was quite horrible," he responded, his tone flat and discouraging. But the lady was not one to take such a hint.

"Of course it was!" she exclaimed. "But however did you escape? Was it very dangerous? We are going to a musical tonight, perhaps you could join us? Oh, possibly not, not attired as you are. But perhaps tomorrow?" On she babbled on with her questions. Thankfully, they arrived at their location long before he was obliged to answer any of them.

Maddy breathed a sigh of relief the moment she shut the door on the gentlemen. She had installed them in the housekeeper's room. The bedroom was tiny, but the bed was large enough for two as it was designed for a husband and wife. Plus, there was a salon out front, one Maddy usually used to balance accounts and plan meals. This would afford them some privacy if they wished to remain apart from the rest of the family. That was safer for all around, for the family if the boy turned violent again, and for them as an escape from Rose's incessant questions.

Mr. Frazier had handled them well enough. Unlike the boy, he was slow to anger and supremely tolerant. And yet something about him set her belly quivering and her chest tightening. Not quite in fear, and yet not in pleasure either. He was everything that was polite—soft spoken and direct with his words—and yet his eyes seemed to watch her, study her, and see much too clearly into her heart. It bothered her, and yet she was the one who insisted that he come home with them.

"What are they doing?" asked Rose from the door to the salon. She was surrounded by nearly their entire staff come to gape.

"Really," Maddy snapped at the crowd. "I would think you all have better things to do right now. But if not, I'm sure I can find something for you."

The threat worked wonders on everyone but Rose.

While the family's three servants disappeared in an instant, Rose simply tried to sidle past Maddy to the bedroom door.

"Are they sleeping? Don't they want a bath or a valet or something? I really don't think Father will like this, but if he can pay, then I suppose it would be all right. It is rather romantic though, don't you think? Mr. Morgan collapsing and all after he saw my beauty. That's what he said, remember? You are very beautiful."

"Yes, of course I remember," Maddy said as she took a firm grip on Rose's elbow and steered her toward the hallway. "Though I don't think he collapsed quite because of you, sweeting. I fear he's suffered a great loss—"

"Yes, yes! Imagine being capture by pirates and coming home to realize your fiancée has married another! Poor man!"

Maddy froze, turning to frown at her cousin. "What do you mean? He said nothing of a fiancée."

"Oh! Of course, you weren't living with us then, and I wasn't even out, but everyone heard the tale. The old one, Mr. Frazier was dead, and who should appear at the funeral but his fiancée, demanding a seat and acting just like one would expect from an actress. Clearly she was there just to find another gull because a month later she's married to Lord Blackstone. Started increasing within the year."

"Oh my. Poor man." She glanced behind her at the closed bedroom door. He had said they needed to rest, but she suspected they wanted privacy more than anything. And food. She needed to send up a tray to them immediately. So she grabbed her cousin's arm and led her down the hallway. "But what of the younger one?"

"Oh, I don't think he's related to anyone at all," Rose answered dismissively. "But isn't Mr. Frazier glorious? The way he handled everything!"

Maddy nodded, pleased that Rose now saw Mr. Frazier as a romantic hero rather than a social disaster. "Now help me decide what to say to your father. He's due back from his club any moment now."

"Oh," said Rose airily with a wave, "just mention the money." Maddy had managed to get them into the hall, but Rose abruptly stopped, her eyes going wide as she looked back into the salon. "Do you think he's very rich? Gold and gems and the like? He doesn't look rich, but he has just come back from God knows what hellish place."

"Rose! You shouldn't say such things!"

"What?" she said with a vague blink. "Hell? Or that he's very rich?"

Maddy grimaced. "Both, and well you know it."

"Of course I know it!" Rose giggled with an impish smile. "I just never thought to hear *you* criticize *my* language!"

Maddy smiled fondly at her young cousin, though the expression was slightly strained. Three years ago, Maddy had indeed cursed rather colorfully and frequently. After all, she had spent all her life with just her father, who had been busy with his patients. That left her to run with whomever caught her fancy, including gypsies who had taught her the most colorful words in her vocabulary. After his death, the adjustment to polite society had not come easily. But in the ensuing years, things had changed. Maddy had learned how to go on, what to say and when to stay silent. Rose, on the other hand, never saw the change. The girl delighted in painting herself as Maddy's older and wiser instructor, even though the girl was eight years younger.

"Come on, Rose, you have to help me—"

"Rose! Madeline! Where are you?" Uncle Frank's angry voice cut through the house.

"Oh, my," Maddy whispered, dismayed by the fury she heard in her uncle's voice.

Rose bit her lip, then winked at Maddy. "We're back in the salon, Papa!" she cried. "And don't shout so, I have the headache."

Maddy shot her cousin a glare. She knew exactly that those words meant, especially since Rose was already adopting a wan pose and placing a limp wrist to her forehead. Sure enough, Uncle Frank wasted no time in heading straight for them while Rose whimpered in pretend pain.

"Papa, I know you're angry," Rose said before anyone else could get a word in. "But try to understand that Maddy doesn't know any better. They don't teach polite things in the country. And now, I fear my head hurts abominably. I'm going to lie down for a bit."

Uncle Frank's eyes narrowed on his daughter. To his credit, he wasn't in the least bit fooled by her display. "How could you bring a violent man to this house?" he snapped. "What were you thinking?"

Rose's hand trembled against her forehead. "Papa, my head. Please—"

"Let her go, Uncle Frank," Maddy said softly. "She counseled against it, but I was determined."

Uncle Frank's eyes narrowed as he glared at her. Then, with a snap of his wrist, he gestured his daughter away. Rose took the chance and fled immediately, which left Maddy, Uncle Frank, and once again their three servants in the hallway.

"They're not violent, Uncle Frank," Maddy urged with a glance at the servants. "You'll see after they're rested. He's the earl's cousin, and the younger one is ill." Her uncle moved into the salon, his set face showing his every intention to barge in on the men without so much as a knock.

"Uncle!" she cried, rushing to get in front of him. "I think it best if we let them rest. Even the older one has hurt his leg. Can barely walk. And the younger is just a boy."

Uncle Frank shot her an irritated look. "Doing it a bit too brown, don't you think?" he drawled. "Didn't they break five of the earl's ribs?"

As many as that? Maddy wondered. "I'm sure it was an exaggeration," she said.

"And who's to pay for their food?"

"They have money. Mr. Frazier has already offered to pay." She didn't add that it would be some time before he could get English coins.

"Humph. My home is not a hostelry for every wayward—"

"I know, Uncle. Perhaps we could discuss this somewhere else. Let them rest. Truly, I think everything will be fine once they get their bearings."

Uncle Frank peered once again at the closed door, but then reluctantly nodded. He was not a man to give in easily, but she was the daughter of a surgeon. He often deferred to her medical knowledge. So they stepped away from the bedroom door, but not even as far as the hallway. Instead, her uncle plopped himself down on the couch in the salon.

"Uncle?"

"I'll not leave them without a guard. Not until I know

it's safe."

"I assure you—"

"They attacked an earl. I'll not be murdered in my bed by savages back from Africa."

She swallowed, seeing that he had decided. So she nodded demurely and took the seat opposite her uncle. She could tell he wanted to talk, and as her uncle's talks could go on quite some time, she found the most comfortable seat she could. But rather than have him start on a lecture, she tried to distract him.

"How did you hear about him?"

"Was all over the club. Kit Frazier, back from the dead and insane. Attacked the earl like a savage—"

"No—"

"Had some mongrel boy with him. Had to be held back by seven men—"

"That's not—"

"And then he up and goes home with my daughter. Some say abducted."

"Ridiculous!"

Uncle Frank folded his arms across his chest. "Really? They're here, aren't they?"

Maddy huffed in disgust. "They can hardly abduct anyone to their own home, now can they? And the boy simply became confused. And then he collapsed."

"On top of you."

She blinked. The way he said those four words made it sound like she'd been ravished on the earl's floor. "No," she stated firmly. "Mr. Frazier had him."

"Hmmm," he returned, his expression unreadable.

"Uncle, I can tell you exactly what happened..." she began, but he shook his head.

"Not just now, Madeline. I have something else I wish

to discuss with you."

She frowned. Her mind scrambled to figure out what he could possibly want. The accounts were up to date, and she had even managed to economize a bit. The servants were generally up to snuff, not like when she's first arrived. She'd even managed to moderate some of Rose's wilder ideas.

"You've been with us three years now, haven't you? And I know you regard Rose as something of a sister, but really, you're more like a mother to her, don't you think?"

Maddy nodded, not sure whether he wanted her to voice her agreement or not. Apparently not, because he stroked his cheek and rumbled on.

"What do you think of her chances this Season? Think she'll catch a husband?"

Perhaps, Maddy thought, *if the man is equally young and has a tolerance for spoiled beauties.* But she didn't say that aloud. This was Rose's father, after all. "She's a beautiful girl and sure to take this Season. She will have offers."

"That's what I thought too," he said. "So she'll be married within the year—"

"Uncle, I'm not so sure that's wise," Maddy said. "Rose is very young."

"She's marriageable," he huffed. "And I can't afford to outfit her for another Season."

Maddy frowned. She knew money was a constant worry for her uncle, but surely it wasn't as bad as all that. "Truly, Uncle, I have pared down the household expenses. I should think that with a little economy..."

"Nonsense. She's having her second Season. Two should be more than enough for such a beautiful gel."

Maddy held her tongue, refusing to fight a battle that had yet to appear. She would do better to wait and see the gentlemen who really did offer for Rose. Perhaps one of them would be perfect.

"Which brings me to the question of you," Uncle Frank abruptly said.

Maddy blinked. Her mind had been spinning about the perfect husband for Rose. She had not been focused on her own future. At least she hadn't at that particular moment. Other times it felt like that was all she thought about. What would she do when Rose married and left the home? Maddy could hardly stay here, an unmarried woman with her widower uncle. But she hadn't the funds to go elsewhere.

"I, um, hadn't realized I was such a burden to you," she said softly, her mind already scrambling to form arguments for her value to the household.

"A burden?" her uncle huffed. "You're not a burden at all! Oh bother, I'm making a muddle of this, aren't I?"

She had no idea what to say to that, so she pressed her lips together. What was he about?

"We've rubbed along together well, haven't we? You manage the house to a tee, and Rose has never been happier. Less wild too, I should think, though she still has the most bizarre ideas sometimes."

"She is maturing into a fine young woman," Maddy said sincerely.

"Exactly. Fact is, nothing's been better since my sweet Susan passed five years ago. Should have mentioned it months ago, but I only just now realized what with Rose about to marry and all, how pleasant it's been with you here."

"Um, well, thank you, Uncle. I like it here too."

"Excellent. Excellent. Glad to hear it. You know we're not related by birth, don't you? Your father was Susan's brother, and a right good man, too."

"Yes, Uncle, I know." She suppressed the pang she always felt when she thought of her father. As much as she might appreciate her life now, everything had been so much better with him. She had been loved wholly and completely then, and not because she could manage a household or knew when to spare the coal and where to find cheaper candles.

"Well, then, Maddy," her uncle continued. "You see, I have an idea, so to speak, an offer I'd like you to consider."

Maddy nodded, forcibly pulling her thoughts away from her childhood. "Yes?"

"You don't find me objectionable, do you? I mean, I'm not repulsive, am I?"

"Of course not." Her uncle had kept himself in relatively good condition for a man his age. His body was the thick sort that held one or five stones extra weight without notice. His lungs were clear, his frame still strong. And if his skin was beginning to soften with fat, that was only to be expected. Many considered him a fine figure of a man.

"Excellent, excellent. So, uh, I was wondering if you'd like to stay on. After Rose is married, that is. With me."

Maddy tilted her head. She could tell that her uncle was trying to ask her something important, but for the life of her she couldn't fathom what. Finally, after looking at his earnest expression for much too long, she simply shrugged. "I'm sorry, Uncle, I just don't understand. You know it won't be proper for me to remain. Especially since, as you say, we're not related by blood."

"Well, yes, as to that, proper is a rather difficult term, don't you think? Forgive me, dear, but you do realize that you're not likely to get a husband, don't you? You're much too old and you simply don't dress to magnify your assets."

She frowned, her pride hurt despite her uncle's apologetic tone. "I dress as I do because I am forced to wear Rose's cast-off gowns. We are not at all the same size."

"But that's exactly the point, don't you see? You're impoverished. A pauper. Without a groat to your name. No one wants to marry a gel too old and poor to boot."

Maddy looked away, tears stinging her eyes. It didn't matter that everything he said was true, that she'd stayed awake nights worrying about just that. It was still cruel of him to say it so openly.

"Oh, here now, don't cry. I know it's hard, but I wanted to put your mind at ease, not worry it further." With a heavy sigh, her uncle shifted to the edge of the couch such that he sat directly beside her though she was in a chair. "I'm not a man of pretty words. I thought since your father was the same, you wouldn't need the poetry."

"I don't," she said, though in her heart she knew she lied. She missed having her father call her beautiful as he chucked her under the chin.

"Well, then, just listen. You're used to nice things and good food. You manage a house better than my Susan. And with Rose gone, I might see my way to some money for your gowns and such."

"Well, that would be lovely, Uncle, but—"

"You must call me Frank."

Maddy stopped, her breath suspended. Why would he want her to call him... A thought crossed her mind, a horrible thought but one she could not shake. "You're my uncle," she said a little too tartly. "My *uncle* Frank."

"But only through marriage. Not by blood."

She stared at him. And as she looked, he reached out a hand that trembled slightly. It was an odd sight to see because as far as she could remember, he never wavered in anything he did. Unless, of course, he was remembering something especially tender about Aunt Susan. And yet his hand trembled now as he stroked a finger across her cheek.

"You're beautiful in your own way, you know that?" he said. "And I want you to stay on after Rose leaves. With me." He swallowed, his finger slowly outlining her mouth. "Will you, Maddy? Stay with me?"

She pulled back, horror sickening her stomach. "Uncle, we can't marry. By law, we're already related."

He flushed, his hand dropped down as he looked anywhere but at her face. "Well, as to that, of course you're right. Legally, there's nothing I can do for you."

Except dower her appropriately so she would be more appealing to someone else. That, of course, had been her secret hope. That Uncle Frank would become so fond of her that he would set her up properly. But what was happening now was...bizarre.

"Uncle Frank, are you asking me to be your *mistress*?"

"Don't answer right away, Maddy," he said. "Just think about the life I give you here, and what you would have out on the street."

She blinked, her mind reeling. "You'd throw me out?"

"Well, I can't have a *proper* girl living here when

Rose is gone, can I?" he asked, his tone turning hard.

"But you would accept an improper one?"

He sighed, the sag in his body showing her that he knew what he was asking of her. He knew what he wanted and how despicable it was. "Think on it, Maddy. What other options do you have? You'll never make it as a wife to some butcher or baker. That's not the life you were born to."

"I wasn't born to be your mistress either."

He shook his head. "I forget that you are more innocent than you seem. Maddy, girls like you who aren't proper are *im*proper."

"Your mistress."

"I swear I'll do right by you. You have my word on it."

She shook her head. "No, Uncle. *No*."

He pursed his lips, staring hard at her. "I approached you too early. I can see that now. You'll see the right of it at the end of the Season."

She pushed up to her feet, not knowing where she meant to go, but she couldn't simply sit there anymore. "I'll meet someone this Season," she said suddenly, the words like a vow. "I'll be married before Rose!"

He pushed himself to his feet, his eyes calm and rather kind. It was the kindness that brought tears to her eyes. He really did think she had no other possibilities.

"You're a sensible girl, Maddy. Too smart to marry the first rake that offers in his cups and too used to the comforts that I give you to marry a footman. You'll see soon enough that I have the right of it. I just approached you too soon, is all."

She pressed her hand to her chest as if she could hold in the pain there. It ached beneath her palm. In truth, her entire soul hurt. "I'll meet someone."

"Maybe," he said with a shrug. "Maybe not."

Then he caught her chin in the barest caress. It was brief because she pulled away, but she felt it with a clear sense of revulsion.

"Don't pull away too quick, Maddy," he said softly. "I'm an excellent lover. I can show you a great many things." And with that, he sketched her a brief bow and left.

CHAPTER 3

Kit grimaced as he listened to the conversation outside his door. He didn't want to hear it. He wanted to be left alone to give Alex the dressing down the boy deserved. The boy had attacked an earl! Yes, Michael had richly deserved a beating and more, but it wasn't Alex's place to deliver it. And worse, Kit knew that the fury hadn't come from any sense of justice, but from a raw place of pain that simply struck out whenever the boy lost control. The pain was understandable. The lack of control, however, could not be tolerated. And so he had to tell the boy. But not if they sat there listening to yet another earl's evil manipulations.

Kit tried to shut out the sound, but no thin scrap of a door could silence the conversation on the other side. What did he care if some girl was forced into becoming her uncle's mistress? It happened all the time, even to the angel with the beautiful voice.

He didn't care. And yet, despite everything, he sat on the bed and listened. He heard everything, from Uncle Frank's solicitation to his implied threat. He caught—or his imagination filled in—his angel's soft gasp of shock when she finally understood her choices. And he even listened to her soft sobs after the bastard left her alone.

He heard it, but he didn't move. And neither did Alex, though the boy was like a taut bow string ready to snap. And damn if Kit weren't considering the same thing. Another rescue, another lost lamb.

He forced himself to lean back on the bed, trying to ease the agony in his leg as he closed his eyes. It was a cruel world, and Kit already had a charge in Alex. He couldn't afford another.

"Sir—" Alex said, but Kit cut him off before the boy could say more.

"Mistress to an earl is a fine place for a woman and better than most marriages. Neither of us can offer her anything better."

Alex hesitated, clearly thinking it through. Then he sat back down with a heavy sigh. And in time—an eternity of time—the angel's sobs quieted. Kit released his breath, stunned by the amount of tension her tiny gasps had created in his body. He heard her move from the salon. Did he imagine the quiet determination he heard in her footsteps? Or did he merely pray that it was true? That somehow, the angel would find a way to rescue herself?

Either way, he reminded himself, he had enough to worry about without her. An entire crew waited at the dock for new orders. Alex needed discipline, and Kit needed money. What did he care about one lost angel? Nothing, he told himself. Nothing at all.

He was still in those terrible clothes, Maddy thought as she checked on them after the musicale. Not the younger one. Mr. Morgan appeared sound asleep in the bed, curled into a tight ball under the covers without even a lock of brown hair peeping out. His clothes were piled neatly in a corner and soft snores drifted up from beneath the sheet.

But Mr. Frazier was fully clothed and sleeping on the floor. Why would a man sleep on the floor? The tray was near his head, meat congealed and ugly on the plate. She frowned, studying the man. His mouth was open slightly, relaxed as he breathed, but that was the only part of him that seemed at rest. She wasn't sure exactly why she came to that conclusion. After all, he was clearly asleep, resting on his side with his hands in front. They were set in a loose curl, not quite a fist, not quite open. He didn't even bother to pillow his head as he rested, but seemed to sleep in a state of a half crouch. As if he needed to leap to his feet at any moment.

It made no sense. How could a sleeping man be crouched? But that is what he looked like, and something in Maddy found the idea both unsettling and infinitely interesting.

She waited a moment, debating what to do. She had to get the tray, if only to keep it from the mice. But she would have to step around Mr. Frazier to get it. She sighed. There was no help for it, so she moved forward as silently as possible and bent down for the tray.

There was no warning and no sound. One moment she was leaning forward for the tray, and the next moment he had seized her. He grabbed her wrist and jerked hard, not away from him, but toward him. She toppled forward, but he rolled easily with her fall, pinning her completely in the space between one breath and the next. And then there were no more breaths, she realized, as his free hand gripped her throat and squeezed.

She couldn't breathe! She flailed at him, banging her fists against anything she could reach. Nothing seemed to affect him. And his eyes seemed so blank in the darkness, as if he wasn't even aware that he was about to murder her.

Her heart was beating triple-time and the ocean roared through her ears. The pressure against her neck was beyond anything she'd ever imagined. Any moment now her throat would give way—crushed beneath his weight—and she'd die.

She switched tactics. Her fists had done nothing, so she dug her nails into his forearm and pulled for all she was worth. It was that sharp pain that brought consciousness into his eyes. Or maybe it had just been long enough. Either way, one moment he was strangling her, his lips pulled back in a growl. Then the next moment, he jerked backward and fell against the wall with a gasp.

She dragged air into her lungs, rasping gulps that burned.

"I'm sorry," she heard him say. "I'm so sorry."

She tried to nod, but she hadn't the strength. She knew what had happened. She'd seen enough animals startled in their sleep. She knew that some—the most wild ones—came awake snarling and fighting first. Obviously, he was one of that sort, but it was an odd thing for a man.

"Please. Is it bad? Can you speak?" Regret trembled through his every word. "I'm so sorry."

Meanwhile, the boy came awake as well. He jerked out of his sleep, leaping off the bed and landing in an angry crouch on the opposite side of the room. Mr. Frazier reacted immediately, holding up his hand. "It's fine, Alex. You're safe. It's fine." But his eyes were on her, the question in his expression. Was she all right?

She nodded. She was breathing without issue, but she knew she would sport bruises. She'd have to wear a fichu until they faded. Thankfully, she had many. She rolled onto all fours, then pushed herself upright. As she straightened, she saw his hands hovering near her body as if to help her, but he couldn't bring himself to touch her.

"I'm fine," she said. Or rather she tried to say. It came out as a croak that had him wincing.

"Tea," he abruptly said. "Would you...you should..." His gaze jerked to the tray. The wine was gone and there was no tea to be found.

She raised her hand to stop him. This time he flinched away as though he expected to be cuffed. But he stilled a moment later, clearly bracing for a blow. She moved slowly, her hand open and relaxed. She touched his face gently, feeling the scratch of beard beneath her fingertips. Internally, her mind fled to the last man's beard she had touched like this: her father's just before he'd died. Ever since she was a small child, she'd liked touching his unshaven jaw and squeaking in mock horror at the roughness.

Mr. Frazier's was just as rough, just as abrasive on her fingertips, and so she left her hand there, stroking softly in memory. He remained absolutely still as she did it. His eyes were wide with confusion, but he didn't move. He allowed her to touch him, his whole body apparently frozen in shock.

Then the moment passed. She came back to the present, realizing abruptly that she sat on her knees stroking a strange man's beard. She pulled back, curling her fingers into her palm.

"My apologies," she rasped, then cringed as the sound abraded her throat.

"I will make you tea," he said as he pushed to his feet. "If there is lemon, it will soothe you even more." He glanced behind him. "Alex, you stay here. Guard our bags."

The boy nodded solemnly, and Maddy saw that his stance had eased out of his crouch. He now stood quietly, his expression carefully emptied. It was frightening really. What had happened to these men that they would wake from a sound sleep into an attack? The Barbary pirates, obviously, but she had not realized how very devastating their abduction had been. And even now, she doubted that she understood even a small part of what they had suffered.

With that thought in mind, she straightened to her full height. Once again, Mr. Frazier hovered close enough to catch her if she stumbled but refused to touch her person. Fortunately, she didn't need his help. Her body was embarrassingly sturdy—Amazonian in proportion—and he had only hurt her throat, not her legs.

"Tea would be capital," she managed, echoing his words from earlier that day. "But I can make my own. Though, perhaps you would care to join me?" She didn't know what she was thinking, inviting a half savage to join her for tea in the middle of the night. But he didn't seem savage right now, and far from discouraging her, this last moment had her more fully *interested* than before.

He didn't answer except to nod. His eyes were on her neck, presumably at the bruises he'd caused.

"It doesn't hurt in the least. Truly." Though her voice was still low and throaty. Then she turned and exited his bedchamber without waiting to see if he would follow. She listened closely for his movements, excruciatingly aware of even his breath. But she heard nothing. In the end, she stopped to check if he planned to hide in his bedchamber.

He stopped less than a foot behind her, the dirty tray held solidly in his hands. How had he managed to even keep the dishes from clattering?

He looked at her calmly, an expectant expression on his face. She didn't know how to respond so she gestured to the staircase with one hand and offered to take the tray with the other.

He frowned at her, clearly not understanding.

She echoed his expression. Did he really expect to follow her like a servant? Apparently so, because when she tried to take the tray from his grip, he would not surrender it.

"You are carrying the candles," he said gently. "It hardly makes sense for you to handle both. And"—he cut her off before she could say anything—"you should lead the way because I haven't an idea where to go."

She nodded. Of course that made sense. And yet it was bizarre to have him follow her as such, like a butler or a footman when he was decidedly not. The contradiction bothered her all the way into the kitchen.

"Set the tray there. I shall make tea and…"

Her voice trailed away. Once they had stepped into the kitchen, he became a blur of activity. He set the tray down, then stoked up the cooking fire. He fumbled a bit with it—as if he had not worked a fire in a very long time—but managed quickly enough. The room would be cheerfully warm very soon.

"Thank you," she said, secretly delighted that he would think to work the fire for her even though her uncle would call it a huge waste. They did not need the room to be hot when only the stove fire was required. But she said nothing as she turned to set the stove fire burning. The kettle was already on it, so it would heat for tea. But when she straightened from her task, it was to see him grab the large bucket for carrying water.

"We already have water in the kettle," she began, "but thank you..."

"Is there a well or a stream?" he asked.

"A stream just two houses down. But we don't need..."

"Please," he interrupted. He looked both uncertain and determined. Odd, but that was what she saw: a flash of awkwardness, but a core of certainty beneath. "I should like to take a bath tonight," he said clearly.

She stared at him. "But I would have to wake the staff to haul the water."

"I will bring the water. The tub is there," he said, pointing in the corner, where indeed a cheap wooden tub lay upside down beneath the flour sack. A harsh lye soap rested beside it.

"But surely you cannot mean to fetch and carry your own bathwater. It is a filthy patch of mud, and everything must be filtered through sand."

He nodded. "It will be the cleanest thing I have done in a very long time, I assure you."

"But it will take hours."

He nodded. "I know."

"But in the morning, there will be—"

"Tonight. Please." He gaze shifted to a place somewhere over her shoulder. "I have scars, angel, that might be frightening to some."

Oh! Oh dear. "O-of course," she stammered.

He disappeared in a flash while she was still biting her lip in mortification. He had scars? Of course he had scars. But where? And how bad? And really, she admonished herself, these were not proper thoughts, but she couldn't help herself. Mr. Frazier's face was rugged, handsome even, with an occasional flash of humor that she found especially appealing. She had naturally assumed that his body was equally well formed. But if he had been seriously hurt, then of course he bore scars. Scars ugly enough that he wished to bathe in solitude. The very idea left her feeling deeply sad.

She glanced at the door, wondering what she could do to help. There was little, of course, except help him with his bath. Despite his intentions, she sincerely doubted he would be able to manage on his own. The water would be filthy, as she told him. It would need to be strained and heated. That required two people, which meant she would be up for hours more and would likely soil her best dress.

She glanced down at her white skirt. As with all her gowns, it was a castoff from Rose. Given the difference in their sizes, Maddy had added panels along the seams to accommodate her larger chest, and yet another flounce at the hem for her height. Unlike her other dresses, she had not been the one to stitch this but had paid a seamstress to do the work. With red and blue ribbons, she thought the outfit rather patriotic and marvelously simple in its design. She loved this dress, and now it would likely be ruined unless she changed.

She was about to do that when Mr. Frazier returned with two buckets full of water. She scrambled to help him despite his objections. She quickly pulled the sand buckets down and set them where they were needed. He poured the dirty water into the sand, and beneath it, water started dribbling into a large kettle that would eventually heat over the fire. It was a task she had assisted in countless times, but never dressed in a gown meant for catching a husband.

The end was inevitable. The water splashed. The bucket rubbed. Despite her care, something somehow smudged two very large streaks of mud across her skirt. She saw them and bit back a sigh of dismay. He heard it, of course, and immediately began to apologize. But she shook her head with a forced laugh. "Never mind. I have dozens of gowns," she lied.

He searched her face but didn't comment, though his brows were narrowed in a frown. And into the silence, the kettle at last began to sing. She moved quickly to it, pulling out cups and tea. But when she turned back around, he had disappeared back to the stream to fetch more water. By the time he returned, she had already set out wafers and cheese and was just about to pour.

She stood to help him, but the filter was already set up. He shook his head firmly and then heaved the bucket up to pour. He moved effortlessly, without even sweat on his lip, and Maddy couldn't help but stare. She knew exactly how heavy those buckets were when full. Even their largest footman huffed and puffed when he brought water. But not Mr. Frazier. Whatever had caused his scars, it had not impaired his abilities except for his limp. And even that was not so pronounced as to require a cane.

"That will take a moment," she said softly when he had set down the second bucket. "Would you care to join me for tea while you wait?"

He flashed her a smile, so fast she thought she might have imagined it. But then he crossed to sit beside her at the large table, sitting down with his usual silence.

"How do you take it?" she asked, excruciatingly aware of how large he was right beside her. Or perhaps not so large, as she was rather tall herself. In truth, they were nearly alike in their height, but he was clearly stronger than she. More powerful too. More everything, in fact, and it made her feel delightfully feminine to sit across from him. Imagine that. Her, of the Amazonian build, feeling small! It actually took her breath away. So much so that she nearly missed how long it took him to answer her question about his tea.

"Sweet," he finally forced out. "I like it sweet."

Perhaps so, she thought, but surely not as sweet as what Rose's tea had been this afternoon. She plopped one large teaspoon of sugar in it and extended cup and saucer carefully toward him. He took it as if they were in the regent's drawing room, with precise fingers and a refined, "Thank you."

It was all very normal, she thought, and yet absolutely bizarre. They were not in a salon, the regent's or otherwise. And even though he was the cousin of an earl, his hands were scarred with cuts and layered with calluses. His clothing was that of a poor sailor, and he had nearly choked her to death. And yet, she sipped her tea with him in companionable silence as if this were truly the most normal thing in the world.

"Were you at a ball this evening?" he asked, gesturing to her attire.

"What?" she gasped as she was jolted from her musing. "Oh, no. A musical evening. Boring really, but unmarried women must be seen."

He nodded but didn't comment. She searched his face for a clue but got nothing. She was sure if he'd heard at least some of what her uncle had proposed to her today. Surely he had a thought or an opinion. Then she nearly kicked herself for her stupidity. Was she hoping for a rescuer? She of all people knew that they didn't exist. In fact, the very idea soured her stomach and she set down her teacup with a click.

"You know," she said a little too tartly. "We must consider the question of your payment. Uncle Frank will bluster and threaten, but do not allow him to charge you more than a shilling a night. He should not be charging you at all, but his Christian charity apparently stopped with me." It took a moment for her to realize what she'd said, and then her mood abruptly plummeted. Apparently, her uncle had something other than charity in mind when he'd opened his doors to her. But that was not for tonight's discussion, and certainly not with this man. He had enough difficulties of his own. So thinking, she continued to babble to cover her own embarrassment. "If he insists, you must agree to whatever he says, but tell him you will pay me. It shall be no more than a shilling, I assure you. I will cover the rest with the household accounts."

He arched a brow at her. The look was especially dashing on him, with his sun-weathered face and his rugged growth of beard. All he needed was an eye patch and all the girls would be swooning. "Do you do that often?" he asked, his voice low enough to produce a shiver across her skin.

"What?"

"Lie to cover for your uncle's boorish manners?"

How was she to answer that? Normally she would consider lying, if only to preserve the family name for Rose's sake. But she had the distinct feeling that he would see through any falsehood, so she simply shrugged. "I'm told that he was once a very kind man. When Aunt Susan was alive, when he was young and in the flush of his youth."

"And now?"

She sighed. "Now, I sometimes lie to cover for his

lacks." Then she lowered her lashes in shame only to be startled when his hand covered hers.

"We all do what we must to survive, Miss Wilson."

Her gaze leaped to his, startled by the depth of feeling in those quiet words. And in his eyes, she saw compassion wholly absent in anyone of her acquaintance. A level of understanding that had her vision blurring with tears. Good God, she could not be about to sob! Not when all he had done was extend a simple kindness.

He must have seen the tears. He must have known how deeply she was about to embarrass herself because he abruptly withdrew his touch. Pushing back from his seat, he looked toward the straining buckets. "I believe I shall leave the question of payment for tomorrow, if you please. I think a bath and shave is all I can manage for one night."

She nodded, knowing that he was covering for her. She was the one who couldn't manage tonight. At the moment, he appeared able to handle any difficulty in his path. "Of course," she said as evenly as possible. "I shall find you a razor."

"And I shall get some more water."

She turned to leave, only to have him stop her. He gripped her wrist before she even realized he'd moved. And when she looked back at him in question, his eyes were burning with intensity.

"Mr. Frazier?" she whispered, startled by his abrupt shift in mood.

"I shall need help," he said, his voice thick. "You said your father was a doctor. That you cared for his patients? His male patients?"

She nodded slowly. "I often helped my father," she

said the words, not entirely sure what she was answering. There was something in his expression, something underlying his words that she did not understand.

His fingers tightened, then abruptly released and his eyes canted away. "I had a fever recently and my hands still shake. I would ask Alex, but..."

"Oh!" she said, beginning to understand. "Oh, no. Alex is still too young. Too much nervous energy in his hands."

He nodded, and she saw relief in his eyes. "I am steady for most things," he said softly, "but razors..." A quiet tremor shook his body. "I do not like razors."

It took her a moment to connect razors with his scars. Had he been cut viciously? By a vile pirate? It was a leap of logic, but not a far one. She swallowed and gave him a smile. "You have nothing to fear," she said softly. "I am extremely steady. I will shave you tonight, and tomorrow will sort itself out soon enough."

His eyes widened, and she thought for a moment there was admiration in their depths. "Do you think so, Miss Wilson?" he asked softly. "Do you truly think that tomorrow will bring better things?"

"Of course," she answered calmly. "What else should one think?"

He had no answer for that except a harsh guttural grunt that might have been laughter, except there was no lightness in it. And when she pulled away, her heart beating in her throat, he immediately shuttered his expression and looked away.

"Mr. Frazier?" she finally said.

"My apologies. Returning to England has me more unsettled than I thought."

"Of course, sir, but—"

"Enough, angel," he interrupted quietly. "Just get the razor. I shall prepare the bath."

CHAPTER 4

Kit poured the last of the filtered water into the large pot over the fire. The wooden tub was already half filed. Within ten minutes, he would have enough scalding water for a bath like a civilized man. Ironic that, since he had never felt less civilized.

He thought he'd put the past behind him. A slave for three years, but free for four. He'd used that time to become less of an animal, to forgive his family, and to become the man he was now. But, seeing Michael and Lily again had been hard. Then to overhear through a doorway that his mother and grandmother were dead. And finally, that Scher, sweet Scher, the love of his youth, was married to his cousin and not more than a month after his disappearance? That was a cruel cut, deep into his soul.

He told himself it didn't matter. He had other things on his mind. Alex for one. Then the angel outside his door being opportuned by her uncle. All of these things distracted him, helped him push the pain away so he could pretend he did not ache. And it had worked for a time.

But now he was with this woman, this naive girl who spoke of sorting out his future when her own was in such disarray. He alternated between wanting to shield her from the world's ills and wanting to shake her for her ignorance! Didn't she know her uncle planned to have her? Didn't she understand how used she was in this household?

Of course she did. She was not stupid. She knew her only hope was to delay her uncle and pray that she found a husband quickly. And in the meantime, she ran the household, forced her uncle to accept two strangers into his home, and still had sweetness enough to talk of his future. The depth of her goodness stunned him, overwhelmed him, and made him insane with hunger.

Good God, he wanted her beneath him, spread for him alone. He wanted to take her as a man claims a woman, and in so doing he would see if her goodness was real. He would either break it or own it, but it would be *his*.

Kit clenched his jaw, refusing to release his howl of fury. Was he a beast then? Was he a slave again, forced to steal any tiny scrap of joy, consuming it quickly before it disappeared? *This* was why he had waited so many years to return to England. He knew then that he was more animal than man, a beast that walked upright and pretended to civility. He thought four years as a free man had changed him. He thought he was ready to return now.

How wrong!

One look at Miss Madeline Wilson, and he was surging with equal parts lust and fury. It hadn't been bad during the daylight when there were people and things to distract him. But now, alone in her kitchen? He wanted her with a hunger that frightened him. She was a gently reared lady and he would hurt her. And yet, he could not send her away. If anything, he wanted to push her, to see just how deep her sweetness went.

She was coming! He could smell her scent on the air and hear the light tread of her steps. He waited, breath suspended for her entrance. He knew the moment she appeared, and the beast inside him relished her soft squeak of alarm.

"What are you doing?"

Stripping so that she would see his scars and know him for the animal he was. That's what he thought, but not how he answered. Instead, his mouth curved into a slightly mocking smile. "I can hardly bathe in my clothing, can I?"

Her face was flushed, her eyes wide with fright. And she had never looked more beautiful. "B-but the water isn't ready!"

He turned to face her full on. He had yanked off his neckerchief, but had yet to pull off his shirt. Still, he had left the rough cotton open, exposing a small part of his chest if she dared to look.

She didn't. She kept her eyes firmly trained on his face, and her expression carefully blanked, though it took her two attempts before she could speak. "I—Um, if you would s-sit right here," she said, gesturing to the chair by the large kitchen table, "I can shave you while you wait." She offered him a white towel. "This will protect your shirt."

He curled his lip at the fine linen in her hand. "That towel cost ten times what my shirt did." Then he tilted his head in challenge. "Have you never seen a man's chest before?"

She stiffened in outrage. "I am the daughter of a surgeon, Mr. Frazier. I have seen naked chests aplenty."

"Good. Then mine shall cause you no shock." So

saying he pulled off his shirt in a single swift movement. He meant to do it quickly, to reveal the horror that was his body as one might uncover a monster at a traveling fair. It had once been a favorite thing to do with the whores. Reveal his body, hear them scream. He could learn a lot about a whore from the way she reacted to his scars.

So he pulled off his shirt and stood half naked before his angel, silently daring her to run. She should be grateful she was only being treated to the sight of half his deformities.

Except she didn't run. She didn't even scream, though he heard her gasp in shock. For a moment, he feared she was like the dead-inside whores who no longer cared about anything, least of all the condition of their customers. But one look at his angel's face and he could see that she was not dead inside. Far from it.

Her eyes were narrowed in thought as she inspected his chest. The large crescent scar was most obvious, beginning at his collarbone, curving around his torso to end at his waist. Most people stared at that, but she saw more than the large sweeping cut. He watched as her eyes picked up the pattern of smaller slashes, deeper, darker wounds.

"You have been whipped," she said softly.

He nodded.

"And stabbed, as well." Then she pointed to a series of parallel lines just above his navel. "But these lines…"

"A razor," he rasped. "Wielded with great skill."

"And designed to give pain." She lifted her gaze to his, her eyes bright with unshed tears. "Mr. Frazier," she whispered. "I am so sorry."

He meant to say something cutting then. He had come across sweet women every now and then, usually innocents abducted as he had been. Girls too shocked or dimwitted to realize the hell would be their lives from then on. He always said something cruel to reinforce that there was no room for tender emotions there.

But he was not in the bowels of a slave ship. He was in a London kitchen standing in front of a woman who had simply offered soft words. Suddenly, he felt ashamed of himself, for ripping off his shirt just to frighten her and for treating her as he did a common whore. He grabbed his shirt, his fingers fumbling with the coarse fabric.

She stopped him with a touch on his arm. "Please sit. It will be easier that way."

He had no choice but to obey. He had abused her enough already. He sat in the chair as she wrapped the starched white linen across his chest. "There's no need to soil—" he began.

"Of course there is," she said as she clipped the drape behind his back with a clothespin. "You can't possibly want the shaving lather dribbling down your chest. And besides, I need something to wipe the blade on."

He had no argument to that. She was right. And perhaps, he thought belatedly, she was avoiding the sight of his scars. Either way, he sat still, his hands gripping the side of the chair as she set about the business of lathering his face. Kit, of course, had felt such civilized wonders before. He'd had a valet once. One with a bad hand at shaving, as he recalled. His angel's hand was sure and steady, her movements efficient enough to show that she had done this many times before.

"Who did you shave before?" he asked, his words

unexpectedly harsh.

Her hands were busy dabbing on the lather about his face, but her eyes were steady as she looked at him. "Patients, from time to time. And then my father during his last months. This is his shaving kit."

There was a melancholy in her voice that pricked his conscience. He had no cause to be jealous of any man she may or may not shave. And from the sound of things, she could very well be performing this duty for Uncle Frank soon enough. That thought soured him enough that he grimaced.

"Stay still," she admonished. "I do not wish to cut you."

He almost smiled at that. Given what he'd lived through, he doubted a little nick would bother him. But she was applying a blade to his throat, so he closed his eyes and appreciated the wonder of her touch. Firm. Efficient. With only the slightest hint of a tremble.

No, he realized with shock. That was not her shaking but him. Why was he shaking? She moved to his side, and her skirt brushed against his forearm. It was coarse cotton, this time. She had changed from her white gown when she'd gone to fetch the razor. Now she wore a dark blue thing that somehow looked more appealing than her white frilly thing.

"You changed your gown," he said, rather than allow himself to think about his reaction to her. "I like this one better."

Her hands stilled against his cheek. And when they did not resume, he opened his eyes in question.

"Why would you say such a thing?" she asked, obviously wounded.

He frowned, confused. "This one fits you better. And

you should be in bolder colors."

"It is a work dress."

"It is not too small with panels on the side and an extra flounce at the hem."

"It is a *work* dress."

"Then your *musicale* dresses should look more like your work dresses."

She had no answer to that. Neither did he. Of all the things to be cross with him about, this was the oddest. But it did set his mind to churning. And before long, he began to speak, moving his lips as little as possible when she resumed her task at his beard.

"At the musicale this evening..." he began.

"Yes?"

"I must have been the topic of the hour."

He chanced a look at her face and saw her lips quirk in a half grimace, half laugh. "Yes, you were."

"And you must have been the woman of the hour too for bringing me to your home."

"Oh, no, that was Rose. She painted quite a picture of you as the doomed pirate returning home to fresh heartbreak."

"Me? But Alex—"

"Alex was cast as the insane servant, defending your honor but so mad as to not know he was attacking an earl."

He swallowed, wondering how all that the boy had experienced could be narrowed down to so few words. "Did they... Did you spend the whole time recounting the tale? Or did you hear anything else?"

She finished with one side of his face and shifted to the other. "Anything else?"

"Yes," he said. He looked at her, the hunger surging

anew. He did not want to ask her these questions. He wanted to be strong and whole for her. But he had to know, and she was the only one here to tell him. "About my family," he finally forced out. "I have three brothers. And there is the question of Scheherazade. How could she... Is she really..."

"Is she truly Lady Blackstone?"

"Yes." He flushed. He had given up thought of her years ago, but still part of him yearned to know.

She sighed, a soft puff of air that cooled his ear where the water had splashed. "Are you sure you wish to know?"

"Yes."

"Very well. I will tell you everything I heard, but I cannot guarantee that it is true."

"Whatever you know would help." And it would distract him from his desire to cross the bare inch that separated them and caress her, hold her, take her.

Obviously unaware of his thoughts, she began to speak. While she scraped at his face, she listed off all that she had heard, her musical voice a temptation all its own. He could have gotten lost in her voice. He closed his eyes and let the sound sink into his bones. But in time, his mind caught up with her words, and he began marveling anew.

Her mind was obviously sharp, her memory excellent, but as she recounted every detail, he noticed a particular emphasis: that of a woman on the hunt for a husband. Listening to her, he could understand how her mind cataloged each person, noted specifics of clothing and conversation, and logged them in her brain as one of two things: eligible for matrimony or not.

It was to be expected, of course, given her situation,

but it was still amazing to hear the way her mind worked. She noted that Mr. Johan pretended to be a scholar, but his glee in relaying his experience at Mr. Frazier's funeral suggested a gossip's heart. Apparently the church had been filled to the rafters, so everyone had an opinion of Scheherazade as she made her final good-bye.

Lady Haverson had been in London at the time of Kit's supposed death. Her girls were not out yet, but she had gone to the parties and heard that Lady Blackstone—Scheherazade Martin at the time—left London straight after the funeral and was not seen for an entire month. And then, up she pops as Lady Blackstone.

Her daughters were a bit more detailed with their information. Emily, who was likely to marry a very nice vicar, said that Lord and Lady Blackstone resided in a town near London. They have two sons and a third on the way, whom they hope is a girl. Susan, who is rather portly but has a good heart, corrected her sister on this point, saying that they had two daughters and were hoping for a son. She found it of particular note that Mr. Rufton—a young buck recently come to town, still a bit wild in his oats—thought they seemed happy together. He had seen them both recently at the Tavern Playhouse and they were quite in love.

And so it went, first with the gossip about Scher and Brandon, and then on to what people had relayed about his family. His eldest brother was married and firmly ensconced in the baronetcy, two others were not. Lucas, his favorite brother, was wandering about the continent somewhere, and the youngest, Paul, was somewhere up north. His cousins were busy propagating heirs. Only one was a serious gambler, another a rake.

Kit's face was clean and the water boiling by the time she finished speaking. He had listened raptly to her voice and her words, marveling at her mind, focusing on the nuances of her speech rather than the fact that she was recounting tales of his own his family as if it were a stranger's. Because it was a stranger's.

"And that is all that I can think of," she finally said. "Though I am sure this will be discussed quite thoroughly in the next few weeks, so there is bound to be more. But perhaps," she ventured gently, her expression tentative, "you would like to find this out on your own? Perhaps visit your brother at the baronetcy?"

Visit Donald? Donald who had been prosaic by the time he was twelve. Donald who always had to stand up to speak. Donald who had chucked him under the chin once and called him a good boy like a dog. What would Donald say to him now? Probably that his brother had turned into a mad wolf and should be put down.

"Yes," he said, lying as fast as he could find the words. "Yes, I should love to see my brother again."

"Excellent," she said with a grin, which made him glad he had lied. She had a beautiful smile. "And now, sir, I believe your bath awaits."

He stood from the chair, feeling awkward as a silence descended between them. Fortunately, there was work to do, so he shifted to the boiling pot. She made to help him, but he glared her back.

"I have worked with much worse, I assure you, and this is too hot for you," he said as he lifted the pot and began to pour it into the tub. It splashed him, as was inevitable, but it was nothing to him who had worked with boiling pitch.

She stood to the side, watching him with a strange expression on her face. Part rapt expression, part horror, and much thought. She was thinking, his angel, as she watched him work, and he wondered what wandered through her mind.

Then it was done. The tub was filled, the water cooled enough by what had already been filtered and waiting. She had brought him perfumed soap and a fine towel. All that was left after he set the boiling pot to the side was to undress and submerge himself.

He looked at her, his angel, who was abruptly coming to the same realization. If she did not leave right now, he would shuck his filthy breeches and reveal himself to her. All of himself, including his thick and jutting erection.

He should have hid himself, but he was feeling too battered from the day's events to hide his body's condition and too embarrassed to know how to smooth over the awkwardness. But, of course, only the lingering shadow of Kit was embarrassed. The beast he was had no apology for his lust. The beast was thinking of dragging her into the steaming tub with him.

"Have you ever seen a naked man before?" he asked, wondering what prompted him to be so blunt.

She nodded, clearly struggling to put on a brave face. "I cared for all my father's needs. He was bedridden for nearly two months."

"I doubt he needed you as I do," he said.

She blinked, then straightened. "Such a thing is not a need, sir, but a want."

"Sometimes it is a need," he said, his mind already filling in images that should not be in his head. Would she turn willing if he dragged her to the floor now? Could he kiss her into compliance, offer her pirate gold and jewels to quiet her conscience? "Have you ever touched a man when he is like this?"

Her eyes jumped to his. "Certainly not!"

"I do not know how it is for a woman, but for a man, that first brush is like a brand—burned into our memory forever. Does she grip him hard and make him her slave? Does she feather a touch that torments with its very lack of substance? Or is it somewhere in between? Firm and yet so sweet as to make a man hunger for her with every breath in his body."

She stared at him then, her eyes drifting slowly down to where his organ pushed at his breeches only to return back to his face. And in her gaze, he read interest, desire, and then a slow creeping coldness.

"You are thinking of her. Of Scheherazade."

He jolted in shock, not because she was correct but because his former fiancée was the furthest thing from his thoughts.

"I am sorry for your loss, sir," his angel said tartly. "But you will find no substitute in me."

"Then you best leave now," he said as he popped the button at his waist. "Only a woman could keep me from that bath."

"Good night, sir," she said, the melody gone from her voice. "Leave the tub when you are done. I will have the footman clean it up tomorrow."

He didn't wait to respond but pushed his pants down to his ankles. He made his movements abrupt, startling even, but he watched from the corner of his eye. Sure enough, she was gone when he straightened, but she had lingered long enough to see him naked. Long enough to catch a flash of the whole of him before propriety made her flee.

The sight of her looking at him was so mesmerizing he relived it over and over again as he sunk into his first real bath in seven years.

CHAPTER 5

"Oh my God, it's true! You're still in bed! Imagine the day that I wake before you! Oh, Maddy! I have had the best idea ever!"

Maddy pushed up from her disaster of a bed and squinted at the clock beside her bed. Just after ten o'clock in the morning. Rose was right. Usually she would be up by now and finished with the morning chores. But as she had spent until nine o'clock this morning tossing and turning while trying *not* to dream of a certain man, ten o'clock felt especially cruel.

"Maddy! Are you even awake?"

"Please, don't shout, Rose," she groaned. "I have a terrible headache." It wasn't exactly a lie. Rose's girlish squeals were indeed giving her a terrible headache.

"But you must listen to me! I have the best idea in the absolute world!"

"Rose, please. Don't bounce on the bed."

"But you're not listening! Oh dear, are you ill? You're not ill, are you? It would ruin everything! For I have the best—"

Gathering her resources, Maddy surged forward and slapped her hand over Rose's mouth. Her cousin gasped in surprise, then started giggling. Her breath was warm and ticklish, and her eyes sparkled with mischief. It didn't take long to melt Maddy's annoyance. After all, Rose was delightful when she had such enthusiasm.

Surrendering to the inevitable, she let her hand drop away from Rose's face. "Now, sweetheart, go ask for some very strong tea, please—"

"But—"

"I know you are bursting with ideas, but I need a moment to wash my face."

"It's the perfect—"

"Go get me some tea, Rose," she said a little more tartly than she intended. "I shall get paper and ink together and prepare to write down every tiny scrap of your wonderful thought."

Rose's face brightened. "That's an excellent idea! There will be all so many notes—"

"Tea, dear. I need that tea!"

Rose huffed, clearly restraining herself as she left. Fortunately, the girl no longer bellowed down for what she wanted, but would rush all the way to the kitchen.

The kitchen! Where everyone would be chattering about the bath that *someone* took last night. Oh Lord, what would Rose make of that? Nothing, she hoped. After all, it made sense that Mr. Frazier needed a bath. It was just that no one had been called to help him. *That* was what everyone would be wondering. *Who* had helped Mr. Frazier? Then they would think Maddy had helped him because that was what she did in this household—helped manage things—and then the speculation would soar from there.

Wild Maddy Wilson—the girl who'd run with gypsies—helped bathe a pirate when everyone else was asleep. My goodness, what talk there would be! And once the servants started, then it wasn't long before the peerage picked up the tale. And before long, her name would be irremovably linked with Mr. Frazier's scandals, all of them, all the way back to his falling in love with an actress. And that would end any of her matrimonial chances this season.

She fell back against her bed with a moan. She hated that her entire life had been reduced to the endless search for a husband. She never used to care what people thought of her. But then her father had died and she had come to live here. And now—just yesterday, in fact, after her talk with Uncle Frank—she had realized just how very much she hated it. The endless gossip and the endless work. Parties night after night and for what? So she could make prattle with pompous men, get her toes stepped on by clumsy ones, or worse yet, sit on the sidelines being ignored while Rose flirted and chattered an endless string of nonsense. Lord, she was tired. And now her reprieve was up because she heard her cousin's rapid tread on the stairway.

Marshaling her strength, Maddy dashed to the door and turned the lock. It wouldn't hold her cousin off for long, but it would last while she went through her morning ablutions. Sure enough, the doorknob rattled.

"Maddy! Maddy! The door's locked!"

"What? Just a moment, sweetheart!"

"Maddy! Why would you lock the door?"

"Hmmm? Just habit, dear. There are men in the house, you know."

"Oh yes, I know! That's just what I wanted to talk to you about."

Heavens. She couldn't have the girl shout it in the hallway. That would only add fuel to the gossip fire. "Hush, sweetheart! You'll wake your father."

Truthfully, nothing could wake Uncle Frank once he fell asleep. It was his only defense against the noise Rose could create.

"Then open the door!" called Rose in an extremely loud whisper.

Maddy in no way felt ready to face the day, but she pulled open the door anyway. "Come in, Rose, come in. And lower your voice."

"Do you think I woke Father? I hope so because I have the most wonderful idea!"

Maddy went back to brushing her hair, trying to use the motion to soothe her disordered thoughts. It didn't work. Certainly not with the thought of Mr. Frazier waking and intruding on her morning as well.

Meanwhile, Rose dropped onto the bed only to jump up again. "You didn't get out any paper and ink!" she said. "Oh, never mind. I shall take notes while you listen. It really is the most marvelous idea."

"Of course it is," Maddy said, her mind spinning to her wardrobe. What could she possibly wear? Not a work dress. They were to have afternoon callers. Though he did say he liked her work dress much better than her favorite one, which now had mud smears on the skirt. And all of her nice dresses were just the same, with panels on the side and flounces at the hem. One even sported three full flounces.

"Maddy, I have decided to host a tea party!"

"Lovely idea. Do you think there's a gown of yours that I could borrow? Something too large for you?"

Rose trilled a laugh. "You know there's nothing I have that will fit you. Just take money from the household budget if you want a new gown. Say it was a gift from my pin money. Papa won't notice."

No. But he would notice if there weren't a maid to clean his room or food on the table. When Maddy had first arrived, the staff hadn't been paid in months because of Rose's "borrowing" of the household money.

"I've told you that we can't do that, Rose," Maddy admonished. Which meant Maddy would have no new clothes. So she selected her least ornate gown with the tiniest panels on the side. It was another white one, of course, but it sported a single rich green ribbon beneath the bodice, which gave her a nice form, she thought. Plus it had a fichu to cover her throat bruises, which she had just noticed in the mirror. Thankfully, Rose wasn't very observant. Still, she pulled her dressing gown tight and high before giving Rose her complete attention.

"All right, sweetheart. I'm sorry I took so long today. Tell me, please, right away, exactly what your wonderful idea is."

Rose huffed in disgust. "But I already told you! I'm going to host a tea party!"

Maddy nodded, waiting for the rest of the news. After all, tea was hardly the most original of ideas. "Well, I suppose that's a lovely idea," she said slowly.

Rose leaned back in her chair, making no attempt to write anything at all. "But you are thinking it's a normal tea. It won't be, Maddy. It's going to be the event of the Season!"

"Well, forgive me, dear, but I don't see how."

"Because I'm going to reunite Scheherazade Martin and Mr. Frazier at my tea."

Maddy stilled, horror blooming uncontrolled in her body. "Miss Martin is no longer a miss, Rose. She's Lady Blackstone, and why would you want to be so very cruel to Mr. Frazier?"

Rose stiffened at the criticism. "Well, he has to see her sometime, doesn't he? Why not at my tea?"

"Because it's cruel! Can you imagine how hard it will be on him? To see the woman he loved married to someone else? And in front of everybody?"

"It is absolutely not cruel," Rose replied heatedly, "because there's more." She abruptly leaned forward, her eyes going dreamy. "You know, don't you, that Papa has said I must find a husband this Season."

Maddy leaned against her post on her bed, frowning slightly. "I know he has high hopes for you this Season, but that doesn't mean you must—"

"He said I must." Rose scrunched up her face in disgust. "He said he will not support me another Season. If I don't get married he will throw me out on the street!"

Rose's voice was very dramatic, as was typical for her. Unfortunately, Maddy couldn't quite dismiss it as untrue. She knew exactly how thin the household accounts were. And given her uncle's discussion with her yesterday, she knew he wanted Rose to marry and leave the home. In fact, he probably said so quite clearly to Rose.

"Nevertheless," Maddy said firmly. "You are his daughter. He would not throw you out on the street. He loves you. And besides, you know it would look very bad on him, and he would find that vastly uncomfortable."

Rose nodded and carefully wiped away a tear. She did indeed look shaken, but Maddy had no way to tell if her cousin really believed in her fate or was just becoming a better actress.

"But, you see, it doesn't matter," said Rose, her face the picture of trembling bravery. "For, you see, I have decided on a husband."

"Of course you have not!" Maddy cried. "The Season hasn't even really begun! You can't possibly have—"

"I'm going to marry Mr. Frazier!"

Maddy's words froze in her throat. It took her a moment for her to repeat her cousin's words in her mind, but even then she couldn't quite understand it. "I sorry. You're what?"

"I'm going to marry Mr. Frazier!"

"But... But why? I mean, he's hardly the type of gentleman you usually want." Rose tended toward handsome, glib-tongued dandies. Mr. Frazier was nothing of the sort.

"He called me beauty, don't you remember? He said I was beautiful and then later called me his beauty. *His* beauty."

"Wasn't that Mr. Morgan?"

"Of course not. That was Mr. Frazier! As if I would pick a servant as my husband!"

Maddy sighed. "Mr. Morgan is not a servant, Rose. And of course you are very beautiful." With her petite body, blond curls, and striking blue eyes, Rose was the epitome of English female perfection, unlike Maddy, who was dark haired, large, overly curvy. "But that still doesn't tell me why you want to marry Mr. Frazier. Many men have called you beautiful. Scores of them."

"Think of it," she said sweetly. "He's cousin to the earl, is rich as Croesus, and will very rapidly become the catch of the Season."

"You're the *daughter* of an earl. To marry Mr. Frazier would be a horrible mésalliance."

"My earldom is decrepit and useless, whereas his is wealthy and thriving. And besides," Rose added straightening her spine in indignation, "haven't you always said I should marry for love? That with my title and beauty, I could pick whomever I want?"

Maddy shifted uncomfortably. "Of course I did, sweeting, but why would you want Mr. Frazier? He's rough and..." She almost said scarred, but she couldn't voice that without confessing how she's seen his scars. "And he's just come back from a horrible ordeal."

"Exactly!" cried Rose. "Don't you see? He's a tragic pirate, returned for his fiancée only to find her married to someone else. That's tragic!"

"One doesn't marry tragic, Rose."

"But I know just how it will happen, if only you can arrange it!"

"Rose—"

"Listen to me! Mr. Frazier and Lady Blackstone will meet again, after all these years, at my tea. Everyone will be there, of course, because they'll want to see. And I shall be in the middle of it all, being kind and serving tea and the like."

"You hate serving tea."

"But I shall do it this time. Because, don't you see, after a few minutes with Lady Blackstone, Mr. Frazier will see that she's a terrible, grasping shrew—"

"You don't know that!"

"Of course I do. That's what everyone says."

"But—"

"Anyway, Lady Blackstone will be hideous to Mr. Frazier because that sort always is. And after she leaves, I will go comfort him. Love will blossom and I shall be married to him by the Season's end. It will be the love match of the century!"

Rose had obviously spent a great deal of time

thinking of what she wanted. None of it was steeped in reality, but that never seemed to bother the girl. And in truth, she did have one thing right. Anything that brought Mr. Frazier and Lady Blackstone together would the event of the Season, at least until another event came along.

"Rose, I don't think your idea is quite practical."

"Of course it is! That's why I've made it a tea, you know. Papa would never allow me a ball. Teas are much less expensive and give more room to talk."

"Well, yes, that is rather well thought out."

"I thought of a musical evening, but those are really quite horrible. Having to listen to someone sing and all."

"Yes, very true, but you haven't addressed the biggest problem."

Rose arched a delicate brow. "No?"

"No. Sweetheart, do you even know Lady Blackstone?"

She stiffened, pulling back with shock. "Of course not! You know it would be ruinous for an unwed miss to know her sort."

"Exactly. So what makes you think she would come to your tea? Especially as she will know it is designed to throw Mr. Frazier and her together so that everyone can watch what happens. She would be a fool to attend!"

"Ah, but then you haven't heard the best part of all!" said Rose, her eyebrows waggling.

"Really?"

"Really! You see, I shall bribe her to attend!"

Maddy stared at her cousin, her mind momentarily stunned into silence.

"See!" Rose cried. "See how brilliant my idea is?"

Maddy shook her head, at last finding the words. "Sweetheart, you have to have money to bribe someone."

"But I do have money!" Rose answered. "I have been saving up my pin money for months and months. And with a little from the household accounts—"

"No. No, Rose. Absolutely not! There is nothing available in the household accounts."

Rose stared at Maddy as if she'd just been horribly betrayed. "But of course there's a little…"

"No, Rose. There isn't at all. And it doesn't matter. By all accounts, Lady Blackstone is the one who is rich as Croesus, not Mr. Frazier. And—"

"It will work!" Rose said, leaping up from her chair. "I know it! I know he and I are destined to be together!"

Maddy looked at her cousin and friend. Yes, Rose was definitely being dramatic, but that didn't change the girl's passionate belief in what she said. She truly did believe she and Mr. Frazier were going to fall in love. It was ridiculous, of course. Mr. Frazier was unsuitable on so many levels, and Rose would eventually see it. But still, that didn't change Rose's romantic dream now.

"You are so very sure of everything," Maddy said softly as she looked at her very young cousin. "It is one thing I so very much like about you. So passionate."

"It's easy to be sure when one is right," Rose said primly.

"Yes, well, I suppose it is." Someday, her cousin would have the pride knocked out of her. Someday, her passion would not be enough, her absolute belief in herself would fail. Someday would be a very sad time for Rose. And Maddy couldn't help but wish that "someday" was very far away. Her cousin was alive in ways that Maddy had lost. When had Maddy last felt that delighted about anything? Not for very many years.

"It will not work, sweetheart."

"Maddy!" Rose cried, climbing onto the bed to come nose-to-nose with her cousin. "You cannot mean to stop this before it even begins!"

Maddy held up her hands. "It is cruel to Mr. Frazier. This is the man you believe you love. Why would you want to hurt him?"

"Because he has to see that Lady Blackstone is not the woman for him! He has to mourn her before he can turn to me!"

"Sweeting—"

"And besides! He has already pronounced it a capital idea!"

Maddy had been pushing off the bed, trying to get some distance between herself and her cousin's wild gestures. But at those words, her head whipped around to stare at her cousin. "What did you say?"

"He thought it a grand plan."

"Never you say!"

"He absolutely did!" Rose shot back. "I told him my idea just this morning and he thought it was wonderful."

"Mr. Frazier is awake?"

Rose blinked. "Well, yes. How else could he have told me that my idea was delightful?"

Maddy narrowed her eyes, searching her cousin's face for signs of exaggeration or deception. She couldn't find any. Of course, that didn't mean much, as Rose always believed whatever nonsense she said.

"No, Rose, this won't fadge. Why would Mr. Frazier

agree to be put on display like that? Just for your benefit?"

Rose huffed as she climbed off the bed. "Because he loves me, silly. He just doesn't know it yet."

Maddy threw up her hands. "Well, yes, of course there's that. But if he doesn't know it yet, it can't possibly be his motivation. So again, Rose, why would he say yes?"

Rose wrinkled her nose in disgust, and her lips pursed into a delicate pout. "First you must promise to help with my tea."

"I promise to do all in my power to assist you in finding the right and proper husband for you."

"That will be at my tea!"

"Rose—"

"Because even if you don't believe Mr. Frazier and I are meant for one another, you know that this tea will be an *event*."

Maddy had no argument to that. "Yes, I suppose it would be."

"Which means every eligible gentleman will come to it."

"Gentlemen don't often come to teas."

"They will to this one. And even if they don't, they'll flock to me—to *us*—later just to hear the tale of what truly happened."

That also was true. It had happened last night at the musical evening. Everyone in attendance had wandered by to speak with them. She couldn't ask for a better opportunity to meet eligible gentlemen. But still...

"I cannot think Mr. Frazier would agree to this."

"But he did!" Rose stomped her foot for emphasis.

Maddy sighed. "Very well then. Let me get dressed. I

will discuss the details with Mr. Frazier himself." She went to open the door, but Rose stopped her by gripping her wrist.

"You promise you'll see that Lady Blackstone attends?"

Maddy grimaced. "No one can promise that but Lady Blackstone herself."

"But you have a way of getting things done, Maddy. I know you can do it. Plus there is my bribe money…"

Maddy held up her hand to stop her cousin. "Let me see what Mr. Frazier says first."

"But you promise you'll help?"

Maddy sighed. "Yes, sweeting, you know I promise. I promised the day I came to this house."

Rose dimpled prettily. "Yes, I know. But I still like to hear you say it."

Maddy pulled open her door. "Go! Let me get dressed!"

"All right. And I'll go tell Mr. Frazier that you want a word with him." Then she dashed out of the room.

"What? No! There's no need!" The words were out, but it was too late. Rose had already disappeared down the hall.

CHAPTER 6

"That's what Mr. Smithson said, but Maddy thought it was funny…."

Kit turned his face to the door to the dining room. Someone was coming down the stairs, and only one person had a tread that steady and yet light. Finally, his angel with the beautiful voice was coming downstairs.

"Maddy's country ways makes her more tolerant than most," continued Rose. "She seems to find the most terrible things amusing…"

Rose continued to prattle on, seemingly unaware that only Alex listened to what she said. They were all at the breakfast table, except for Maddy. While Rose chattered, her father read the racing pages, Alex toyed with his food, and Kit waited, his belly taut, for that first glimpse of Maddy. After she left the kitchen last night, he had lingered in his bath, fantasizing about her. And then in his bedroom, he had been tormented by dreams of her. The torment was real, of course, as his visions were nightmares. Last night, he saw Maddy beaten, whipped, and worse. Now he needed to see her again just to convince himself she was unharmed.

"Anyway, she tells me that everything shall go smoothly, if only we apply ourselves. That is Maddy, more efficient than any servant and no burden at all to us, right, Papa?"

Frank Pershing, the Earl of Millsford, grunted rather than answer. He didn't even look up.

"See? She's wonderful, and I am ever so thrilled to have a sister. Do you know, her first months here, she even did the cooking! Said our cook was terrible and robbing us blind!"

Where was she? Kit wondered. Everyone else was here, lingering over breakfast. Kit had finished his much earlier, but he had waited, anxious to see her. And then Rose had appeared, her hair all askew and her eyes wide with excitement. She'd been surprised that Maddy hadn't risen yet, which only increased his alarm, illogical though it was. She was likely sleeping in after her long night of it. But still, where was she?

Then Rose appeared a second time with the urgent news that his angel expressly wished to speak with him. Heat had speared through him at the words, but he quickly quashed his hunger. It was daylight, and he would be a man, damn it, not a beast. But then she still did not come down! Instead, it was the earl who had wandered in, farting as he walked.

And now, hallelujah, Maddy appeared! Not from the stairs, as he expected, but from the servant's entrance to the kitchen. She was wearing another god-awful white gown that only emphasized how sallow her skin was. His eyes went immediately to her neck, where he knew she sported bruises. Bruises that *he* had caused. But a fichu and some paste covered the evidence. And thankfully, she moved easily enough, so perhaps he had not done her permanent harm. She was carrying a plate of eggs while the cook trailed beside her holding a fresh pot of tea.

"So there was nothing amiss this morning?" she asked, her brows narrowed in confusion.

"Not a lick. Why would there be?"

"No reason. I just thought..." Her eyes shifted to Kit's and he smiled benignly. Obviously she thought he would leave the debris of his bath for others to clean up. Years ago, Kit would have. But the last seven years had changed him, and in some ways for the better. Meanwhile, she turned back to the cook. "I just thought I heard something last night. Must have been dreaming."

"Well, it's no wonder what with strangers in the house and all," the cook responded while shooting him a dire look. Kit raised his eyes in surprise. The cook obviously treated his angel with a motherly kind of affection and was warning him off. He liked that, and he gave the servant a nod of respect. To his amusement, the woman grew flustered and retreated quickly to the kitchen. Which finally gave him time to focus all his attention on her.

"Good morning, Miss Wilson. How are you faring today?"

She lifted her gaze and smiled brightly, but the expression didn't reach her eyes. What he saw instead was worry as her gaze slid from him to Rose. The girl picked up on the attention immediately, launching into yet more meaningless prattle.

"That was an excellent choice of gown, Maddy. I do think that's my favorite of my old dresses."

Maddy gave her a pained smile. "Thank you, Rose. And thank you for detaining Mr. Frazier long enough for me to have a word with him."

"I've been talking to him about the tea and he believes it's a capital idea."

Maddy raised her eyebrows in surprise, and he could not suppress his surge of heat when her gaze returned to him. "Indeed, sir? I had not thought you would agree."

Kit frowned, searching his memory. "Er, I'm sorry. I'm afraid I was daydreaming."

"My tea!" cried Rose with a laugh. "You love the idea!"

Of tea? What was there to object to in tea?

"Yes," inserted Maddy softly. "A tea party where Lady Blackstone would be invited."

Scheherazade. Of course. *That* tea. For the first time since Maddy had entered the room, he allowed his eyes to drop. His mind quickly ran through the reasons for and against the party. The list wasn't long. He needed to see Scheherazade—once in private, once in public. It was the way things were done in London. He also understood why Lady Rose wanted to host the event since it would make her cause célèbre for a couple weeks at least.

He pasted on a smile, but he could not quite meet his angel's eyes. So he shifted to the easier of the two women. "You have been most gracious in offering your home to us while we get our bearings," he said to Lady Rose. "It would be churlish to refuse any event you planned."

Rose dimpled prettily even as she flashed a look of triumph at her cousin. "You see! He understands completely. We shall have it next week!" She hopped up from her chair. "I shall begin compiling the guest list immediately. Oh and, Papa, never fear, I shan't require you to attend." Then with an impish giggle, she spun on her toes and left.

Meanwhile, her father at last closed up the betting pages. He looked hard at first Alex then Kit, his gaze narrowing in threat. Alex bristled immediately, but Kit knew better than to make an outward show of his anger. Instead, he remained still, a placid expression on his face.

"You can stay through the tea, but no longer," the earl half growled. "And you'll pay me for it. But the women are mine."

"Uncle Frank!" Maddy exclaimed, but none of the men so much as blinked in her direction.

"Yours?" asked Kit with a slow curl to his lip. "Then you have branded them with hot iron? You have cut them or bought them—"

"Don't be ridiculous!" the earl snapped.

"I don't believe I am. The daughter is yours by law. The mistress is not your mistress yet and therefore—"

"You will shut your filthy mouth!" the earl bellowed as he slammed his palms flat on the table. To the side, Alex shot to his feet, but Kit gestured him back with a flick of his wrist.

"Gentlemen please!" Maddy squeaked, but Kit could not break his gaze with the earl to give her a reassuring look. Instead, he leaned back in his chair to stare cold and steady at the earl.

"Do you know what I learned as a pirate slave, my lord? How to whip a man within an inch of his life. How to wield a knife to castrate or to kill. I *have* branded men, women, and children with hot iron. Do you seriously think slamming your palms onto a wood table will intimidate me?"

He watched the message sink into the earl's small brain. Kit was a savage, and he did not take threats well. But then neither did the earl.

"I want you out of my house within the hour," the

man growled.

"And disappoint your charming daughter? I am to attend her tea, remember?"

"Rose be damned! You will leave my home!"

Kit waited a long time. He held the earl's gaze long enough to make the man sweat. But in the end, he conceded. With a slight tilt of his head, he agreed. "Within the hour." He glanced at Alex. "Would you please pack your bag?"

With a huff, the earl spun on his heel and stomped out, leaving a thundering silence in his wake. Alex gave him a shaky nod before disappearing. And still, Kit did not move. He would not leave his angel before the very last second. So he sat, his expression carefully blanked while she stared first after her uncle then at him. Finally, she shook her head and reached with a shaking hand for her tea.

"Why would you goad him like that?" she asked, her voice not quite under control.

"He is the one who claimed to own you."

She brushed the comment off with a wave of her hand. "He's an earl. He feels he owns the very air we breathe. What difference does it make to you?"

His eyes shifted to hers. Did she really not understand? "I *have* been owned. For three hellish years, I was the property of a corsair named Venboer. I sweated and bled for him. And I made sure others did the same. Ownership is a serious business, Miss Wilson. He should not make claims he cannot support."

Her expression shifted then. Frustration gave way to surprise and then a gentle sympathy. But she had no words for him. He could see her struggle to find something to say, but for the first time, he did not want to hear her voice. He didn't want empty platitudes or inadequate words. So he stopped her with a touch on her arm.

"He does not own you, Miss Wilson. Do not allow him to pretend that he does. All too soon it becomes fact whether you wish it or not."

She looked at where his hand rested on his arm. He didn't know what that meant to her, but he saw his dark, slave's tan against her white flesh. He saw the scars on his skin against her pristine softness. And he felt her gentle tremble through her skin.

"I won't," she finally said. Then she looked at his face. "But now you have to leave."

"Would that pain you?"

She bit her lip and didn't answer. He could see the confusion in her eyes and knew that he had discomforted her. Likely she had never met a man as wild or bizarre as him in her entire life. That thought soured his mood, so he covered by reaching beneath the table to pull out his satchel. She blinked in surprise when he drew it out. Clearly she'd had no idea he'd kept it with him. But he'd be damned if he abandoned this bag to the maid—or the earl's—prying eyes. It took him less than a second to draw out a Spanish gold coin and set it on the table before her.

"I have wealth," he said softly. "Just no English money."

"Put that away!" she hissed. "The staff is honest, but they're not exactly trustworthy when gold is flashed."

He pushed it toward her. "It's for you. Take it to a bank and exchange it for English sterling. A few coppers to the household account, and the rest for a new dress. As my thanks for helping me last night."

Her lips pressed tight as she looked at the coin. Then her body shrank away from it as if it were poison, and when she lifted her eyes to his, they were burning with fury.

"You called me a mistress," she said, her cultured voice in no way covering for her anger. "And now you seek to pay me with gold. I helped you out of Christian charity, Mr. Frazier."

"Christians cannot be paid? I assure you, the missionaries in Barbados certainly were."

"Well, I am not in Barbados. And I am certainly *not* any man's mistress. So you will take your gold and you will be gone from this house as you promised. I begin to think you are much more savage than your clothes would suggest."

He arched a brow. "You have seen my scars, Miss Wilson. And you are only *now* thinking that?"

She released her breath with a huff, but it in no way lessened the animosity in her eyes. "You are a puzzle, Mr. Frazier. One I do not care to solve."

His chin dipped in acknowledgment as he pushed his chair away from the table. "Then I will be off." He picked up the coin off the table. "You should have a dress to replace the one I ruined last night. I will visit a bank today for English money, then make sure you are recompensed—"

Her eyes flashed and he immediately adjusted his statement.

"That the earl is recompensed for my night's care."

She inclined her head. No queen could appear more regal. "I would be grateful for that, sir."

He caught her chin before she could pull back. Her skin was soft, but the bones were firm. Her lips parted on a gasp, and he found himself staring at the hot, wet center of her mouth.

"Gratitude," he murmured, "is not what I want."

Then he took a kiss. He couldn't stop himself. But he did manage to keep from ravishing her mouth. He pressed his lips to hers and felt the heat of her breath as it invaded him. He touched his tongue to the seam of her mouth, wet the exquisite expanse of her lips in a single, long stroke, and then he forced himself to withdraw.

Her eyes were wide, her body frozen in shock. But her lips were red and glistening from his kiss. And she did not scream. He counted that a windfall.

"Good day, Miss Wilson," he said. And then he turned and fled before her shock had a chance to fade.

Maddy made a point of yawning behind her fan, shooting Rose a look to see if the girl was watching. Rose grimaced back but acknowledged the silent request with a dip of her head. Rose never liked leaving a party early, especially when she was the center of attention, but Maddy needed to get home. She needed to pretend to go to sleep so she could escape the house and get on to her real errand.

Meanwhile, Rose continued chatting. Everyone wanted to know about Mr. Frazier and his terribly violent companion. Rose kept it coy, of course, neither giving out too much information nor too little. It was easy for her to keep the audience entertained, especially since she fabricated most of her information. No one bothered to ask Maddy her opinion. Rose was much more entertaining, and Maddy preferred not to speculate anyway.

Unfortunately, that's all she'd been doing all day: speculating. What exactly had Mr. Frazier meant when he had kissed her like that? Did he truly see her as a mistress? As *his* mistress, perhaps? She didn't believe so. One kiss was absolutely not an invitation to carte blanche. Perhaps, he meant to be honorable by her. As much as she might wish it, she didn't believe so. He didn't seem like a man looking for a wife. And even if he were about to propose marriage, would she accept?

He was so different than anyone she had ever met. Sometimes he seemed more like the gypsies of her youth in their passions and intense, focused emotions. But whereas they were loud in their joys and sorrows, everything about Mr. Frazier seemed contained, quieted, and kept under the strictest control. She saw flashes of humor, such as when they restrained Alex. They had seemed so in accord then, though they'd only just met. Then last night, he had been moody and dark. One moment he was in pain, yearning for information about his own family, then the next moment he was angry, his hands clenched into fists, his mouth tight with fury.

Which brought her right back to this morning's kiss. She had sensed no anger from him then, at least not toward herself. His touch had been sweetly passionate in the gentle exploration of his mouth on hers, and her response had verged on alarming. Her heart had started pounding in her chest, her belly had quivered, and a tide of hunger washed through her. Desire had burned through her, and yet he had pulled away. She didn't know if the look he gave her was one of banked passion or if she were simply reading her own needs in him.

It was all so confusing and incredibly wonderful at the same time. And yet it was folly, sheer folly! How could she even think of a deeper connection with a man who had almost murdered her? God knew she never wanted to disturb his rest again!

But, of course, this was all ridiculous speculation. Normally, she would dismiss these thoughts entirely, but her mind kept wandering back to that kiss. Well, that and her horrible conversation with Uncle Frank. If she were to become a fallen woman, would it be better to be with the uncertain but decidedly intriguing Mr. Frazier? Or the known quantity of her Uncle Frank?

Ugh! The very idea of Uncle Frank was repulsive, though she supposed starving on the street was repulsive as well. Thankfully, she did have other options. She could become a paid companion. She had even kept her eyes open for just such an opportunity. But everyone assumed she was Rose's paid companion and so they believed her already employed.

She could become a governess. In fact, she might be very good at it. But she was holding on to hope of making a match this season. That would solve all her problems. If only there were a man interested in applying for the position, so to speak.

"The tarts not to your liking?" asked a warm male voice to her left.

"What?" She blinked and encountered the very calm and very brown countenance of Mr. Mitchell Wakely.

"You were pursing your lips, as if tasting something sour."

"Oh. No. Sorry. I remembered the tarts from last month's musicale, and so declined."

"Ah," he said with a warm smile. "Then you have a fortunate memory."

"Or the tarts are simply very memorable," she countered. "I doubt you will forget next month."

He nodded. "Very true. So what, may I inquire, had

you looking so sour?"

She tilted her head, unwilling to share those particular thoughts with anyone, and opted for flirting instead. "That's very unkind of you, Mr. Wakely, to suggest I looked sour."

"But I was merely referring to your expression. Right now, I would say you look quite delightful."

"You are too kind."

"I assure you, Miss Wilson, no one has ever accused me of that."

She arched her brow. "On the contrary, I believe I have heard that often about you."

"That I am kind? No, you have not. Bland, brown, annoyingly inquisitive, certainly. Dog terrier-like mind with the puzzles, perhaps, but not kind. Never, ever kind."

She looked away because she had indeed heard every single one of those words when referred to him. His skin tended toward a dull tan, his hair and his eyes were brown, and his attire did nothing to change that impression. She did know that he enjoyed puzzles and that he was often seen with the political set. She also knew that he had modest income and was on the search for a wife. Which made him the perfect man with whom to chat right now.

"Well then, sir," she said smartly. "Allow me to say it. You seem very kind to me."

He touched his hand to his chest and gave her a slight bow. "I am touched. But you have not told me what soured your thoughts."

"Nor am I like to, sir, until we are very much better acquainted."

"A challenge!" he crowed, though not overly loud.

Mr. Wakely was never overly loud. "Or perhaps, I should view it as more of a puzzle. Shall I try it?"

She leaned back slightly, not sure what to make of Mr. Wakely's sudden attention. As much as she wanted to believe in his interest, experience had taught her to question such a thing.

She tapped her fan closed and regarded the gentleman somewhat coolly. "I do not know what you mean, sir."

"And you do not like that. Not knowing, that is. And there you understand exactly my daily condition."

She frowned, trying to follow his twisted words. "Very well, sir, you may try. And I promise that I shall tell you if you guess correctly."

He grinned, and suddenly his rather dull face became much more interesting. "Well, as I saw you yawn a moment before, I shall guess that you are tired and wish to go home."

"Too easy an answer, sir. And here I thought you were counted an excellent puzzler."

He held up a finger. "Ah, but I have not actually made my guess yet. I am merely speaking my thoughts aloud."

She made no response, choosing instead to arch a brow. She thought that was one of her best expressions as it smoothed out her skin's tendency to darken under her eyes. And though she didn't have any wrinkles yet, she was certainly not in her first flush of youth, so the look also brought attention to her eyes and not the less-than-perfect peach tone of her skin.

"I see you are not convinced, but like a terrier, I must keep on until I have found the truth. I believe that while Lady Rose spent her night resting in the blissful sleep of a beautiful miss, you were up dealing with the added work caused by two unexpected guests, one possibly mad."

"Neither guest is mad, I assure you."

"No, but they aren't exactly well either. And even so, there is always linens to change, baths to arrange, and an extra couple mouths at table. Perhaps with delicate stomachs." He glanced to the side where Rose trilled a laugh that could be heard across the room. "Lady Rose is a delightful girl, but never say she assisted with any of that."

"I would never say anything about it at all. Domestic matters are not for polite discussion." Her response was more tart than she intended, but his reference to a bath had unsettled her nerves. And his guesses were indeed amazingly accurate.

"Of course you wouldn't," Mr. Wakely returned, completely unaffected by her tone. "You are much too circumspect to say such a thing. I find I like that about you."

Maddy didn't know what to say. She found herself looking into his brown eyes and feeling the unaccountable need to cry. What was wrong with her? Three times now in the space of twenty-four hours, she had found unacceptable tears threatening. It was ridiculous! And yet, she could not deny that she found herself grateful—eternally grateful—that someone had noticed her character!

She swallowed and looked away. "Even if what you say is true, sir, why would that produce a sour expression?"

"Ah, but don't you see? The hour is not late by Lady Rose's standards, but you must be up again, early in the morning to do it all again."

"Don't be absurd. Our guests have removed

themselves from our home. There is no additional work, no new people to entertain or feed."

"And is that," he said softly, "perhaps the reason for your sour expression? That these rather interesting men have left your abode?"

Her gaze jumped to his as surprise radiated through her body. He was completely wrong, of course. Her thoughts had been on the possibilities of her future, not on Mr. Frazier's whereabouts. And yet, something in what he'd said echoed true. More true than anything she had been thinking on all day.

"You promised," he said when she was silent. "You said you would tell me if I guessed true."

"I did indeed," she answered, her mind still whirling. "But I'm afraid I cannot gratify your curiosity. As I don't precisely remember making a sour expression, I certainly cannot answer as to what I was thinking at the time."

Disappointment skated across his features. "I cry foul, Miss Wilson. I had not thought you would stoop to lying."

She shook her head, doing her best to be honest *and* circumspect. "Not a lie, Mr. Wakely. Sometimes a lady's thoughts are so torturous that even we have no wish to revisit them."

"Then your expression comes from something deeper than extra work and more profound than departed guests."

She gave him a soft smile. It was the best she could manage at the time. "Only one guess allowed, Mr. Wakely. And now, I'm afraid Lady Rose and I must be going. The performers have finished and our hostess looks like she intends to press more tarts upon us all."

He shot an alarmed look over to the dessert table. No one was there except for a rather bored footman, and so his gaze hopped immediately back to her. "Now that, Miss Wilson, was a definite lie."

"No so," she said as she pushed to her feet. "Look behind you." There, indeed, stood Mrs. Hughes with an extremely overladen tray of her chef's terrible lemon tarts.

He turned around to look, and in that time, Maddy managed to shoot Rose a stern look. Fortunately her cousin also had little love for the lemon tarts, so she began her good-byes. By the time Mr. Wakely turned back, they were all caught up in the general leave-taking of fully half the party.

Minutes later, she and Rose were climbing into their carriage and heading home. And now Maddy had yet more things to speculate about: What exactly were Mr. Wakely's intentions and how did she feel about them?

Fortunately, she had little opportunity to stew. Immediately upon returning home, Maddy pretended to yawn and seek her bed. Then she changed her clothes and donned a shapeless brown wrap that reminded her of a female version of Mr. Wakely's attire.

That thought had her smiling even as she pocketed the last of the household coins. Moments later, she descended the servants staircase and crept through the kitchen and out of the house.

CHAPTER 7

Maddy descended from the hackney and wrinkled her nose. The neighborhood that hosted the Tavern Playhouse was not in a sweet-smelling area of London. Fish and stale drink were the primary scents this evening as the wind was blowing from the docks. But there was no help for it. She had a task to do.

She pursed her lips, walking slowly around the building as she planned her course of action. Fortunately, it was a warm evening for early spring. The windows were cracked to allow in the breeze. It also allowed her—and a few street boys—a view inside.

The main doorway led straight to the central tavern, where men gathered to drink and jeer at the production. The stage area was at the back of the room and she could hear a male singer, though what she saw were scantily clad women dancing.

Those girls would not be Lady Blackstone. That's who she was looking for: the lady herself or someone who would get a message to her. Maddy continued wandering around the building, stepping gingerly past a gin whore and the refuse pile on which she slept.

Luck was with her tonight. A back door was open to

let in the night air. A man sat there, his big face calm though he seemed to be scowling at someone inside. She stepped forward. She didn't try to sneak past him. It simply wouldn't be possible. So she stood waiting while he glared at some boys backstage. And then he turned to look at her with the same angry scowl on his face.

She tried a soft smile, but it wavered in the face of his stare. "Please. I need to see Lady Blackstone." She dropped the hood of her cloak and allowed the moonlight to shine full on her face. Hopefully, her clean appearance and cultured accents would gain her some credibility.

It did. The man's brows drew together in a puzzled frown. But then he simply folded his arms across his chest.

"I merely wish to speak with her. I have no need for money or influence. I just need to discuss—"

"Angel! What are you doing here?"

Maddy flinched backward away from the light. She had no wish to be seen, even by the only man who called her angel. Especially by him. But there he was, standing behind the big man and looking much better than he had just this morning.

"Come inside," he said. Then he glanced at the big man blocking the way. "It's all right, Seth. She's a friend."

The guard nodded, and Maddy was surprised to see that there was a softness in him. When he looked at Mr. Frazier, a sadness came into his eyes and the pinched look left his mouth, as if the two men had shared a past that wasn't especially kind.

"Come in, angel," Mr. Frazier repeated.

"Thank you, sir," she said to the guard, who nodded

to her.

"That's Seth, by the by," said Mr. Frazier. "He's mute, but we all understand him well enough. And God knows he understand us!"

"Oh..." began Maddy, but there was no time for more as Mr. Frazier tugged her away into the flickering lights behind the stage.

"Are you cold?" he asked as he rubbed her arms up and down. It was too familiar a movement, but she found she didn't object. His hands were on top of her cloak. She was hardly being improper, and yet it felt as though she were allowing a gross liberty made worse when he tucked her close to his side.

"I had forgotten the cold," he said. "There was a time I thought I'd never feel it again."

She had no answer to that. She didn't want to bring up painful memories, so she chose to remark on his new appearance. "You've bought new clothing. It looks quite nice."

The attire was modest by Uncle Frank's standards, but she found the outfit to be perfect for Mr. Frazier. Simple lines that showed off his excellent physique. Of course, looking at him dressed like this, she couldn't help but remember the scars that crisscrossed the skin underneath. Was it strange that it made him even more handsome to her?

Meanwhile, he tugged at his cravat and managed to look better rather than worse. "I managed to free up a few groats. What money I had before I left is all gone now. Here I'd been thinking that I'd have seven years of income waiting for me."

"But they declared you dead."

"Yes. They declared me dead," he echoed hollowly.

"My brothers got my money. And spent it, no doubt."

"But surely they will return it to you, once they learn that you're alive."

He shrugged. "It wasn't much. They may have it with my blessing."

They fell silent, listening to the singer and the pound of the dancers' feet. The crowd was hooting and calling, so it was hardly silent where they stood. And yet, it felt quiet. She felt the weight of it in the very air she breathed.

"You haven't told them, have you? You haven't written your family to say that you are alive."

He glanced sharply at her. "I wrote a brief missive to my eldest brother. I do not know how to find Lucas or Paul."

"Did you post it?"

He looked away. And that in turn prompted her to step away from his body enough to stare him in the eye. "Surely you should contact them. Do not let them hear of it from someone else."

He blanched at that. He knew she was right. And yet, he stubbornly refused to speak.

"Mr. Frazier, they are your family."

"So are Michael and Lily, but they left me to rot."

She could see the fury in his eyes, hatred radiating from every tight muscle in his frame. And yet anyone else looking at him would think him relaxed. She reached forward and touched his arm, feeling the muscles ripple beneath the fabric. "If I had to guess, I would say that the earl and his countess acted alone. Your brothers probably didn't even know you were alive."

His mouth tightened but she did not allow him to turn

away. When he tried, she simply stepped back into his line of sight.

"Mr. Frazier? Did they know you lived?"

"I don't know," he snapped.

"And you don't want to know, do you?" she abruptly realized. She couldn't begin to imagine the betrayal he felt from the Earl and Countess of Thornedale. How much more terrible would it be to know that his parents and brothers had done the same?

"They didn't know," she said firmly. "They couldn't have."

He looked in her eyes, and she saw him struggle. Part of him desperately wanted to believe it was true, but the other part clearly felt betrayed in the worst way. So much so that he couldn't force himself to believe.

The sight was heart wrenching, but she couldn't properly do more than she was right now. She couldn't embrace him or even touch his skin. So she used her voice instead, trying to reach him with her words. "They didn't know. And they will be so overjoyed to see you again, you cannot imagine the happiness that will ensue."

He searched her face, for what she had no idea. And in that moment, the music stopped, the act finished, and people began crossing behind the stage.

"Come," he said, grabbing her arm. "We can get to the Green Room now."

"But—"

"Shhh! Not until the Green Room. And cover your face." He didn't wait for her to do it, but tugged the hood of her cloak up. Then he rushed them across the unlit portion of the stage. People could see her, of course. There was no curtain at the front of the stage, just an army of boys setting out props. She hunched even farther when a cheer went up from the crowd at the sight of her female form, but she was anonymous in her dull cloak. Then they were across the stage and heading down a dark hallway.

"Make way, guv'her," said a boy as he carried a small table on stage.

"Mind your head," said another as he danced across a walkway above them, a large bucket dangling from a rope that he carried.

Mr. Frazier moved rapidly, pressing her into a tight, dark space between a wall and a rack of costumes. He pushed her deep, keeping his back to the chaos, his body shielding her from harm. But, of course, she had been in little danger from swinging buckets or boys with props. What was dangerous were her thoughts as his body enfolded hers.

His legs were on either side of hers, and he braced her with his knees. His hands were on her waist, large and possessive. His chest bumped against her breasts, not hard, just enough for her to feel the tightening of her nipples in response. And then there was his face, tucked to the side of hers, his chin resting against her temple. She heard his breath as short, quick pants, and his hands tensed around her hips.

Heat. That's what she noticed the most. His body radiated such heat she might have thought he was feverish. It left her breathless.

"Mr. Frazier," she whispered. "I believe the danger has passed."

He looked down at her, his eyes dark shadows. Then he glanced upward at the boy with the bucket. The child was leering down at them, his lips pursed as he made a loud kissing noise.

Maddy felt her face heat to the roots of her hair, but Mr. Frazier did not seem remotely embarrassed. Instead, he looked to her with an arch to his brow.

"Well, I am in a quandary," he drawled.

"Mr. Frazier!" she hissed. "You must step back!"

"Can't quite yet, you see. Grit up there has seen us."

"Grit?"

"The boy's name because he has a lot of it."

She sighed. Of course that was the boy's name. Couldn't be anything more sensible like Tom or Joseph.

"Grit has seen us now, and there's a price to be paid or my reputation's lost."

"I care little for your reputation, Mr. Frazier," she said tartly. "Mine, on the other hand—"

"No one knows who you are here," he said softly, his head lowering toward hers as he spoke. "I called you angel—"

"Which you really should not—"

"But I did." One of his hands left her waist to come up to her cheek. He stroked her so softly that a shiver skated down her spine. "I did, angel. And I have been dreaming of kissing you forever."

She looked up at his eyes. They were again dark pools, but she imagined a mischievous light there. A spark of humor that had been missing in him before. "We only just met yesterday. And you kissed me once already."

The hand on her hip tightened, pulling her closer to him. His breath feathered across her cheeks and then it heated her lips. "That was years ago," he whispered.

"Mr.—" Too late for protest, halfhearted though it was. Truthfully, she had been thinking of his kiss as well. Daydreams, fantasies, nighttime desires all meshed together into this moment. So much so, she told herself, that perhaps this caress of his mouth on hers was yet another dream.

But it was real in so many wonderful ways. His body was hard and hot against hers. His hand on her cheek slipped behind her neck to support her head. And his mouth on hers was infinitely delightful. Not hard, not soft, but a constant mixing of both. While his lips moved on hers, his tongue began a quick tease. A lick here and there, a darting thrust, and soon she found herself opening to him, a soft murmur trembling through her mouth to him.

He took it, and he took her. He slanted across her mouth, thrusting inside. Never before had she experienced so carnal a kiss. He thrust into her, he stroked every part of her, and God help her, she loved every moment of it. She opened herself to him, releasing a soft sigh of delight. And at the sound, his hands tightened, his body pushed harder against her such that she felt his organ like a hot brand on her belly.

She trembled beneath the onslaught, her mind still numb with shock, even as her arms wrapped around him. His hand on her hip shifted, rolling to her behind, where he cupped her boldly. She did not intend to return the pressure against his groin. This was well beyond anything any man had done with her before. But her body wasn't listening to her mind. Her thighs tightened, her stomach too, while he ground his delicious heat into her.

His mouth left hers to press kisses along her jaw and throat. His hand at the back of her head slid down her front to stroke her breast. She cried out, the sound lost behind the roar of the audience. The play was starting. Some part of her mind grasped on to that rather than speak the obvious: This was improper. This was dangerous!

"Oh!" she gasped. "No!"

His free hand left her breast to start rucking up her skirt. His knee was beginning to press between hers.

"Mr. Frazier! Stop!" She tried to push against his chest, but she had no strength in his arms. He was a solid wall against her and he was gripping her thigh, pulling it high.

She couldn't do this! She could *not*! She had a second at most to save herself, so she took it. She made a fist as the gypsies had taught her, and then she struck. She slammed downward onto him. Her aim was true, hitting his organ through his breeches, And then, before he could do more than rear back, the bucket slammed against his head. Grit, the stagehand from above, glared down even as he kept swinging the bucket close enough to hit again.

"She said no, guv'nor!"

Mr. Frazier roared in shock as he clutched his head. The sound echoed backstage but simply mixed with the noise of the crowd out front. He stumbled backward, pain twisting his face into a feral snarl. Maddy stared at him in shock as she saw the same mindless fury enter his face that young Alex had worn when he was pummeling the Earl of Thornedale.

"Mr. Frazier!" she cried. "Mr. Frazier!"

He did not seem to hear her. And then something even worse happened. She did not understand it, nor could she fight it.

A boom roared on stage. It was part of the production, she supposed. A loud bang complete with female screams. The audience roared its approval, but that only added to the general mayhem of sound that came from just a few feet away.

Mr. Frazier ducked. He more than ducked, he flattened to a crouch on all fours, dropping so low that his face touched the floor. And then another big bang hit, followed by the cries of the audience. It was a large crowd so the sound was deafening. Mr. Frazier shrank into himself while his gaze darted one way and the next. The air was smoky to begin with, but down by the floor, he was kicking up dust that surely blinded him.

"Mr. Frazier," she said as loudly as she could manage. Then she touched his shoulders.

He flinched as a wild dog might. He recoiled and glared at her with a snarl. But she didn't move. She had faced a few angry dogs in her time. At this moment, Mr. Frazier was no different.

"It's all right," she said as she extended her hand. "It's just the play." She touched his shoulder. And when he didn't draw back, she allowed her fingers to caress his face. His flesh was slick with sweat, his eyes still wide with fear. But she could see intelligence in there now. The more she touched his skin, the more awareness returned to his body.

Then there was a rolling sound. Drums. A steady crescendo like thunder breaking across the world. Before she could stop him, he launched himself at her. Grabbing her by the waist, he tossed her over his shoulder. Then with effortless strides, he ran down the hall and into a cellar.

CHAPTER 8

Mold. Wet. Screams. Cold.
Battle.
Can't breathe. Heart beating, beating, beating in my ears.
Are they coming?
Who is it?
Good God, what is happening?
"Mr. Frazier. Mr. Frazier!"
"Hush, Jeremy. Don't cry. I'll protect you."
Straining with every ounce of his strength, he shoved aside a full barrel of something—potatoes?—creating a dark space for the boy. He set the boy down there in the space he'd created. The child could hide there for days, tucked away behind the stairs and the barrel.
"Who is Jeremy, Mr. Frazier? I'm Maddy. Maddy Wilson, your angel."
"Stay down, Jeremy. I have to go up and fight."
The sounds of men's voices was growing louder. Was the battle over? Were they safe?
No! No! Don't go up there!
Kit frowned as his mind fractured. Part of him was blindly hopeful, believing the crew of *Fortune's Kiss* was victorious. The battle was over, the pirates tossed

overboard. Another part screamed uselessly. *It isn't safe! It isn't over! Don't leave the boy!* But the majority of his mind was trapped in darkness, lost behind an impenetrable wall of pitch and blood.

What was wrong with him? Why couldn't he think?

"Mr. Frazier. We're safe. We're in the Playhouse Tavern. There's no one here named Jeremy."

Footsteps. *Hide!*

"I'm going to go up and see what has happened," he said to the boy. "If I don't come back, stay here. You're good at hiding. No one will find you. You'll be safe."

No! Take him with you. Take him topside.

The door to the cellar levered open, and a lantern flashed bright in his eyes. He crouched low beside Jeremy, then slowly sidled around for a better vantage point. Was it the captain? Was it the crew? If they were pirates, he would fight. He would keep the boy safe.

Where was his knife? Why didn't he have a knife?

"Oh, look, Mr. Frazier. It's your friend from the doorway. Don't you remember? He blocked me from entering the playhouse, but you told him I was your friend."

"Jeremy, hush!"

He felt the boy's hand on his arm, warm and gentle, and large for so young a boy. He shrugged it off. He couldn't fight with a child hanging on his arm. He slid a little farther away, tensing so he could leap upon the huge man coming down the stairs. He was a white man, his face too pale for a sailor. No beard. And English clothing.

One of the sailors! And he had a boy with him. Another cabin boy? He thought Jeremy was the only one. Didn't matter. They were English which meant they were in danger too.

He stepped into the light. "Hsss! Hurry up. There's a hiding place for you with Jeremy. Seth, you and I will have to protect them. Do you have a knife?"

Seth slowed his steps, staring at first him then Jeremy with a puzzled expression.

"He thinks I'm some boy named Jeremy," said a voice. A woman's voice. There was a woman on board?

"Come down, boy." He gestured to the young adolescent on the stairs. He knew Seth was mute, so the man could hardly issue orders in battle. "Hurry up!"

The child looked to Seth, who nodded slowly. Thankfully, that was all that the boy needed to get him to scramble over the barrel to stand beside Jeremy.

"Good. Now Seth and I will go up and see the lay of things…"

No! No! Don't abandon Jeremy!

He closed his eyes, shaking his head as he tried to sort through the emotions roiling through him. Thoughts. Feelings. *Fear!* That's what he knew. That's what was real.

"Kit, you are safe now. The battle is over." It was the woman's voice again. Where was she?

He nodded, his head beginning to ache abominably. "I know. I know. The battle is over. The *Fortune's Kiss* is lost."

"It was a terrible thing, wasn't it? Horrible. But it is over now. You have come back to England."

"No, no." He pressed his palms against his eyes. "It's not over. You're still alive. Stay with me! You mustn't ever leave my side, do you understand? *Never* leave my side!"

"Of course," she answered. "Don't worry. I won't

leave your side."

Shudders wracked his frame. He was so cold down here. Why was he cold? It shouldn't be cold! It was blistering hot, the sun beating down to burn his flesh raw. He remembered it so clearly. The burn. Burning. The ship on fire!

"Jeremy!" he bellowed. He tore his palms away from his eyes and he scanned the cellar. He saw Seth and a stage boy, plus his angel, all standing there staring at him. He whipped his head around, searching for Jeremy.

"Where is he? Where is Jeremy?"

Seth stepped forward, but Kit spun around, his fists raised to fight. The big man froze in place.

"Where is Jeremy?" he demanded.

His angel reached for him. He bared his teeth at her, but she was undaunted. He couldn't hurt her. She was his angel. And her voice was so beautiful.

"Jeremy isn't here," she said gently. "Do you know where you are?"

He blinked, his eyes going in and out of focus. Memories rolled through his mind, unfolding over him, the weight suffocating his mind. He couldn't breathe! And, God, he hurt. Everything hurt! His legs gave way and he landed hard on his knees.

Then he felt her hands on his face. She shouldn't touch his face. He tried to pull away, but she held him still, her scent weaving about him. Lavender and spice. She soothed his cheeks and brushed his hair from his eyes, just like his mother used to. He looked up at her and twisted away, just as he had as a child. But not far. Never far because he liked her scent. And the sound of her voice.

"Mr. Frazier," she said. "Kit, please look at me."

He could not refuse her. His mind was still oppressed, shackled to memories and buried beneath a surging ocean of weight. But her voice. Her face. That was not painful. He could look at her. He could hear her. And let the rest sink into silence. Her thumb stroked across his cheek and he smiled.

"Do you know who I am?" she asked.

"Angel," he answered, though it took him a moment for the word to struggle past the weight.

"Do you know where you are?"

He winced. That required too much work, too much searching and his body began to tense with the effort.

"Never mind," she said quickly. "I know, and that's good enough for now."

He didn't have the strength to disagree. So he allowed his mind to collapse again and narrowed everything to just her. She glanced over to the side. To where Seth stood with a deep scowl on his face.

"I think he just needs a little time. Do you mind leaving the lantern?"

From the corner of his eye, Kit saw Seth shake his head. He set down the lantern, then folded his arms across his chest. The man wasn't moving. But he did jerk his thumb at the boy called Grit. Grit nodded, then climbed across a barrel of potatoes before dashing away upstairs.

"You know," said his angel, "it is decidedly uncomfortable standing here like this. I should like to sit down. Do you mind, Kit?"

He shook his head. Of course he didn't mind. Though he murmured in protest when she stopped touching his face. She was stepping away from him, and with the loss of her presence—her scent—the memories surged again.

"There now, that's better," she said. She settled on the floor, her back against a wine rack and her legs extended in front of her. Her skirt lay short of her feet, and so he could see her trim ankles.

"It must be uncomfortable there on your knees," she said to him. He frowned and she smiled. Now that she mentioned it, his legs were abominably sore. "Come sit beside me."

He shook his head, but the movement unfroze his body. He half rolled, half collapsed forward. She caught him. And with her help, he settled with his head on her lap. It was a good position. He could see her ankles this way. And he could smell her lavender and spice scent. It was so very, very English.

Her hand settled on his arm while the other brushed his hair off his forehead. He liked the soft stroke of her hand, like the lap of the waves. The ground wasn't moving, but her fingers were, and so he could close his eyes and pretend he was on the boat. Or at home in England. Or anywhere he would like to be. Just so long as she kept stroking his face.

He slept.

Maddy let her head drop back against the wine rack. Kit was sleeping now. She tried to admonish herself for referring to him by his given name, even in her own thoughts. But after this last display, she couldn't keep him at arm's length anymore.

He was wounded in mind if not in body. She had seen enough of her father's patients to recognize a man struggling with enormous pain. Who was Jeremy? she wondered. Likely a boy Kit had tried—and failed—to protect. Had the noises from the play made him relive the battle when he was first captured? She believed so, but of course couldn't be sure.

All she could do was sit here and let the man sleep. Her father had often said that sleep was the best thing for mental pain. She could only pray it was true for Kit. And so she would do nothing to interfere with the man's rest despite what this might do to her reputation.

She looked up at the huge doorman named Seth. He hadn't moved from his position on the stairs except to glare at a few boys who had come to the cellar door. It was unnerving, the man's absolute silence, but reassuring too. He seemed like a solid, silent bulwark against the outside world.

She sat on the floor for hours. She heard the noise of the performance as it ended. She heard men's laughter and the actresses' coy giggles. People came to the cellar, but their silent guard glared them away. And Kit slept on. In time, Maddy too let her eyes drift shut and she dozed.

"My God, it's true."

Maddy opened her eyes to see a tall, dark-eyed man descending the stairs. He was stripping off his great coat as he came down, and so she at first had the image of a great large bird, but he stilled quickly enough when she squeaked in alarm.

"I'm sorry," he said softly, as he slowed his steps. He had dark brown hair, matted down from his hat, and his gaze seemed to devour Kit. "How long has he been like this?"

Maddy had no idea, but the guard lifted three fingers.

"Three hours," the man said as he stepped up beside Maddy. "And you have sat here patiently this whole time."

Then his eyes slid back to Kit as if he could read answers from the curled form. "How can this be? Michael said he died." He crouched down then reached out to touch Kit's face, but stopped before he connected. Maddy took a breath as much to clear the sleep from her mind as anything else. But in that one moment of inattention, she must have jostled Kit. He woke in a sudden flurry of movement.

He grabbed the newcomer's wrist and used it to shove him away hard. Then he rolled to his feet in a crouch in front of Maddy. He was protecting her as he snarled at the new man.

Maddy hastened to find her voice. She touched his back and tried to sound reassuring, though she croaked her words. "No, no! He's not come to hurt you."

She felt Kit's back ripple but nothing else. Kit was staring at the newcomer, his body so tight she feared it might break.

"Kit," said the newcomer, his voice low and gentle. "Do you remember me?"

"Brandon," he answered, though the word came out as a harsh grunt. "Thief."

She saw the word hit the newcomer like a blow. He flinched backward, but then he steadied. "We thought you dead. We went to your funeral, for God's sake. Oh, Kit, what happened?"

Maddy's eyes widened as she fit the pieces together. The newcomer was Brandon Cates, Viscount Blackstone. The man who had married Kit's fiancée.

"Ah," she said, her voice thankfully steadying into a conversational tone. "This is rather hard, isn't it? To be woken from a sound sleep straight into an awkward situation. My goodness, I am parched. Are you thirsty, Kit? I vow I would simply love some tea. What about you, my lord? Isn't tea a capital idea?" Good God, she sounded like an idiot.

The viscount looked at her for a moment as if she had lost her mind. After all, Kit was still crouched before them. Fortunately, he was able to recover his wits and was soon nodding at her.

"There is nothing like English tea, is there, Miss..."

"Madeline Wilson, my lord. A pleasure to make your acquaintance."

"Ah yes. The intrepid Miss Wilson. It must be very cold there on the floor. Would you like some help to stand?"

He leaned forward, extending his hand, only to pull up short as Kit jerked into his way. It was no more than a slight shift, but it was clear that Kit would not let the viscount anywhere near her.

"Well, Kit, I suppose if you will not allow him to help me up, you will just have to do it yourself." She winced as she rolled her ankles about. "I do find myself quite stiff."

Kit still had not said anything beyond the two words that labeled the viscount a thief. She wasn't remotely sure that he knew where he was or what was happening. But there was consciousness there, she was certain of that. He was not insane. Merely somewhat uncivilized at the moment. So the best course of action was to be civil around him such that he could remember how to act.

She gently trailed her fingers down his arm until she gripped his hand. He watched her do it, his body taut with a kind of lethal awareness. But he didn't strike out. And when she reached his palm, he gripped her fingers.

She maneuvered her legs under her, gasping slightly

as the blood flowed through her limbs. She meant to push up off the floor with her other hand, but Kit was there before her. He reached under her far arm and raised her up. He leaned over, hooked his free arm around her ribs, and gently stood up, carrying her with him. It was the most extraordinary feat of strength and grace she had ever experienced. And as she was of rather large proportions, she found herself quite breathless with awe when he at last set her on her feet.

She looked into his eyes. They were nearly face-to-face. She felt his heat again, but mostly what she saw was the pain in his eyes. He was not insensate. He was not confused. He knew that he had been found asleep on a woman's lap after a period of madness. And the man who had discovered him was none other than his cousin—a viscount—who had married his fiancée.

"Oh, Kit," she breathed, "we shall sort it all out. I promise."

His eyes dropped to her lips. She would swear he was thinking of kissing her. Or perhaps that was her own wickedness. She licked her lips, wishing more than anything that they could return to that moment before his madness. She wanted to be mindless in his arms again. And maybe this time, she wouldn't stop him. After all, it must be nearly dawn now. She would soon be discovered absent from her bed. If she were to be a fallen woman, she might as well be one in truth.

"Seth has put the kettle on," said the viscount, breaking through her wicked thoughts. "I told him to make it strong. You know how they like to water things down here, don't you, Kit?"

Kit turned, looking at his cousin with a dark stare. "I remember," he said clearly. "It saves money on tea and encourages the sale of the stronger stuff."

"Exactly so," returned the viscount with an encouraging smile. "We should go drink some now while it's hot. And then, I would expect that Miss Wilson needs to get home. It's a couple hours before dawn," he said more to Maddy than to Kit. "Plenty of time to get you in bed before light."

Before anyone knew where she had spent the night, he meant. Which told her that there was still hope of salvaging her reputation.

"Thank you. That would be lovely."

"I will take her home," said Kit firmly.

The viscount inclined his head in agreement, but his expression was troubled as he looked at the two of them. She was still wrapped in Kit's arm, held up by his strength. She could probably gently disengage herself but was loathe to do it. He wanted her tucked close, and she would stay there for his peace of mind.

"Well," said the viscount, "whomever takes her home, I want tea first. Kit how about you help me while we allow Miss Wilson a moment to collect herself?"

But Kit didn't move. He held her firmly, his eyes searching her face. So she smiled at the viscount. "Go on, my lord. We shall be up directly."

"Very well," said the viscount slowly. "But I shall be…I'm right up here. In case of anything."

Kit didn't move until the viscount disappeared. Only then did he slowly release her and step back, a blankness taking over his expression. The sight was chilling. She knew he was tucking away all that pain he suffered, hiding it from himself as well as everyone else. But she didn't want such a thing for him. He needed to feel his pain, not run from it.

"Don't hide," she began, but her voice faltered. She

didn't know what to say.

"I have abused you most abominably tonight," he said in an undertone.

"No—"

"I have. I cannot apologize enough."

"There is no need for that," she said, wishing she could say more. There was no need to hide his anguish from her, to retreat into polite banter, to become civilized again, even though that was exactly what she had wanted a moment ago. "I understand the need to be wild sometimes," she said. "I have wished it a million times since coming to London."

He didn't answer, but she saw a silent misery enter his eyes. He didn't believe her, didn't think she understood pain or even the need to scream at the world like a beast howling at the moon.

"I don't understand what you suffered," she said firmly. "But I do know about feeling wrong from the inside out."

"There is nothing wrong about you," he said. "Nothing at all." And then before she could say more, he stepped away from her. "There is a necessary just off the Green Room. Come, I will show you where it is."

His wits were fully returned. She would get no more glimpses into his past now, and she didn't dare question him. Not now when they were finally climbing out of the cellar. But she wondered, and she vowed to find out someday. Not for her own curiosity, though she had plenty of that. For Kit because she very much feared these episodes would haunt him until he made peace with them.

But in the meantime, she had to freshen her gown. She had to have tea with the man who had taken Kit's fiancée away. And she had to do it all as if Kit meant no more to her than a man—any man—whom she had just met two days ago.

CHAPTER 9

"What happened, Kit? How did... How did this all happen?"

Kit swallowed his tea without tasting it. He sat in the Green Room with his cousin Brandon while his angel did whatever women did during their toilette. He didn't answer. He wasn't really sure what to say. In truth, without his angel here to ground him, he felt himself slipping into the cold, angry horror of his years as a slave.

"You know," his cousin commented. "When I first came back from India, I spent months as a snarling monster. I abandoned my friends, crawled into a brothel, then drank and whored until I couldn't hear the screams in my head."

Kit looked up at his cousin's face. It wasn't as haggard as he remembered. His skin seemed healthier, his body less angled and harsh. "You've put on weight," he said, startled to find that he could indeed talk rationally.

Brandon smiled and looked down at his belly. He didn't have one, but he ran his hand over his stomach nonetheless. "Well, a good life does that to a man."

"She is happy then?" Neither of them needed to say her name. Scheherazade. The woman Kit had once loved and Brandon had married.

"I believe so," he said, his expression open as Kit had never seen before. "I thank God every day for her. I will do anything she needs to make her happy." He swallowed. "Kit, I am sorry for everything, but you have to know. I will not give her up."

He felt his hackles rise. Not because he had any claim to Scheherazade. He'd given her up as lost a very long time ago. She was more of a nostalgic memory than a true desire. But there was something primal about staking a claim on a woman. A lifetime ago, he had claimed Scher for his bride, and now here was Brandon doing the same. He reacted as a beast, his hands tightening into claws. Not because he wanted the prize, but because someone dared challenge him for it.

"Thank you, sir," said his angel from behind him. "You have been most kind."

Both men turned to see Maddy stepping into the Green Room behind Seth, who was leading the way.

"Will you be joining us for tea?"

The big man shook his head even as he gave her a slight bow.

"He has to be up early with the stage boys," said Brandon. "I fear that we have kept him much later than usual."

"I understand completely," Maddy said with a slight nod. "But I'm afraid we were never properly introduced. My name is Maddy Wilson." She held out her hand to the big man, who bowed formally over her fingers.

"His name is Seth Mills," supplied Brandon. "And he is greatly honored to meet you."

Maddy smiled warmly at the large man. "Oh, but the honor was all mine. You were a wonderful help in the cellar."

Then something happened that Kit had never seen. Seth blushed. What started as a soft rose in his cheeks rapidly became a flaming red that made his ears appear to burn. The man bowed again then ducked away, still half bent.

Brandon watched, his mouth open in shock. Kit was no better, though his mind remained stuck on something else. Not the sight of Seth's fiery blush, but the way Maddy exuded warmth toward the big man. How easily she brought joy to everyone around her. Then she smoothly crossed the room to join them at the table, effortlessly reaching for the teapot and offering to refresh their cups. In short, she was a lady and much too refined to be sitting on a cellar floor with him.

"I don't believe I've ever seen him blush like that," Brandon said, his voice laced with amusement. "You are a woman of many surprises, Miss Wilson."

"I don't know about that, my lord. My father would say that I am a woman who ends up in surprising—and vastly inappropriate—situations."

"He sounds like a man I should like to meet."

"You can't," Kit interrupted, his voice thick with emotions he could not name. "He's dead." Then he silently cursed himself. He sounded like a churlish child.

Not surprisingly, Brandon stared at him. Maddy, however, graced him with a sad smile. "Yes, he has been gone for some time now. I am staying with my Uncle Frank, the Earl of Millsford."

"Ah yes. I know the man." From the sound of it, Brandon didn't much like him either. Kit couldn't disagree.

The other two continued to chat, speaking about mutual acquaintances and their respective families. The conversation flowed as it would in any parlor of the *ton*. Once, Kit had been a master of just such polite discussions. But now, he was unable to say anything, to do anything, while his cousin sat right there and charmed his angel.

It was ridiculous, and Kit felt his fury grow. At himself. At his cousin. Even at Maddy, who laughed and poured tea like she was a lady born. She wasn't. Her only pretense to a title was her uncle who wanted to make her his mistress. Her lineage was no better than his, and yet watching her now, he knew she was destined for a brilliant match. An earl at least, if not a duke. She was a *lady* and he was a *slave*. The differences could not be more clear.

Kit abruptly stood up, and his chair scraped loudly in the room. Maddy gasped in surprise, and Kit once again damned himself for being a cad. "It is late," he said, working hard to keep his voice genteel. "You should get home."

Maddy recovered quickly. Of course she would. "Of course, you are quite right," she said, but then her gaze slid to Brandon. "But I do have one rather impertinent request, my lord."

Kit didn't like her looking at Brandon, but he couldn't stop her. So he held himself still and waited, hating every moment that she looked at Brandon and not at him.

"I came to the playhouse tonight expressly to find your lady wife," Maddy said, her expression apologetic.

Brandon frowned but moved smoothly behind her to pull out her chair. Hell and damnation, why hadn't Kit thought of that? Gentlemen assist ladies to rise. How could he have forgotten?

Meanwhile, his cousin was speaking. "Why would you be looking for Scher?"

"It is for Rose," she said her cheeks flushing. "My cousin, Lady Rose, wants to have a tea where Kit...er, Mr. Frazier and your wife both attend."

"Ah," responded Brandon, and in that one word was a wealth of understatement. He knew exactly what Rose's motivations were for having the tea. The hostess who could catch both Kit and Scheherazade in the same room would have the event of the Season.

"I know it is a terrible imposition," she continued.

"My wife is increasing."

"Yes, and I would not wish to endanger her health in the least."

Brandon released a quick laugh at that. It was startling. Kit could not remember ever hearing the man make so lighthearted a sound. "As to that," Brandon said, "have no fear. The woman is tireless. Doesn't even get morning sickness."

Maddy nodded. "Then it is the spectacle you object to. I quite agree but promised Rose I would ask. Thank you, my lord, for hearing me out."

Brandon nodded, but his gaze was on Kit, his expression serious. "Do you wish to attend this party?"

Kit did not know how to answer. No, of course he had no interest in Rose's tea. Certainly not a public one where his every move would be scrutinized and discussed for weeks on end.

"I need to see Scher, Brandon," he said softly. "After my capture, I would dream of her. I would think I was back home and we were getting married. I would think so many fanciful things. It kept me sane." He looked at his cousin, trying to find the words to explain. "But there were nightmares too. Where she was hurt or dying and I couldn't get to her. I couldn't help." Just like the nightmares he had had of Maddy this morning. "I just need to see her, Brandon. Just...see her. If not at this tea, then some other time, some other place. Soon."

Maddy touched him then. He saw her movement long before her fingers reached his arm, and so he was able to remain still while her heat speared through his body. "But why would you want this to be public?"

He couldn't look at her. He couldn't put words to his need to see Scher was alive and well. Perhaps he should have done so when he'd first purchased his freedom four years ago, but he'd had no money for passage and knew he was more animal than man. It had taken all this time for him to believe he was fit for civilized company. Clearly, he'd been wrong, but that didn't change the need.

Fortunately, Brandon understood. "He doesn't care how he sees Scher. He just needs to know."

Kit nodded, and in time his cousin came to a conclusion.

"I will speak to Scher. We will do what she thinks best. Agreed?"

"I have waited seven years," he said. "I will wait a day more."

"Kit," Maddy admonished softly. "This will be a shock to her."

"A day," responded Brandon. "I will send our answer to the earl's home."

"But—" interrupted Maddy. No doubt to explain that he was *not* really staying at her house.

"That will be fine," Kit interrupted. Then he took

Maddy's hand. "We must be leaving now. The sun will be up much too soon."

"Really?" she said, frowning out the window. "How can you tell?"

He couldn't tell. Not in London where the buildings crowded close and smoke clogged everything. But he shrugged and lied because he did not wish to look like a fool. "There is a rhythm to everything, even here in London. And it tells me that you have dallied here too long."

He thought he was lying but realized at the last moment that it was the truth. There was a rhythm in London. One that he had once known intimately. Perhaps he did not have the knack of it exactly now, but it was coming back. Already he could feel the city as it prepared to wake.

"He has always known the time," said Brandon. "Even as a boy who could not read a clock, he knew the when of things."

"Then," said his angel as she squeezed his arm, "I should listen to you and be off."

"Take my carriage," said Brandon before they could leave. "The coachman is very discrete and I have already warned him to be ready. I shall spend the night here, so he knows to return when you are done."

"You are most kind." Maddy bestowed one of her most beautiful smiles on his cousin, and Kit found himself fighting the urge to haul her away from Brandon's too charming presence.

"We must go."

"Good night, my lord."

"Good night, Miss Wilson. Kit."

Kit didn't respond. His hold on his tongue was

tenuous at best, and so he ushered Maddy quickly out the door. The carriage was waiting, and so they were on their way within moments. But once moving, a terrible silence descended between them, all the more awkward because he searched for some way to break it. But everything that came to mind was either surly, impertinent, or ridiculous. In the end, he simply spoke the truth.

"I shall be at your tea, no matter what happens. Just furnish me the date and time."

"You needn't worry. I'm sure it will be a strain."

"I said I will be there!"

He watched as Maddy pressed her lips together. She had been trying to help and in return he had accosted her. He had not forgotten what he'd done before the madness seized him. The shape of her body, the feel of her thighs, the heat of her kisses, all became the thing of feverish desire here in the dark carriage. There were not words that could atone for the abuses she had suffered tonight. Then her voice came to him, soft and melodic through the darkness, breaking him out of his useless brooding.

"Do you truly intend to spend the night at Uncle's house tonight?"

"What? No, no. I have let rooms."

"Oh! Good. Good." Was that disappointment he heard in her tone? Or relief? He could not tell. "Was the price very dear? Can you afford it?"

"No. I mean, yes, I can afford it. And, no, it wasn't dear. I find my needs are relatively simple."

It was so dark in the carriage that he could not see her face. And yet, her voice was so soft that he imagined her smiling when she spoke.

"You are much like my father in that. Our home in Derby was very simple."

"What of your mother? Did she like it so plain? I cannot imagine my own being content with a staff of less than ten."

"Ten!" she gasped. "Imagine all those people underfoot! No, as my father spoke of her, Mama wanted very little as well. She died of childbed fever, so I never knew her."

"I'm sorry. It must have been hard growing up without a mother." He liked speaking this way, whispering together in the dark.

"I—well, yes, sometimes. But I was very happy with just my father."

Her words petered out, but it wasn't an uncomfortable silence. And then her voice whispered through the darkness again.

"Might I... Would you, perhaps, furnish me with your address? We would like to send you an invitation to the tea."

"I will do whatever you ask, Miss Wilson," he said, not at all surprised when the words came out like a vow. "I owe you everything for how you have helped me these last two days."

"Mr. Frazier...Kit...please. You have given me such excitement these last days. You cannot know how my days drag on with the very *sameness* of it all. I should be thanking you."

"Be careful what you wish for, Miss Wilson," he drawled. "I once longed for excitement, foreign travel, and a chance to make lots of money. I got my wish, you know. Just not how I thought."

She fell silent then, and he imagined that she mulled

over his words. What did she wish for, he wondered. Could he make any of her desires come true?

"I have a gift for you," he said as he pulled it from his coat pocket. "Something to show my thanks." It was a broach weighted with gold and old jewels. He had ripped it from one of Venboer's victims and secreted it away before any could see. He had intended to sell it to a jeweler years ago, but had never brought himself to do it. And now he was giving it to her.

"My goodness!" she gasped as he pressed it into her hand. "It's so heavy!"

"It's gold. And very old, I think."

She shifted to the window, holding it out so that the moonlight could shine on the piece. "Oh my! I cannot take this! It is much too valuable."

"Of course you can. No need to tell anyone. Hide it away. Save it until you have need of something to sell."

She looked at it, turning it over in her hands. The moonlight flashed on the dull metal as she peered at it first one way then another. "I cannot tell what the design is."

"A peacock, I think. Or what is meant to be one."

"A peacock. Oh yes, I see it, I suppose. Though it's not very clear."

No, it wasn't. And truthfully, it wasn't even remotely the right piece for her. His angel should be wearing something with a simple structure, but oh so elegant that it took the breath away. Something very much like her.

"I should give you something better," he said. "I learned something of gems when I was away." He couldn't manage to say the words: When I was a slave. Not now when they were speaking so easily. "I could design you something better, I think."

"I wouldn't think of it!" she cried. Then she gently set the broach back on the squab right beside his leg. "But I cannot take it. You know I cannot."

His throat thickened with hurt. Did she not understand how he had fought for this piece? Did she not know the thing's value? Not only in gems, but in blood? He couldn't speak, so he turned away, his gaze seeking out something—anything—in the darkness beyond the window.

"Kit..." she said softly, her voice soothing him even when he wished her far away. "Anyone who saw it would think me a whore."

"No one need see it!" he rasped. Didn't she understand what he was trying to say? That of all the things he valued in this world—all his pirate booty hoarded and counted and prayed over until he could buy his freedom—this was a piece he kept. This was part of the treasure he brought home with him. And this was what he gave to her.

Then the carriage pulled to a slow stop. They had arrived at her home. Her sigh filled the carriage as she gathered her skirts about her.

"Be well, Mr. Frazier," she said softly as she made to push open the door.

He stopped her. He moved without planning it, grabbing the broach off the squab with one hand while his other caught her wrist and peeled apart her fingers.

"I have nothing else to give you," he said urgently. "I have no sterling with which to buy you an appropriate gift." He pressed the broach into her palm.

She didn't speak. The coachman was pulling open the door for her, but Kit refused to let her go. "Keep it hidden, if you must," he said softly. "And when I am more settled, I will bring you a better gift and you can return this to me."

"Then why should I take it at all? You can bring me posies in a few days' time."

He shook his head. He didn't know his own mind from one minute to the next. He couldn't know what he'd do or even where he'd land after Alex was safely settled with his parents. He would remain in London long enough to speak with Scher. Then he had to find funds to outfit his ship and a cargo. That could take him any number of places beyond London.

"Keep it safe for me," he said. "So you know that I will come back for it."

She sighed. He heard it distinctly in the darkness. "Kit—" she began, but he cut her off.

"Please, angel. I trust you to keep it safe." His words made no sense, even to him. He knew only that he valued the broach, and that it was important that she have it.

He felt more than heard her sigh of acceptance. And then there was no more talk as the coachman opened the carriage door.

CHAPTER 10

The hansom cab pulled up in front of a modest home in an almost exclusive neighborhood. Unlike the first day when they'd arrived in London, the knocker was on the door and Kit could see movement through the windows. Alex's family was home.

Kit looked at his companion, recognizing the stark fear on his friend's face. How did one return to family, home, to *normal* when everything inside you had changed? Kit hadn't managed it yet. His reunion with Michael had ended in disaster. Last night's moments with Brandon had been difficult at best. And he just didn't have the heart to try again with his brothers. It would kill him if Lucas had known. Of all his brothers, if Lucas had known of his enslavement and done nothing, then he would go mad from the pain.

So Kit remained at outs with his family, but he refused to allow fear to keep Alex apart from his. Reaching out, he touched the young man's arm.

"They are your parents, your brothers, and sister. They love you."

Alex shook his head. "I'm different now. Everything's different now."

Kit shrugged as if it were of no moment. It was a lie,

but one he would hold on to. "You are a man now. That is to be expected."

Alex's voice dropped to a whisper. "I still have nightmares."

"Your mother held you during your nightmares as a boy. She is desperate to do so again, I assure you."

Alex flashed a look of both horror and longing at that. It was so comic that Kit released a sharp bark of laughter. The sound was startling to them both, and soon they were grinning. And then the moment was past as the cabbie rapped sharply on the roof.

"Oy! Come along now!"

With a silent nod, Alex squared his shoulders, pushed open the door, then stepped out into the street. Kit followed, his heart in his throat as he prayed for this to end well. Just this once, for this boy, let the family reunion be a good. Let the boy heal.

They never made it up the walk.

A squeal went up from inside the house. Kit saw a flash of a female face in the window, before the girl was gone. Then the front door flew open and another delighted squeal arose. *Thank God for little girls,* Kit thought, as a girl of about thirteen ran down the steps. She'd hitched her skirts up to her knees and her hair streamed behind her in a disordered mess. But she was beyond excited to see her brother.

With a rather impressive leap, she launched herself into Alex's arms, and he caught her as only a brother could: with strength and love and a groan at her weight.

"God, you've gotten heavy," Alex grumbled, then he buried his face against her neck and hugged her tight.

"And you've gotten strong!" she gasped.

Then Kit could hear no more of their words because

more squeals and good natured roars came from the door. Mother, father, and two brothers came rushing out of the house, and behind them stood a butler, footman, and a pair of maids. This was no small household, Kit realized, and he found himself mentally upgrading his estimation of Alex's background.

Meanwhile, he stepped backward outside of the mayhem. It was hard to remain unemotional as Alex's mother openly sobbed, alternately clutching her son to her and pouring her tears out onto her husband's shoulder. Alex's father was similarly affected, though with less noise. He simply touched his son once on the cheek while tears spilled down into his beard. Then the father was pushed aside by two younger sons both in their gangly, awkward years.

It was the girl who finally noticed Kit. She had backed away from the group, letting her mother clutch Alex again. She turned to Kit with bright curious eyes before moving closer. "Are you the one then? Did you rescue my brother?"

It took Kit two attempts to answer, but he finally got the words out. "I tried," he said, his voice thick with emotion. Then he took a step sideways, purposely emphasizing his limp. "But I only got us part way. In the end, he had to rescue me."

The girl studied him with a serious expression, her gaze seeing much too clearly for one so young. "I think," she finally pronounced, "that Alex is very lucky. And that you are a man who creates luck." Then before Kit could recover from that shock, she spun around, her hair ribbons fluttering behind as if they were trying to catch up. "Papa!" she cried. "Papa!"

Her father turned to her, though it was difficult to manage around both wife and children in a tight clutch.

He had to hush everyone before he could finally raise his brow in question.

"Papa," the girl pronounced. "We must invite this gentleman to dine."

Maddy was still gripping the broach that evening, but this time it was in her pocket as she argued wearily with her family. Both Uncle Frank and Rose were peering at her with varying degrees of suspicion and annoyance. It was just after dinner, right before they departed for their evening's entertainments. Why was it so hard for her to beg off for one night?

"It is nothing," she said for the hundredth time. "I have run myself ragged trying to arrange for your tea, Rose. And with the unexpected guests, there have been chores to do. That's all."

"Are you sure you're not ill then?" pressed Rose.

"Just a headache, sweetheart. You will have much more fun at the party without me, I am sure."

"But it's just a quiet gathering. You know Father will be bored chaperoning me. Then he gets short-tempered. Are you sure you can't come?"

Far from being annoyed by the description, Uncle Frank added his own slow nod. But as soon as he spoke, Maddy realized his thoughts had run an entirely different direction.

"Perhaps I could escort you there, Rose, and then ask one of the other ladies to chaperone you. I will come back here and care for Maddy."

It took a moment for Maddy to understand what her uncle was thinking, and longer still for her to believe he was serious. And in that time, Rose had brightened considerably.

"Oh yes, Papa, what an excellent suggestion."

"No, it is not," Maddy said firmly. Coldly.

Rose turned to her in shock. She doubted she had ever heard Maddy speak in so furious a tone, but Maddy's eyes were on her uncle. She needed him to comprehend—in no uncertain terms—that she had no interest in beginning a liaison with him tonight. Or any other night.

"You are my uncle," she said firmly. "I can never see you in any other capacity than that."

Uncle Frank narrowed his brows, the message clearly understood. Rose, of course, had no knowledge at all and frowned at them both.

"Well, certainly he's your uncle," the girl said. "What else would he be?"

Maddy offered her cousin a gentle smile. "A nursemaid, sweeting. He was offering to be my nursemaid," she lied.

"Perhaps you ought to rethink," Uncle Frank inserted with hard, crisp syllables. "You have only this Season to catch a husband. Are you sure you wish to miss even one night?"

Maddy heard the underlying message. She had only this Season left under his roof. After that, she would either have to get married or become his mistress. She bit her lip, offering a silent prayer to God that a man find her attractive soon.

"I am positive that I wish to be a home tonight," she said. "In darkness with a cold cloth over my eyes. Blessedly, silently, *alone*."

"Well, fine," said Rose with a sniff. "No need to become a shrew. I didn't realize we were so *noisy*."

Maddy sighed. She hadn't the patience to deal with Rose's temper right then. She was more concerned with her uncle's thoughts. But his expression was infinitely bland and wholly devoid of warmth. He took hold of his daughter's arm and began steering her out the door.

"Come along, Rose. You'll shine brighter without her sour presence. Besides," he added as he patted his daughter's arm, "she has plenty of servant's work to keep her occupied."

Maddy watched them go, pain cutting through her heart. Up until now, her uncle had never made her feel small. She had taken up the reins of the household because someone needed to. She had taken on the task of steadying Rose's flights of fancy because she was older than the girl and could look out for her. And whereas Rose never tired of telling people that Maddy lived on their charity, Uncle Frank had never suggested that she was anything but welcome. He fed her, housed her, and allowed her to have a Season in order to catch a husband. Never before had he even suggested she was a servant, even obliquely.

Obviously, that was over. She had rejected his advances, and his pride was wounded. Every woman knew how delicate a man's pride was, and an earl was even more prickly. Yet the pain still cut deep. He and Rose were her only family. And now she saw exactly how little he loved her. With a muffled sob, she dashed for her room.

She didn't cry. She'd shed all her tears years ago when her father died. But she wrapped herself around a pillow and buried her face in the linen. One day, she told herself over and over, some man would find her attractive. Some man would marry her. Someone would love her again.

"Angel. Angel, don't cry."

Maddy jerked awake as a hand touched her shoulder.

The candle still burned, so she had a good view of a man crouched beside her bed.

"Hush, angel. It's me."

Kit. In her bedroom. She blinked and rubbed a hand across her face, startled to find her skin wet.

"What are you doing here?" she croaked.

"I came to see you."

She pushed up from her bed, blinking again to make sure she was not dreaming the bizarre sight of Kit Frazier kneeling beside her bed. She peered over the edge to see more clearly. It was definitely Kit in his shirt sleeves and bare feet.

Bare feet? She had to be dreaming. She scooted backward, frowning when her dress pulled at her shoulders. Had she fallen asleep in her clothing? Of course she had. She'd run upstairs and collapsed on the bed, not even bothering to undress. And then she'd fallen asleep. It was all perfectly logical. Reassured, she adjusted her body then leaned back into the corner. Her bed was pushed against two walls, so she could easily rest there while she got her bearings. He watched her move, his eyes serious, his face dark and forbidding in the flickering light.

"This isn't real," she told herself. "It's a dream." She spoke the words out loud, hoping they would wake her, but they didn't. The apparition that was Kit shook his head.

"I am real, angel. I heard you crying."

"I don't cry."

"You were."

She shook her head. "I haven't in years."

"I saw it often on the boat, people who cried when they slept."

"Doesn't sound like a very happy boat," she said. Then she frowned. Of course it wasn't a very happy boat. It was a slave ship. "I beg your pardon. That was a stupid thing to say."

"No need to apologize. It was certainly not a very happy boat." He shrugged, rising up from his crouch to settle on the bed beside her. This close she could see that his shirt was undone at the neck, allowing her a peek of tan skin beneath.

"Did Jeremy cry? In his sleep?" She was acting very bold, she realized, asking questions she should not. But as it was a dream, she wasn't particularly worried. Except, of course, she knew she was lying to herself. This wasn't a dream at all.

Mr. Frazier flinched at the question, but he answered it readily enough. "Jeremy died on the *Fortune's Kiss*. I told him to hide. I didn't know that the pirates intended to sink it."

She blinked, the last vestiges of sleep ripped from her. "They sank the ship? With Jeremy on board?"

He nodded. "I was captured the moment I went topside. I'd never seen death like that before. Men gutted, dead but still bleeding. I had no weapon and no real fighting skill. Just as well because any type of resistance meant death. Instant and merciless. Venboer—he was the pirate captain—didn't have the men to subdue difficult slaves. Anyone who fought back was killed."

"My God…" she whispered.

"I didn't say anything about Jeremy. It's ridiculous, looking back at it now, but I kept thinking that a boy his age shouldn't see death like that. So I held my tongue."

"Of course you did," she said. Her hand twitched. She wanted to touch him in some way, comfort the haunting pain in his eyes. But to do that would be to go too far. She would have to admit that this was real, and that he really was in her bedroom. And he was barefoot. For some reason, that fact struck her as the most bizarre. That a man was in her presence barefoot.

"I kept silent. I was herded off the boat and onto the pirate ship. I didn't know what was happening, didn't understand anything. Not until they fired their guns."

"Why would they sink a perfectly good ship?" she asked.

"Venboer didn't have the men. He could barely control the slaves. He certainly couldn't spare the men to sail the other ship."

"So he sank it? With Jeremy hiding on board?"

He nodded. "That is the way of things."

"What a waste." And then she realized how ridiculous that statement was. He had been taken by pirates. A boy had died. The captain and a good deal of his crew had died. The loss of one ship was hardly the biggest crime. She sighed and rubbed a hand over her face. "I beg your pardon. I am being especially stupid right now."

She watched his lips quirk in a flash of a smile. "It seems so long ago. I haven't thought about Jeremy in years." His expression sobered. "I don't know why I chose to relive that time last night. I must have seemed like a madman."

She shrugged. "Perhaps a little, but it's only to be expected." She let her head drop back against the walls. "And I suppose you relived that memory because it was the beginning. I expect you have thought about that day a million times, wondering what you could have done differently. I know I would."

He tilted his head in confusion. "The ship was

attacked by pirates. At the time, I was in the galley complaining about the terrible food. There was nothing I could have done to change anything."

She nodded. "I know. And there is nothing I could do to change my father's illness either. Or that I eventually came to live here. And yet, I still think and wonder."

He shook his head. "I gave up wondering many years ago. Only a fool wastes energy on yesterday. Today has enough challenges."

She bit her lip. He was right, of course. But there were still moments she ached to relive even one day of her old life, one day when her father was still vital and strong.

"Tell me why you were crying," he said softly.

"Tell me why you are in my bedroom barefoot."

His eyebrows raised in surprise. "It is too difficult to climb a wall in shoes." He gestured out her window. She saw now that the glass was lifted. He must have scaled the wall and climbed in.

"But there is nothing there but wall and a few spots of ivy!"

He nodded. "Exactly. That is why I had to take off my shoes. My coat and cravat are down there as well."

Of course, she thought with a laugh. Why ever would she think something different? "But why would risk your neck in such a way?"

He gave her an arch look. "I lived for seven years on a ship. I climbed ropes during storms, cut sails in the dark, even scrambled between ships at war on the ocean. Even with my injury, your wall is not a risk."

No. Put like that, it wouldn't be. "But why?" she pressed. That was the question he had avoided. "Why would you climb in my window?"

He lifted one shoulder in a kind of shrug. "I had to see you."

She mulled over his words, sifting through them to find the truth. "I was supposed to go out this evening. The Season is beginning. I will not be at home for many nights to come."

He dipped his chin in a nod.

"So you intended to sit here and wait for me? Until I came home hours from now?"

Again, a quick dip of his head. She let hers fall backward against the wall in shock.

"What if anyone saw you? My reputation would be destroyed!"

"No one would see me."

"But of course they would!"

"No one would see me," he repeated. He spoke with such confidence that she was tempted to believe him. Which was ridiculous, because she could not entertain a man in her bedroom without someone noticing! And yet, he was here, sitting on her bed, talking with her as if it were the most natural thing.

"Mr. Frazier—" she began.

"Kit. Please call me Kit."

"I most certainly will not!" she said firmly, even though she had been calling him Kit in her thoughts for a while now.

"Please," he said, and she heard a note of desperation in his voice. "It helps me remember where I am. *Who* I am. On Venboer's ship, my name was Slave."

"Just 'Slave'? Weren't there a lot of you?"

He nodded. "It was a game Venboer played, a way to show us that we were all one and the same to him."

She bit her lip, beginning to understand a little of

what he suffered. After years as a pirate slave, coming back to London must feel like a dream to him.

"But you are safe now," she pressed. "You *are* in London. You *are* free."

His gaze slid from hers to the guttering candle. "We were not allowed fire on the ship. No candles. No light. Too dangerous, especially when many slaves would rather die than continue on." He reached out to touch the flame. She watched it flicker over his fingers and wondered that he did not burn. Then he pulled away and looked at her. "Candles help me remember. Clothing helps me remember." He leaned forward. "You help me remember."

She felt her lips curve in a rueful smile. "I do not believe I helped you last night."

"Never say that!" he said sharply. "If it weren't for you, I don't think I would have returned at all." He rubbed a hand over his face, and she saw how haggard he appeared. "It has been four years since I bought my freedom, and yet still, some nights I am afraid to go to sleep. I am afraid that I will wake in the morning—"

"And this will be the dream."

He nodded, and she saw such vulnerability in his eyes.

"Kit…" she whispered, her heart breaking at the sight. And then her stub of a candle finally gave out. The flame flickered one last time and extinguished. She gasped in surprise, but that was nothing compared to his reaction. One moment he was sitting there in candlelight, confessing his fears. The next moment, there was darkness and he leaped on top of her bed. It took her a moment to realize he'd spun around too. He was crouching with his back to her, his body blocking hers as he looked out over the room. Was he protecting her? She touched his back and felt the muscles tighten beneath her fingertips.

"Kit. Kit! There is nothing there. Just the candle going out."

He didn't respond at first. His body remained tight, his every muscle prepared to strike. Then she heard him take a deep breath, releasing it slowly. "I know," he finally rasped. "I know that in my mind, and yet..."

He didn't have to finish his sentence for her to know what he was thinking. His rational mind knew the truth, but he could not shake the fear from his body. It was an instinctive reaction, honed over years at sea.

"I'm going to scoot to the side," she said gently. "There's another candle in my dresser drawer."

She made sure not to move until he nodded. Then she trailed her hand along his back and to his thigh so that she would not startle him as she moved. It was a moment more before she could spark the flint and get a light. But once it was done, she released a breath in relief. She turned back to him, seeing his body relax as the light burned through the room. She saw too that his cheeks were red with embarrassment.

"I thought this would be easier," he said quietly. "I thought I could come back to London and still be a man." He closed his eyes and let his head drop back against the wall. "I came to apologize, angel, and to thank you. I'm sorry if I frighten you."

"You don't frighten me," she said with absolute truth. "And change is hard. Even good changes. It takes a while for the mind to catch up."

He looked at her, and she saw gratitude in his eyes. Then he slowly shifted until he sat down on her bed, his back to the wall.

"Would you like me to light another candle?" she offered.

"One is enough." Then he glanced down at the dirty footprints he had left on her bedsheets. "I owe you new linens."

She laughed, surprised at how light the sound was. "I have slept on far dirtier things, I assure you." Then as he watched, she pulled off the sheet and turned it over such that the clean side would be against her skin. "See. Now no one will notice, least of all me."

He stared at her and slowly shook his head. "You are a marvel, angel." Then his expression darkened. "Tell me why you were crying."

She let her eyes drop away from his. "I don't cry," she repeated firmly.

"Is it your uncle? Did he hurt you?" He abruptly leaned forward, his eyes flashing in the candlelight. It was only mildly frightening to see him so, but it was his words the chilled her. "I will kill him for you, if you like. With him dead, Rose will inherit. She is almost of age, is she not? You can convince her to keep you on as companion, and then the two of you could live here without him. You won't have to think about him ever again."

She stared at him, her mind barely keeping up with his words. He couldn't possibly be offering to murder her uncle for her. "You're not serious, are you?" she whispered. "You can't be."

She saw him clench and unclench his teeth. But in the end, his spine rolled back against the wall. "No," he said. "No, I'm not serious. But it is wonderful to imagine, isn't it? I used to lie awake and dream of ways to kill Venboer."

"No!" she gasped, though a tiny part of her did

wonder what it would be like to live alone with Rose without Uncle Frank's constant questioning about the household expenses. To be able to buy a dress without thinking how she would justify it to him. And without wondering what he was thinking every time he watched her from his library chair. He just sat and watched her as she went about her tasks. The idea of living without him was intoxicating. And yet equally appalling.

"No," she repeated firmly. "I don't want him dead. I just want…"

"What?" he prompted when she fell silent. "What do you want, angel?"

A husband. A home. A life such as she would probably never have. "I don't know," she finally said aloud. "I just wish that things were different, that's all."

"Like back when your father was alive?"

"Yes."

"Yes." He exhaled a sigh. "Wishing is for fools. You know that, don't you?"

"Yes," she said, her tone very much more dull. Then she looked into his eyes and saw an answering longing in them, a wish so deep and so powerful that she could read it in the very striations of his eyes. "Then I suppose I am a fool."

His lips quirked. "So am I."

He took her hand, tugging her gently closer to him. She allowed him to, though she didn't move next to him as he obviously wanted. Instead, she let him hold her hand and relished the feel of his large palm, the rough texture of his calluses, and the simple joy of being touched in so gentle a way.

"Alex's family is back in London. I took him to them today."

She jerked her gaze up to his face. He had spoken so deadpan, so blandly, that she knew the words were important. Men never allowed their emotions free rein, and he was more closed than most.

"Was it terrible?" she whispered, thinking how awful it would be for Alex if things had gone badly. He was just a boy, really. Too young to be—

"It was exactly as a reunion should be," he said. "Tears, hugs, teasing, more tears, and a celebration the likes that I have never seen. Angel, they love him so much and they were beyond thrilled to have him home."

"Oh," she whispered, understanding coming slowly. "I'm so glad for him."

"Yes."

"But it's terribly hard, isn't it? To see such happiness and know that it isn't there for you."

"I am happy for Alex," he said clearly. Then his gaze grew abstract, his lips softening into a gentle smile. "His mother couldn't stop crying. She's probably still sobbing."

Maddy smiled, her eyes misting in memory. "Tell me about it," she asked. "Every moment. Every tear. Please."

He looked at her then, and she saw from his eyes that he understood. She needed to share in Alex's joy as much as he needed to tell it. And then together, they could live for a while in happiness, even if it wasn't their own.

He spoke slowly, taking his time. He had a gift for storytelling, and though he kept his voice low, his story filled the room. Through him, she got to know each member of Alex's family, and before long, she was curled up into Kit's side so that she could feel the vibration of his words. And when he was done, the room still echoed with the memory of laughter and good food. She sighed in delight, holding every second to her heart.

She felt his arm tighten around her. Some part of her had known all along that he would do that. His kiss was inevitable from the moment he had appeared by her bed.

She should pull back, she thought. She should move away and order him to leave her bedroom and never come back. She should, but she didn't. Instead, she lifted her face to his. He touched her cheek first. A quick brush with his fingers. And when she turned toward his caress, she saw his eyes widen and his nostrils flare. She didn't speak. She hadn't the breath. She only knew that she wanted this to happen. And she didn't want to think at all. When his mouth finally found hers, she released a sigh that took her mind with it. No thoughts. No fears. Just a simple, single kiss.

Until it became more.

CHAPTER 11

His caress feathered behind her cheek, then delved into her hair. His gentleness was only a ruse, she knew. Within seconds, he was cupping the back of her head and holding her in place as he plundered her mouth. And, oh, she liked it. What a glory it was to surrender to his possession as his tongue swept into her.

There was no teasing like last time. No nipping at her lips. Just a slow, steady, thorough possession. His mouth slanted completely over hers. His tongue dominated as he thrust into her. And when she tried to tease him by sucking him deeper into her mouth, he reacted as if she had pushed him beyond his control.

He growled into her throat and, with his free hand, pushed her down on the bed, following her without breaking the seal of their mouths. She might have gasped in surprised, but there was no breath for that. He continued to thrust and parry with her even as his body settled hard and heavy on top of her.

They were both fully clothed—except for his lack of shoes—but the feel of his weight was intimate beyond anything she'd ever experienced. She was shocked by it, and yet, nothing had ever felt more exciting, more thrilling, more exactly what she wanted at that very moment.

She reached up to touch his face, to stroke his cheeks, to run her hands through his hair. She did it, but only absently. It was a soft feeling on her hands when everything else was so delightfully hard. And hot. Good God, his organ was so large as he thrust against her pelvis!

She should not be feeling these things. She should not understand these things! But she was the daughter of a doctor and had been raised in the country as well. She knew exactly what a man looked like, but she had never felt it like this before. He pushed against her in a steady rhythm that drove her wild.

Without her willing it, her legs fell apart. One slid off the bed such that her heel landed on the floor. That allowed him to settle more fully against her, and to her shock, more deeply against her core.

He pulled away from her mouth with a gasp and trailed kisses across her jaw and along her neck. "Don't be afraid, angel," he whispered. "Don't be afraid."

She wasn't. Or she hadn't been until he spoke. But his words started her mind working again. Why would she be afraid? He wasn't going to hurt her, was he?

His fingers found the buttons of her gown. It was a work gown, not a fashionable one, so the buttons down the front were perfectly accessible. While his organ continued to push against her, the rhythm delightfully steady, he began undoing her bodice, kissing down her throat as he went.

She shifted against him, her mind starting to cry alarms. But the movement only opened her groin more fully to him. There were layers of fabric between them, but he was so large she believed she could feel his every ridge. She even drew her free leg up his calf, tightening her legs to feel him more intimately.

He had unbuttoned her gown almost to her navel now, and her shift was wet from his kisses. He pulled himself upward, one foot dropping to the floor as he levered himself against her. She shivered at his thrust, her whole body arching in wonder at the exquisite feel. And as her head was thrown back in delight, he grabbed hold of either side of her shift and ripped it apart.

She opened her eyes at the sound and saw the bunch of his arm muscles as he brushed the torn fabric aside. She saw the raw expression of hunger on his face as he looked down at her. And then she watched it shift to awe. *Awe.*

"You are so big," he said. "I had not realized beneath those ugly gowns." He ran his fingers along the side of her left breast.

She bit her lip, wishing to hide away. "I'm sorry," she murmured.

He didn't appear to hear her. "So perfect," he said as he cupped her breast. Then he let his eyes drift shut in obvious pleasure as his other hand framed her right side.

She trembled at the feel of him holding her, his hands so large that he easily shaped her. And when she looked down, she saw tan fingers on white skin, as his thumbs rolled over the rose peaks of her nipples.

"Oh!" she gasped. No one had ever touched her like that. No one had ever rolled her nipples between their fingers, had squeezed and lifted her in such delight. Her belly began to tremble with each stroke of his hands. Her buttocks tightened and she ground against him. Never would she have thought this could feel so good.

She felt his hair brush across her shoulder and then the heat of his mouth across her left breast. Kisses. He was kissing her skin, even as he continued to lift and mold her breasts. His tongue drew circles over her collarbone and breast. And then, he shaped her into a perfect peak that he nipped with his teeth.

Her body had left her control. She was using her legs to drag him closer to her as he moved in a rhythm that was too slow. He began to suck on her nipple, drawing it into his mouth with a pull that was too strong, then just perfect, then not enough.

She grabbed his shoulders, needing something to hold on to. He pushed against her, his thrusts coming harder. She arched into his every stroke while his mouth continued to tug at her nipple. She felt as if her body would burst with the heat as a straight line of fire raged between breast and groin.

She cried out at the glory of it all, her undulations pulling her breast from his mouth. But she felt him rasp her name. "Angel. Angel." Repeated over and over as he rammed against her.

Then it happened. A wave of pleasure so amazing that her entire body seemed to lift off the bed. She cried out as another wave rolled through her. He too slammed against her, his face frozen on a gasp of wonder: eyes wide, mouth open, and such amazement that she knew she would remember it forever.

Twice more he slammed against her. At least double that many waves of pleasure swept through her. Then he collapsed, dropping his weight full and heavy upon her. His face landed to the side of hers, his breath hot against her neck and shoulder. And still her body moved as yet more waves washed through her. Smaller. Slower. And still wonderful.

Was this what it meant to make love? Was this what married women experienced every night? If so, no wonder everyone rushed to the altar. She lifted her arms, wrapping them around Kit. He was boneless on top of her, but his weight was lovely. And now she could appreciate the soft feel of his hair.

She tilted her head and pressed a kiss to his temple. And when he didn't respond, she contented herself with holding him in her arms. As she closed her eyes, she pretended they were married. She was holding her husband, she told herself. And tomorrow night, they would do this again. So thinking, she allowed herself to drift into a light sleep.

Kit's mind was awake long before his body could move. Thoughts collided inside him, slamming against his consciousness even as his body lay in languid release.

What had he done? She was a gently bred woman, and he had just rutted over her like a…like the slave he was. He had pinned her down, ripped her clothes, and then feasted on her body. That he released into his pants and not her sweet channel was both a blessing and an embarrassment. What kind of animal was he? With a groan of self-disgust, he slid off her. She sighed as he moved, her eyes drifting open as her near hand played with his hair.

"Is it always so wonderful between husband and wife?"

He flinched at her wording. They were not married nor were they likely to be. Not unless he could get his affairs in order. "I have no idea," he said with complete honesty. "I have never been wed."

"Oh," she said with a dreamy smile. "Of course."

"But I can say that this was special," he said softly as he looked into her eyes. "*You* are special."

She flushed and glanced away, but she looked pleased

with the compliment. "I suppose all men say that afterward."

He tugged her chin back to him, forcing her to look into his eyes. "There was a time when I said many silly things to women. Exaggerated compliments, ridiculous statements. I have lost the knack of it. I can only tell you the truth." He took a breath, knowing that his next words were not adequate to his feelings. "I will remember this night for the rest of my life. It will not diminish with time, it will not fade or soften. I will remember you, your touch, your caresses, and your exquisite body." He rubbed his thumb across her lips. "Thank you for tonight."

She looked at him, her color pinking to a delicate rose, but she didn't smile. She liked what he said. He saw a misty gratitude in her eyes. But the sight never reached her mouth or the rest of her body, which had gone very still.

"I have given away too much, haven't I?" she asked softly. Then her gaze darted to the door. "If someone heard, if someone knows what I have just done—"

"No one heard. No one knows," he said, praying that it was true. "But I should not linger." Then he pushed up from her side, regretting the loss of her heat, her touch, her scent.

She straightened as well, pulling the edges of her shift together. He winced at the sight of her torn clothing, of the mess he'd made of her hair and her bed. And yet, she had never looked more lovely to him.

"I am sorry," he abruptly confessed, and he wondered if he lied. "This was very bad of me."

She shook her head. "It was my choice as well."

He stood up from the bed. His pants were an unholy mess and cold as well. Grimacing, he looked around.

"Do you have a cloth I could use?"

"Yes. One second." Straightening up on her knees, she shrugged out of her dress. The fabric pooled about her waist and her breasts bobbed free before him. Just the sight had him stiffening again. God, she was beautiful.

"Angel..." he murmured.

But she was busy pulling off her torn shift and handing the soft fabric to him. "Use this."

He looked at the worn cotton in his hand. He couldn't. Even though he was the one who'd ripped it, he couldn't sully her attire with his filth.

"Oh!" she said, misunderstanding. "You wish some privacy, I'm sure." She started buttoning up her dress, carefully hiding away her glory. If he hadn't seen with his own eyes, he would never guess the fullness of her figure beneath the ruffles and fichus. If he had the dressing of her, she would be lauded as a diamond this season. Beautiful beyond compare and lusted after by everyone in London.

When she was all buttoned and tucked away, she smoothed her hair and climbed off the bed. He was still standing there like a fool, staring at her, and already hard again. She poured the remains of a pitcher of water into a basin, then headed for the door.

"I shall just refill this and be back. A couple minutes."

"Angel..." he began, but his voice trailed away. He didn't need privacy. He needed her. And yet he desperately needed to be far away from her, not tempting himself to re-make the same mistake. This time without any clothing between them.

"Don't worry," she said in a bracing tone. "I shall give you enough time." Then she cracked the door and peered out. A moment later she was gone.

He closed his eyes, but that was no help. The memory of her full skin, of her breasts high and full bouncing before him, of her writhing in ecstasy beneath him—all of that was waiting the moment he closed his eyes.

Cursing himself, he forced himself to deal with his mess, but he refused to sully her torn shift. Instead, he tore a wide strip off the bottom of his shirt. It was new and the best in his limited wardrobe, but he counted it as nothing. Using that, he cleaned himself up as best he could, before rebuttoning and tucking all away.

He folded her shift into his pocket. His soiled linen was tossed out her window to land near his jacket and cravat.

He should leave her, he knew. Just being in her bedroom tempted him beyond reason. But he couldn't. He had come to her room for a reason, and it was not to seduce. He desperately wished it were different. It would be beyond awkward to ask. But he had to know. And if he climbed out now, he would be back within the hour to ask his question. So he stayed, his hands shoved into his pockets and his stance uneasy. At least his right hand was encased in her shift.

She returned too tardy and too soon. She scratched softly at her own door, and he pulled it open as fast as he could. Her cheeks were rosy from exertion and her smile was filled with mischievous delight.

"I feel like a girl sneaking treats from the kitchen at night. No one is about. The servants are gone or retired. We are completely safe!"

She wasn't safe. Someone still could have heard them. Someone might even now be below the window discovering his clothing. "I, um, I need to leave, but I have to ask something first."

She nodded as she set down the full pitcher. Then she turned to him, her expression open and expectant. Sliding away from what he needed to ask, he stumbled into another question.

"Do you still have the broach I gave you last night?"

She smiled. "Of course I do." Then she pulled it out of her gown pocket. The gold flashed dull and garish in her palm. "I shouldn't carry it around with me, but I couldn't think of a safe hiding place. So…"

"The problem is that I need a fence."

She frowned at him, not understanding what he meant.

"A jeweler or someone who will buy the piece, melt it down and make something better."

"But this is an old and valuable broach! It shouldn't be melted down."

He shifted awkwardly, and he forced himself not to hunch like a dog before her. "I need to get some English coin. I cannot pay a tailor with jewelry. I need someone who will buy pieces like this and give me English pounds."

"Oh!" she said, finally understanding. "Of course. But must it be a jeweler?" she said, her brow furrowing as she thought.

"It can be anyone, I suppose. But who…" His voice trailed away. She was thinking, her brow creased, her eyes narrowed on something only she saw.

"There is a woman. A baroness who has a fondness for romantic tales." She flashed him a smile. "She and Rose are very much alike in that. But whereas Rose has almost no pin money, the baroness has a great deal. And her husband absolutely dotes on her. I think, if you spin her a good story, they would pay well for this piece."

He looked at her, amazement coloring his thoughts. A woman with a rich, doting husband was exactly what he needed. But... "I do not know that I am up to spinning anything beautiful these days."

"Nonsense," she said. "It shall be easy once you start. I loved every word of Alex's story."

"But that was real."

She shrugged, her lips soft. "It doesn't matter. Real or not, your words will be perfect."

He shook his head, but she was looking at him with such light in her eyes. His head stilled, his objection dying on his lips. In the end, he sighed. "I will try," he promised. For her, he would try anything.

"Excellent." But then her brow creased with worry. "But I don't think they are in London yet. They will be, never fear. The baroness loves the Season. A few days. A week at most."

He nodded, his mind spinning. He might not be in London in a week's time. Alex's father had asked him to come by tomorrow. It was possible that the man wanted to invest in Kit's shipping venture. If nothing else, he might give Kit a loan to restock the ship. Then as soon as there was cargo, Kit would leave. Shipping was the only way he could earn a living, and cargo waited for no man. Or woman.

But there was something he had to do first. Something he had to put to rest before he could leave England again. A memory of Scheherazade that needed its final good-bye. And smart as she was, his angel read the need right off his face.

"I suppose," she said slowly, "that there is something else you want to know, isn't there?"

He nodded, misery welling up inside him. He had no desire to be with Scheherazade. Whatever he had once felt for her was long gone, and certainly his boyhood desires were nothing compared to what he felt for Maddy right then. But he had come to England with the express intent of returning Alex to his family and reassuring himself, once and for all, that Scheherazade was well cared for. It was her memory that had kept him sane on the boat. And it was his nightmares of her death at his hands that had kept him in Africa when he might have returned home. More even than a reunion with his brothers, he needed to see that she was alive and well. Once he saw that, then he could at last move on from his past.

None of those thoughts found their way to his lips. He couldn't express the tortured reasoning behind his needs. And in the end, Maddy simply stopped waiting for his explanation. With a blank expression, she stepped over to her dresser and pulled a letter from a pile of papers there.

"Lord and Lady Blackstone sent a brief missive agreeing to attend Rose's tea next week," she said, her body stiff and her tone flat. "There was a second letter with it," she said as she handed him a pristine envelope addressed in a tidy hand. "This letter was for you."

CHAPTER 12

Kit took the letter with a shaking hand. It was from Scher. He knew it. And he needed to read it, but in front of Maddy? In front of the woman he had just seduced? He couldn't do that, especially now that her face had gone flat.

"I have hurt you," he said, stating the obvious.

Her expression hardened even more. "Life has hurt me," she finally said. "And I miss my father."

She missed more than just her father. She missed her childhood and the innocence of that time. Just as he missed the carefree man he'd been before Michael tossed him on a boat and declared him dead.

"What does she say?" she asked, her tone almost bland.

He broke the seal and pulled out the sheet, but his vision swam as he tried to read it. Closing his eyes, he took a deep breath. He was a man, damn it. He had survived in the worst hell known to mankind. He had even killed. He could read one damn letter from the woman he once loved. He rubbed his face and opened his eyes.

"'Dearest Kit,'" he read aloud. "'I am stunned but so thrilled to hear that you are alive. Please, dear friend, will you come visit me tomorrow at tea time?'"

He stared at the missive, his mind numb with emotion. His knees went weak and he found he was sitting back upon Maddy's bed.

"I don't understand," she said. "Isn't this exactly what you wanted? To see her again?"

He nodded. It was. It most certainly was. And yet... "I have been in my new rooms a day," he said. "I have already received a dozen letters just like this. Old friends, acquaintances, people I once knew."

She touched his cheek, the gesture tender even though she held the rest of her apart from him. "You thought to get something more personal from her?"

He nodded.

"She is married, Kit. She has two children and is increasing with her third. You have been gone from her thoughts for nearly seven years."

"She hasn't been gone from mine!" he exploded, coming off the bed and stepping away from Maddy's too intimate touch. "Every day, I thought of her. Every breath was because she waited for me. Everything I did—and I did such terrible things, Maddy—was so I could come back to her."

"And yet you didn't. You bought your freedom when?"

"Four years ago," he said, the words paining him as he spoke.

"You stayed away for four more years. Why?" Her eyes were dark, her body still, but he knew she was listening with her whole heart. And that she would not judge him.

He sighed. "I was more animal than man. I feared I would hurt her."

"Or be reviled by her?"

"Yes."

He heard her hand fall to her side. "I cannot imagine how hard this must be for you."

"I don't love her, angel. I swear to God in heaven that it is not how I feel toward her."

"Then what is it?"

He shook his head. "I don't know. She was everything to me for so long. Everything I had lost, everything I thought I wanted. But then I changed. I became an animal to survive."

She touched him then. Despite the way he had hurt her, she pressed her fingers to his back and let her warmth seep into him. "You are not an animal now."

He turned around, catching her when she would have slipped away from him. He wrapped her in his arms. Her body was stiff and unyielding, but she softened quickly enough. Within the space of two breaths, her body melted into his. He closed his eyes as his head dropped to her hair. She was real. She was not some mirage of a memory of another time. And he drew his strength from her. His angel.

"I cannot see her," he suddenly decided. "Not when she writes me like that."

For a long moment, she had no response. He, on the other hand, felt her breathing, the erotic press of her lips against his neck, and even the rapid beat of her heart. But then he felt her strengthen, as her body slowly drew apart from.

"You will go see her, Kit."

He didn't want to release her, but he would not cage her against his side. He owed her that much at least. "Angel—" he began, but she stepped away, folding her arms across her chest. And damn he was a bastard for noticing that her nipples were tight, her breasts full and pump.

"You must go," she said.

"No. No, I won't." Did he sound like a stubborn child? "I shall go see my brother instead. I should like to see the house where I grew up again. Even if he has painted it a ghastly color. Green. Pah!"

Her eyes lightened at that, but her mouth remained implacable. "You should go see your brother. It is well past time. But you must go see Lady Blackstone first. Tomorrow at tea, Kit. You must."

"Why?" Why should he go when she was but a fading memory? Why should he look at the past when the present was so much more enticing?

"Because you cannot move on until you put the memory of her to rest." There was more she wanted to say. He read it in the tightness of her body and the way she pinched her lips shut.

He looked away, unable to see her looking so prim. Especially since he knew the fire that burned just beneath her skin. "Agh," he said, self-loathing churning in his gut. "I am useless this way! I cannot think. I cannot even fight for the woman I want."

He heard her breath pull in with a hiss. "She is *married*, Kit. There is no fighting for a woman who is pledged to someone else."

"I know!" he snapped. He hadn't meant Scher. He had meant her, Maddy, his angel. He wanted her. Just looking at her made him hard with want. But with all the storm of emotions in his head, he could not find the words to express that. "You don't understand me!"

"I understand that you are longing for something that

is gone. I, too, spent months crying for my father, wishing for my friends back home, desperately pleading with God to make it different. I miss that life, Kit. With every breath I take, I miss it. But it is gone."

"I cannot do it," he said, the revelation cutting so deep, he could barely breathe.

"You can," she returned. "You are stronger than you think."

"Not without you," he said. "Not alone, I'm not. I can't..." He raised his arms in despair. "I just can't."

He saw her close her eyes, fighting some internal struggle. Then when she opened them, he saw that she had surrendered. To what, he didn't know. To him, perhaps. To the impossible position he had just placed her.

"Then you won't go alone," she said. "I will tell Rose that I must go convince Lady Blackstone to join us for tea. She will get her father to loan me the carriage. We will go together tomorrow."

He looked at her, seeing her willingness to help him, and he was humbled. "I owe you so much," he said. "And have abused you most abominably."

She looked at her clasped hands. "You may thank me by making your peace with Lady Blackstone tomorrow, by attending Rose's tea Tuesday next, and then by repairing whatever fences you need to with your brothers."

He would. He would do what she asked because he could not bear to hurt her more. "Of course, angel." He took a step toward her, but she held up her hand.

"I think you should go now. Rose will be coming home soon, and she always wants to talk about the evening."

He glanced at the clock. Rose would not likely be home for another hour at the earliest, but he didn't argue. He knew it was a convenient excuse to get him out of her bedroom. He grimaced. She should not need to lie to get him to leave. He should not have climbed in here in the first place.

"Thank you, angel," he said, knowing the words were so inadequate.

"My name is Maddy," she said. "Now go."

He nodded and went for the window. He had no choice with her body so rigid, as if she held herself together by willpower alone. He knew that feeling well, and so he did the best thing for her. He left. As quickly as possible, though his heart wanted nothing more than to take her back to bed and caress away the pain he had caused. But that would only make matters worse.

He paused only once. He climbed down the wall easily enough, landing with a soft thud. And when he had gathered up his things, he stopped to look up at her window. She was there, silhouetted against the candlelight from her bedroom. Her skin was touched by moonlight, and her hair was askew, making a soft halo about her face. She had never looked more like an angel. But she did not want that name, so he ceded to her wishes.

"Thank you, Maddy," he said loud enough for her to hear. Then he added two more words under his breath. "My angel." And he ducked away.

Maddy watched him disappear into the night. He moved silently, and when he donned his dark coat, he was also invisible. But she saw him. In her mind's eye, she saw every part of his body, that which she had seen and that which she had only dreamt. She felt like she knew him intimately, just as he probably felt he knew her.

Except it was all a lie. With a sigh filled with remorse, she stepped away from the window and locked the pane tight. He would not creep in on her unawares again.

Oh, but it had been wonderful. Such pleasure! She hadn't known it could be like that. And they hadn't even done the most intimate act. She wondered if it would be even better then. Or if a man invading her body would be painful and uncomfortable. And most important, would she ever really know?

She was a respectable woman, gently reared and niece to an earl. Her lineage was excellent, if not her dowry. She had every reason to hope for a match this Season, and weeks yet to catch one. She should be on her knees thanking God that she had not given away her virginity this night. That Kit hadn't pressed for her to strip out her clothing and give him all. She doubted she would have refused. She was that mindless when she was with him.

But she was still a virgin. And she could still make an acceptable match. Which meant a husband, a home, and children. Everything she wanted. But only if she refused Kit the next time he knocked on her window. Only if she cut him out of her heart right here and right now.

He was not proposing marriage. He was obviously still in love with Lady Blackstone. Maddy was merely his relief of the moment, and she could not be such a stupid, reckless woman around him. Even now, she worried that she was tainted somehow. That eligible bachelors would look at her and know what she had done.

No more! From this moment on, she would act with the utmost propriety. Her bedroom window would be

latched shut. No intimate conversations in private—
whether it be the kitchen, the back of a ballroom, or at
her bedroom window. And as for tomorrow...

Her mind stuttered to a halt. Propriety demanded that
she absolutely not go with Kit to visit Lord and Lady
Blackstone. Unmarried girls simply did not travel with
gentlemen who were not related to them. But she had
promised, and more than that, she believed that he
could not face Lady Blackstone alone. If she did not
pick him up in the carriage tomorrow, then he would
not go on his own. Which meant he would be trapped in
pretend fantasies of the life that might have been.

She couldn't condemn him to that. But she would
have to take steps to ensure that she didn't weaken. She
had no sense around him, but there was a solution.
After all, *two* unmarried ladies could travel with
propriety to a lady's house. *Two* unmarried ladies could
also travel in a coach with an unmarried man, though
that was less proper. And best of all, the second
unmarried lady in question had already decided that she
would marry Mr. Frazier. Rose would naturally leap at
the chance to spend time with her imagined fiancé.

It might not be fair to Mr. Frazier to expose his
vulnerabilities to Rose, especially since Rose was a
terrible gossip. But that was the price he would have to
pay. If he wanted Maddy there beside him when he saw
his Scheherazade, then Rose would have to be there as
well. That's how proper women behaved. And from this
moment on, that's exactly what Maddy intended to be:
excruciatingly, horribly, and without a doubt *proper*.

CHAPTER 13

For the rest of her life, Maddy would never forget the look on Kit's face when he first opened the carriage door. She and Rose had arrived at his rather shabby address. Rose had been busy exclaiming over her pirate love's reduced circumstances when the coachman opened the door and Kit popped his head inside.

His eyes lit on Rose first. The girl had positioned herself closest to the door in the exact place where one first looked when entering a carriage. She said she always caught a person's most honest expression in that moment, be it joy, envy, or anger. Maddy did not put nearly as much credence in the moment as her cousin did, but she nevertheless watched Mr. Frazier's expression closely.

He looked joyful. That was her first thought as he pulled open the carriage door. His eyes were lit from the sunlight and his lips were curved in a smile of welcome. But then his gaze took in Rose first, Maddy second, and his eyebrows raised in surprise while the rest of his expression carefully blanked to polite interest.

"Hello, Mr. Frazier," Rose said in her high, sweet voice. "I'm so touched that you invited me to accompany you on this most difficult mission. But never fear, I shall make sure to keep everything light and delightful."

Maddy hadn't exactly said that Kit had requested Rose's presence. She had, in fact, suggested that Kit would likely be surprised by her presence. But somehow her cousin had twisted that around to her own liking and was now grinning happily as Kit maneuvered himself inside. He had to sit next to Rose, of course, as she had layered the blankets and reticules in the space beside Maddy.

Meanwhile, Kit nodded politely to Rose. "Then I shall rely on you," he said, but his gaze traveled to Maddy's with a questioning lift to his eyebrow.

"As you know," she said, answering his unspoken question, "a lady cannot travel unescorted. It wouldn't be proper."

"But a maid is so boring," inserted Rose. "And I was so in need of a diversion. This shall be just the thing!"

"Of course," he said, his gaze enigmatic. "I am pleased that you could come."

Was there a hint of sarcasm in his voice? She wasn't sure, and Rose certainly didn't think so as she dimpled prettily. In any event, it didn't matter. Maddy was here with him, as she'd promised, and she'd done it in a way that was eminently respectable.

And yet, she couldn't shake the memory of his first look as he opened the carriage door. Joy. Excitement. Happiness. It had all been in his face as he looked for her. And it was all gone now that Rose was here.

"You look quite handsome in that outfit," Maddy abruptly said. "The darker colors suit you." He was in a smoky gray in a severe style. His cravat was simple, and the fine white lawn of his shirt contrasted sharply with the golden tan of his skin. In truth, he looked like a savage suited up as a man, and yet the appearance was devastatingly handsome. Especially when he smiled. Were he to wear that at a ball, every young miss would swoon in delight.

"It is quite lovely," said Rose. "Don't worry. It will only take some practice—or a good valet—and you shall master the cravat in no time."

He arched a brow at Rose in surprise. "Do you not like the simplicity of the Maharata knot? I remember spending hours on the exact fall of a cravat before, but now..." He shook his head. "I cannot seem to find the need."

"Oh, but you must!" countered Rose. "It is the only way a man can wear lace, you know, or something like lace. Like a waterfall of fabric, right under the chin. It's most stylish. Very popular."

Mr. Frazier's eyes crinkled at the corners when he smiled. He had probably spent a great deal of the last seven years squinting against a very bright sun. "I can certainly tell that you like lace and flounces, Lady Rose," he said. "Have you been trying to create a waterfall in your gowns?"

Rose clapped her gloved hands in delight. "You noticed! I knew you would. You are a man who has suffered a great deal, and they are always the most perceptive. Almost makes me wish I could be captured by pirates!"

Maddy winced, her eyes darting to Kit. Rose sounded as if she were praising horrible years as a slave so that he could notice her flounces. To trivialize what he had experienced was beyond tactless, and yet, he simply smiled warmly.

"Nonsense, Lady Rose, I find you eminently

perceptive just as you are. For example, I find it especially perceptive of you to force your cousin to wear your cast-off gowns. She cannot look half as good as you do in those dresses as it is clearly not her style. Thus, you appear generous in giving up your gowns and yet ensure that she is in her worst looks. Very clever, Lady Rose. Very clever."

Rose pursed her lips in clear dismay. "But...but that is so unkind, sir. I think Maddy is lovely! And she is so tall that she gets to add an *extra* flounce!"

For her part, Maddy wanted to run outside and hide. She had no idea what Kit meant by tweaking Rose. How dare he accuse the girl of being unkind! The truth was that Rose just assumed everyone looked lovely in a dozen layers of lace.

"Really, Mr. Frazier," Maddy began. "This is most improper."

Kit raised his eyebrows. "On the contrary, nothing could be more proper than to discuss fashion ad nauseam. Do you know, I find lace and flounces most lovely on you Lady Rose. But as you can see, Maddy is older than you. To put her in such a young, sweet style only emphasizes how young she is *not*."

Rose frowned. "Oh. Well, that is true, I suppose. But I had hoped to disguise that fact. It is hard for an ape leader to find a husband."

Maddy stiffened. "I am *not* an ape leader! Such a woman is twenty-nine or thirty. I am years away from that." She was, in fact, less than six months away from twenty-nine. But some facts she kept to herself.

"An excellent age. I myself am in my thirties," Kit said, his gaze falling steady on hers. She found herself staring back, losing herself in the very steady, very silent presence of his gaze. Which was extremely odd as the man was *not* being silent and was certainly *not* steady.

Then he turned back to Rose. "But you know how trying to hide something merely makes everyone notice it all the more."

"Well, that's certainly true. Like poor Baron Halperin and his bald head. The more he combs his hair over the top, the more everyone notices it."

"Exactly!" he crowed. "See, I knew you were smart. So you are just the person, I think, to do a daring experiment. Though I must warn you," he added, lowering his voice. "It might be a bit scandalous."

Rose tilted her head, her eyes sparkling with interest. There was nothing she liked more than a bit of daring, and that was a dangerous thing.

"Mr. Frazier," Maddy said repressively, "I find I like my dresses quite well enough, thank you." It was a lie. She *hated* her dresses, which he no doubt knew. But there was no money to pay for new ones, so stirring up Rose was to no point. Her uncle would not free up money to pay for new gowns.

"Well, of course you do," he said sweetly. "They were a gift from your generous cousin, and you must appreciate them and her because of it."

Maddy sighed. "She has given me her dresses to wear, her home to live in, and her food to eat. I would not dream of asking for anything else."

"Of course you wouldn't, Maddy," cried Rose, clearly getting into the spirit of whatever Kit intended. "Having grown up in the country, you are most grateful for *everything*."

She made it sound like Maddy had been raised in a cave. "My home was quite lovely—"

"Tell me more of this bold experiment, Mr. Frazier," Rose interrupted.

Kit grinned. "Well, you know how you have been working to hide Miss Wilson's age? Dressing her young like you?"

"Yes. I thought it was the wisest choice."

"It was the *only* choice, Mr. Frazier," Maddy put in darkly. It had no effect whatsoever.

"What if we dressed her differently?" he asked Rose. "What if we boldly accented her fatal flaw, so to speak."

Rose wrinkled her nose. "Accent her age?" she asked dubiously. "But whatever for?"

"Well, what would you think if Baron Halperin suddenly stopped trying to comb his hair over his bald spot? What if he simply cut his hair and showed the world his bald pate?"

"I would think it most sensible of him," Rose returned logically. "After all, he wasn't fooling anyone."

"Exactly!" Kit crowed. "And so we shall dress Maddy in mature styles to fit her age. And not just her age, you know. The dresses must emphasize her other flaws— her height and her full bosom."

"Mr. Frazier!" Maddy snapped, her face flaming.

"Come, come," he returned. "We are making a bold experiment here. If you were to emphasize your flaws, then perhaps…" He glanced at Rose.

"They would fade away as if nothing! Just like the baron's bald head! Oh, Mr. Frazier, I think it is a capital idea! After all, we are fooling no one. They all know she is old and tall and poor."

Maddy's eyes burned with tears. They were itemizing every aspect of her person that she had spent years trying to hide. "Shall I also draw red circles around my spots so that everyone can notice them too?"

"But you don't have spots," said Rose.

Well, at least they hadn't noticed them as she covered them carefully with her makeup pot. Though, thankfully, she didn't have to do it often.

"What do you think, Rose?" inserted Kit. "Are you brave enough to embark on a great experiment with me?"

"Oh yes!" cried Rose. "I think it a marvelous idea."

Of course she did, thought Maddy sourly. Rose also thought that the Irish had fairies called brownies who cleaned their homes. The girl had heard it from the cook and had expressly asked Maddy to acquire an Irish fairy instead of a new maid.

Maddy sniffed. "It's all well and good for you two to talk of experimenting, but I am not a doll for you to dress."

"Oh, Maddy, don't be like that," wheedled Rose.

"I cannot pay for new gowns," she hissed, furious that she had to blink back her tears. Damn him for bringing up her dreams like this, even getting Rose to crow about it like it was possible. "Do you not think I would like new clothes?" she snapped, glaring at Kit. "Don't you know that I wish to be beautiful like everyone else? Well, I am not, and I never will be!" She twisted then to stare out the window, mortification making her back prickle. How dare they do this to her?

Rose's voice, soft and very young, pierced her misery. "But you are not ugly, Maddy. How could you think that?"

"It is because she had been dressing wrong, Lady Rose," answered Kit when Maddy could not force herself to turn around. "Trying to hide things that everyone knows anyway."

Maddy let her forehead drop against the cold glass of the window. It was ninety minutes to Lady Blackstone's home, and they had barely gone twenty of it. "I am quite content with my wardrobe," she said miserably, though now even Rose knew she lied. "Can we please discuss something else?"

"No," said Rose stubbornly. "No, we cannot. I won't have you thinking you are ugly! You are just not quite the thing."

"But if we attempted this bold experiment," inserted Kit, "then perhaps that will change. Perhaps she will become just the thing. And you, Lady Rose, will be the leader! You will begin to dictate what is fashionable and what is not. Imagine it!"

Maddy fell back in her seat with a groan. She did not have to see Rose's face to know the girl was imagining just that: Lady Rose as the fashionable leader of the *ton*. But, of course, it would be Maddy standing there in all her old, tall, and poor proportions.

"There is no money, Rose," she said clearly. "I have no money."

"But your uncle does," inserted Mr. Frazier. "Rose, does your father perhaps pay your milliners bill? Does he ever question you about it?"

Rose shook her head. "Never. But Maddy doesn't go to Madame Celeste. She's much too expensive."

"But what if Maddy did?" inserted Kit. "What if you told your father that you needed a few more gowns."

"Oh! But I have already told him that. My ball gown isn't quite right—"

"Excellent. What if, instead of a gown for yourself,

you commissioned new gowns for your cousin instead? Your father would pay the bill without even knowing it."

Maddy folded her arms across her apparently massive bosom. "He would notice it if I suddenly appeared in new clothing."

"Ah, but you can merely say that you have been saving up from the household accounts."

"Then he will cut the household accounts!"

Kit pursed his lips. "Really? Is he truly that stingy that he will not pay for meals on the table? A valet to care for his clothes, a maid to dress your hair?"

"Oh, Papa doesn't care about those things," inserted Rose blithely. "And he said I could buy whatever gowns I need for my Season."

"Perfect!" exclaimed Kit. "So buy your cousin new gowns instead! You shall become a great fashion leader within a few days!"

Maddy sighed. "The earl pays closer attention than you think, Rose. He will notice."

"But by then the deed will be done," returned Kit.

"That is not the way to act, Mr. Frazier." Why didn't he understand? Rose was already too prone to act without thinking, to blithely believe that the ends justified the means. By encouraging this one flight, who knew what Rose was likely to do in the future? Maddy shot a stern look at her cousin. "Besides, I believe your father said you could buy *one* new ball gown. Only one."

Rose flushed and looked down at her hands. "Oh. Well, yes. Perhaps I overstated a bit. But truly, my father is the most generous of men."

"One *elaborate* ball gown could buy two or three new

gowns of the kind I think would suit Miss Wilson," said Kit encouragingly.

"But then Rose would have to give up her new ball gown." Maddy looked hard at Rose, seeing that the girl indeed had not realized that Kit's idea meant that she would have to forego her treat. "Rose has been looking at fashion plates for weeks, drawing them on every piece of paper she can find. She has dreamed of this new gown. I couldn't take it from her." After all, it was Rose's money. Maddy was only there as charity.

"Oh my, that is hard," Kit said, his expression filled with sympathy. "But you know, nothing worthwhile has ever been accomplished without great sacrifice. Losing your ball gown must cut deeply. I understand your hesitation. But recall that we are engaged in a bold experiment. You might become the fashion leader of the *ton*." Then he sighed dramatically. "No, no, you are right. One gown is too much to ask you to give up."

Maddy sighed as she looked at her cousin. She understood the irony lacing Kit's tone. He clearly meant that one gown was *nothing* to sacrifice. Especially given that he had spent the last seven years nearly naked. But Rose had not been swept up in a pirate raid. It was not in the girl to sacrifice anything. It simply wasn't.

"I'll do it!" Rose abruptly cried. "I will. Maddy, I want you to be beautiful. I want you to catch a husband. And *I* want to be the one to get you a husband!"

"Oh, Lady Rose!" gushed Kit. "You are the most generous of souls! I count myself most fortunate to be here in your presence." He grabbed her hand and pressed lush kisses into her palm.

Not surprisingly, Rose blushed a most becoming shade. She was beautiful, Maddy thought, a most fortunate face with a good heart. Sadly, the moment of generosity couldn't last.

"It won't work," she inserted softly. "Her father will notice and then we will both suffer."

Kit rounded on her then. He had been acting so civilized, so proper, that she had forgotten that he had a darker side. So she was shocked speechless when his anger lashed out her.

"You will *not* take this from her," he snapped. "She is having good, honest impulses. She wants to see you married. She is horrified that you believe yourself ugly. You will *not* take that from her!" He looked down at Rose who appeared equally stunned by Kit's change. "And your father will *not* punish either of you. I will see to it."

Rose nodded slowly. What else could she do with Kit looking so fierce? But Maddy was made of sterner stuff.

"I am not a doll for you to use and discard however you will," she whispered.

She saw his eyes widen and remorse flash through his expression. He knew she was not speaking just of new gowns, but of what they had done last night. Of how he had treated her even before that in the playhouse. Perhaps he was trying to do a kind thing, manipulating Rose such that Maddy got new gowns. But she could not shake the feeling that he was still doing what *he* willed for her, without the least consideration as to what *she* wanted.

"You are not my doll, angel," he said softly. "And new gowns can only aid you in finding a husband."

And there he'd said the one thing that could change her mind. Of all things, she needed a husband this Season or she would be forced into very uncomfortable choices. Anything that aided her quest was perforce necessary. Even if it meant lying to Uncle Frank and taking new gowns from her cousin.

"Are you sure, Rose?" she finally said.

The girl nodded with clear resolve. "Absolutely! It shall be the best experiment ever!"

Maddy smiled at her earnest cousin. "Then I thank you. From the bottom of my heart, thank you."

Rose flushed even prettier, but it was Kit who drew Maddy's gaze. He nodded to her in his own acknowledgment, as if thanking her for giving in. "You will make a most stunning bride," he said softly. "I do hope you will invite me to your wedding."

"Of course…" Maddy said without thinking. And then the truth of it hit her broadside. If he needed to be *invited* to the wedding, then she would naturally not be marrying *him*. Of course she knew all that. She knew he was not in a state to wed anyone just yet. His affairs were still in disarray. Good heavens, his mind was still in disarray.

But after what they had done last night, after all that she had experienced, a certain part of her had clearly hoped. Despite her resolve to be proper, she had spent last night dreaming of doing more with him as husband and wife. But he was not going to offer for her. If she had any doubt, here he was stating it clearly: I hope you will *invite* me to your wedding. Her vision swam with tears, and she turned her gaze to the window. Perhaps she could make some bland remark on the scenery that she couldn't even see.

No need. Kit noticed where she was looking and began a rolling discussion on the English countryside. No, she reminded herself, his name was Mr. Frazier. She had no business using his Christian name, even in her thoughts. Especially in her thoughts. And with those stern thoughts, Maddy suffered through an eternity of prattle until they arrived at the home of Lord and Lady Blackstone.

CHAPTER 14

They had arrived. Kit threw a panicked look at Maddy but she was still determined to avoid him. He didn't blame her. If he were a gentleman, he would have already offered her marriage. But he wasn't a gentleman and he hadn't been one for a very long time. He would not saddle any woman with his fits.

She did not know the nightmares he faced whenever he closed his eyes or that he slept with a knife clutched to his chest. She did not know how close his rage was to the surface, and that he struggled to keep it hidden away. She didn't know who he was inside, and so she naturally expected that he would offer for her.

But he had made his position clear now, much to her obvious pain, but he could not help that. She would be better in the long run with a good, solid Englishman as her husband. While he, on the other hand, now had to face the most urgent of his demons: Scheherazade, the woman he had once loved above all others.

They stepped out of the carriage to view a rather dull home. Compared to the huge edifices built as monuments to titled ego, Viscount Blackstone's home was downright modest. Two floors, perhaps some depth to the building, and a modestly decorated lawn.

Wherever would all the servants sleep? But, of course, he realized, Scher was used to doing for herself. She would not want a bunch of footmen underfoot.

He had just turned around to assist Lady Rose from disembarking when the front door opened with a bang. Kit tensed, his entire body tightening from the sound. Consciously, he knew he was far away from a battle, but his skin still prickled with his own mixture of terror and excitement.

"Stop! Oy, blimey, Christopher, stop!"

A small dark form shot past. Within a moment, Kit had the child in hand and held up by his starched collar. It was a boy of perhaps five years old, his legs pumping and kicking despite being held aloft. And in his hand was the last of an apple tart, which quickly disappeared into his mouth.

Kit felt his lips curve into a smile. He remembering doing the exact same thing as a child. And again as a slave whenever food had come his way.

"Don't let him touch me!" gasped Lady Rose. "He's covered in tart!"

"Really, Rose," Maddy admonished. "I think Mr. Frazier has him well restrained."

"You never know when a child like that can squirm away!" Rose returned haughtily.

"Especially little Christopher," came a voice from the front step. It was Scheherazade. Kit would recognize her voice anywhere, and the sound seemed to shudder into his skin, making him tremble in reaction. His hand went weak and he lowered the child to the ground. The boy was wily though and managed to twist away. In the background, he heard Rose squeak with alarm, but it was Scheherazade he listened for as she sighed heavily before calling out to her child.

"You will not escape, young man, just because we have callers. There will be a reckoning, I promise you!"

Her tone was bracing, obviously meant for her son, but Kit took it into his heart and used it to steady himself. He was a man, damn it, and he would face her. So thinking, he forced his body around to see Scheherazade and a governess standing in the doorway. But he couldn't quite face his lost love, so he focused on the servant. She was a rough-looking woman of middle years and thinning iron gray hair. In her arms, she held another squirming child—a girl of about two years—who was obviously struggling to run after her brother.

"I'll get him, m'lady," she said as she watched the boy take off around the house.

"Good luck catching that speed demon," returned Scheherazade, looking plump in her overly large dress. "Here, give me Suzanne."

The girl transferred happily to her mother's arms, settling heavily on the woman's belly. Scheherazade was certainly increasing. About six months along, he estimated, and more beautiful than he remembered. Her face had a healthy glow and was no longer gaunt with fatigue. Her strength seemed to have increased too, as she easily maneuvered the little girl, despite her pregnancy girth. But most of all, he noticed her eyes as they settled on him. Green, steady, and blinking against a sheen of tears. "Kit," she whispered.

She didn't speak the word loud enough for him to hear, but he saw the shape of her mouth and knew she breathed his name. He started forward, intent on taking her and her child into his arms. But at that moment, Brandon also appeared. He was tall, dark, and his size easily filled the doorway.

Scheherazade turned from Kit to her husband. She said something Kit could not hear, then Brandon smiled at his daughter and lifted the babbling girl from her mother's arms. But even as Brandon blew kisses at his daughter, he kept Kit within his line of sight.

Was there worry in the man's eyes? Did he wonder if Scheherazade loved her husband? She did. He could see that as clearly as he saw the clouds in the sky. But it didn't stop him from stepping forward.

"Hello, Scher."

"Oh, Kit..." she said, and with those words, he closed the distance between them and swept her up in his arms. She was so much larger than he remembered, her body softer and infinitely more womanly. And even more disconcerting was the way she held him so tight. She clutched him to her without the reserve he remembered so clearly.

He buried his face in her hair and inhaled deeply. She'd always smelled of ale and grease paint, but not today. Today her scent was of rose water and apple tarts. His Scheherazade had never smelled so...so sweet. Like a mother or a cook. But when he pulled back, he saw her eyes and remembered the woman he once loved.

There was pain in her gaze and a longing that echoed through his entire soul. Memories assaulted him. Not real ones, but the pretend ones, imagined fantasies that he had held tight to his heart all those years as a slave. He gasped and leaned forward, struggling beneath the weight of what he'd once felt. His brain didn't even register the movement until he was already leaning forward to kiss her.

Then pain clamped onto the back of his neck, squeezing such that his shoulders tensed in agony. He struggled to hold on. He had worked through pain much worse than this. But the grip at the back of his neck was relentless and amazingly strong.

"Release my wife, Kit." Brandon's voice was implacable.

The beast in him snarled, his lips curling and his hands tightening. But he wasn't at full strength, not with his cousin's fingers boring deep into his neck. Meanwhile, Scheherazade stepped from his arms to confront her husband.

"Brandon, let him go!" the woman gasped. "It was just a kiss hello."

"Scher—"

Kit took that moment to spin around, easily dislodging Brandon's grip. He might have attacked then, simply out of habit. But his cousin was still holding his daughter, and Kit would do nothing to endanger the child.

"Did you notice that it has become a beautiful day?" came another voice. His angel. Maddy. "I vow it never feels this lovely in the city. Do you think, Lady Blackstone, that we could have tea outside? Is there a table or something set up in back?"

"There is indeed," Scher returned as she smiled warmly at Maddy. "You must be the intrepid Miss Wilson."

"And I am her cousin, Lady Rose. We were having a lovely conversation on the drive here. All about how I intend to become a fashion leader. You wouldn't know much about that out here in the country, but I vow I will become the most important heiress in all of England."

"I am honored to make your acquaintance, Lady Rose," Scher returned smoothly. "Please, let us all step inside for a moment while I have Cook set up tea on the lawn."

Scher turned and led the way inside. Lady Rose scampered up behind, babbling all the way about a new idea she had to dress Maddy differently so as to draw attention to her flaws. Maddy followed more slowly, her eyes dark and troubled as she looked from Kit to Brandon.

"A pleasure to see you again, Lord Blackstone."

"An honor, Miss Wilson," Brandon returned, bowing formally to her.

She smiled, then looked at Kit. It was clear she wanted to say something. Perhaps an on-dit that might cut the tension that continued to mount between him and his cousin. But what could she say?

"You are snarling, Kit," Maddy said softly. "Do you hate my gown so much?"

She was teasing him. She knew his expression was for his cousin, but it had the desired effect. He consciously reined in his feral impulses and turned his sneer on the paneled, ribboned, and flounced monstrosity that she wore. "It is an affront to the senses," he drawled. "I do believe it even sounds ugly."

In his peripheral vision, he saw Brandon's eyes widen in shock. One did not speak to a lady as such, even if it was about a hideous gown. But as he knew would happen, Maddy smiled in response, obviously relaxing into the teasing banter.

"Truly? Does this sound ugly?" She purposely rustled her skirt. "I used to think it was wonderful."

He shuddered in mock horror, the tension flowing from his shoulders as he forced the movement. "Silks, Miss Wilson, those sound lovely. What you are wearing must have been made from barn hay."

"Oh, how cruel you are to Rose, sir!" she cried in mock horror as she took his arm and began gently leading him up the steps. His side prickled as he passed Brandon's hard stare, but he didn't swing his fist into the man's eyes. It would alarm Maddy too much. Then they were inside the front foyer and he was able to whisper to her.

"Thank you for suggesting we sit outside. I find it easier to breathe in open spaces."

"I know," she said.

He started. How could she know that he had spent years trapped below deck? That any home—even so open and airy a place as Scher's house—still reminded him of wood soaked in blood and sweat and echoing with the sobs of grown men? Above deck—in the sun—was safer than below. Above deck, the wind smelled better and carried fewer diseases. Above deck was for the masters while below was for the slaves.

"Inside is not so bad so long as I can hear your voice," he said truthfully.

"But your forehead is not so pinched with a bright sky above you." She tugged him forward as they followed Scher and Rose through the house. "Come, let us see if that beleaguered nurse has caught the little boy."

He went easily as he always would around Maddy. He was aware of Brandon, of course, still holding his daughter while his eyes bored into Kit's back. And he watched Scheherazade bobbing her head while Lady Rose chattered about fashion. He saw her pause and give an order to a maid. And he saw her maneuver gracefully around an upturned chair, a discarded child's blanket, and a small army of wooden soldiers set on attacking a large China doll.

"Kit," Maddy called softly as she squeezed his arm. "What are you thinking?"

That Scheherazade was beautiful pregnant. And that Maddy would be as well. Maddy had that same thinness that had dogged Scher. But given her size, Maddy's bones appeared more pronounced, more carved than Scher's ever could. With a little more weight and the right clothes, Maddy could be a rare kind of beauty. Not a rosy-cheeked doll like her cousin Rose, but statuesque in the classical style. Like a Roman goddess come to life.

"Kit?"

"One day," he said softly, "you will be round with a child, and your husband with think himself the luckiest man alive."

Maddy's eyebrows rose sharply in surprise, but pleasure lightened her features and touched her cheeks with color. "You are acting very strange, Mr. Frazier. I do not know what to think of it."

"Do not think, sweet angel. Just keep talking to me." It would keep him sane. And likely prevent him from killing his cousin.

"I shall make a bargain with you, sir," she said softly as they began to maneuver though the toy soldier battlefield. "I shall endeavor to keep talking, if you swear to never again try to kiss another man's wife."

He paused, his foot suspended in air as he looked at her face. She was serious. Gravely serious and frightened for him as well. Then he slowly set his booted heel down on the floor.

"I had not intended to. She just looked like I have always wanted for her. Plump and happy, children at her feet." He shook his head, confusion once again tightening his throat. "I cannot...I do not..." He looked into her eyes, trying to blot out the memories—the fantasies—that whirled through his mind. "This doesn't feel real to me, angel. None of it." He rubbed his hand over his face. "Talk to me. Let me hear your beautiful voice."

"Well, of course, Mr. Frazier," she said with a too bright smile. "I believe I can summon up some nonsense." Then she began to chatter. About what, he hadn't a clue. He listened instead to her open vowels and the steady, lilting cadence of a gently bred English woman. It was Maddy, his angel with the beautiful voice and the worried eyes. She feared for him, he knew. She should, for he was perilously close to insanity. And yet with her arm tucked securely in his and her voice flowing through his ears, he believed he could remain civil. He could talk with Scheherazade, even exchange pleasantries with Brandon, and not descend into madness. With her beside him, he could do it.

And then he walked through the back doorway and realized he was very, very wrong.

Maddy saw the feral hunger enter his eyes and threw herself completely into spouting nonsense. She talked about gardening, of all things, about which she knew much more than any gently bred woman should. Her father, she told him, had valued the medicinal properties of many herbs and had sent her often to learn from the village witch. She was not really a witch, of course, just an herbalist who was lonely for a child of her own. If things had gone differently, perhaps her father and Miss Ruseman might have formed a deeper friendship. Perhaps. But then he had grown ill and her entire life had changed as a result.

"That must have been very hard," said Lady

Blackstone. "I lost my mother as well and felt very lonely without her."

Maddy smiled wanly at Lady Blackstone. Maddy had been speaking to Kit as a way to keep him calm and make the dark violence fade from his eyes. It had started to work. She had felt the muscles of his arm relax. But then the woman had spoken—his fiancée and the woman he obviously still wanted—and his entire body had coiled tight again.

Was there ever a more impossible situation? She had thought it would be good for Kit to see his former fiancée at her home with her husband and children around. What better way to show him that Lady Blackstone had moved on? She was beyond his reach now. Instead, he had boldly accosted her the moment he'd seen her. He'd tried to kiss her!

Maddy struggled to find some sort of polite banter to fill the silence. Rose was unaccountably silent, her expressive eyes hopping from one person to the next. Did the girl understand the undercurrents in the room? Probably. Rose was a great deal more intelligent than most people thought. Thankfully, the nurse chose that moment to appear, dragging a sulking little boy behind her. She wasn't rough, by any means, but Maddy recognized the look of a woman who had reached her limit.

"Ah, so you have found the tart thief!" Maddy cried much too loudly.

Lady Blackstone swiveled in her son's direction. "And what a dirty mess you have made of yourself," she said sternly. "Just when I wanted to introduce you to someone special."

"Dragged me down to the creek and back, 'e did," said the nurse. "But I knew 'e'd get tired eventually, didn't I, boy? And next time, you'll be wise to listen to me and your mum, won't yeh?"

The boy had a fierce scowl for his nurse, and his mother abruptly burst out laughing. "My God, Christopher, you look exactly like your father when you do that."

"He does not!" cried Lord Blackstone in mock horror. "I would never appear so dirty before beautiful ladies. And I certainly always listened to my mother."

Lady Blackstone arched a brow at her husband. "I believe your mother also taught you to never lie," she said sternly. Then she waved to her son. "Come here, sweetheart, I want you to meet the man you were named after."

The party was loosely gathered around the terrace, with Maddy and Kit gracing a bench brought up from the grounds. It was no longer proper for Maddy to hold on to Kit's sleeve, but she was close enough to feel his leg clench and hear the sharp intake of his breath. His gaze slid hungrily to the little boy in muddy clothing and with dirt across his cheek. The child was still held in the iron grip of his nanny, but he was able to study Kit, his steady regard making him appear quite advanced for his years.

"Goodness, you are really quite filthy," despaired his mother as she pulled him away from his nurse. Rose wrinkled her nose as well and twitched her skirt away from the boy. But Maddy was charmed. It had been a long time since she had been able to talk with a child, especially one this young. Children, as a rule, were banned from polite society.

"Just tell your mama that getting dirty is what little boys do," she said sweetly. "And also"—she added as the tea tray finally arrived—"it is hungry work." Maddy picked up a sweet biscuit from the tray and raised her eyebrows at Lady Blackstone. "May I give it to him?"

The child's eyes immediately went to the cookie, and at his mother's nod, Maddy was able to pass it to him.

"I am only allowing it," said his mother sternly, "because I want you to be especially gracious to Mr. Frazier. Mr. *Christopher* Frazier."

And finally Kit found his voice, though his words came out in a thick rasp. "Call me Kit," he said. "U-Uncle Kit."

The boy didn't say a word, of course. He was busy chewing on his sweet.

"He does look a great deal like his father," said Maddy as a way to fill the silence.

"Yes. And he has his father's temper—"

"You named him after me?" interrupted Kit. "In my...memory?"

Lady Blackstone nodded. "It was Brandon's idea, but I liked it the moment he said it. A daughter would have been Christine."

Maddy watched as Kit's gaze jumped to Brandon, who confirmed everything with a nod. But then something happened as he gazed to the boy. A kind of trembling fit began to shake his body. It was small at first, a suspension of breath that only Maddy noticed. But then his hands began to shake where they were fisted by his sides. She tried to help him. She touched his arm, but by then the fit was shuddering through more of him. She could see his thighs twitching and knew he had ceased to breathe.

"Kit," she said, desperate to allay the coming disaster. "It's such a lovely day. Perhaps we should go for a walk." But it was too late. His entire body was shuddering.

Lady Blackstone stood up and quickly gathered her son into her arms. Lord Blackstone abruptly passed the girl to the nanny as he slid in front of wife, obviously protecting her.

"Rose!" snapped Maddy. "Take the boy inside to the nursery."

"What!" gasped Rose, her nose wrinkling at the sight of the dirty boy.

"Do it!" Maddy hissed, and she shoved her cousin forward. Lady Blackstone had already moved toward the doorway with her son, pushing the nanny ahead of her. Rose stumbled behind as Maddy took hold of Kit's forearm. Even through the covering of fabric, she could tell his muscles were locked tighter than iron. And his gaze had yet to leave the boy.

"Lady Blackstone, please!" Maddy cried. "Please don't leave. He needs to have it out now."

Her hostess paused, her gaze steady on Kit, whose trembles appeared to have peaked.

"Please," Maddy repeated. "Please don't abandon him now."

She knew the moment the woman decided what to do. With an abrupt nod of her head, she shoved her son into Rose's outstretched arms. The child cried out, squirming to get back to his mother, and Rose was no better as she tried to hold his tiny body away from her dress. It was Lord Brandon who came to the rescue. In one quick move, he pulled his son out of Rose's arms and set him on the ground.

"Christopher! Go to the nursery. *Now!*"

The boy was about to protest, but one look at his father's face and he spun on his heel and ran.

"Lady Rose, if you would do me the greatest favor

and make sure he gets upstairs safely. Last door to the right." The words were spoken politely, but there was no mistaking the commanding tone in his voice. Rose nodded meekly and followed the child. Which left Maddy with Lord and Lady Blackstone all looking at Kit. Until finally, blessedly, his fit passed.

CHAPTER 15

Kit found his footing, but his world was teetering out of control. His vision wasn't even clear as the lawn seemed to bob and weave before him. He was sinking in an ocean of emotions as wave after wave of fury swamped his consciousness. Never before had he come face-to-face with all he'd lost.

"Kit!" It was Maddy's voice, a single high note of worry, but it did little to beat back the tide.

He thought he'd dealt with everything that had happened. He thought he'd come to accept his lot in life, but now he saw so clearly what had been stolen from him. It wasn't that he wanted Scheherazade. As a woman, she was little more than a fond memory for him. But her life, her children, her obvious *joy* in all that surrounded her—that is what he'd lost the day his bastard cousin had thrown him onto a boat.

"That boy," he rasped as he stumbled in the direction of the back house door. "He should have been mine. This life!" He spun wildly, trying to indicate the house, the grounds, the joy he saw in every line of Scher's pregnant body. "This life was mine!"

A dark figure steadied him, a masculine hand that restrained as much as supported. Brandon, of course, one of the two cousins who had taken everything from him. First Michael declared him dead and shipped him off to Barbary pirates. Then Brandon stole his wife and child.

"Leave me alone!" he screamed, shoving hard at his cousin's form.

Brandon rocked back on his heels, but he did not release his hold. "You have lost yourself, Kit," he said.

"Myself?" he said with a wild laugh. "I have lost *everything*!" He straightened and twisted his arm, easily breaking Brandon's grip. "Stolen!"

"I stole nothing!" Brandon snarled, and inside Kit, the slave crowed. Finally a fight. Finally an outlet to the fury that seethed within him.

Kit crouched before his cousin, his hands loose as he judged the best place to grab the taller man and drag him down to the ground. Once there, no one could best him. He saw Brandon read his intention. The man's eyes widened in surprise, but that in no way slowed his reaction. By the time Kit had decided on his attack, Brandon had tightened his own hands into fists and was angling for a better position on the terrace.

And then a large pregnant woman pushed her way between them. "Stop it! Both of you!" Then she unleashed her fury at Kit. "How could you think he stole me from you? We thought you dead!"

"He's not thinking," came another voice—his angel's—from the side. "Can't you understand? He's angry. He's lost so much, he just wants someone to blame."

"Fine," Brandon said as he gently set his wife aside. "Blame me. I courted her. I seduced her. And then I married her and built a life I never thought possible."

Kit landed his blows, one to Brandon's soft belly and the second to his jaw. Slave howled with glee as his cousin dropped like a stone. Not unconscious, though. The man was more hardy than that, but Kit was ready.

He leaped, but caught Maddy instead. She had stepped into the fray at the worst possible moment. He had just been bringing back his fist, intending to rain blows down upon Brandon, but she stepped into his swing. His fist missed her, but his arm wrapped around her neck. And the force of his movement twisted him onto her. His knees caught her stomach and his chest collided with her much softer one.

He heard and felt her exhale as they collided, but she was prepared. Despite the force of their impact, she wrapped her arms around him and held tight. Even her legs spread to trap him, but her skirt hampered them both. They fell sideways, missing his cousin by less than an inch, and rolled against the tea table.

Slave snarled, already trying to lift off her. It was Brandon he wanted, but she held on like a damned monkey. And her grip was too tight for him to easily lever himself off of her.

"Angel!" he growled. "Angel!"

"I won't…let go! I won't."

He was fighting her, the table wobbling above them as he banged into it. In his peripheral vision, he saw Brandon roll to the side. In a moment, the man would be on his feet with Kit on the floor. And Angel as well! They could be killed like this! It was too vulnerable.

"Angel!" he gasped as he fought to both protect her and force her to release him. But it didn't work. She wouldn't let go. Then the teapot crashed to the floor right beside them, shattering as it landed. Shards of china and burning tea splattered his face. Hers, too, as a thin line of blood appeared on her cheek.

"Angel!"

"No! I'm not leaving you!"

He stilled as her words penetrated his churning thoughts. He felt too the burn on his skin from the tea, and the tight clutch of Maddy's arms as she held him with all her considerable strength. "I'm not letting you go," she said again, her entire body vibrating with the force of her words. "I'm not."

The rapid-fire thoughts in his mind began to slow. Sensations poured in, but now he could process them. He felt Maddy clutching him and realized she was solid enough to support his weight. He saw Brandon gain his feet, but not move to attack. And he felt his own heart beating erratically, not to fight, but because of her words.

"I'm not letting go. I'm not. I won't."

Inside his mind, Slave still raged. The fury remained, but somehow Maddy's words made the rest settle. His hands lost their grip on her clothing. He stopped pressing into her ribs. And his breath stuttered out of his chest like a sick horse.

Then it happened. His mind finally stopped raging. Slave was silenced. His body stopped fighting. And in the quiet that remained, an agony began to grow. Like black water rising in his soul, there was no fighting it and no stopping it. It was beyond pain, beyond anguish. It was simply loss—raw and unfettered—and it buried him beneath the tide.

He screamed. He bellowed. He must have raged in a fit beyond imagining. He had no conscious awareness of it. There was only the black water killing him. And her. Wrapped around his body, whispering over and over and over.

"I won't let go. I won't let go."

Time ceased to have meaning for Maddy. At first, all she knew was the anguish of the man in her arms. He didn't realize it, of course, but it wasn't just him that she embraced. As he shuddered in his arms, she too cried. She railed at the fate that had killed her father and sent her to care for a spoiled Rose and a lecherous uncle. She vented her fury at the Marriage Mart and the men who daily judged her lacking. And she cried for the man who had lost so much more than she had and who saw no way free of his pain. She cried as he did, and the release was as healing for her as she prayed it was for him. Either way, they made a pretty pair rolling about on the terrace.

She came back to herself before he did. After all, she'd had a few years to mourn her childhood, whereas he had just come face-to-face with the loss of the woman he loved. Maddy felt the aches in her body begin. Her arms trembled where she clutched him. Her head hurt where she had banged against the table. And her cheek stung from the shattered teapot. All these little annoyances began to push into her thoughts, but she resolutely ignored them. She would not release Kit until he was ready to face the world again.

And into this frozen tableau stepped Rose. Maddy should have expected it, of course. Rose would never hide away when something was happening. Besides, the girl believed herself to be the destined bride of the romantic pirate. She could not be that from upstairs.

So while Maddy still lay on the ground with Kit, the French doors opened and Rose stepped onto the terrace. Or rather, she tried to but was stopped by the sudden bulk of Lord Blackstone standing right in front of her.

"Oh my, Lady Rose! I am so glad you came down,"

he said as he stepped bodily into her path. "I was most pleased that you could help me with my son. He is such a rapscallion," he said as he advanced firmly upon her. Rose had no choice but to back up—back into the house—or be bowled over.

"Well, of course, my lord," she said. "But as the children are well settled now—"

"Do you know," said Lady Blackstone as she too followed her husband, easily blocking any view of Maddy and Kit on the floor, "I believe it's going to rain. I think we shall have to settle inside. Lady Rose, have you seen my front salon? I vow it is most acceptable for tea. Not quite as comfortable as your home in town, I'm sure. In fact, would you care to give me some advice on the proper way to arrange it to look more stylish?"

"Well, of course, I would, Lady Blackstone. But—"

"Right this way, Lady Rose," said Lord Blackstone.

Then their voices faded from hearing. Maddy exhaled in relief. Thanks to their hosts' quick thinking, Rose wouldn't see her current disreputable situation. Rose was always taking her to task over her country ways. Imagine what the girl would say to this! The thought was amusing enough that she found she could smile. And as Kit had come to his own place of peace, she soon realized that he was looking at her. Sadly, his expression was anything but amused.

"It's all right, Kit. I'm not insane." Though she felt it. After all, she'd just landed not once but twice beneath a man during a brawl!

he rolled slowly off her, shifting his weight such that he could free one hand from beneath her body, though their legs were still intertwined. She eased her grip as well, trying not to wince as blood seeped back into her fingers. Her efforts were in vain. He saw every flicker of her expression as his gaze never left her face. And when one of his hands was free, he lifted it to her cheek, wiping away the tears and the blood.

"I have hurt you," he said softly.

"And yet I am still here. And still smiling, I might add."

His fingers trailed across her mouth and she tasted salty wetness on her lips.

"How do you feel, Kit?"

His expression shifted then, flowing through myriad emotions, none very clear. In the end, his eyes simply turned tragic. "They are so happy," he said softly.

She didn't need to know who he meant. He referred to Lady Blackstone and her husband. "Yes," she said as gently as she could. "Very much in love."

Kit nodded, the movement almost too tiny to perceive. But they were nose-to-nose, so there was nothing in his body that she did not know, including a warm and very present thickening in his groin.

"And Alex is happy too. His family embraced him, his father wept, and his mother..." Kit sighed. "His mother is still alive."

It took a moment for Maddy to remember that Kit's mother was dead. And the head of his family was Michael, the Earl of Thornedale, who had declared him dead while secreting him away on a doomed boat. "Do you begrudge them their joy?" she asked quietly. She did. A tiny part of her hated them all for being so happy when she was not.

"I don't want Scheherazade," he said softly. "I swear to God that I don't. But I want her life. I want Alex's family. I want..."

"To be happy again."

"Yes." He closed his eyes and dropped his forehead against hers. She was becoming more aware of his organ, thickening hot and hard against her hip. If only she could succumb to the physical desire they felt for each other. If only she could let him come to her at night again, let him strip away all of her cares as easily as her clothing. Then, for a time, she would feel happy. She would likely feel ecstatic!

He groaned and rolled away from her. Not far, but enough so that she could no longer feel the press of his organ against her. "What has become of me?" he said, his gaze looking up at the sky. "Angel, I can barely breathe for the emptiness."

"It is like your soul is gone, and your body just a shell," she said, thinking of her life just after her father died. "And all you feel is—"

"Loss. And anger."

"Such anger," she whispered.

He turned his head toward her, and she read tenderness in his eyes. "I am so sorry about your father," he said.

Her mouth curved into a healing smile. "I'm so sorry the Earl of Thornedale is an arrogant idiot. Either one could be forgiven, but combined…"

"Do you know, he is considered influential in politics."

She groaned. "God save England."

His lips twitched in humor, but the lightness quickly faded from his eyes. So she levered herself upright such that she was sitting and looking down into his rugged face. "Do you remember what Alex's sister said to you?"

He covered his eyes with his forearm. "She is but a child."

"She said you were a man who made his own luck."

"I have nothing," he said, still hiding behind his arm. "A ship that is not seaworthy and a crew who needs to be paid. No cargo and no reputation with which to find one." His arm dropped away and he looked into her eyes. "I can't even pay next month's rent on my rooms. I got them for Alex, so he would not have to sleep on board. And because the ship's repairs would send me to land anyway. But I have no money for next month's rent. In four weeks' time, I could very well be in debtor's prison."

"You had less than that as a slave," she reminded him. "And yet you bought your freedom."

He sighed. "I was lucky, then. And patient. It took months, but Venboer came to trust me a little. And with that little freedom, I found opportunities. I became a thief, first to steal food, then gold and jewelry. I secreted it away, hoarded it." He shook his head. "I did such things, angel."

"You made your own luck. And in time, you bought your freedom. And from there, you created more luck. You survived as a freed slave in Africa. And now you have a ship and a crew, and you have given Alex back his life." She leaned forward and stroked a finger across his cheek. "Such a man can do anything."

His expression shifted, but not to anger. She could see the fury drain from him, and the emptiness fill with…something. Not passion, not hunger, not even hope, but a curious mixture of all three. Plus awe, she realized when he spoke. His words held awe.

"How is that you can say such things?" he whispered. "After all that you suffer, how can you believe them?"

She smiled. "With you, it is easy." How she wanted to kiss him then. She could read the desire in him as well.

But they were outside in full view of anyone who cared to look. So she forced herself to remember that she was an unmarried miss, a woman who needed to guard her virtue closely. She pushed to her feet with a sigh. "Rose can be distracted only so long, you know. And she is not a fool. She will want to know what happened to us."

He nodded, and she saw his mind reluctantly shift to polite excuses. "We were taking a walk to see the creek." He shot her a mischievous look. "Your countrified ways, you know. You insisted on looking and then you slipped and fell."

"I did no such thing! My footing is always secure!"

"Very well, then I slipped and brought you tumbling in after me."

"But we are not wet, Mr. Frazier. And anyone with half a mind would know that we did not fall in a creek bed."

"On the contrary, Miss Wilson," he said as he quite deliberately rolled his backside in a puddle of spilled tea. "I am quite wet and you are quite dirty. I most sincerely doubt that a London chit will notice the difference."

Well, a London girl might, if she had a scientific or logical bent. But that was definitely *not* Rose, and so Maddy ended up nodding in agreement. "It will have to do, I suppose. I can think of no other polite excuse for my appearance."

He pushed to his feet, coming to stand before her. His hair was mussed, there was still blood on his cheek, and his clothing appeared exactly as one would expect from a man who had been brawling.

"Mr. Frazier..." she began, though she had no idea what she intended to say.

He stepped right up to her; then he took her head in his hands and he pressed his mouth to hers. She had time to stop him, but she didn't. She wanted to feel his mouth. She needed to open herself to him and let him plunge inside.

It was over too quickly. The push of his tongue, the invasion of her mouth was only long enough to make her body arch into his.

"You must call me Kit," he said when he had stepped a polite distance away.

"And invite you to my wedding," she said, her heart breaking as she reminded herself just how unwanted she was.

His gaze dropped to the ground, his cheeks flushed with embarrassment. "I am not a man, angel, but a beast wearing a man's form."

"Don't be ridiculous—"

"You don't understand!" His voice was harsh, his expression abruptly feral. The shift was so sudden and so startling that she gasped. Then he sighed, obviously pulling his body and his mind back under control. "You were right to make me come here," he said and she blinked at the sudden shift in topic. "I needed to see this, needed to face what could have been."

"Can you let it go now?" she asked, her heart in her throat.

His nod was slow but unconvincing. "But I should finish the task," he said slowly. "Go visit my brother."

"It's a good idea," she said calmly, though inside her heart crumbled at the thought of him leaving London. "He is your family. He will help you remember who you were before all this."

She said the words, even made them especially

bracing, but not for him. They were for herself. She had to go back to Rose and to Uncle Frank. They were *her* family and quite possibly her only future. After all, he had just said in the carriage that she would not be his wife. Did she think that another episode would change that undeniable fact? If anything, it only underscored how very unsuitable he was as a husband.

Only a fool would feel such aching sadness that he was leaving London. He was not a viable candidate for a husband, and it served her no good to spend time on his difficulties. Two full minutes of this silent tirade braced her spine and refocused her on her goal: a husband, a marriage. With someone who was decidedly *not* Mr. Frazier. And at the end of those minutes, she looked up to see him watching her, his blue eyes shuttered, his expression closed.

"I am ready," she said firmly.

He didn't respond except to hold out his arm. She took it carefully, only allowing the tips of her fingers to touch his arm. And she kept the maximum possible distance between them as they crossed into the house.

It wasn't hard to find Rose. The woman was chattering about settee fabrics. Kit took the lead the moment they entered the salon. He apologized profusely for their disreputable appearance, explaining about his fall near the creek. And if Rose looked at them both with narrowed eyes, she didn't question his statement. She couldn't, what with Lord and Lady Blackstone laughing so loudly about his clumsiness.

And then, just when Maddy thought they had escaped unscathed, her cousin smiled sweetly and clapped her hands. "Well, I am so glad that you are here now, Mr. Frazier. We can discuss the details of my tea. You promised to attend, you recall. And now Lord and Lady

Blackstone have agreed as well."

"Rose," said Maddy with a sigh. "Rose, it won't do. Lady Blackstone cannot travel that far. Not in her condition."

"Nonsense," returned Rose blithely. "She was just telling me that she goes to her playhouse at least once a week. It is hardly much farther to my home, you know."

"But—" began Maddy.

"I will of course go," Lady Blackstone interrupted, her gaze shifting from first Rose to Maddy and then finally to Kit. "But only if Mr. Frazier will agree to escort me. Is it possible, Kit? Do you think you could join me and Brandon on the ride into the city?"

Everyone turned to Kit, including Maddy. She was closest to him, so she could see the minute struggles on his face. In the end, he lost his battle with his cheery exterior. His social smile faded, and his eyes held regret. "I am sorry, beauty," he said to Rose. "I'm afraid I have to leave London as soon as possible."

"What?" Rose gasped. "Now? But where will you go?"

Kit shrugged. "To my brother Donald. I'm afraid I need to borrow some money. I have a ship and a crew that require cash immediately."

"Well, as to that," Lord Blackstone said, the rumble of his voice deep and slightly embarrassed. "I made some inquiries after we, um, met the other night. Scher and I would like to help, Kit. We'd like to invest."

Maddy felt the shock hit Kit's body, a shudder that trembled through his body into hers. "I... What?" he gasped.

Lady Blackstone reached behind her to clasp her husband's hand. "The playhouse generates cash, Kit.

Not a lot, but a steady profit. We would like to buy an interest in your shipping venture."

Kit gaped at them. "Shipping venture?"

"You have a boat, right?" inserted Rose. "That's a shipping venture. They want to give you money so you can stay in London and attend my tea!"

Maddy looked to Kit. His eyes were wide, his body still tense with shock, though she wasn't entirely sure why. Perhaps he couldn't believe in what was being offered. "Goodness," she drawled, "that sounds very lucky, don't you think?"

He turned his gaze to her, but his expression remained unreadable except for his general surprise.

"There's nothing lucky about it," growled Lord Brandon. "I've been looking for a venture. I made inquiries, talked to his crew."

"You talked to my crew?" Kit asked.

Lord Blackstone nodded. "Went to your ship first thing after...well, when I woke in London. Met a man named Puck and learned an earful, all of it good. The crew's good, but the ship isn't. We can help you with that. Pay for the repairs as an investment in your company."

"In you," pressed Lady Blackstone.

Kit didn't speak. His body was so tight, Maddy wondered if he could.

"Well, that's excellent!" crowed Rose. "Repairing a boat takes time, doesn't it? Long enough that you can still attend my tea!"

"Rose, please," admonished Maddy. "Not everything relates to your entertainments."

Rose huffed in response, but there was little time for more as Lord Blackstone pushed to his feet. "We can accomplish this now, if you like, Kit. I have some documents already prepared. You can see if they're too your liking. Then you shall have the funds you need to begin repairs immediately."

Again, everyone looked to Kit, who at last broke out of his stupor. "I just tried to break every bone in your body, Brandon. I called you a thief and frightened your children in your own home."

Lord Blackstone's face broke into a surprisingly carefree smile. "The children thought it was grand fun, except for Christopher, who deserved a spanking at the least. As for calling me names, you should hear the things that Scher calls me."

"Brandon!" gasped his wife, but her blush said that she was not offended.

Meanwhile, Lord Blackstone's expression sobered. "I owe you a great deal, Kit. And my brother owes you much, much more. Allow me to repay a tiny portion of that debt. Please."

The change came slowly, a tiny shift in body imperceptible to all but Maddy. Eventually, Kit's breath released and his head bowed in agreement. "Thank you," he breathed. "And," he added as he turned to Scher, "thank you for the gift of my namesake. In time, I should like to be a proper uncle to him."

Lady Scher's smile revealed a rare beauty. Not one of face, though she certainly was lovely enough, but of heart. Her body seemed to glow and her smile warmed everyone, Maddy included. "I should like that above all things, Kit."

"Oh excellent!" cried Rose as she clapped her hands. "Everything is working out just as I planned!"

"Almost, Lady Rose," Kit said as he slowly stepped apart from the group. "The thing is, beauty, that I am not ready for polite company." His gaze shifted from Rose to Maddy. "I have learned that much and more this afternoon, thanks to you."

"Kit..." Maddy whispered, but he shook his head, cutting her off.

"I will take your money with gratitude, Brandon. I will set the repairs to my ship in motion, and then I will go see my eldest brother, maybe even look for the others. Lucas, for one. I think I should like to see him." He turned back to Rose. "I am afraid, beauty, that means I shall not have time for a tea."

Rose pushed to her feet, distress written in every line. "But surely that won't take long. You can be back before Tuesday next, can't you?"

"No, beauty, I won't. In fact," he said with a deep breath, "I wonder if I shall be fit for polite company ever again." And with a last look at Maddy, he turned and nodded at his cousin. They left the room immediately without any more good-bye than that.

CHAPTER 16

"I know what you did with Mr. Frazier."

Maddy started out of her gray fog of misery to look at her cousin. They were in their carriage on the way back to London after an interminably long tea. Rose and Maddy had lingered long after Lord Blackstone and Kit had disappeared to their business discussion. Even after the men sent word that the ladies should return to London alone, Rose had lingered, hoping that Kit would change his mind. But he didn't, as Maddy knew he wouldn't. He needed time to sort out his moods, to relearn what it was like to be an English gentleman. Only after that would he attempt polite society.

It was wise of him, she knew. But she couldn't help but pray he healed quickly. That his business with Lord Blackstone worked marvelously fast. And that someday soon he would appear as a proper caller at their front door. She prayed for it, but she didn't expect it. She, more than anyone, knew how long it took a heart to heal.

Meanwhile, Rose finally gave up hope. She ordered the carriage, and then climbed in with an irritated swish of her skirts. Maddy followed, certain that she would spend the next two hours pretending to listen while

Rose complained about the fickleness of certain parties in first accepting her invitation then changing his mind. There had been some of that, but then Rose had fallen strangely silent. Maddy had been too grateful for the reprieve to question it. Until, of course, her cousin came up with that horrible statement.

"I beg your pardon?" Maddy said, vainly struggling to marshal her wits.

"I saw what happened on the terrace. It wasn't as if you were quiet, what with all the roaring and crashing into tables."

"Rose, it wasn't what it looked like."

"It looked like Mr. Frazier tried to kill Lord Blackstone and you stepped in the middle. Again! Really, Maddy, didn't you once tell me to *never* step between two men when they are fighting?"

"Well, yes, I have said that," she began, but Rose was winding into quite a scolding.

"But you couldn't help yourself, could you? You couldn't let them punch it out as boys do. Everything would have gone better if you had, you know."

"Rose, you can hardly blame me—"

"Imagine if they had beaten each other to a bloody mess. Neither of them would have been seriously injured. Unlike the soft earl, both Mr. Frazier and Lord Blackstone are in the peak of health. They would have punched each other, satisfied whatever notion of honor needed to be satisfied, and then Kit would not have felt humiliated. He would not have collapsed on top of you, sobbed like a little boy, and then felt it necessary to leave London!"

Maddy blinked. Every once in a while Rose surprised her by saying something completely logical and quite perceptive. But still, she didn't think she deserved the blame for this latest fiasco.

"Rose, I think it's rather more complicated than that."

"Of course it is!" her cousin huffed. "Mr. Frazier isn't well. But that's exactly why he needs to go about punching things. Better his family who won't spread it about than some hapless lord or servant or butcher."

Maddy bit her lip, wondering if what Rose said was right. Was that all Kit needed? Some time to punch out whatever violence was in him? It sounded ridiculous. His pain went much deeper than a few fist fights could cure. And yet, she had seen her father's patients recover from the most horrible things by hard labor, a few drunken brawls, and time. Most especially time.

"I'm sorry, Rose," she finally said. "Perhaps I was very wrong to interfere."

"Of course you were. And now he is gone!" Rose wailed.

Maddy had no response especially since her own heart was chanting the same refrain. "But why are you so upset, Rose? You hardly know Mr. Frazier. Is it because of the tea?"

"I don't care about any silly tea!" Rose snapped. Then when Maddy arched a brow, she waved her hand in dismissal. "Well, of course it would have been nice, but I was able to witness the dramatic reunion of the doomed pair, wasn't I? My tea will be a huge success merely because I can recount the details."

"Oh, you wouldn't!" cried Maddy. The thought of everyone knowing how Kit had collapsed in pain was beyond unbearable.

"I won't say anything scandalous, Maddy! I shall just say that you got caught up in the brawl. Everyone will ask about that cut on your face anyway."

"Not about me, you ninny!" she returned with heat. "About Mr. Frazier. About…well, everything."

"Well, everything is exactly the point, isn't it? Don't worry," she said with a dramatic sigh. "When I am finished, he will come out as the romantic hero of a modern tragedy."

"And Lord and Lady Blackstone?"

"They are victims as well, don't you think? After all, they thought he was dead. And they did name their son after him. I thought that was the perfect touch, don't you?"

"I doubt they did it so you could have a dramatic tale," returned Maddy in excruciatingly dry tones.

"I don't see why you are in such a crabby mood," Rose snapped. "It isn't your fiancé who is harrying off to God knows where to return only God knows when!"

Maddy gaped at her cousin in shock. "He isn't your fiancé, Rose. I don't believe he has a mind to marry at all."

"Well, of course he doesn't, but then men never know these things."

"Good heavens, where are you getting these ideas?"

"Everyone knows that!" Rose said indignantly. But when Maddy stared hard at her, she had the grace to flush and huff back into her seat. "If you must know, Bethany's mama says that Lady Ashcroft trapped her husband by…"

The story went on for quite some time. It involved various people and absolute facts that were really just speculation. It was the fodder of the aristocracy and had created in Rose the belief that with the right provocation, men by nature would fall prey to their baser instincts. They fell desperately in lust with the right woman, and then—because they could not have a proper woman any other way—perforce must propose. Marriage, love, and children would follow in some fashion or another.

It was all ridiculous, of course. Rose painted men as simple creatures of appetite who had to be directed the right way for the desired result. Like aiming a horse to water. Eventually, every man got thirsty enough and would propose so long as he got to drink.

It was an interesting idea and one Maddy had to mull over. After all, she had not been successful to date in capturing a husband. Perhaps it was because she wasn't seductive enough. But that still didn't answer the basic question.

"Yes, yes, Rose, that is all well and good, but why do *you* want to marry Mr. Frazier?"

Rose frowned at her. "Well, I should think that was obvious."

Maddy threw up her hands in disgust. "It's not! And do not say some ridiculous prattle about true love. I do not believe it. You are no more in love with Mr. Frazier than I am."

Her cousin arched a look at her, a sudden mischievousness coming into her expression. "Well, that is an interesting thought," she drawled. "*Are* you falling in love with him, Maddy?"

"Don't be silly!" she snapped with much more heat than she intended. She certainly cared for the man, just as she might care for any person who was in pain. And if she were truly pressed, she might admit to a great deal of, well, animal lust for the man. She had spent many hours in fantasies that began with the sight of his naked chest their first night together. But that was not love. And it certainly wasn't marriage. "I am looking at a quite different man for a wedding ring."

"Mr. Wakely, perhaps?" Rose asked, her eyebrows waggling.

Mr. Wakely? Maddy had to think back until she remembered Mitchell Wakely. He was the quiet gentleman who had spoken so nicely to her at one of the interminable musical evenings. He had a respectable portion, a logical mind, and a nice smile. "Yes," she said firmly. "He is on my list."

"Well, I think he's perfect for you."

"Thank you. But we were speaking of you and Mr. Frazier. Why do you want *him*?"

Rose leaned forward. "I'll tell you, but you have to promise not to steal him from me. He would make good sense for you as well."

"I have already told you I have no interest in Mr. Frazier!" Maddy said loudly. "My sights are set on Mr. Wakely and perhaps some others." She rattled off the names of gentlemen who had caught her eye.

"No," Rose said, her nose wrinkling. "I think Mr. Wakely is your best hope. After all he is—"

"Rose! What are your reasons regarding Mr. Frazier?"

Rose pursed her lips. "Oh, very well! First off, you know he is the catch of the season."

Maddy knew no such thing. "He's not handsome, dresses poorly, and has fits. That cannot make him a good catch."

Rose waved all that away. "He's handsome enough and clothes can be changed."

"But—"

"Don't you see? By the end of my tea, he will be the most exciting man on the social scene. No gently bred man could possibly compete with a doomed pirate, now returned home."

Maddy pressed her lips together. It didn't bear repeating that was Kit *not* on the social scene and had no interest in becoming a romantic hero.

"Second," continued Rose, oblivious to Maddy's disapproval, "you may not realize that father's money isn't exactly what he pretends."

Maddy knew that the earl was a pinch penny if ever there was one. It wasn't that the earldom was broke. Far from it. Just that Uncle Frank had no interest in paying for anyone's interests but his own.

"Your father is careful with the money he spends on us," she said, doing her best to be diplomatic.

Rose nodded her complete agreement. "Well, Mr. Frazier is rich as a nabob—"

"He is not!"

"Well, he will be with Lord Blackstone's money, and so my smallish dowry won't be a problem."

Maddy shook her head. "Mr. Frazier does not have the money you think."

"Pish posh! He has piles of jewelry. Alex told me so!"

Maddy stared at Rose, who had the grace to blush. "Well, you see…I, uh, I know about the bath."

"What!" Maddy nearly exploded off her seat. As it was, her hands gripped the squabs just to keep some pretense at calm.

"I couldn't sleep," she said, "and I heard Mr. Frazier going in and out of the kitchen."

"You were spying on me!" whispered Maddy. There was no way the girl could have heard Kit going in and out of the house unless she were already downstairs at the kitchen door.

"Not on you, silly!" said Rose with a giggle. "On him! He's very strong, don't you think? I never would have guessed if I hadn't seen it for myself."

Maddy bit her lip, horrified to know that Rose had seen her that night. It had grown in her thoughts to become the perfect evening of intimacy between herself and Kit. That it had been witnessed by someone else made her feel... Well, it felt wrong.

"In any event, since he was occupied downstairs, I took the chance to go into his bedroom."

"Oh, Rose!"

"Alex was there, and we had the most lovely chat. He was quite easy to charm," she said, her cheeks dimpling in false modesty.

"Rose! That's most unfair to—"

"Anyway, he told me about Mr. Frazier's jewelry. Even showed some of it to me. Old, ugly jewelry!"

Maddy bit her lip, putting aside her cousin's appalling behavior. So Kit had more of the same pieces like the one he'd given her. "He needs to find some way to sell it."

"Then he will have piles of guineas!"

Maddy sighed. "But money is not enough of a reason for marriage, Rose. You are the daughter of an earl. You could have any man you want."

"And I want him! Don't you see? He is the catch of the Season and quite handsome to boot. He has money and all his teeth, and he is already half in love with me."

That jerked Maddy's attention back to her cousin. "He is?"

"You heard him call me beauty. And he's quite charming around me."

Yes, he was, Maddy realized. "But, Rose, he's gone."

"But he'll be back. He left before and he came back."

"He didn't go away," Maddy snapped. "He was a captured slave."

Rose shook her head. "He'll be back. And when he comes back, I will have laid the groundwork. He will be the most celebrated man this Season, thanks to me. And I will be his faithful beauty, waiting desperately for his return!"

Maddy stared at her cousin. It was clear that the girl had it all worked out in her mind. "You can't mean to put yourself on the shelf waiting for him."

Rose heaved a dramatic sigh. "Yes, I know. It wouldn't be at all necessary if you hadn't chased him away, you know."

Maddy refused to be lured into that argument again. "Surely there is some other gentleman who catches your fancy." She began to list off the men who constantly hovered about during parties, but Rose kept shaking her head.

"None of them are like Mr. Frazier," she said firmly.

The girl wasn't listening. Maddy could hardly blame her. After all, Maddy's own heart was still mourning today's debacle. So she had to say the words, both to herself and her cousin. "You have created a fantasy that isn't real. He's not a tragic pirate figure, he isn't even a full man right now. Not in his mind."

"Of course he is!"

Maddy held up her hand. She couldn't give the full details of what she'd seen. She certainly couldn't say that the man had abducted her to the playhouse cellar, believing her to be a dead cabin boy. "Mr. Frazier told me himself that he has fits. That he sometimes thinks he's in the past, living something that happened a long time ago."

"But that is to be expected, isn't it?" said Rose. "The sooner he sets himself up in society, the sooner he can forget about all that happened before."

"It's not that easy, Rose."

"Of course it is. And now that he sees he can no longer have Lady Blackstone, he will naturally start thinking of other ladies. Like me, his beauty."

"Rose..."

"Oh, stop it, Maddy! You make your plans for Mr. Wakely and leave me to mine with Mr. Frazier."

Maddy would have continued to argue, but the best way to handle the girl's illogic was to let it pass. Eventually, Rose would become caught up in some other romantic story. So Maddy pressed her lips together and looked out the window. They had reached the outskirts of London and would soon be home. Once there—

"I don't think we should go out tonight," said Rose suddenly.

"What?"

"It wouldn't be right, if I'm to mourn Mr. Frazier's absence."

Maddy arched her brow. "But if you really *want* to go out..."

"No," Rose said with determination. "I don't really. We'll have to go to tomorrow's ball, of course, because that is the real beginning of the Season. But for tonight, I shall have to grieve." Then she abruptly brightened. "I know! We shall look at fashion plates together. For your new gowns!"

Maddy gaped at her cousin, unsure what to think.

"Are you sure you want to pay for them, Rose? Your father will probably find out."

"Of course we have to get you dresses! Don't you see? When Mr. Frazier returns, he will see that I followed his advice. I bought you those gowns and became the reigning fashion leader, just as he said. He could not fail to fall desperately in love with me then!"

Maddy wished she had the moral fortitude to refuse. She didn't. So she nodded and soon they were having a lively discussion of exactly the types of gowns which would suit her best. They kept up the argument the rest of the way home and well into the evening hours. It turned out to be quite a lot of work. Rose did love to add bows and layers upon layers of lace. But in the end, they decided upon a few styles that should suit. And the entire discussion had the added benefit that Maddy didn't think about Kit once the entire time. Or so she told herself.

The lie became harder to sustain after she retired for the night. Then Maddy was left alone with her thoughts and the memory of everything that had happened. She propped the window open again, knowing that he would not visit her. Kit was gone, and that was a good thing, she told herself. He needed time to heal. He would be visiting his brother and reestablishing family ties. He would be away from the constant reminder of other people's happiness. And, of course, he would not be constantly underfoot as she was trying to attract Mr. Wakely.

All in all, everything was going exactly as it should. But she still lingered in her bedroom window. She still stood there in the moonlight and dreamed of what might have happened that first night in the kitchen. If she had lingered nearby during his bath. If she had done any number of things differently.

She couldn't have, of course. She was a proper young lady who shouldn't even be thinking these things. But she was also a country girl, and some fantasies would not be denied. She knew the mechanics of love, and now she had experienced their wonderful sensations.

Would it be as delightful with Mr. Wakely? She tried to force herself to speculate in that direction, but her mind would not be directed. No matter how she tried, Mr. Wakely's face was always replaced by Kit's rough beard and sun-streaked hair. Kit's scarred body that nevertheless seemed beautiful to her. And Kit's gloriously possessive and desperate kiss. Never had she imagined that one could feel such hunger from a kiss.

Was that love? she wondered as she stood in her window and dreamed of him. Most certainly not. It was lust, plain and simple. And yet… And yet…

She sighed and turned away. She was a practical girl who lived in the real world. She didn't have the luxury of existing in fantasies like Rose. So she would turn her attention to catching a husband. Lust or love would not enter into it, unless of course, it was on Mr. Wakely's part.

She remained solid in her decision as she climbed into bed. It had been an exhausting day, so it was little wonder that she fell into a doze almost immediately. And even less of a surprise that once she lost the rigid controls on her mind, her dreams immediately went to Kit.

She relived every kiss, every press of his body against hers. She experienced again the caress of his fingers and the need that ached through her belly. It was lust and she gloried in it. Here in her sleep, she could be as wanton as she liked with no one to tell her differently.

And then, as she shifted restlessly in her bed, she felt something else. Something new and yet so familiar as to bring a smile to her lips.

Kit was here in her bed, exactly as she wished him to be. And he was very, very real.

CHAPTER 17

Kit needed to be on his ship. He needed to repair the boat, fill its hold with cargo, and then sail far away from anyone who spoke English or even knew what a white man looked like. He should set England at his back and never turn around. Instead, he was standing Maddy's window like a lovesick waif.

He had been here for an hour or more. He had watched her prepare for bed, and then saw her stand at her window. He had memorized the expressions that drifted over her face, clearly illuminated by the moonlight. What he saw couldn't be true. She couldn't possibly be feeling the same wistful despair that haunted him. But he saw it there on her face: a sadness so deep that nothing would erase it, and yet a touch of resolve kept it from consuming her. He saw it in the clench of her jaw and the whiteness of her fingers where they gripped the window pane. She did not want to feel so lost, and so she pushed it away with a force of will. And that in turn created the wistfulness. What if things had gone differently? What if he had not gotten ill and been squirreled away on a boat by the thrice-damned Michael? What if her father hadn't died and she'd stayed in the countryside?

How could her feelings so closely echo his? And when she turned away and blew out her candle, he knew that she would climb into her bed and cry just as she had that other night. The tears would come in her sleep, and they would flow like a river.

He couldn't leave her to that. Not his angel. Not tonight, when he could alleviate her pain, if only for a moment.

He was lying to himself. He knew it even as he climbed the wall to her bedroom. The last thing Maddy needed was him in her life. She didn't know how perilously close to the knife's edge he was. Certainly Brandon's money would give him a seaworthy vessel. That did not ensure a cargo, much less a profit. Any number of things could go terribly wrong on the most mundane voyages, as he had cause to know. A simple shift in the weather could leave him broke, at the best. And that was nothing compared to the demons in his own mind.

He was not fit for any woman, least of all his angel. And yet he couldn't stop himself. He needed tonight as much as she did. So long as he kept himself under control, there would be no risk to her virginity.

So he climbed into her bedroom. He found her tangled in her sheets, her sweet lips open on a gasp. He reached out and touched her cheek, feeling the wetness of her tears. She was wearing a simple cotton night rail, worn thin with age. What was she dreaming? he wondered. Her nipples were tight points that pushed against the soft fabric. His free hand found her breast immediately, shaping it and stroking across her nipple with his thumb. Her body arched into him even as her eyes flew open in surprise.

"Don't say anything, angel," he whispered urgently. "I

couldn't leave without seeing you again." His hand on her breast would not stay still. He brushed across her nipple, he squeezed her full shape. "I won't take your virginity. I swear it! But let me touch you tonight. Let me give you something."

She licked her lips but didn't speak. It didn't matter. He reached down and began unbuttoning her gown. He would not rip this one. God, what he wouldn't do to sink into her right then. He was achingly hard, his organ pushing insistently against the buttons of his pants. But tonight was for her. He had dishonored her enough. He would not do more.

"Just don't scream," he said as he used his knuckles to brush apart the seam of nightgown. Her skin was luminescent in the moonlight, and his hands now on her naked flesh showed as a dark stain growing across her skin. Was that what he was? A horror that shouldn't be allowed to touch her?

He stilled his movements, but he couldn't force himself to pull back. Beneath his fingers, he felt her breath tremble through her body and her heart beat so fast.

"Do I frighten you?" he asked.

"Never," she whispered.

"I should," he said honestly, as he looked in her eyes. "I am not a sane man."

"I am so lonely," she said, her eyes misting with tears. "I think I have gone mad as well."

"No, angel," he said, his hands beginning to caress her again. "You're not alone. Not tonight."

Her eyes fluttered half closed with pleasure. Her mouth opened on a soft gasp, and her back arched to lift her breasts more fully into his hands. "Make the pain go away, Kit. Please."

"Yes," he said. He could deny her nothing. And this was something he could do, if only for a little while.

He was kissing her breasts, sucking one nipple into his mouth while rolling the other with his hands. Dreamed Kit or real, she didn't care. His hands on her body felt so good, and the sensations he built inside her made her body tremble with pleasure.

It was wrong for her to do this. She knew that. Just as she knew this was really happening and not a wonderful dream. But she didn't care. He made her body come alive. Her breasts—the huge blobs that made all her clothing tight—felt incredible with what he did. With every pull from his lips, sucking the nipple deeper inside his mouth, she felt more beautiful, more wonderful than ever before. Her body no longer was an embarrassment, but a joy.

"Will you be naked for me?" he asked against her skin. His hands left what they were doing to stroke up to her shoulders, pushing the fabric aside. She didn't even hesitate as she shifted on the bed, allowing the cotton to roll off her shoulders. Then at his urging, she lifted enough for him to drag the fabric down her back. She meant to have it pool at her hips. She meant to bare only her upper body to his gaze. But he was too quick for her.

With one quick pull, he drew it—and the covers—down and away from her entire body. And then—to her shock—she lay completely naked before him. She sat up, surprised into full alertness. Her hands went to cover groin and breast, though, of course, she was so huge, she could not even begin to make herself appear decent.

"No, angel," he breathed, his hands coming up to

stroke the back of her arms. "Don't hide. You're beautiful."

She flushed and turned her head away. She was a tart, plain and simple. To allow a man into her bedroom was the worst sin, and she was an immoral wretch for allowing it.

"Don't cry," he said. "Oh, sweet angel, don't cry."

He was tender as he gathered her into his arms. He pulled her head to his shoulder, and he stroked her back with long, soothing caresses. She tried to hold back the tears, but they came out anyway, wetting his shirt and making her shoulders heave. She was not a woman who cried, but tonight she sobbed. Great big, gasping heaves against his body as she had not cried since her father died.

He held her throughout it all. His body was solid where she pressed against him, muffling her sobs against the muscular curve of his shoulder. He didn't speak, or if he did, she didn't hear him. She just poured out her misery into his arms, and in time, her tears eased.

He was ready with a handkerchief. And while she blew her nose, he rose and wet a cloth from the bowl in her room. That gave her time to readjust on the bed. She leaned her back against the wall and tugged the covers up to her neck. He noticed immediately, of course, but he didn't say anything. Instead, he waited patiently while she wiped her face with the cloth and set it aside. But then there was silence until he whispered his question.

"Why do you sob when I say you're beautiful?"

She tried to look away from him, but he pulled her chin back to his with a firm hand.

"Angel, tell me."

"Because Rose is beautiful. She's small and delicate and everything that is lovely. I'm…well, I'm as huge as a cow."

"You are no such thing!"

She didn't answer. She had a mirror. She knew what she looked like compared to Rose. And even if she didn't, she had the daily experience of gentlemen passing her over for her more stunning cousin.

"You don't believe me," he said gently. He leaned forward and carefully took hold of her hand. He wormed his fingers into her palm, tickling her there until her fingers opened. And then he slowly drew it to his groin. His organ was hot and hard, burning against her hand.

"You are beautiful, Maddy."

She would have laughed if she had the nerve. She didn't. It was too interesting to feel the shape of him through his pants. And yet common sense made her speak.

"This proves nothing," she said. "There were boys back home who were said to be attracted to the sheep." She reluctantly pulled away from him and lifted her gaze to his face. "Perhaps you are one such man."

His brows shot up to his hairline. "I most certainly am not!"

She did laugh then, and the feeling was so wonderful. Her sobs had left her wrung out. The entire day had been one roiling storm of emotions, and now she had nothing left as she faced him. She simply felt empty. And yet, her body still tingled as he looked at her, his expression beyond tender.

"You are a stubborn woman, my angel. But if you will not believe my body, let me try and sway you with words."

"Kit..." she began, but he cut her off.

"I tell you I find Rose too tiny for me, too delicate and too spoiled." He said it so matter-of-factly that Maddy straightened in surprise. That motion released her grip on the sheet enough that he reached forward and tugged the fabric down, exposing her large and bulbous breasts. She tried to pull it back, but he captured her hands and held them still.

"Men love big breasts such as you have. And wide hips to support a baby. If anything, I find you too slender for your height."

She winced. She knew she was excruciatingly tall. One of the boys in her village used to call her big bear because of her height and her untidy mop of brown hair.

"But that's not the only reason I find you beautiful, angel. Your body is strong, and that is that extremely desirable. Rose would break at the first sign of hard work, but you have hauled water, been abducted by a madman, and kept me from killing my cousin all without the slightest bruise."

"You weren't precisely mad."

"I was," he said firmly. "And I find your strength incredible." His hands trailed to her arms, where he squeezed her muscles. "To find such power in a gently reared woman is amazing."

She flushed. She had never thought of herself like that. If anything, her physical strength was labeled common in the worst possible way. But he made it sound like it was a gift.

"I think about that first night often," he continued. "You in that ridiculous gown—"

"Why do you hate my dresses so?" she huffed.

"Because they hide your curves, sweet angel," he said, his gaze going back to her breasts. There was no mistaking the hunger in his eyes. "And they look like a doll's clothes on a woman."

She said nothing. Her mouth was dry as she watched him look at her breasts. He really did find them beautiful. As if mesmerized, he reached out to stroke her. She wanted him to. With his touch distracting her mind, she could believe everything he said.

"You have been a woman to me from that first day," he said as he cupped her breast. "Bold enough to help me contain Alex. Strong enough to insist that I be brought to your home. A strange madman in your midst and you clean his wounds, prepare his bath, all while managing an earl's household."

He was tweaking her nipple, stirring the current of pleasure that only he made her feel. She closed her eyes to better savor his touch and was surprised that she felt little shame when he tugged the sheet away from her legs.

"I think you have the most wonderful legs, angel. Long like a colt and yet so graceful." His free hand went to her thigh, squeezing the flesh there. "I dream of you gripping me with your legs while I thrust inside you. I want you to hold on to me as if there could never be another."

Her eyes flew open at his graphic words. The image he depicted made her heart beat so fast that the skin of her chest heated. How she wanted to experience just what he said.

"I'm want to pleasure you now, Maddy. I will not take your virginity, but I want to give you such joy that you will not forget me when I am gone."

"I could never forget you, Kit."

He smiled, and it seemed for a moment that he doubted her words. Then he began to lean forward, but she stopped him. She pushed a hand to his mouth and held him away from her.

"Why won't you marry me?" she asked. "Is it because..." She bit her lip, unable to say the words aloud.

He pulled her hand gently down and away from his mouth. "Because what?"

"Because..." She glanced away. She couldn't look at him when she said it. "Because I am a tart. Because I have let you see me naked and touch me where only a husband should?"

"Oh, angel, no, that is not it at all." There was such a roughness in his voice that Maddy turned back to see his face. It was stark with pain and a feral kind of need. "I am a madman. Surely you of all people know that."

"You are not!" she said firmly, rising up from where she leaned back against the wall. "You just get confused sometimes."

He shook his head. "You have seen my scars. They are the smallest of what happened to me." His eyes went vague and she knew he was looking at his past. "I did things to survive, Maddy. Horrible, terrible things."

"I don't care."

"Because you don't know." His gaze had cut back to her. "I have to leave, angel. I have to go far away from here and remember what it is to be a man."

She bit her lip, knowing it was true. "I could wait for you."

He shook his head. "You do not have that kind of time. You need a husband now."

"But you could—"

"No!" he rasped. "Even so strong a woman as you would break eventually. I have seen it many times."

"That's ridiculous—"

"I have done it, Maddy! I have broken women and men. I helped capture them, I whipped them when they cried, and I sold them into slavery."

"That wasn't your fault!" she cried. "You were forced into it. You were a slave yourself!"

His gaze was dark, his expression hollow with guilt. "That doesn't excuse what I did."

"Of course it does!"

He sighed. "And it doesn't change what I became."

She saw the truth of it in his eyes and in every line of his body. He believed himself an animal.

"Let me kiss you, angel," he whispered. "Let me remember what it is like to love a woman."

Those were the words that undid her. They so clearly expressed what he needed to do, and what she needed to feel: love. If only for a night and only a love of the body. She wanted it desperately. And so this time when he leaned forward to claim her mouth, she met him halfway.

She let him plunder her lips, open her mouth and thrust his tongue inside. She let him lift and mold her right breast with one hand while the other gently supported her down to the bed. Then he left her mouth to rain kisses upon her body. He touched her neck, shoulder, and breasts, where he suckled until she grabbed his shoulders as an anchor against the sensations he built.

Belly and hip came next, as he shook off the reach of her hands. He slipped off the edge of the bed when he began to kiss the top of her thigh. She did not know what he was doing, so she raised her head in confusion.

"If I am beside you, nothing will stop me from taking you."

"But—"

"Press a pillow to your face. It will muffle your sounds."

"But—"

"Do as I ask, angel. I will not hurt you."

She knew he wouldn't. And more, she knew that whatever he intended would be both deeply scandalous and incredibly wonderful. So she did as he bid.

"Trust me, angel," he said against her skin.

She did. So she let him gently—firmly—spread her thighs apart. His lips were still on her leg, his tongue stroking circles across her skin. She was glad, then, that her face was buried in a pillow. She burned with embarrassment, but she did not stop him as she felt him gently shift between her legs. He set her calves on his shoulder while still pressing soft kisses into her inner thigh.

Then she felt his fingers stroking her open. His touch flowed from her center upward, outward, opening everything to his touch. Never had anything felt more intimate, and she tightened her thighs, lifting away from him in reaction. But there was nowhere for her to go and soon she felt something even more shocking.

He was kissing her there! His lips pressed tiny kisses up her thighs until he was at the apex. Then she felt his tongue, swirling about her folds, licking while she arched in wonder. Fire shot through her belly and her heart felt like it would explode. But nothing compared to the sensation of his tongue so wide and so strong as he pressed…she didn't even know where. But he did it again, and she felt a scream building in her throat.

Her body arched and her legs tightened. She wanted him to do it again and again while the tension in her belly grew. Instead, she felt his fingers pushing into her. First one, sliding in so easily, and yet she felt its width and every knuckle. He pulled it out only to push in again, and she whimpered without even knowing why. It wasn't enough. She wanted more.

She got another push, this time of two fingers, and she liked the thicker feeling, the stretch that he gave her. Her movements on the bed were slowing, her mind caught up with the sensations of his fingers pushing into her.

But he withdrew them again; this time though, he flowed his thumb upward to press against that wonderful place. It was too fast a movement and too soft, so she arched to push against him.

"You cannot believe how beautiful a sight this is," he said as he stroked her again, this time harder. "I love watching your breasts in the moonlight. I love seeing your body move when I touch you."

Her legs were spread as wide as they would go, her body alternately arching into him then flowing down, only to push upward again.

"Press the pillow against your face, angel. Do it now."

She hadn't even realized that the fabric had fallen away. That the lift and lower of her hips had dislodged it. She grabbed it now, pushing it tight against the scream he built in her. His fingers were pushing inside again. And this time when he withdrew, he rolled a long circle over her spot higher up.

She whimpered, the sound caught by the pillow. And then he pressed his mouth to that place. He sealed it with his lips and thrust his tongue against her. He moved rhythmically, pushing hard then sucking, pushing hard, then sucking. Her entire body pulsed with his mouth. Her legs tightened. Her blood pounded in her ears. And the heat—sweet heaven, the fire that raced over her skin!

He pushed with his tongue again. And again. And then he sucked hard.

She burst apart. Her body convulsed in waves of pleasure. Her mind soared, and yes, she screamed.

He held her while she arched on the bed. He pressed kisses into her thighs that sparked tiny bursts of flame under her skin. And the tremors continued, one after another. Growing smaller with each passing moment, but still filling her with such sweetness.

This was what physical love felt like. This is what lucky ladies experienced in their marriage bed. And this is what she wanted with Kit. She let the pillow fall from her face, her body still suffused with delight. She looked down at him, not even ashamed of how she lay sprawled with him between her thighs.

"That was incredible," she breathed.

He grinned like a schoolboy. Then he pressed a long kiss against her thigh before slowly straightening up from the bed. She held out her arms. She wanted him lying against her, his body pressed hard and full on top of her.

"Come lie down for a bit," she said.

He looked at her, his gaze dark and hungry. Then he suddenly covered her with the sheet. "I dare not."

She frowned and pushed up on one elbow. "Just for a bit, Kit."

He shook his head. "I have seen men take women in their sleep."

"But—"

"The men, Maddy. They were the ones asleep. We were packed in so tight sometimes, men and women all pressed together. Men dropping with exhaustion, their eyes closed and their mind turned off. They became animals, thrusting and taking without even knowing what they did."

"But you're not—"

"I want you that badly, sweet Maddy. I will."

She bit her lip, then abruptly made her decision. "Then do so," she said.

His nostrils flared, and his body went tense. "You would have me take you your virginity? Ruin you forever?"

"Yes," she breathed.

His hands tightened into fists by his side and he took a step backward. She lifted up, boldly letting the covers drop away from her breasts. His gaze went immediately to them, and she inhaled deeply just to make them more visible. He closed his eyes.

"You would have me lose what little honor is left to me?" he rasped. "The one thing I never did as a slave was rape a woman. You would have me lose that?"

She shifted onto her knees. Her breasts bobbed and the covers slid completely away. "You cannot rape a willing woman."

"You don't know what you are saying!" he cried, his voice going deeper with each word.

"I do," she said firmly. Then she quickly leaped off the bed and rushed to shut the window. She slammed it down, the sound loud in the silent house. "I intend to be caught with you, Kit. I will trap you into marriage."

His eyes flew wide and a look of panic flashed

through his expression. "You want me by force?" he gasped.

"I do." She lifted her chin, stunned at what she had just declared.

He looked equally struck, his mouth slipping open as he stared at her. But then he seemed to recover. His mouth closed first, and he released his breath on a long, steady exhale. His hands relaxed by his side while his shoulders slowly straightened. A look of gratitude crossed his features—so quickly she thought she dreamed it—and then his entire face became shuttered. Then worst of all, his eyes became cold.

"I won't do it," he said.

The words were so far from what she expected that her mind could not grasp them. "W-What?"

"I won't," he repeated, his voice low but no less clear. "You can scream if you want. Bring the entire house down on us, but no matter what you do, I will not marry you. You cannot force a man who cares nothing for his reputation."

She blinked against the tears. She understood every word, and yet she could not believe what he said. "But you want me. You think I am beautiful."

"I do. You are. But the answer is still no."

She gasped, the pain cutting through her so deeply that she pressed a hand to her chest. Suddenly, she felt naked standing before him. She saw him step forward reflexively, as if to go to her, but she twisted away. She abandoned the window to grab her dressing grown and wrap it tightly around herself. And when she was covered, she lifted her head to look at him.

He stood in the middle of the room, his hands thrust deep into his pocket, his expression tortured. *How dare he,* she thought. *How dare he look so miserable right now?* She wanted to say something cruel. She knew that by morning, she would have a dozen jibes to throw at him, but right now she just wanted him gone.

"Angel," he rasped. "You think you want me now. I am the first man to show you pleasure. Of course you think to build a life on that."

"I am not a fool!"

"Neither are you experienced." He rubbed a hand over his face, and when his hand fell away, he looked more miserable than she had ever seen. "Angel, I am not what you want. I cannot give you the life you deserve."

"How dare you," she hissed. "How dare you sneak into my bedroom, show me such things, and then tell me I do not know what I want. I do not understand what I *deserve*. Of all the arrogance! Will you next tell me I cannot marry who I chose and put me on a boat for my own good?"

She saw her words hit him like daggers. His body recoiled in horror at the comparison to what the Earl of Thornedale had done to him. "Angel—" he began, but she cut him off.

"Maddy," she ground out. "My name is Maddy!"

He bit his lip and nodded, his expression guilty, and yet still stubborn. She saw it in his tightened jaw. No matter what she said now, he would not change. He would not marry her.

"Get out," she hissed.

He jerked as if slapped, his gaze going first to the window then back to her. He opened his mouth to say something to her. She didn't want to hear it. She didn't even want to see his lips move, so she spun around, giving him her back.

She heard him hesitate, and for a brief moment her heart surged. Maybe he would apologize. Maybe he would change his mind and go down on one knee before her, begging her to be his bride. Maybe.

Then next sound was the windowpane lifting up and a rustle of fabric as he climbed out. A long moment later, she heard the soft thud of his feet as he jumped to the ground. Then nothing.

Kit was gone.

CHAPTER 18

"You have changed the ribbon to blue silk. An excellent choice, I believe, and it completely alters the appearance of the gown."

Maddy twisted in her seat to look at the newcomer to their little party on the edge of the ballroom. She didn't need to look. She knew the cadences of Mr. Mitchell Wakely's voice down to every nuance. Just as she knew he had no interest in hearing her simper in response. So she didn't. She arched a brow in challenge.

"Apparently not enough of a change, as you seem to recognize the dress."

"Ah," he said with his own arch look, "but I find that the details can change everything. For example, I don't believe I have ever seen you wear that pin before." He narrowed his eyes. "What is that supposed to be? It looks like an upside down tree."

She chuckled as she looked down at the pin. "You're quite right," she quipped. "From this angle, it does indeed appear to be a tree. How clever of you to figure it out!"

"Wherever did you find such an interesting ornament?"

She almost lied to him. She almost said that it was an

heirloom she'd only recently discovered. That alone would up her market value by a few hundred pounds. But she couldn't lie to her future husband. Or rather the man she hoped would become her husband. Instead, she opted for a version of the truth that would not prick her conscience.

"It's not mine," she confessed. "I'm holding it for a friend. I believe we decided it was a peacock."

"Hmmm," he said as he narrowed his gaze even tighter on the jewelry. She hoped he was looking at the shape and design of the piece, but his next words dispelled that notion. "Quite an expensive lot of jewels to be leaving with a friend."

"Well," she said with a shrug that she hoped appeared casual. "It is a rather ugly piece."

She suddenly started fussing with the folds of her scarf, deciding to cover up the jewelry. It felt wrong, somehow, wearing Kit's broach when trying to attract a different man. But she had needed something to pin her scarf, something to change the look of a ball gown worn a dozen times too many. She was tired of borrowing from Rose, who had gotten rather snippy lately about everything, and so in desperation, she had reached for the broach. And now Mr. Wakely was touching her hand, stopping her from hiding the piece.

"No, no, leave it. I believe it is a peacock after all."

"But—"

"Leave it, Maddy. But don't tell anyone that it's not yours."

She flushed at his words, and she looked away. She ought to chastise him for using her Christian name, but she hadn't the heart. Nearly two months had passed since Kit's departure from her bedroom. Almost the entire Season was gone, and no one had offered for either herself or Rose. Which meant that life was rapidly becoming untenable for them both.

At least it was easier on Rose, not that the girl seemed to see it that way. Her father might bluster about the expense, but he would not toss his own daughter out. Maddy, on the other hand, had no such quarter. She had just this morning been surprised by a private visit from her uncle. He had been plainspoken, as was his wont. He had repeated that she had no hope of an offer this late in the Season. And as Rose would soon be of age, she had no need of a chaperone. Therefore, he wished to make his arrangement with Maddy official. He would even write up a contract making her his mistress. She would continue to care for the house and grace his bed. In return, he would pay her a handsome sum when he tired of her. It was all the rage, he said. And was just like a marriage.

Except, of course, it wasn't. She had refused him in no uncertain terms. And he had given her notice. In one week's time, she would be out on the street. How she wished she'd had the presence of mind to throw her uncle out of her bedroom. But she hadn't. She'd simply stared at him, tears burning in her eyes, but she'd refused to let them fall.

Then, after he'd left, she'd made her decision. She would become a governess or a seamstress. Or a chimney sweep if need be. But she would *not* become her uncle's mistress. She intended to visit an employment office first thing in the morning. That was, of course, assuming she could not bring Mr. Wakely up to scratch tonight.

"I am pleased to find you here tonight," she said by way of opening.

"I can always be found where there are beautiful

ladies." The words were routine banter, heard a dozen different ways at any ball. But the way he looked at her when he said it made her flush even hotter. Did he really think her beautiful? What with Rose not five feet from her?

"Ah," he said in approval. "I like it when there is color in your cheeks. You have been much too peaked lately."

That came from managing an earl's household by day and husband hunting by night, but she didn't say that. Instead, she decided to come to the point. She had thought and thought on how she would do this. After all, one usually didn't baldly ask a man if he intended to offer marriage. But she couldn't wait any longer. She glanced to the side at Rose, who was flirting rather outrageously with a bevy of young men. Then she glanced at Mr. Wakely.

"Do you think we could take a turn about the ballroom? It will be a few minutes before the next set starts."

"Yes, it is rather close here," Mr. Wakely said as he was jostled by yet another of Rose's beaus. "Shall we head toward the windows? It is a little cooler there, but not much."

"An excellent idea," she returned as she took his arm. And as she did, she couldn't help but wonder—would she be doing this for the rest of her life? Spending every moment at his side and in his bed? Did she want that? Of course she did, she told herself sternly. It was either Mr. Wakely or the poorhouse.

So she resolutely pushed aside thoughts of any other men, most especially a dark, tortured pirate slave, and centered herself on how exactly she should ask Mr. Wakely to marry her.

"The Season is almost done," she began, her gaze going to the open windows. "Will you be staying in the city or visiting your relatives up north?"

"Oh, I shall remain here. Always work to do for a banker."

She laughed, then abruptly cut off the sound. It was too high and almost horse like. Sadly, the uncharacteristic sound did not go unnoticed. Mr. Wakely slowed his step to cast her a curious look.

"Is something amiss, Miss Wilson? You seem rather nervous all of a sudden."

She swallowed and reminded herself that he valued plain speaking. "Ah, well, that is perhaps because I am."

His brows shot up at that and his steps came to a halt. "Is there a particular reason?"

Plain speaking, she repeated to herself. Plain speaking. "My uncle is throwing me out in a week's time. At the end of the Season." She said the words, then felt her eyes widen in shock at what she'd said. "Oh, sweet heaven! I cannot believe I said that."

Mr. Wakely's eyes had darkened to near pitch. And given that his eyes were light green, that was saying something indeed. "Come, let's walk a bit farther, shall we?"

"The balcony is just beyond there," she said once she'd swallowed the lump in her throat. "We should be a bit more private—"

"No. If we keep our voices low enough, we should be private enough in the ballroom. So long as we keep moving."

Maddy nodded, though she really doubted they would have more privacy in a crowded room. Still, she deferred to his wishes and began a sedate and very proper stroll around nearly everyone of the *ton* who was still in London.

"Why would your uncle do such a drastic thing?" he asked after a moment. His tone was so bland, she at first thought he had asked after Uncle Frank's dyspepsia.

"He has tired of paying for my keep," she said.

Mr. Wakely arched a brow. "I doubt you are that expensive. You have only three good gowns purchased by Lady Rose, as she is wont to tell everyone. And if you were to leave, he would have to pay for a housekeeper. You are a cost savings to your uncle, not an expense."

She bit her lip, pleased beyond measure that someone understood her value. "Thank you," she finally managed. "I have learned to economize."

"You've done a great deal more than that, I warrant. Which brings me back to the first question. Why would he do such a drastic thing? He is not unaware of your value, I assure you. The earl knows enough about his money to see that."

This in turn caused her to step to falter as she gaped at him. "Truly?" she said. "You think he knows—"

"Of course he does!"

"But—"

"He knows, Maddy. Now smile and keep walking."

It took her a moment, but she managed to do it. All this time, she simply thought he didn't see what she did for him—for Rose and for his home. But he did? Uncle Frank knew how very much she managed?

"Really?" she said more to herself than to Mr. Wakely. "He really knows."

"Yes," he said, then he patted her hand in a polite gesture as he smiled at a nearby matron. "So why make his, um, most recent choice?"

The choice to throw her out of his house. The answer was obvious, of course, not that she wanted to face it so squarely. He was forcing her hand, guessing that she would succumb to his advances rather than face the street.

"I won't do it," she said firmly, repeating the vow she had uttered just this morning. "I will not do it."

Mr. Wakely arched his brow and spoke, his voice low and slow. "You will not be cast aside?"

"What? No! I won't become his mistress just to have a roof over my head!"

"Ah. As I suspected."

Maddy didn't really hear his words. She was too busy fuming less and less silently. "To think I believed him the kindest of men when I came to London. I never thought he would stoop so low. I thought he was ignorant of household things. But to know what I am worth, to know that I am a help, and yet still demand more! And such a demand! Oh, I vow I will scratch out his eyes!"

Mr. Wakely didn't respond. He simply walked with her and occasionally admonished her to lower her tone. She could tell by the taut feel of his arm that he was angry, but no one else would know as he nodded to various people they passed.

Eventually, her passionate diatribe wound down. After all, this was not really new information. Whether done out of ignorance or lust, the situation remained. Her uncle would throw her out in less than a week's time. And on that unsavory thought, her words finally sputtered to halt.

After a moment or more of silence, Mr. Wakely spoke. "What do you intend to do then?"

"I intend to apply at an employment agency tomorrow morning. I could be an acceptable governess."

He nodded. "I am certain you could. But, um, I'm afraid you will not be hired. Not as a governess in any gently bred home."

Again, his words were delivered so blandly, his tone so polite that she did not at first understand his meaning. "What? Why not?"

"I'm afraid, Miss Wilson, that any reputable agency would make some inquiries regarding your past before recommending you to a client."

She nodded. She already knew that. "But my past is exemplary. If anything, it is rather bland."

"Not if...I beg you, Maddy, do not cry out..."

Maddy tried to stop walking. She tried to face him square in the eye, but he would not let her. He forced her to keep meandering aimlessly through the maze of people. "Mitchell, what are you trying to say?"

He grimaced, and she could tell he had no love of what he was about to tell her. "You will not be hired if you have been an earl's mistress for the last three years."

It was easy to keep silent. She didn't understand the least thing he'd said. "But that is what I am saying. That is his bargain with me. He will not throw me out if I *become* his mistress."

Mr. Wakely shook his head. "But he has let it out that you have been gracing his bed for years now. Almost since the very moment you came to London."

"That's ridiculous!" she snapped. And it was perilously close to a scream.

"Of course it is, and I suspected it was a lie more than a month ago."

"A month ago," she murmured. *More* than a month ago. Which meant that her uncle had been spreading his slander from the very beginning! It took long moments for the truth of that to sink in. And for her to take the next logical step. "But that means I never had a chance to find a husband! He ruined me from the very beginning!"

"Er. Well, yes. But very quietly, as these things go. He made it clear that he would ruin anyone who made such a thing known."

"But he is the one who created the rumor!"

"Yes. Obviously. And I believe his strategy has backfired somewhat in that it has clearly hurt Rose's chances. It's all rather unsavory, don't you know, courting a girl in front of her father's mistress."

"But I'm not!"

"I know! I know!" He rubbed a hand over his face and directed her to a bench. It was in an open hallway and people were constantly moving back and forth, but this tiny space was empty.

Maddy sat down, feeling her entire world shift. It wasn't so large a shift, really. Her uncle was angling to have her as his mistress. She knew that. And yet she had trouble processing the cold calculation of it all, the spurious rumor, the ruination of her chances before it had even begun. "He is my uncle," she said, her words and her entire body feeling very small.

Mr. Wakely had no words except a sigh. His expression was miserable, and his hand continued to pat hers with unspoken sympathy. But this news was so much beyond what she had imagined for this night. When she had made her plans this evening, she had imagined it ending with a kiss. A passionate kiss shared between an engaged couple.

"That's why you didn't offer for me last month," she said. "Because you thought I was his mistress."

He swallowed and looked aside. "As I said, I realized it was a lie some time ago."

Her gaze leaped to his. "But then—"

"I am a banker, Miss Wilson. Management of money requires the strictest moral code. No one would give a man of uncertain character access to their funds. A man in my profession must appear to have the highest moral standard."

She frowned, not understanding what he meant. "But I have always found you to be most proper, most circumspect."

He nodded, taking the compliment for what it was. But his words went somewhere else. "As I said, a man in my position must have every *appearance* of holding himself and the world to the highest moral standard. His work ethic must be unshakable, his hobbies must be modest, and...um...his wife must be above reproach."

She stared at him, at last understanding his difficultly. Mr. Wakely was a younger son. He did not have a title nor any kind of steady income beyond what he earned every day. He was educated at the best schools, had friends in the highest levels of society, but at the heart of it, he stood on the shaky pedestal of public opinion. Were his character to come into question at any time, then he could lose his livelihood completely.

"That is why you haven't offered for me. Because my character has been assassinated."

"I care for you, Miss Wilson. And I think, perhaps, that I could love you."

Hope leaped into her heart, but one look at his face told her that he was not prepared to offer for her. She looked away, misery making her eyes water and her chest squeeze tight.

"I am not easily swayed by public opinion, Miss Wilson. And I believe a great wrong has been done to you."

But it wasn't enough. She could tell by his apologetic tone of voice. Then, to her shock, she felt his knuckles under her chin. With the gentlest of pressure, he drew her face back toward him. He still remained a proper distance apart from her. People still moved up and down the hallway. But there was an intimacy in his gesture that she felt deep in her heart.

"I have been waiting to see if this is love, Miss Wilson. I find you stalwart and loyal. You have a level head and a good heart."

She winced. He described her as a good dog.

"These things carry a great deal of value for me," he continued.

"But it is not love," she said. "It is not passion."

He sighed. "Truth be told, I am not a very passionate man."

She searched his face for some clue but found nothing. "Then what? Why have you courted me all these weeks, dancing with me at ball after ball, only to dash my hopes now?"

He tilted his head in an apologetic shrug. "I have been testing the waters, so to speak."

"To see if this was love?"

He nodded. "Yes. And also to see how my clients reacted. My interest has been noted."

Yes, it certainly had. Rose already had them married

with six children. She spoke of it constantly enough to make Maddy snap at the girl when days and weeks went by with no proposal.

She bit her lip. "And what has been the reaction?"

"Fully half of them have heard of, um, your reputation. At least two directly from the earl himself."

Maddy hurt too much to even whimper at that.

"If this is love, Maddy, then I will marry you anyway. I would prefer to wait until I am better established. I am still quite young as a financial advisor, and already my business has been hurt. I need to see if the situation recovers itself or gets steadily worse." He sighed. "It will do neither of us any good to marry only to end in the poor house."

"How long?" she whispered to her fan. "And how…how will you know if this is love?"

He sighed and was forced to step backward as a bevy of young girls swept through the hallway toward the ballroom. The set was beginning. The musicians were tuning their instruments.

Meanwhile, Mr. Wakely extended his hand. "I should take you back to your cousin. You have a dance partner for this set, do you not?"

Did she? She didn't even know, and suddenly she didn't care. What good was a dance when everyone thought her a tart? Uncle Frank's tart!

"How will you know?" she asked, her voice coming out thick and harsh.

His expression was miserable, and a small part of her was glad. Let him suffer for not telling her these things earlier. Let him stew in his guilt for not helping her avert disaster a month ago. If nothing else, she could have at least told potential suitors the truth.

The idea was ridiculous, she knew. Nothing cemented a rumor like denying it. And yet, she wanted to vent her fury at someone and poor Mr. Wakely was the only one here.

"How?" she repeated, more loudly now. "And when?"

"I don't know," he answered honestly. "I'm sorry, so very sorry, but I just don't."

It was all the answer she was going to get. She knew him well enough to see that in this he would not waver. Then he surprised her again. "Let me call on you tomorrow. We can talk more then."

She nodded. What other choice did she have but to wait on his pleasure? Perhaps she would enjoy being a chimney sweep, she thought with a slight gurgle of hysteria. Apparently that was all a woman of unsavory reputation was suited for. Except, of course, she was much too large to perform such a task.

"Ah!" she cried with false cheer as she pushed to her feet. "There is my partner for the next set waiting right next to Rose. Thank you, Mr. Wakely, for your escort. I believe I shall manage the last few steps alone."

She felt him hesitate, the tension in his body unmistakable. "Miss Wilson..." he began, though he clearly didn't know what to say. "Maddy—"

"Tomorrow, Mr. Wakely. Do please call on me tomorrow."

He hesitated. For a man who was always reserved and always certain, that simple moment spoke volumes. But it wasn't enough. She needed more than his discomfort. And so with a brittle smile, she gave him her curtsey and walked away.

She managed to make it through the next set, thank heaven, though she had no idea who it was with or what was said. She stopped trying to flirt, and barely held on to being pleasant. Why bother when it was all useless anyway?

Soon she found herself back on the sidelines, sitting with the wallflowers and praying that the evening would end. That, or perhaps a heavenly message carried by angels would suddenly appear in front of everyone. It would say with unassailable veracity that she was no man's mistress and never would be! And if a huge lightning bolt incinerated her uncle at the same time, she would not grieve in the least.

She was so enamored of this idea that she almost missed it when a gentleman appeared before her. His clothing was obviously new, the color an unfashionable dark brown. But his shoes were rather nice. Comfortable boots clearly worn in places well beyond London ballrooms. Her father had owned a pair just like that.

"Excuse me, Miss Wilson, but I wonder if you might give me the pleasure of this dance?"

Maddy froze. She knew that voice. She had dreamed of it nightly for the last six weeks. He couldn't possibly be here. Not tonight of all nights. Not when everything and absolutely nothing had changed. He couldn't be here.

But he was. He stood before her with his hand outstretched and a pleasant smile on his clean-shaven and still tan face.

"Kit?" she breathed.

"Dance with me, Maddy," he said. "Please."

"But it's a waltz."

He smiled, the sight looking more relaxed than she had ever seen. "All the better."

CHAPTER 19

Sweet heaven, she was beautiful. Kit could barely speak over the pounding of his heart. Every day—and every night—of his absence from London, he had thought of his angel, dreamed of her, fantasized about her. Always he had put her in an ugly dress and slowly peeled the horrible thing from her sweet skin.

But tonight's gown wasn't hideous. In fact, the white silk draped her beautifully, shimmering the lightest kiss of fabric across her full breasts and narrow waist. Gowns were not supposed to be tailored tightly to a woman's curves, mostly because the ladies of the *ton* did not have Maddy's figure. Similarly, her dress was not quite tucked against her waist, and yet it was cut to reveal exactly how exquisite a body she possessed. A simple blue ribbon crisscrossed between her breasts and flowed ever downward to emphasize her glorious height. The only thing that kept it from being completely seductive was the modest blue scarf she wore, pinned by that ugly broach.

"You are stunning!" he breathed. "I want to force you back into the ugly castoffs because this dress makes you too beautiful."

She was staring at him, her mouth agape, and her

cheeks blanched to a ghostly white. But at his words, she recovered a little. Her mouth closed and her cheeks flushed with the barest hint of pink. But it was too soon gone and he now realized how pale she looked and how gaunt.

"Have you been starving yourself?" he asked, suddenly alarmed. "Are you ill? Maddy, what is amiss?"

She blinked and he watched her gather her wits. In a moment, she went from total shock to a composed lady of the *ton*. She grew taller, her mouth pinched shut, and her gaze shuttered closed behind half-lowered lids. He found he much preferred her in stunned disbelief.

"Mr. Frazier, I did not realize you had returned to town." At least her voice was not completely under control. It trembled ever so slightly.

"I arrived two days ago. It took me all of that time to find where you would be tonight and obtain an invitation."

She clearly did not know what to say about that. Her gaze skittered away and her hands fidgeted in her lap. Something was gravely amiss. He was about to press her for more details when a voice cut through their isolated discussion.

"Mr. Frazier! It is you!" said Lady Rose as she came to his side. Reluctantly, he turned around to greet the confection in flounces. Clearly her seamstress how outdone herself. The girl wore fully eight layers of lace.

"Lady Rose," he said as he bowed over her hand. "You look like a confection atop a cake!"

"I know!" she said with a girlish giggle. "The more plain Maddy gets, the more I am pushed to frills."

"Come, come," he said with a grin. "Turn around and

let me see the frills fly."

"Oh, Mr. Frazier!" she cried, though her eyes danced. "That's not exactly appropriate deportment for a young miss."

"Ah, but I like a little scandal in young ladies. For me, sweet Rose. Spin just once."

"Welllll," she drawled as she wrinkled her nose in flirtatious delight. "Only because you asked so nicely. And only once! Otherwise Maddy will have my head for behaving badly."

"Never," murmured Maddy from the side, but Rose wasn't listening. She was already beginning to twirl. Slowly at first and then with increasing speed while her ruffles lifted. She did seven or eight full turns before spinning back to a gasping halt, her blue eyes sparkling and her cheeks flushed red.

"Oh my!" she cried breathless as she fake stumbled against him. He caught her, of course. It was what she wanted as she hung overly long on his arm. "I am quite done in!"

"Nonsense," he said, laughing with all good humor while silently trying to think of a way to be rid of her. "You are the peak of health. In fact, you are so perfect that I must see if you have a dance available."

"Oh, Mr. Frazier!" she cried in mock dismay. "I didn't know you were coming tonight."

He lifted her wrist and looked at her card. As he expected, it was completely filled. "No space for me. Well, perhaps tomorrow night. If you but tell me—"

"Vauxhall," she said on a gasp before he could even finish his question. "An end-of-the-Season gathering before everyone leaves for the country. The Countess of Thornedale has taken a box."

Lily, his bitch of a cousin. Would Michael be there as well? "Excellent," he lied with another courtly bow. "I shall be sure to find you. And now," he said, indicating a gentleman waiting anxiously behind Rose. "I believe your partner is most hungry for a taste of your beauteous presence."

"Oh, Mr. Frazier!" Rose said with a giggle, clearly pleased. "Flattery does not move me."

"Liar," he said as he tweaked her cheek. She gasped at the impertinence, her hand rushing up to cover her face. "Of all women who deserve Spanish coin, Lady Rose, you top the list. And the cake!" he said indicating her gown.

She had no answer to that, though her eyes sparkled in the candlelight. Good. He had no wish to continue this conversation any longer.

"The set is beginning," he reminded her gently.

"Oh! Oh yes!" she gasped, then she turned to her dance partner. But her gaze remained on him and she ended up walking sideways onto the dance floor.

He watched her all the way. It was an easy sacrifice to make to keep the girl happy. He had no doubt that when she was unhappy, everyone in her household suffered, most especially Maddy. So he smiled and waved as she danced while his mind remained fixed on the woman seated behind him.

"You are wearing the broach," he said softly, his gaze at last able to return to his angel.

Her hand went to the piece. "Would you like it back?"

"No, no! I still need to find a buyer..." His voice trailed away. Selling his jewelry was the last thing he wanted to speak about. But then he saw a spark of animation in her eyes as she began to speak.

"Actually, Mr. Frazier, I think I can help you with that. That Norwegian baroness I told you about? She has a true fondness for peacocks."

"Norwegian?" he asked. Did they even have barons in that frozen clime? Apparently so because she half shrugged, half nodded.

"Actually, I believe the term is sysselmann or something like that. I have no idea if it equates to a baron, but everyone calls her baroness and she really is a dear lady."

"And you think she would buy that broach? The one I gave to you?"

Maddy flushed and looked down at her hands. "Well, as to that, you only gave it to me for safekeeping. As you can see, it is quite safe. I know I shouldn't have worn it. Rose asked about it immediately, but I told her it was paste. She wrinkled her nose, called it ugly, and flounced away." Maddy sighed. "She has been in a bit of a temper lately. Though she does seem very pleased that you have returned."

"And what of you? Are you pleased I am here? Is Rose why you are looking so wan? You are so beautiful tonight that I can scarce believe it, and yet I cannot shake the feeling that you are ailing."

She flashed him a false smile. "Nonsense, Mr. Frazier. I am quite well. And the baroness will be extremely grateful, I am sure, if you were to present this broach to her."

Kit frowned. "As a present?"

"For sale, sir. Discretely, of course."

"But—"

"She is extremely wealthy, Mr. Frazier. She would pay you more than what any jeweler would. Especially if you told her a story along with it. You know, about how you got it, where it came from, the more romantic the better."

"There was nothing romantic about how I got it," he said, his voice flat.

"Then speculate for her, sir. Spin a tale of how it *might* have come into your possession."

"Maddy..." he began, but he cut off his objection when she reached forward to touch his hand.

"People...*ladies* need to believe in romance, sir. We need to think that someone, somewhere has found true love even if it has escaped our grasp." There was a hidden meaning beneath her words, an urgency to her body as she squeezed his arm. "Tell her a tale of romance, Mr. Frazier, and she will pay you handsomely for it."

"Even if it is a lie?" he asked.

Her hand fell away from him, and he immediately mourned the loss. "Romance," she said firmly, "is always a lie, but we like to pretend anyway."

He saw it then, saw why she looked so peaked, why her body was listless and her eyes dull. She had broken sometime in the last six weeks. While he was away, something or someone had broken her heart and all that was left was disillusionment. How well he knew that pain.

"I have stayed away too long, haven't I?" he asked softly.

She pursed her lips and looked away. "I have no idea, sir. I simply point out a solution to your financial problem. You can ignore it if you think—"

"Can you set it up for me? Make the introduction?" He had no interest in selling his jewelry, no interest in painting a false story of love for an elderly baroness or sysselmann or whatever. But his angel was slipping away from him. It was as if he could see her fading before his eyes, and he would do anything to keep her with him a moment longer.

"Of course," she said. "But it might take a few days. Perhaps as much as a week. Do you have a card so that I may contact you?"

He did. Printed just today. He handed it to her, hoping to press it into her hand and linger there, touching her skin. But she pulled away, and all he felt was a brief whisper of cool skin against his fingertips.

"Thank you, Mr. Frazier," she said as she tucked his card away. "I am afraid I must decline your request to dance as my feet hurt abominably."

"Of course," he said, though he knew she lied. She wanted to be rid of him, and the pain of that cut deep indeed.

"And, Mr. Frazier..." she said after a quick glance around her.

"Yes?"

"My bedroom window will be closed and locked tonight. And every night."

There was no mistaking her message. She meant to keep him at arm's length. He could hardly blame her. They had not parted on good terms. In truth, he had been horrible to her, but there had been no other choice. He couldn't have taken a wife for fear that he would kill her in a rage. And now he was paying the price for his cruelty.

"Of course, Miss Wilson. I would expect nothing less from a proper lady such as yourself."

She winced at that. It was a telling gesture, if only he

knew what it meant. Did she feel guilty for what they had done together? Or was there more?

"Maddy..." he began, but she cut him off.

"You look better, Mr. Frazier. Much, much better."

He smiled. "I am better."

"I am glad," she said softly.

There was more in her eyes. Some kind of yearning, perhaps. Or maybe it was his own fevered imaginings. Either way, it was a gone in a moment. She shuttered her gaze, then pushed to her feet. He held out his hand to help her, but she shunned it. Instead, she smoothed her gown about her, making sure the folds of the scarf completely covered the broach.

"I believe I shall find the ladies' retiring room," she said by way of dismissal. "I find the Season has been more exhausting than I once thought."

"I could escort you—"

"Good evening, sir," she said as she brushed past him.

"Did you see how handsome he looked? Oh goodness, his time away seems to have helped him enormously. And he still remembered me. He called me beauteous! Did you hear him say that? Beauteous. Most gentleman don't even know the word, but he did. Oh, I'm so thrilled that he's back. And just in the nick of time! I had begun to despair of this Season all together. But now he is back!"

Maddy winced as Rose's voice echoed in the dark carriage. Any hopes that her infatuation with the man had faded were put completely to pasture. The girl's romantic fantasy of marrying a pirate was stronger than ever. Still, Maddy did her best to dampen her cousin's expectations.

"Just because he's back doesn't mean he wants a

bride," she said when Rose paused to take a breath. "And we know nothing of his *true* circumstances. Your father will want to know the specifics before you can entertain any kind of suit."

"Oh, Father isn't nearly as picky as you might think," she said with a distasteful twist to her lips. "He told me just yesterday that it was past time I brought a real prospect up to scratch. As if I haven't been *trying*!"

Maddy narrowed her eyes, searching her cousin's face for signs of subterfuge. "What exactly did your father say to you?"

Rose heaved a dramatic sigh. "Only that I'm of age in a month's time and that I had to stop acting like a little girl. He wants me to dress and act more like you and less like me!"

"Is that why you wore that…um…that particular gown tonight? In defiance of your father?"

Rose huffed a little nervously. "Well, yes, I suppose I did. I mean, what does Papa know about ladies' fashions? Or about how to attract a husband? This is the way to do it, I am sure. Did you not hear what Mr. Frazier said? That I looked like a confection atop a cake! That just proves I am right about this gown!"

Maddy sighed. They were back to Kit again. "Really, I don't know that you should take fashion advice from Mr. Frazier. His clothing was rather restrained." It was, in fact, excruciatingly handsome. Not black, but a dark chocolate brown. White linen cravat and a shirt with a simple vest. Maddy had never seen him in better looks.

"But he was right about your dresses, don't you remember? I think Mr. Frazier is quite right in his fashion opinion. And it doesn't matter, does it? As he is the one I am going to marry, his is the only opinion I care about."

"But, Rose!" Maddy began. Unfortunately, her cousin waved her to silence.

"I saw you walking with Mr. Wakely. Did you get him outside for a passionate embrace? Is he mad for you yet?"

"No. No, I didn't."

"Well, you should! Otherwise how will you ever get him to propose?"

Maddy swallowed and turned to look out at the street. She should tell Rose what her father had done. According to Mr. Wakely, the rumor about Maddy was hurting Rose's chances as well. But Rose loved her father. Maddy couldn't quite bring herself to reveal the worst of what Uncle Frank had done. So she opted for a softer version.

"I don't think I'll be marrying Mr. Wakely," she said softly.

"Don't say that! He'll come around. You just have to make him more passionate!"

"No, Rose, I don't think it will happen. Which means I will be leaving in a week's time."

"You need to let him kiss you, Maddy. Stop being so proper! And besides… What? Wait, what did you say?"

Maddy leaned forward, taking Rose's hands in hers. "You know, you have grown up quite beautifully. I am pleased to have been a part of that."

"Well, of course, but what do you mean 'leaving'?"

Maddy took a deep breath. "Your father had decided that he is tired of paying for me. He has asked me to leave next week."

"What!" Rose's hands went flying in wild, dramatic gestures. "That's ridiculous! He can't send you away! I like having you at home!"

Maddy smiled, her heart warmed. "I like being there with you, too. But he was most clear."

Rose stared at her a moment, her brow furrowed in thought. "Did he speak calmly to you or in exasperation?"

"Calm."

"Oh, that's bad. But was he in a temper about something? Have we spent too much money on candles?"

Maddy shook her head. "He was perfectly calm and rational. I could tell that he had put in a great deal of thought." Months of thought apparently, as his plan had begun well before the Season even began.

"But that's just silly," Rose repeated. "Wherever would you go?"

"I believe I shall apply for employment." Though as what, she hadn't the foggiest idea. Especially if her reputation precluded her from being a governess. A housekeeper might even be too high a stretch.

"But surely Papa will change his mind."

Maddy shrugged and leaned back against the squabs. "I don't believe so."

"And Mr. Wakely—"

"No, Rose." She sighed, feeling more resigned now that she had spoken the words aloud. She would find employment. And if Mr. Wakely deigned to ask for her hand, well, she would simply have to think of matters then.

"Well, that is ridiculous!" Rose huffed as she folded her arms across her chest. "I shall have words with Papa first thing in the morning."

Maddy didn't comment. And she didn't dare hope that Rose could convince her father to change his mind.

After all, he had gone to a great deal of effort to force Maddy into an illicit affair. He would hardly change his mind just because his daughter begged him. And even if Rose succeeded, would Maddy even want to stay? The very idea of what he had done made her skin crawl. She wanted to be out of the house immediately, if she could. She certainly had no wish to look him in the eye unless it was to spit in it.

"I will be fine," she said aloud, more to herself than to Rose.

"Of course you will," returned her cousin staunchly. "You will come live with me and Mr. Frazier after we're married."

"Oh, Rose. You cannot count on—"

"Hssst! Stop it, Maddy! Now that he has returned—and no longer ill, I might add—nothing will stop him from having me. Did you hear what he said to me? Do you know that he's coming to Vauxhall tomorrow night just to see me? Don't worry, Maddy. It will all work out. Though I do wish you had given me a bit more time than a week! Really, Maddy, that is cutting it quite close!"

Maddy didn't respond. Rose would believe what she willed. After all, Kit had certainly made quite a spectacle of himself, flattering Rose and getting her to spin around like that. Perhaps he was in town looking for a wife. Perhaps it was Rose whom he wanted. Perhaps a million different things.

But whatever it was, she could be sure of one thing. She would be no man's mistress. Not her uncle's. And not Kit's. That's why she told him she would lock her window tonight. He needed to understand that there would be no more midnight visits. It didn't matter that her uncle had made her into a tart in the eyes of the *ton*.

She was a proper girl, and she would *not* give in. She would become a chimney sweep first. Or a maid. That was more likely, she supposed. She would become a maid.

"Don't sigh like that, Maddy," said Rose, her voice uncharacteristically subdued. "I can't bear it when you're sad."

Truly? Maddy thought with a fond twinge in her heart. Rose might live most of her life in fantasy schemes, but her heart was true. "Very well," Maddy said as she forced a lightness into her tone. "I shall rely on you."

"Good!" said Rose brightly. "But we must figure out a plan first!"

Maddy couldn't help but laugh. Rose always had a plan. At least this time she was asking for help with it. "Actually," Maddy said slowly, her mind working out the particulars. "I am supposed to help Mr. Frazier with a task. But perhaps you would be better suited for it."

"Really? What?"

"Well, he is…um…" How to phrase this without revealing the truth? "He is going to help me sell this broach I'm wearing. To Baroness Haugen."

"That old bat?"

"Rose! She's very sweet!"

"She's as big as a house! And she talks constantly!"

"Well, perhaps, but she is very fond of peacocks. And as a lady can't engage in commerce by herself, he is going to…um…pretend that this broach is part of his pirate booty and sell it. I'm to arrange an introduction for them, but perhaps you would like to do that? That would allow you to spend more time with Mr. Frazier and be a help as well."

"Hmmm," said Rose, obviously thinking hard. "Hmmm."

"Rose—"

"I have it!" The girl practically exploded off her seat in excitement. "I know just what we will do!"

"You will arrange for the introduction?"

"No, no! You can do that. You are much better at these things than I am."

"But—"

"No, listen! You go meet with that old bat. You are much more patient than I am in listening to her blather on. Make sure to sell it to her and convince her to wear it at Vauxhall tomorrow night."

"But, Rose! That is much too soon!"

"No, it's not! It's the last major event of the Season. She might be back in Norway by the day after tomorrow."

"I believe her country home is in Gloucester."

"It's the same thing!" Rose huffed. "She won't be here."

Maddy frowned, doing her best to understand what Rose was getting at. "But, dearest—"

"No, listen. You arrange for her to buy the thing and wear it tomorrow night. I shall see it on her at Vauxhall and make quite a fuss over it. Everyone else will chime in, of course, because I am the fashion leader after changing your gown style and all."

That wasn't exactly true, but Maddy didn't dare contradict her. There had been quite a lot of praise for her new dress style six weeks ago, and Rose had naturally taken all the credit, but that was a very long time ago in the *ton*'s mind.

"And then," Rose continued, "Mr. Frazier will

become all the rage. His jewelry will be in demand everywhere."

Maddy made to catch her cousin's hands, but Rose was moving about too quickly. "Don't you think your plan is a bit convoluted?"

Rose huffed. "Well, there are a few ifs and maybes, but they will all work out. Never fear. I know just how to handle it."

And the amazing thing was that Maddy could actually see it. Because of Rose's status and beauty, she did command some degree of sway. If she declared pirate booty to be all the rage, then Mr. Frazier could very well find his pieces in demand.

Rose leaned forward. "You just have to make sure she buys it tomorrow. And wears it to Vauxhall. You must be sure of it, Maddy! Everything depends upon that!"

"I don't know that I can do it."

"But you must, Maddy!" Rose pressed. "Everything depends upon you!"

Maddy huffed, but knew she would give in. It was hard not to. Certainly Rose's demands could be wearing, but her enthusiasm was infectious and her heart was usually in the right place. What was one more task for her cousin? She would think of it as one last thing for Rose before... Well, before she was forced to leave and her entire life changed.

"I promise to try," she finally said.

"Excellent!" Rose squealed. "And if Father won't see reason, then you shall come live with me and Mr. Frazier immediately after the wedding."

Maddy laughed. That was too much of a stretch, but it felt good to pretend. Especially if she didn't think at all about who it was that her cousin intended to ensnare.

"You know, most newlyweds prefer to live alone."

"Don't be silly. You'll have your own wing or some such thing. We'll be entirely private. I'm sure he can afford it, especially since his jewelry will be all the rage. We'll make a fortune!"

Of course they would. And everyone would live happily ever after. Fantasy was a lovely thing, Maddy decided. Something she should indulge in more often.

"Now," began Rose, just as Maddy was starting to relax into a make-believe dream, "I know just how you should approach the baroness. First thing in the morning you shall write the old bat an urgent note. Tell her you have the most amazing surprise…"

CHAPTER 20

"I didn't expect that you would contact me this early," Kit said as he sauntered up beside Maddy.

She was in Mayfair, strolling alone, as Rose had insisted that commerce should be done without a maid in tow. In truth, the girl had probably wanted protection from her father in case things turned ugly. Apparently, there had been times when the man had taken a hand to spank his young daughter. Nothing like that had ever happened while Maddy lived with them, but the memory was burned into Rose.

In any event, once the time for Maddy's meeting with Baroness Haugen had been set, she had dashed off a note to Kit and then been ordered out of the house by Rose. Father-daughter discussions were to be handled in private, she'd said. Maddy'd left for Mayfair moments later.

But that was done now, and truth be told, Maddy had enjoyed the fine air as she strolled down Mayfair. How Kit had found her among all the other souls, she had no idea. But find her he did, stepping up beside her as she was looking in the window of one of London's premiere jewelers.

"See anything you like?" he asked when she didn't

answer his first question.

She shrugged. "They're all lovely."

"Come now, surely there's one that strikes your fancy," Kit pressed.

She bit her lip and decided to confess the truth. "That one." She pointed to a necklace that boasted a ruby cut in the fanciful shape of a heart. "I know it's childish. Rose would be in alt over it. But my father used to carve corks into the shape of a heart for me. He said it was how he'd proposed to my mother, promising to make it a diamond someday."

"Did he ever do it? Did she get her ring?"

Maddy shook her head as she turned away from the beautiful gems. "Country doctors are paid in vegetables and fruit pies. There wasn't ever the kind of money for that, but I don't think she minded. I wouldn't, not if the home was happy."

"You're a rare woman," he said as he took her arm.

"No. Just a practical one."

"As I said, a very, rare woman."

She laughed, letting her mood lighten with the beautiful day and the joy of having a handsome man beside her. And he was looking quite handsome today in a jacket of blue superfine that set off the sparkle in his eyes.

She gestured to a waiting cab. "We should hurry if we are to get to the baroness before afternoon callers."

He nodded, but he didn't stop walking. Glancing at his face, she saw his expression was strangely serious.

"Is there something amiss?"

"Yes. No. Oh, bother," he said. "I should like to say something to you, angel. Er, Maddy. Something private, and I fear this is the best time despite the crowd. The rest of the day is likely to be quite full."

Well, her day was full as usual. After their visit with Baroness Haugen, she intended to go to an employment office. She had no idea how long that would take, and she still had to make it home for tea with Mr. Wakely before dressing for Vauxhall.

"You are looking quite sour, Maddy. I begin to fear this is a terrible time."

"No, pray continue. I was only thinking about my day and all that needs to be done."

"Does Rose run you ragged? Or your uncle?" His voice dropped on the last word. And his eyes had turned stormy. She knew he was asking if she had succumbed to her uncle's plans, but she felt no reason to enlighten him. Certainly not given what they had done together without an offer of marriage.

"Running an earl's household takes time," she said primly. "And Rose is as delightful as she is demanding, so you can guess what that means."

"I can also guess that you are put out with me." When she opened her mouth to disagree, he merely held up his hand. "Do not deny it. I have behaved badly toward you, and I regret the harm I caused you."

"There has been no harm," she said, trying to invest truth into her words. "My reputation remains what it was before you came."

"And left," he said. "I left you, and I'm sorry."

She bit her lip and decided on plain speaking. "There were no promises between us, Kit. Any hopes I built were entirely my own."

"No, Maddy, they were not. But I was not a sane man. I could not… It wasn't possible…"

"And now?" she asked. "How do you feel now?"

He shrugged. "Better. Not so lost, anymore. The time with Donald's family was healing. I saw Paul too, which was good, but Lucas is still traveling." He took a deep breath and released it slowly. "They didn't know anything about what Michael and Lily did. They wouldn't have stood for it."

"Oh, Kit, I'm so glad." Finally, he had the family reunion he should have had.

"I've finally made peace with it, I think. Donald wants to make a complaint on my behalf. Quite the thing to see my prosaic brother out for Lily and Michael's blood."

She smiled at the idea. She too had fantasies of hurting the earl and his countess.

"But Michael's an earl, and far wealthier than us. I won't have Donald beggar himself just to publically call Michael a lying dog. There's no point in it. Especially since I am finally on the mend."

She turned to him, seeing the bald honestly in his face. "That really is excellent news, Kit—"

"But I am not whole yet either."

She bit her lip, suddenly afraid. "Not…whole?"

"Not enough yet. My affairs are balanced on a knife's edge. The boat repairs are expensive and not as simple as you might think. And then there is what happens at night…" He shuddered. "That is when the demons come to call."

"Nightmares?"

He nodded. "I think I will be haunted by them for the rest of my life. I fear…" He swallowed. "I fear I would be too dangerous for a wife."

Ah. So there it was. He was making it plain that he did not intend to marry her. She looked away, her heart once again crushed. She hadn't expected the pain that washed through her. Hadn't she cut him from her life some six weeks ago?

"The dreams will fade in time," she said, and wondered if she spoke to him or herself. Eventually her fantasies would fade too. They had to.

"I am always fine on a sunny day. I do not know about tonight, though."

"But—"

He pressed a hand to her mouth. Even through his glove, she felt the heat of him. And she saw the hunger in his eyes. "You deserve a man, not a savage. And that man must be able to afford you. Right now, I cannot even buy new shoes."

"I like your shoes," she said softly. But one look at his face told her there was no arguing with him. His jaw was tight with determination the likes she had never seen. He would do anything to reach his goal. In truth, the look was a little dangerous, and yet she saw only Kit, the man who had touched her so sweetly and who had never, ever hurt her.

A month ago, she might have argued with him. Even a week ago. But she had lost the will to fight with the one man who genuinely cared for her. So she nodded and looked away. When she spoke, her words came out in a rush. "Rose will be hurt. You must tell her this. She believes you will offer for her tonight."

"The devil you say!" he barked, his words not angry so much as completely surprised.

"Rose has her own way of viewing the world."

"I have no intention—"

"I know. But you should tell her."

He released a rush of breath. "Where would she get

such an idea?" He took her hand and drew her around to face him. "It's you I want, Maddy."

How beautiful he looked when he said those words. How earnest and how perfect to hear them. If her heart was crushed before, now it beat triple-time, but every pulse brought another bite of pain. He wanted a mistress, not a wife. And God help her, she was considering it. If her choice was between Kit and Uncle Frank, then there was no contest. If she were to be a tart, she would be Kit's tart. Fortunately, she had another option.

"You have been gone a long time, Kit. Six weeks. Nearly the entire Season."

"I know. I'm sorry."

She began walking again, and he matched her pace. They could not stand in the middle of the street speaking like this. It was bad enough that she had no maid trailing behind her.

"There is a gentleman who intends to offer for me. A good man, one I like very much." She paused, wondering how much of a lie she would spin out of her relationship with Mr. Wakely. "When he offers, I intend to accept."

"So he has not proposed yet?" Kit asked.

"No. But he will." At least she prayed that he would.

He tucked her hand close to her side. "Then there is still time for me."

Did she tell him? Did she let him know that she had only a week before she was turned out on the streets?

"Do you love him?"

Mr. Wakely? "I don't know," she answered honestly. He was kind, and she certainly enjoyed his company. "I do not believe poor girls get the luxury of love."

"But you should, Maddy. You should have everything!"

His words were passionate, and for the first time she caught a glimpse of the boy he must have been. Young, earnest, and filled with the belief that all would be exactly as it ought. She smiled despite herself. "You sound like Rose."

He winced. "That awful?"

"No. Sweet. Kind. I am glad you have found that part of yourself again."

"Do you know how I found it?"

She shook her head, unable to guess.

"By thinking of you, angel. By thinking of what it would be like to live with you every day and night for the rest of my life."

She arched her brows, stunned into silence. That sounded like a marriage. But then his face fell and he looked away.

"I am speaking of the good times, angel. But reality has its darker side."

"I don't understand."

"When I was happy, it was because I was thinking of you. But that was only…"

Now she understood. "Only part of the time. Did you…" How to describe his fits? "Did you think you were back on the boat again? With that cabin boy?"

He nodded. "And worse. Much, much worse. I slept in my brother's barn. I feared for his family."

"That's terrible!"

Kit shook his head. "It was my idea, plus I preferred it out there. It was quieter, and I could think."

She had no answer to that, and so they walked in silence. He was not ready for a wife, he said, and perhaps he had the right of it. But she had no more time to wait. In the end, she slowed her steps before a waiting cab. "We must go to see Baroness."

"Of course. Do you have the broach?"

"In my reticule. I even placed it in a silk pouch that Rose had lying around."

"Excellent. Then let us go charm a Norwegian baroness."

She had another suitor! Kit's mind reeled as he helped her into the cab. Of course she had a suitor! With the way she looked in her new gowns, she likely had a dozen or more. Except he had thought the exact opposite was true. Both last night and today she had a wan look on her face and an air of general despair. Not many would notice it, but he had watched her come alive under his caress. Her spirits were clearly depressed, and so he had assumed that her Season had gone badly.

He looked at her now as she composed herself neatly in the cab. She sat painfully tall, with her hands folded into her lap. Every line in her body bespoke a person using sheer willpower to keep from screaming. He knew the feeling well.

"If there is a suitor, Maddy, why are you so afraid?" He hadn't meant to say the word afraid. He meant unhappy or angry, even. But she visibly started at his question, her entire body jerking, and he knew he'd used the right word. "You are afraid of something terrible."

She opened her mouth, probably to deny it, but then abruptly shut it again. Her eyes canted away and she began to lean back against the squabs. "I fear for your health, of course," she said too calmly. "You seem much better, and yet I remember your episodes."

She was lying, looking for a convenient excuse, and yet the words still hurt. But rather than dwell on his failings, he focused on her.

"If nothing else, angel, we have always been honest with one another. I had hoped that would continue."

She blinked rapidly, fighting tears, so he leaned forward to touch her chin. A gentle tug brought her face around. "Tell me what demon you fight. I shall defeat it, I promise you."

Her expression grew wistful as she gave him a trembling smile. "There is no demon except life. And you have monsters enough of your own."

"No—"

"Yes," she returned firmly. Then she pulled away from him. "Now as to the baroness, you must be sure to spin her a romantic tale."

"Yes, I know," he answered, his tone more curt than he intended.

"But do you know that her husband is in shipping?" she countered. "He owns, oh what was the name?"

"Sysselmann Shipping?"

"Yes! Do you know it?"

"I… Yes. I've spent much time at the docks lately." He flashed her a rueful smile. "Pirate gems will only go so far. I thought to find employment while the ship is repaired."

"And you think to do it with Sysselmann?"

He shrugged, not knowing how to answer. As much as he despised the way he had learned about sailing, he did know a great deal. He could use that knowledge for benefit. "I thought perhaps I could make suggestions. Show them ways to guard against pirates."

"Oh, Kit!" she cried, "I think that's a marvelous idea!

You would be turning a terrible ordeal into something positive."

"That is exactly what my brother said."

She arched a brow. "And is he wrong?"

Kit leaned back with a sigh. "No. It turns out that my brother is not nearly the pompous ass I remember, even if he did paint the house green."

She smiled. "Or perhaps you are not the wild youth you once were."

"I'm certainly not that," he said with an attempt at a laugh. It didn't last. He was more interested in the echo in her words. "Feeling nostalgic? Were you wild as a child?"

"Oh, very! I had no mother to watch me night and day. Don't tell, but I used to play with gypsies!"

"Scandalous!" he cried in mock horror.

"Terribly so. The vicar's wife took me to task dozens of times."

"But you ignored her completely, didn't you? I can see that you have always gone your own way and done as you think you ought. I admire that about you. It shows a rare kind of strength."

He watched her mouth open in surprise. Clearly she had not expected such insight in him. Did she think he didn't know how hard it was to daily service a master he didn't respect? How hard it was to dream nightly of a childhood long gone? Then she said something that completely shocked him.

"You *are* better," she said. "You are thinking of the future, seeing truths in other people, and last night you laughed."

"I have my good times," he hedged. He did not want to encourage her to think him completely sane.

"More and more, I should think."

"Yes. And this is one of the best. Sitting in a carriage, just talking with you about the future." He wished he had the words to explain. A month ago, he could not have done this. Not sit so contentedly in the dark. Too many ghosts haunted him.

She had no chance to answer. They were at their destination. Bloody hell! She had a suitor, their afternoon was filled, and despite everything, he had not yet said what he expressly wanted to say. She made to move out of the carriage, but he grabbed her. His motions were too abrupt, his grip too tight, but he had to say this now. If he didn't, then the moment would be lost. The day would be lost.

"Maddy, listen to me. You have to know… Whatever happens, whatever you face…" He swallowed. "You are safe. I shall protect you, I shall help you. It matters not when or where or what. I shall be there for you."

She frowned, searching his face as if looking for an answer. He had none for her. So he drew her hand to his face, pressing his lips to the back of her hand, and he whispered his vow.

"Whatever it is, Maddy, I will help you. You are not alone."

CHAPTER 21

"She loved birds, rare and beautiful birds, but had never seen a peacock…"

Kit continued to weave his silly tale, based on stories he had heard. Fantasy, illusion, anything with a glimmer of possible truth, as long as it made the baroness's eyes glow with delight.

"He was a poor man. A sailor who had traveled the world over. Unfortunately, the jeweler he went to had never seen a peacock either, so this piece was designed by a man—"

"Who had never seen the bird!" interrupted the baroness. "Oh, Mr. Frazier, this is the most delightful story! Did he give it to her?"

"He did," Kit answered with a desperate glance at Maddy. She was smiling at him, her eyes dancing nearly as much as the baroness's. Clearly, she also had a romantic streak. Too bad everything he said was a lie.

"Don't stop there," urged Maddy. "How did he give the gift to her?"

Kit squirmed in his seat. His life as a slave had been stripped down to simple honesty. Do this or die. Obey without question or die. There was no room for subtleties. It unsettled him to return to the gray light of half-truths. And it bothered him even more that it was so easy for him to spin his tale.

"You understand," he said gently, "that I do not know if any of this is true."

"Oh, pshaw, young man!" returned the baroness as she refilled his teacup. "Of course this is all flimflam, but I want to hear it anyway."

"Very well, then, but I have no idea how the sailor presented the princess with his treasure."

"Oh!" interrupted Maddy. "But that is all the better! We can all say how we think he should have given her the gift. I think a rough sailor would never have been let into a princess's presence. He must have scaled the garden wall and given it to her that way."

"What a marvelous idea," returned the baroness. "But do you think..."

The ladies bantered ideas back and forth until they decided on one that was appropriately romantic. Kit was grateful to be let out of the tale. The truth was so much uglier than what they imagined. And Maddy was so much brighter as she talked with the baroness, her hands flitting about as she spoke, her entire body filled with life.

It was good to see her like that. He knew how she appeared when climbing the sexual steps to fulfillment, but now he saw when she was simply happy. Relaxed, animated, and happy. Good Lord, she was beautiful.

"I believe," said the baroness, "that he must have looked at her just as Mr. Frazier is looking at you right now."

Kit blinked, coming back to himself with a start. What had the woman just said? "I-I beg your pardon," he stammered. "I w-was trying to recall—"

"Oh, don't spoil it, my boy," said the baroness with a fond smile. "Not when she's blushing so prettily."

He looked at Maddy, who would not meet his eyes. She was looking down at her hands, but there was a sweet rose color to her cheeks. And then it happened again. He lost his thoughts as he simply watched the shift of light and color in her face.

He had no idea how long he sat there. No one else said anything to interrupt his reverie. He only knew he came back to himself to see the baroness drinking her tea, her eyes dancing with merriment. And Maddy was still looking down at her hands.

"Er, um, I'm so sorry. Where is my mind these days?" He swallowed, feeling awkward and embarrassed.

"You were telling us how the sailor gave the princess his beautiful creation," supplied the baroness.

"Of course. Well, as to that I don't really know, but it is clear that she did eventually receive it. And I was told that she wore it prominently at a festival one night."

"A festival?" asked the baroness. "What kind? I mean was it like our winter festival?"

In Africa? "No, Baroness. It was…well, um…"

"Perhaps it was like Vauxhall, a party of sorts outside," inserted Maddy. "Like tonight."

The baroness shook her head. "It was a fertility festival, wasn't it? You needn't be embarrassed, sir. After all, I have had four children myself. I understand all about fertility."

He doubted she understood the kind of drunken revels he had seen, but nodded nonetheless. "Well, yes. And, of course, the sailor saw her wearing it."

"Did he find her then?" asked Maddy, her voice quiet with a kind of wistfulness. "Did he sweep her away for them to live happily ever after?"

No. More likely she was abducted by villains who raped her and then sold her on the slave market. But Maddy was looking at him so sweetly, and he knew that as strong as she was, she also longed for someone to sweep her away.

"Yes," he whispered, wanting with all his heart to be her hero. "Yes," he repeated more firmly. "They had a desperate escape, of course, running from her father's men. But he was a good sailor with good friends. They were smuggled aboard a ship and made off as fast as the tide could take them."

"Oh marvelous!" cried the baroness as she clapped her hand. "Where did they settle? And how did you come to have the broach?"

Kit ducked his head, buying time to think as he sipped his tea. Eventually, he found his answer. "They went to an island and settled there. It was filled with beautiful tropical birds, of course, and they had a wonderful life."

"With lots of fat, happy babies," finished the baroness. "That is always important."

"Yes. Lots of them. But…well, many years later the island was hit by a terrible storm. Our princess was a great grandmother by then. She died in that storm and was buried wearing the broach."

"Oh, how sweet," breathed the baroness.

"Sadly the village had to move after the storm. Everything was devastated. I do not know where they went."

"Well," said the baroness with a small nod, "those islands do get hit by storms and the people move around quite easily. Quite a normal way of life for them, I'm told."

Kit stared at her, momentarily stunned by the woman's ignorance. There was nothing about a tropical storm that was normal or easy, but he couldn't say that. Fortunately, he was saved by Maddy, who tilted the ugly piece to the light.

"It is marvelous how it has survived through all that, isn't it? Really, once you know its history, it fairly takes the breath away."

"Yes, it certainly does," said the baroness as she looked back at Kit. "But if it was buried with the princess, then how did it come to you?"

Kit sighed, allowing some of his real heartsickness to flow through the sound. "It is not a pleasant tale, Baroness."

She arched a brow, but he could tell he had caught her attention.

"Grave robbers, Baroness. You know I was on a pirate ship. Pirates see no sanctity in graves."

Maddy frowned. "But did the village have so much that their graves were worth robbing?"

Kit turned to her. Did she truly believe any of this tale was true? "Well—"

"Hush, Miss Wilson! The lady was a princess, and princess's graves are *always* worth robbing, isn't that right, Mr. Frazier?"

"Of course, Baroness. Of course."

"And did you steal it from your masters when you escaped?"

Kit flinched. Is that the story that was being bandied about? That he had escaped? "No. I was given the piece because it was ugly. I had served well, and this was my share of the take." Shame soured his gut and he set aside his tea. He did not like remembering what he had done on the ship or that he had been rewarded for doing his service well. Of course, this particular piece wasn't shared booty. He had found it, taken it, and hidden it away before his masters were any the wiser.

"Well, never mind that," said the older woman. "The point now is that you have a beautiful piece to sell me, and I insist that you do so, sir. I will not countenance anyone else owning such a thing."

Did she have no guile whatsoever? Kit wondered. She had just handed him the opening to charge her an exorbitant price for an ugly bit of jewelry and a romantic story of lies. Kit hesitated, but he could not stop himself from beginning the negotiation.

"I'm afraid the jewels are most valuable, Baroness."

"And I was just this morning talking to a London jeweler," Maddy inserted. "It is only because of our friendship that I thought to speak with you first."

"Quite right, quite right indeed," said the baroness as she leaned over and patted Maddy's hand. "But never fear. My birthday is coming up and I have already told dear Migel that this is what he is getting me for my birthday. He has allowed me only so much, and then..."

They sat down to dickering. Surprisingly, Maddy and Kit fell into a perfectly matched rhythm. She had little understanding of the worth of gems themselves, but she knew the baroness and knew exactly when to ease off the discussion and when to press. In truth, she could have done the sale completely on her own. She just needed Kit there to explain what each and every stone was and their individual value and history. Truthfully, he hadn't even realized how much he had learned about gemstones, but it was the stock and trade of a certain grade of pirate. As he had not wished to learn anything about pedaling slaves, Kit had learned about gems.

In the end, the baroness purchased the broach, a ring, and a single ear bob that she intended to convert to a pendant. And she paid by banker's check, bringing in her husband, who dashed off the note as easily as if he were paying the butcher.

And that, of course, gave him the chance to introduce himself to the baron and owner of Sysselmann Shipping. Maddy was the one to mention—to the baroness—that Kit was interested in a business venture. That he had marvelous ideas on how to stop pirates. She was speaking to the baroness, but the baron heard it. Within moments, Kit had an appointment to discuss business matters at the shipping office in a few days time.

All in all, it was a perfect afternoon. For the first time in over seven years, Kit felt he had financial security— for the time being, at least—and a possibility for a brighter future. It was an amazing moment and one he had to stop on the front step to appreciate.

"Kit?" Maddy asked, turning to look at him. She was smiling in inquiry, her satisfaction with the afternoon beaming through her expression. "Oh, this has been a wonderful afternoon, hasn't it?"

He nodded, unable to speak. How did he explain the bizarre mixture of feelings that were coursing through him? But apparently, he didn't need to explain. She took one look at his face and grabbed his arm.

"Come along with me. We'll take a stroll through a park I know near here. Hardly anyone fashionable goes there, which is why I absolutely love it."

"You don't prefer Hyde Park?"

She sighed and they began walking together. "Hyde Park is, of course, very lovely. I have strolled and sat in carriages and generally paraded myself in front of every

possible gentleman who might someday think he
wanted a wife. But that's not really enjoying a park, is
it? It's hunting for a husband, and so incredibly tedious
I usually come home with a headache."

He raised his eyebrows at her bitter tone, sensing the
deeper truth. "So you do not really enjoy London
society? You are here for the husband."

"Well," she hedged. "I suppose if all the Marriage
Mart nonsense were removed, there are things I like in
London. The theater is marvelous, and there are ladies
like the baroness who are quite fun. But I was raised in
the country. Sometimes the city is just so…"

"Noisy? Crowded? Dirty?"

"Busy. Always doing something, going somewhere,
talking about something. And yet…"

"Insubstantial. As if it were a whole lot of talk
about…"

"Things that matter so little to anyone at all."

He tilted his head, needing to explore this side of her.
"Would you be a political hostess then? A reformer
seeking to better the plight of orphans?"

She laughed, showing more joy in life than humor in
what he said. Either way, it was a beautiful sound, so
perfect from her. "No, not political that way. But I
should like to have more talk with the medical men in
the city. My father had some very innovative ideas,
practical ones that he thought should be discussed
among men of medicine."

"And he told them to you?"

"Oh yes. I wrote them down, but have done nothing
with them. I thought I would pursue it after I was
married—"

"And your time was once again your own?"

She nodded, but her gaze wandered to the trees. They had just walked through the main entrance to a small stretch of grass and park benches. She didn't pause to sit but continued meandering along the path. "I am so glad the baroness was charmed by you. Is that check enough, do you think? Will you be set for a while?"

"It will cover my expenses for a few months. Your share should last you quite some time as well."

She stumbled slightly, her eyes going to his in shock. "My what?"

He touched her cheek, marveling again at her beauty. Her skin was not so much flawless as healthy and free of powder. Her mouth was parted slightly in surprise, and best of all, her eyes were empty of guile. She truly had not expected a share of his sale.

"It is a called a finder's fee, Maddy. Or a commission if you like. You will get thirty percent of anything I sell to the baroness."

"But that is…" Her eyes widened in shock as she calculated the amount in her head. "Oh! Oh my goodness!"

He smiled at her. "You deserved it. I could never have made that much without you. I never would have met the baroness at all!"

"But…but…"

He pressed his fingers to her lips. "You deserve the money. Do not even try to dissuade me."

Her eyes sparkled, flashing in the sunlight. "All right, I won't. But thank you!" She flung her arms around him and hugged tightly. He returned the embrace, loving her natural enthusiasm. Better yet, he adored that he was the one who had brought her such easy joy.

"I am only being fair, Maddy," he said as he buried

his face in her hair. She smelled like the angel she was. "You earned every pence."

She pulled back, her lips curved in delight. "Is this what it feels like to be in commerce? I vow it is not so terrible! In fact, I believe it is the best thing ever!"

"Really?" he said, his mind already fading out beneath the feel of her body pressed against his, her arms still wrapped around him. And before she could pull away completely, he leaned forward and captured her mouth in his.

She stilled, but only for the smallest fraction of a second. A moment later, she opened to him, meeting his tongue with her own and teasing him with an enthusiasm that surprised him. Had he taught her that? Or had she learned it with her other suitor since then?

The thought spiked a flash of jealousy in him, and he found himself pulling her harder against him. They were beside a tree, and it was the work of a moment to press her against the trunk. Then he was free to pillage her mouth as the pirate he was.

He expected her to fight him. What little mind he had was warning him to go easy with her. She was a gently bred woman and such an assault would surely terrify her. Except she did not fight him. She met him with such fiery passion that he was stunned.

He broke away, his breath coming in great gasps, but his hands were not still. He had meant to grip her hips, but he found his hands were higher, his thumbs rolling over her tight nipples. Her head was thrown back, her breasts lifting as she gulped deep breaths. And her eyes—sweet heaven—her eyes were looking straight at him, glazed with desire.

"Angel?" he whispered. His hands slowed their caress and he was finally able to force them down her sides to rest gently on her hips.

She swallowed, coming back to herself with visible anxiety. Her gaze dashed around, scanning the area. Thankfully, the only people nearby were a nanny and her charges many yards away.

"Don't be afraid," he said. "No one saw."

She nodded as her gaze came back to his. "I'm not afraid," she said, her voice steady and strong. "And I'm not an angel," she said. "I have lately been considering the value of other professions."

He stilled, his mind whirling. She could not possibly mean... But she... But...

"Angel," he rasped. "What of your suitor? What of..."

"A lie," she confessed. "Because I was angry with you for being gone so long."

He blinked. "But... But..."

"There is a man, but he is a banker. His livelihood would suffer were he to marry me." She looked away, her shoulders slumping with the movement. "I have lately learned of a horrible thing..."

She told him it all. A halting confession, a recitation of facts that in no way portrayed the perfidy of her uncle. By the time she was done, the slave in him was raw with fury. The earl was not long for this world. Slave would kill him while he slept. He would choke the life out of that fat bastard, and he would laugh as he did it.

"Kit. Kit, do not look at me like that! I swear I never... Not with Uncle Frank! We were never...I only ever with you. I—"

"Hush, Maddy," he said as he pressed his fingers to her lips and silently wrestled the slave in him into silence. "I know. I know, and you need not fear your uncle anymore."

She reached up to his hand, stroking it gently while gratitude shone in her eyes. Then she slowly pulled his hand down. "You have given me the money to be free. And…and if you have other jewelry, then perhaps I know other ladies. None quite as rich as the baroness, perhaps, but many of them would pay a great deal for pirate treasure. We would have to be discreet, of course. But you are quite the rage, right now, thanks to Rose. There is a great deal of money to be made. If you…if you will allow me to help you."

"Of course I will," he said. But she didn't understand how much this afternoon of lies had cost him. Spinning romantic tales of pirate gold? What a lie! And yet, looking into her eyes, he could not deny her. "But there is not much left. The baroness bought the best of it."

She nodded, and her gaze dropped away. "Of course," she said softly. "It was but a dream. But at least now I shall have enough for a small room while I wait for an employment opportunity." She lifted her chin and met him with a defiant gaze. "I had intended to apply as a governess, but I fear my reputation will harm me there. So I shall be a housekeeper, I think. I do that anyway and very well."

"Maddy—"

"I shall pretend to be a widow. Mrs. Wilson married to a soldier who died in Spain." She bit her lip, her gaze challenging him. "Which means, since they all believe I am a whore anyway, that I need not be so careful with my reputation."

He stared at her and she stared right back at him. She could not be suggesting that they… That she… God, he was hard as granite, and he could not think!

"So you see," she said slowly and rather awkwardly.

"You really, well, you shouldn't call me angel anymore. I-I really am not."

He took a deep breath, feeling his lungs shudder with the gasp. "You don't know what you are saying."

She pushed her lips together and arched her brows. It was a perfect imitation of a courtesan's arch look, but he knew it was a lie. Still, the sight shocked him to the core. She should not be talking like this. She should not be *thinking* this!

He stepped backward, the movement difficult because his body was rock hard with lust. "I shall kill your uncle."

Her lips curved into a soft smile that quickly faded when she realized he was not exaggerating. "Kit. Oh no, Kit. You cannot." But he was turning away from her, his mind and body at war and both too far gone for reason. "Kit!"

She grabbed his arm, pulling him back toward her. He used the motion, spinning around until he caught her. His force was so great that he lifted her off her feet to set her rather hard down on a bench. She sat with a gasp and he continued the motion, flowing to the ground until he was kneeling before her.

"You will not become a housekeeper or a governess and certainly not a damned tart!" he snarled. "And you will not have to tolerate that bastard for one damn second more—"

"Kit..." she began, but he shook her off. Pulling out the check from his pocket, he shoved it at her. "Take it. Take it all, Maddy. It will be enough for a while. Certainly for a room. You can get better when Rose inherits—"

"Kit!" she cried, her eyes flashing fire.

"But do not go back there now. Not until I can—"

"Mr. Frazier!"

He gasped, the use of his proper name too shocking from her. His words stopped. His breath stopped. And that gave her time to straighten up from the bench and step carefully away from him.

"Angel—"

"Don't speak of those things again, Mr. Frazier. He is my uncle."

"He has made you into his mistress! He has ruined your life and any future—"

She held up her hand to stop him. It was an imperious gesture and one he forced himself to obey.

"I will not have you murder anyone for me. Villainous as he is, I will not have it." She leaned forward. "Kit, it would ruin your life and do nothing to save mine." Likewise, she took the check and pressed it back into his hand. "And I will not take your money either. Only what I have earned. Good God, Kit, do you think me so delicate that I cannot survive this?"

"Angel—"

"*Stop calling me that!* I am no delicate creature! I have sat and watched my father wither away before my very eyes. I stood helpless while everything he owned was sold off and I was packed off on a mail cart to London where I knew no one. Uncle Frank gave me a home and a purpose in caring for his house and for Rose. So what that he manipulated things to his advantage? Everyone wants more, everything is done as a manipulation for something else. Even that check. I know every word you uttered was a lie. Even the baroness knew, but she likes a romantic tale and so we gave her one. Why? For the money. For independence.

For survival."

He stared at her then, his heart clamoring in his throat. He stared and was hard put not to sob. When had she become so cold? When had she become as cynical as a slave?

"No," he whispered, unwilling to see her in such a harsh light.

"Yes," she repeated firmly. Then her expression softened. "Tell me something, Kit, did you kill the pirate who owned you?"

"Eventually."

"But you bought your freedom at first, right?"

He nodded.

"Then allow me to do the same. Allow me to purchase my independence without murder or bloodshed."

He swallowed. She was too innocent to see that it would mean nothing to him to kill her bastard of an uncle. He had killed before. He had murdered and not thought twice about it.

Except, of course, that was a lie. He *had* thought about it. And dreamed it. Most especially now when it was over. It haunted him. Even if she did not do the deed, her uncle's death would haunt her too. She would feel like she was responsible and would eat herself alive with guilt. He could not do that to her. He could not doom her to live as he did, with terrors by night and uneasy pretense by day.

"Maddy," he whispered, though in his mind he still called her angel. "You are so much stronger than I ever imagined."

"And you, Kit, are the answer to my prayers. Will you let me sell your jewelry? Will you help me gain my independence?"

"Yes," he said. Of course he said yes, though he would have to *find* more jewelry for her to sell. He would do anything for her. And he would also have a long visit with her Uncle Frank.

CHAPTER 22

Maddy didn't make it to the employment center. She barely made it home in time for dinner. Instead, she asked Kit to show her all the jewelry he wished to sell. That necessitated a trip to the bank where the gems were held in a safety deposit box. He was right that there wasn't a great deal, and much of it was bent or damaged in some way. But she committed his supply to memory and began thinking of wealthy aristocrats who could be induced to purchase them. That had taken all afternoon such that she barely had time to catch a cab back home. But on the bright side, their trip to the bank had also allowed Kit to deposit his check from the baron and to help her open an account in her name alone. She had money! She had sat there and watched him figure her percentage of the sale and saw the clerk write it down. That money would be credited to her account by day's end. She was no longer impoverished, and the feeling was beyond anything she'd ever imagined.

Money of her own! How liberating it was! Was this how courtesans felt when their protectors handed them presents of money or jewelry? Was this how the lowest street tart felt when she was paid? No wonder women chose to step across the moral line. She had options now. Enough money to live in a modest room for months! She was not wholly dependent on anyone, least of all Uncle Frank. And better yet, she had not lost her principles to achieve this sweet heaven of coinage.

Sadly, the moment she returned home, all her exuberance disappeared. The butler informed her that she had had a visitor that afternoon. Looking at the card, Maddy felt her breath freeze in her throat. Mr. Wakely! In the excitement of the sale to the baroness, she had completely forgotten their appointment! She could have sealed his proposal today, she realized. Instead, she had been away from home with Kit.

With her spirits suitably lowered from that horrible realization, Maddy trudged up the stairs. She would have to hurry to dress for dinner. But the moment she made it to the top of the stairs, Rose came barreling out of her bedroom with a squeal of excitement.

"You're home! Finally! I have been on pins and needles all afternoon to know. Did you accomplish it? Did the baroness buy that ugly thing? Will she wear it tonight?"

Maddy held up her hand, her lips curving at the girl's enthusiasm. "Yes and yes, sweetheart. Now give me a moment to change for dinner."

"Oh, don't bother. Father's at his club tonight, so it is just us two. We'll order trays brought up to my room and you'll tell me all about what happened!"

Maddy paused, her eyes narrowing as she looked at her cousin. "So you have spoken with your father?"

Rose shrugged as she grabbed Maddy's arm and dragged her down the hall. "Father wasn't in a talkative mood," she groused.

A moment later they were in Rose's bedroom,

stretched over her bed. Rose lay on her stomach, her feet kicking into the air, while Maddy reclined back against the post.

"Sweeting," Maddy said, the tension mounting in her belly. "What does that mean about your father? Were you able to talk with him at all?"

Rose huffed as she flipped over onto her back to stare at the ceiling. "I told him that it was beyond horrible of him to throw you out of the house. That I wouldn't stand for it. You're like my sister and I want you here with me."

"Oh, Rose!" Maddy said, touched that Rose could think of her so dearly.

"He patted me on the cheek and said that you weren't going anywhere." She kinked her head back toward Maddy. "Then he added that I shouldn't think of you as my sister. You're more like a friend or a mother who has come to stay for an extended visit. Whatever did he mean by that?"

Maddy swallowed and clenched her hands tight in her lap. It meant, of course, that Uncle Frank expected her to succumb to his pressure and become his mistress. What he didn't know was that Kit had given her another choice than to be bedded by her uncle. But she couldn't say that to Rose. No good could come from revealing the man's perfidy to his daughter. So Maddy chose a coward's lie.

"I have no idea whatsoever," she said firmly.

Rose narrowed her gaze, her eyes searching her cousin's face with too much intelligence. Maddy did her best to look completely unreadable. It would only take a moment and then Rose would become distracted by something new.

Sure enough, after two long breaths, Rose heaved a

sigh of disgust. "Very well. So tell me about the old bat. She bought the broach?"

"Rose! You shouldn't say—"

"Yes, yes, I know," she said as she flipped back onto her stomach. "But tell me what happened."

It was an easy request to fulfill. Maddy was still brimming over with everything, and it was wonderful to have a sister to share it with. She launched into a detailed recounting of the sale. She relayed every bit of the story of the princess and the sailor, and even allowed Rose to embellish the tale, making it even more spectacularly romantic.

"So she will wear it tonight?" Rose asked as she bounced up onto her knees.

"I suggested it just before we left and she thought it a capital idea."

"Whee!" Rose squealed in delight as she leaped forward to hug her cousin. "Thank you, thank you, thank you! You have arranged everything perfectly!"

Maddy hugged her cousin back because Rose was always delightful, even when she made no sense. "You're welcome, my dear, but I don't know exactly what I have arranged."

"It will all happen tonight!" she gasped. "My pirate prince will hear me praise that ugly thing to the skies. I shall wish and moan and wonder just how I could get my hands on such a fantastic thing. With my influence as a fashion leader, I shall make pirate treasure just the thing for everyone."

Maddy couldn't object to that. Not if she were going to get a commission on each of those sales. "But...pirate prince?"

"Well, that is Mr. Frazier, of course. And I shall be

his beauty. That story he told—about the sailor and the princess—that was clearly about me and him. Oh, how did he know I have such a love of rare and beautiful birds?"

Maddy blinked. "You do?"

"Well, I like birds. They're pretty and sing nicely. I know! I shall wear my gown that makes me look like a bird."

"What gown?"

"Don't you remember?" huffed Rose as she leaped off the bed to search her wardrobe. "Mr. Wakely said so quite distinctly. That when I wore this I looked as pretty as a partridge sitting in a pear tree!"

The mention of Mr. Wakely quieted Maddy instantly. "Do you think he will come tonight?" she asked Rose. "I missed his visit this afternoon. Did you entertain him?"

"Hmmm? Who?"

"Mr. Wakely."

"Oh. Well, yes, of course. Though he is a bit dull sometimes. Still, I told him a lovely tale about how you were visiting a gentleman friend who was deeply sad. A wasting disease, I believe, and that you were most broken up about the loss."

"You told him what?" Maddy gasped.

"Well, I could hardly tell him that you were at the old bat's engaging in *selling* things." Her tone could hardly be more disgusted. "Besides, it never hurts to let a gentleman know that there are others interested in you."

Maddy couldn't help but laugh. "A gentleman with a wasting disease?"

"Yes, well, that just made the story sound better. Anyway, he said he wouldn't be at Vauxhall tonight.

Something about it being too frivolous for a man in his position."

Too scandalous, probably, to be seen there with a woman of her reputation. Maddy sighed. "Did he say if he would call again tomorrow?"

"Hmmm. I don't remember. Caro and her mother came by and we started talking about her older sister. She's increasing! Barely two months married and already…"

Rose continued to chatter while a maid brought up their dinner trays and Maddy let her thoughts wander. Mr. Wakely would not be at Vauxhall tonight. Regrettable, but at least that left her free to pursue her mercenary goals. Any of the *ton* still in town would be at the gardens tonight. She could mix as she liked, quietly whispering about pirate jewelry. Yes, all in all, it was fortunate that the proper Mr. Wakely would not be there to see her engage in commerce.

And, of course, it would be best if Kit and Mr. Wakely did not meet. Business partner and suitor were best kept far, far apart. Especially in the rather enchanting pathways of Vauxhall.

Kit prowled the edges of Vauxhall, sliding easily through the shadows. He should have dressed more formally, he realized, and not in black trousers and open pirate shirt. A black cape completed his outfit. It was a dash of whimsy on his part. If everyone thought him a pirate, let him play the role on this night, when half the revelers were in costume and the other half were nearly out of their costumes.

He slid past a working girl as she pulled her fare down toward the darker pathways. Tonight the *ton* celebrated the last of the Season until fall. Tonight the working girls would get more expensive pigeons to pluck. And tonight, he meant to prove to himself and to Maddy that he was a civilized man.

Except he wasn't civilized. Maddy's revelations about her uncle had brought the slave in him to the fore. His more relaxed attire and the wilder festivities had his darker side pushing the bounds of his mind, especially now that it was nighttime. And to cap off this disaster, he was set to meet with Michael and Lily again, the two people most responsible for his capture and enslavement.

He should have worn a civilized outfit for a civilized man. He should have put on a damned suit of armor to lock the savage inside. But he hadn't, and now he was here, ducking past drunken revelers while searching for the one woman who made it all worthwhile.

Maddy. His angel. Where the bloody hell was she?

There! Dancing with some elderly fop. She wore another one of her good gowns, this one of pearlescent white. There were no ribbons or flowers or flounces on this one, thank God. Just simple white draped beautifully, and an equally plain mask that dangled uselessly from her arm.

She was laughing as she curtsied to the elderly gentleman. He was scarecrow thin and pasty faced to boot. But he smiled at her sweet laugh and winked in response. The man was at least sixty years old, and yet the sight of him winking at Maddy made Kit growl under his breath.

"You should not scowl like that," a voice said behind his ear. "It scares people."

Kit spun around, the movement half animal, half simple shock. There before him stood his older brother Lucas. Taller, paler, the smartest of his brothers and a man who looked equally stunned as he stared right back at Kit.

"So you really are alive then," he said, his voice choked with emotion.

Kit had no voice at all. The best he could manage was a halfhearted shrug. Apparently it was all that was needed as his brother enveloped him in a heartfelt embrace. And Kit surprised himself by gripping his brother right back.

"Omph!" Lucas said as he finally drew back. "You've grown a bit stronger there, little brother. Nearly crushed my ribs. Have you a voice? Or was that stolen by yon miss as well?"

Kit glanced back to where Maddy continued in the patterns of the dance. Her cheeks were flushed and her smile warm. A new life had come into her today, and he was grateful to be the cause. But why in the devil's name was she flirting with that elderly cad?

"Kit! You're doing it again."

Kit came back to himself with a start and forced himself to look away from Maddy to his brother. "When…" His word came out as a savage growl and he had to stop and clear his throat. "When did you arrive? I waited for you at Donald's but you never came."

"Got to the family estate yesterday and heard the news. Swore I wouldn't believe it until I saw your face."

Kit arched a brow. "And now that you have?"

Lucas's expression grew sober. "The scowl is new, little brother, and the face is harder."

Kit nodded. "Harder. Yes. That's a good word." When he'd been a slave, he'd dreamed every moment of returning to the easy life he'd lost. And now that he was back, it all seemed so much harder than before.

"Shall I buy you a drink, brother? We can talk about

travel and women. Foreign lands and women. Vast new lands and..."

"Women?"

"Exactly!" his brother crowed. It was a surprising sight, his bookish older brother attempting a lecherous waggle of his eyebrows.

"When did you lift your head out of a book?"

"Ah, well that is a tale and a half. Shall we—"

"No."

Lucas's eyebrows rose at Kit's harsh word. And when Kit could not find the words to explain his savage mood, his brother turned back to look at Maddy, who was entering the last steps of the dance.

"What's her name?"

"Angel." The word was out before he could stop it.

"Interesting—"

"Maddy Wilson," Kit corrected himself. "And I need to speak with her."

"Ah," Lucas said, a wealth of meaning in his tone. "The set is ending. Perhaps I should go ask for a dance." He glanced over at Kit, his words obviously meant to bait.

Kit merely shook his head. "She will head back to her party now." Then he pointed before his brother could ask. "She's with Michael and Lily."

"Really?"

Kit nodded. "The connection is with Lady Rose, the poufy-dressed blonde in the front."

"All the better," his brother quipped. "We shall go pay our respects to—"

"I can't." Now that the push was upon him, Kit was finally able to voice the first of his many problems this night. "It's because of them, Lucas. All of it. They put me on the boat, then declared me dead. They knew about the pirates, and they refused to pay..." His words choked off.

He didn't need to elaborate further. Lucas was the smartest of the Fraziers, by far. All it took was one look at Kit's face and he understood the bulk of it. The fury that always seethed beneath his skin. The pain of everything he had lost. And the absolute disgust of the arrogance that had wreaked so much havoc in Kit's life.

"Stay here," his brother abruptly said. "I believe I shall go pay my respects for you." Then he was off, his long legs covering the distance into the box in mere seconds.

Kit stood in the shadows watching his brother with one eye and Maddy with the other. She was chatting with the fop as they made their leisurely way back to Michael's box. Lucas was bowing over Lady Rose's hand before turning to greet their cousin, the Earl of Thornedale. Michael smiled warmly, extending his hand in greeting. Then Lucas, his bookish, pacifist brother, tightened his fist and planted a facer to Michael's jaw.

The earl fell sideways. Thankfully he was already seated, so he had little room to fall. And as Lily came rushing up in shock, Lucas gave her a withering look, turned his back on her in the cut direct, and calmly walked away.

And Kit felt the strangest thing. It had been so long since it had happened, he had to touch his face to be sure it was real. It was. He was grinning.

Oh no! Not again! thought Maddy as she stared at the chaos erupting in her host's box. Someone had just planted a facer on the Earl of Thornedale. Someone who looked like a taller, gaunter, and much paler version of Kit. Someone who was right now walking directly toward her.

"Oh my! Oh my, my," murmured Viscount Rothsby to her right. "That really isn't the thing."

"It isn't the thing to allow your cousin to be captured by Barbary pirates either," she said. "And then try to negotiate over the ransom price."

"Oh really?" said the viscount as he looked at her. "Is that truly what happened?"

"Oh bother, I probably shouldn't have said that. But yes, my lord, it is." Thanks to the earl's influence, Kit's story had centered on his dashing escape from the pirates. The part where the earl had refused to pay the ransom had been conveniently forgotten.

"Well then," the viscount returned with a raised eyebrow. "I suppose that a facer was well in order, don't you think?"

"I do, my lord. I most certainly do." And that was all the time for conversation they had as the violent stranger was now bowing before her.

"Miss Wilson," intoned the viscount beside her. "Please allow me to introduce you to Mr. Lucas Frazier. The second eldest of the Frazier clan, I believe."

"Just so," the man answered as he bowed over her hand. "I am most honored to make your acquaintance."

"And I you," she said as she dropped into a polite curtsey.

"I wondered, Miss Wilson, if you would do me the honor of walking with me for a bit? You needn't worry about propriety as your cousin has already agreed to join us."

She looked at him in confusion. "Rose? But..." She shifted to look around him to where the earl's box was in chaos. And in the middle of it, fluttering her hands like a lost bird, was Rose alternately looking at where the Michael was arguing with Lily and back to Maddy and Mr. Lucas Frazier.

"Do you agree, Miss Wilson? A simple walk along with your cousin?"

"Of course."

"Excellent!" he crowed. And after a brief nod to the viscount, he took himself back to the box, where he extended a hand to Rose. She didn't even hesitate as she rushed forward. Mere moments later, the two had joined Maddy where the viscount was bowing his good-byes.

"You're a charming woman, Miss Wilson," he said over her hand. "And I think you are quite correct. My daughter would simply adore some pirate jewelry for her birthday. It will make her just the thing."

Maddy could barely keep from clapping her hands in delight. She covered by gripping her skirts in another sketch of a curtsey. "Felicitations on her special day, then, my lord."

Then she turned and found herself face-to-face with an entirely different Mr. Frazier. While she had been taking her leave of the viscount, Kit had somehow appeared beside her. His eyes were dark, his clothing bordering on scandalous. And when he held out his hand to her, she did not think twice about disobeying his unspoken request. She put her hand in his and together they strolled after Rose and his brother Lucas.

It was some time before she realized they were heading down a very dark path.

CHAPTER 23

"My goodness, Kit! You look…you look…" How did she describe him? His clothes, though very nice, were the least of the attractive package that was Kit tonight. There was a taut feel to him now, wild and unrestrained. As if standing next to him was like standing in the middle of a thunderstorm. "You're very dashing," she said, though the word was barely adequate.

He arched a brow. "Do you like dashing?"

She swallowed, feeling a blush heat her cheeks. "Yes," she confessed. Yes, she liked it quite a lot.

"Then I am glad that I chose this costume."

She tilted her head to look at him from head to toe. "Is it?" she asked. "Is it really a costume?"

His lips curved into something that was half smile, half snarl. "I have worn nothing like this before in my life."

"And yet you seem more at ease in it. More you."

She saw understanding grow in his eyes as his expression slid from anger to confusion. "I am not comfortable in a dandy's lace. My leg prevents me from being a sailor ever again. I suppose I am still searching for what fits."

"You will find it," she said, sure that he would, but silently wishing he would figure it out quickly. Where would she be when he finally decided he was ready for a wife? Then to cover her sudden need, she looked for his brother and Rose. "They are moving too far ahead of us." And into a pathway that was even more improper than the walk they currently meandered.

"Let them, angel. My brother knows I need to talk to you." And before she realized his intent, he whisked her sideways onto a path that was altogether devoid of light.

"Kit!"

"Maddy please," he rasped as he pulled her tight into his arms. "Please, you cannot know the feelings that are at war inside me now. It is like I am going to explode."

She softened against him, her heart easily overcoming her anxiety about propriety. "You have felt that way before," she said. "It will pass."

He nodded, and his forehead came to rest against hers. "It is so hard," he said. "So powerful…"

"Tell me what you are feeling. One by one, just name them." His body was tight against hers, his grip almost bruising. But she was a strong woman. Even at full strength, it would be very hard for him to break her. So she stood still, waiting patiently.

"Did you see my brother hit Michael?" he asked.

"Yes. Yes, I did."

"It is the best thing I have seen in an age." His teeth flashed in the night. "Do you think that evil of me?"

"That you enjoyed the sight?"

"Yes."

"No." She quirked her lip in a rueful smile. "If I were a man, I probably would have done that and more. The earl deserves it for what he did to you."

He swallowed and a small bit of tension faded from his body.

"Don't stop there, Kit," she admonished. "There is more. Tell me it all."

"I cannot stand the sight of you in another man's arms."

A tingle of delight slid down her spine. It was small of her, but she liked that he was jealous. "Do you mean Lord Rothsby? He is married and twice my age."

"I know. I don't care."

She smiled and squeezed his arm. "His daughter is turning eighteen soon. He wants to buy her a piece of pirate booty to make into a necklace. The uglier the better as it will make a good story, and she is a girl who likes stories." She peered at him closer when he didn't answer. "Isn't that a good thing, Kit? I have made us another sale."

"It is a wonderful thing," he answered immediately, but there was no release in his body. If anything, his tension ratcheted higher.

"But what is the matter?" she pressed. She had very little room with him holding her hips so tightly. But she could raise her hand and stroke the hair from his face. She could touch his cheek and coax his gaze to hers. "Are you afraid you do not have enough jewelry?"

He shook his head. "I spoke an hour ago with a man who sometimes comes by what we need."

"Oh! How excellent!"

"You are entering commerce, angel. Dancing with men to sell your wares." She stiffened at his words, but he continued regardless of her reaction. "I know you do not sell yourself, but there will be those who think you do. Men who—"

"My own uncle thinks I do or will," she returned more tartly than she intended. "And many men have tried to steal a kiss or more from the impoverished cousin." She rolled her thumb across his lower lip, partly to gain his attention, partly because she liked the feel of his mouth. "I care less and less what men in this world believe, and more about the money I will have. And the freedom it buys me."

He closed his eyes. "Angel, I would buy you the world if I could."

"I don't want the world," she said, the words flowing from her lips before she could think too deeply about what she said. "I only want you."

She felt her words shudder through him, but when it passed, his body remained as tense as before.

"I will frighten you, angel. I will hurt you."

"You have never done so before."

"I frighten myself. You do not understand how—" He cut himself off, his face a grimace of pain.

"How what?"

"How desperately I want you." He took her mouth then. It was a harsh kiss, slanting over her mouth, forcing his tongue inside. She opened herself to him, wanted what he did, loving the raw intensity of his need. Then he broke off and his words filled the air between them.

"I came here tonight to take you. I cannot stand the thought of you one second more in your uncle's home. It is worse when I imagine you alone in some room you have let, vulnerable to so much evil. So I ordered a boat to wait nearby. I want to abduct you, steal you from everything you know and make you mine."

Far from terrifying her, the idea had her body tightening with desire. And in that moment, all of her choices lined up before her. Like lines on a ledger sheet, she saw her future.

She could be her uncle's mistress, wholly dependent upon him but at least safe in a life she knew. She discarded that thought immediately. Second, she could take the money she had already earned and find a room somewhere. She would search for some form of honest employment, but she would constantly be hampered by her reputation. And worse, she would still be dependent upon someone else, living in their household, subject to their rules.

It was an honorable choice, but one that appealed to her less and less. She would be completely removed from society and would never see Rose again. And her new business venture with Kit would end before it ever really began since she would not be able to move through society to sell the jewelry. It was honorable, certainly, but it still lowered her social status. Mr. Wakely, for example, might stoop to marry a suspected courtesan, but she did not think he would find his wife among the housekeepers of this world.

Then there was the last choice. Become Kit's mistress, right here, right now. Yes, she wanted marriage, children, and legitimacy, but those weren't among her choices. Not even Mr. Wakely could say if he wanted to marry her eventually. Kit wanted her now, and she wanted him.

Plus, mistresses were allowed in society, just not *proper* society. She would still be among the people she liked, living in London, which she enjoyed. And she would have access to the people who would buy Kit's jewelry.

And she would have Kit. In her bed. In her arms. In her body. The very idea made her shiver with anticipation. And that overrode any of the thousands of objections she had not thought through yet. In truth, she knew she wasn't thinking clearly at all, but that was all part of the excitement. She felt alive for the first time since before her father died. "Take me, Kit," she said. "Let's go."

Now she understood what he meant about a war going on inside, just underneath his skin. She felt his tension as if it was her own. Every tremble in his fingers, every shuddering breath was echoed by her. But with each passing moment, she felt his hands skate across her skin. She remembered what he'd looked like with his shirt off as she shaved his cheeks. She recalled the touch of his body on hers. And she remembered the sweet glory of release.

He had taught her that. And he could teach her so much more. So she danced her fingers across his chest, slipping beneath his scandalously open collar. And as he stilled to better feel her touch, she did the boldest thing of her life. She rolled her hips against him, pressing her groin into the hot length of him.

"I choose you, Kit. And I will not wait any longer. My whole life has been about waiting!" She leaned into him and slid her breasts against his chest. Her nipples drew tight and hard. And when he still did not move, she took hold of his hand and brought it to her breast.

"Now, Kit," she said. "Do I need to strip here in front of you?"

His hand tightened reflexively, sending a jolt of pleasure through her. But his face was stark with pain. "Angel…"

It turned out she was bolder than she ever before

believed. As he whispered that stupid nickname, she lost her patience. Having fought so hard to keep her virginity, she never thought she would have to fight to lose it! So she reached down and gripped him. Without hesitation. And as hard as she could manage through the tight confines of his clothing.

With a sudden growl, he grabbed her around the waist and threw her over his shoulder. She released a squeal of alarm but quickly muffled it. She wanted to be abducted. And she did not want to scream loud enough for anyone to stop him!

Fortunately it wasn't far. He moved smoothly through the dark pathway. Even upside down, she could tell that there was little light. Then, when she was becoming lightheaded from her position, he abruptly stopped and set her on her feet.

"Get in," he said.

She blinked and looked about her. They were at the water's edge with a small boat moored beside. The boatman winked as he jerked his chin to a cushioned seat in the front. She flushed, momentarily embarrassed, but her feet moved quickly enough. With Kit holding her hand to steady her, she stepped into the boat, but she did not sit down. She couldn't as Kit stepped in behind her.

He was the one who took the cushioned bench. And then as she looked at him in surprise, he adeptly turned her around and pulled her into his lap. She was seated securely facing forward. His hands came around her belly and his hot cock pressed against her backside.

"Look ahead," he whispered against the back of her neck. "Watch the sights and know that no one can tell who we are. We are just two lovers riding the Thames."

She liked the sound of that. She liked the beautiful

view of boat lanterns across the water and the shadows of the city. She liked the sweet breeze that cooled her skin, and the muted sounds as they pulled away from the dock. She relaxed back against Kit and let her head rest against his shoulder.

Lovers. They were going to be lovers. She couldn't wait.

"I dislike small boats, angel," he said. "I believe I need something to distract myself."

She started to lift her head up to ask him what he meant, but then she arched on a gasp. His hands slid up to cup her breasts. And his thumbs began a slow brush across her nipples. Her breath came out in a stuttering rasp, but the rest of her swelled beneath his caress. Oh, she loved it this! And yet, it was too little. She wanted his hands on her breasts, she wanted to be skin to skin with him.

She shifted restlessly, trying to touch him behind her back. But there was nothing to grab hold of and no angle to reach more. Then she felt his lips curve against her neck. "Easy, easy," he breathed. "We have all night."

"Kit—"

"Shhhh," he soothed. "Lie back. Let me touch you."

She had no choice but to comply. It was late spring, so her clothing was thin. She had left her wrap behind her, and so there was little barrier between the heat of her body and the stroke of his hands. He roamed freely over her breasts, her waist, and along her thighs. Her legs relaxed immediately, but her skirt kept her from allowing anything more. And then he abandoned her legs to run upward again, to cup her breasts, to stroke her nipples, and then to trace the edge of her bodice. She sighed in delight.

"You are so beautiful," he said. "And I am going to show you such things."

She felt beautiful. She felt hot. And she felt like this boat ride had to end very soon.

"When, Kit?"

He lifted a hand and pointed to a spot just ahead where another dock waited. She saw other boats with other couples, and they had to wait an eternity to disembark. Then they were ashore and he was leading her up the streets to his bachelor apartments. A moment later, she waited impatiently as he unlocked his door.

Finally, they were alone.

CHAPTER 24

"Last chance to escape, angel."

She laughed. She didn't want to escape. She had never felt so free in her entire life. So in answer, she turned to face him. With a smile that she hoped was filled with seduction, she reached behind and began to unbutton her gown.

His eyes heated and he slowly stepped forward. "Please, allow me," he said as he brushed her arms away.

She straightened, liking the burning intensity in his eyes. He stood in front of her, but his fingers were deft as he unhooked the buttons down the back of her gown. She felt the bodice loosen, hold for a moment on her breasts, then slowly slip away. Her sleeves caught on her elbows, the rest of the fabric stopped at her waist. And now, finally, she could smile seductively at him as he stroked a reverent hand across the edge of her shift.

"How can you look at me with awe?" she whispered. "You have already seen everything."

"I never tire of it."

She smiled and allowed her gown to fall to the floor. She stood before him in just shift and stockings. "But what about you? When can I see all of you?"

He visibly flinched at her question, but she refused to let him hide. She reached out and gently pulled his shirt from his pants. He swallowed in anxiety but did not stop her.

"There are more scars, angel. And the whole is frightening."

"I think I shall kiss every one of your scars," she said as she pulled his shirt free.

His eyebrows lifted in surprise. "Every one? That will take a very long time."

"Every single one," she vowed as she discarded his shirt.

She looked at him then, saw the dark tan of his skin and the crisscross of white scars. There were ridges from deep wounds and puckered round shapes from burns. But they were all Kit, and they did not frighten her.

She trailed her fingers along the crescent-shaped wound, starting at his collarbone and curving around his torso to end in his belly. She pressed her lips to that one first. She felt him gasp, and his body trembled. His arms came around her but more to steady himself than her. She kissed it again, a little lower this time, using her tongue to stroke the white line. His breath rasped harsh above her, and his hands tightened. Then he abruptly jerked her backward.

"Kit?"

"Do you know what you kiss?"

"You," she answered.

He shook his head. "That is my name. My slave name," he rasped. Then pulled her into his bedroom, but not to his large bed. Instead, he took her to the dressing table mirror. She had to wait while he lit a candelabra, but his intent was clear. Once there was light, he made her look at his reflection.

"My name was Slave. Later, I became Head Slave. But we were all slaves, and so sometimes they would call me Moon Slave. Not Kit. Not even Englishman. But this. Moon Slave because of the shape of this scar."

"How did it happen?"

"That first night after I left Jeremy. I went on up top and joined the fight." He snorted. "I was such a fool! I had no skill with knives and no defense against trained killers."

"This wound should have killed you."

He nodded. "They had surgeon of sorts. They would have left me for dead but one of the sailors told them I was an English lord. Said to contact Michael for my ransom."

"That was fortunate."

He arched a brow. "You think so?"

She nodded, coming around to face him. She left her hand on his chest, then slowly trailed it down around his torso toward his flat belly. "I think I want you alive, not dead. Moon Slave or Kit, I cannot imagine never knowing you. When will you believe that you do not disgust me?" She smiled and quickly nipped at his nose. "You do not even frighten me."

He caught her around the waist then. She hadn't even separated from his face more than a half inch when he grabbed her waist and lifted her off her feet. Two steps farther and he was half setting, half dropping her on the bed. She laughed as she bounced, but then quickly sobered when he did not follow her down. Instead, he looked at her with eyes that burned.

"Kit?"

"This is your first time. I need to be gentle."

"I am a strong woman."

His lips curved slightly. "Yes, I know. That is one of many things I adore about you." He stroked her face, then allowed his hand to move across the width her shoulder. "You will not break easily."

"I will not break at all," she returned.

"Really?" he challenged. Then his hand trailed down her arm, past her elbow, until he cupped her hand in his. Then he slowly but firmly guided her hand to his groin. He pressed her hand to him, letting her shape him as she had earlier. She hadn't thought it possible, but he felt larger than ever.

"Do you understand the mechanics?"

"Do you love me?" The words were out before she even realized what she asked. Her thoughts were on his organ, hot and hard beneath her fingertips. But her mind, obviously, was thinking about something very different.

"I..." He swallowed.

"No, never mind," she said suddenly embarrassed. Some courtesan she was, asking about love! Everyone knew that there was no love between a man and his mistress.

He knelt down before her and gently turned her face to his. "I think of you all the time, Maddy. By day, I plan how I can see you. At night, I close my eyes and lose myself in you. Eventually, I fall asleep. And then, angel, I dream of burying you."

She frowned, trying to understand his words. Why would he dream of—

"I dream that you are Jeremy lost and alone on a ship that sinks around you. I dream that you are one of the many women I have seen raped and murdered. Or worse, sold in the slave market. I see you brutalized, stabbed, even whipped by my own hand." He swallowed. "Angel, is that love? Or madness?"

She didn't know what to say. She had no words to soothe the terrible things that haunted him. So she leaned forward and pressed her lips to his shoulder where a burn had puckered the flesh. She moved then toward his neck, using her tongue to lave a small piece of beautiful, untouched skin, before quickly finding the top of a whip mark. She continued kissing him, pulling him closer to her as she pressed her lips to every scar she could reach. The back of his shoulder, the cuts beneath his arm, the lean cords that led down toward his hips. And then she could not reach farther so she slipped her fingers beneath his waistband and unbutton his pants.

He didn't move during any of this. Not until his clothing was fully open and his organ pushed free. She brushed the cloth off his hips and down with one hand. With her other, she stroked him. Here was untouched skin, smooth, taut, and so hot she thought he might burn her hand.

"Lie back, angel," he rasped.

She did, scooting upward on the bed until she lay before him. Her shift was long, covering her hips, and her stockings were tied beneath the hem. He climbed onto the bed beside her. While his eyes held hers, he gently took hold of the bottom hem and drew it slowly up her body. Inch by inch, she was revealed to him.

He tossed the shift aside without looking away. Then he leaned forward to kiss her lips. Slowly. Carefully. Barely even touching her with his tongue. It was as if he feared to hurt her. So she coiled her fingers into his hair, loving the silky feel of it against the back of her hand. She pulled him close. She opened her mouth and she began to thrust her tongue into him.

She felt his reaction immediately. His body tensed and his mouth went wild. He thrust into her, he stroked her. He took her mouth as she wanted him to take her body. Then he pulled away with a gasp.

"You have to be ready for me. It will hurt otherwise."

She understood what he meant. She was the daughter of a doctor, after all. But knowledge and experience were two different things.

"Then make me ready for you," she said with a smile.

His eyes darkened and his nostrils flared. His hands went to her breasts—at last!—and he once again lifted and shaped them as she had come to love. His mouth descended next, biting at her nipples, before suckling, pulling in a rhythm that had her crying out in delight. Her heart was pounding, her skin felt as if it were on fire, and she arched on his bed as her blood began to heat.

He didn't stop what he was doing to her breast. But one of his hands slid over her belly, steadily downward through her curls. She opened her legs. Indeed, they were already spread for him, but the feel of his finger pushing between her folds had her bucking. She cried out as he pressed hard against that wonderful place, and with her body lifting and lowering of its own accord, she felt that marvelous tension tighten. Then he pushed a finger inside her.

"Yes!" she gasped. "Please, Kit. More." She couldn't speak what she wanted. She couldn't find the focus to say that a single finger wasn't enough. That his tongue on her breast wasn't enough. She wanted him. "Kit!" she cried as he pulled his finger out then pushed it back in. "Please, oh, please!"

She grabbed him then. She pulled his mouth from her breast so that she could look him in the eye. She had no words, just gasping hunger as he continued to stroke her. She shuddered, her belly impossibly tight. Her mind nearly shattered.

"I don't care if you love me," she gasped. "I don't care. I love you."

His hand stilled, his body froze, but hers did not. She whimpered as she pushed against his fingers. It felt so wonderful, and yet it wasn't enough. "I love you," she repeated. "Oh, Kit! I love—"

He moved on the bed, spreading her legs as he knelt between them. His hands wrapped her thighs as he lifted her up into position. "Again, Maddy!" he rasped. "Say it again!"

"I love you."

He entered her. One slow, steady, thick invasion. She cried out at the size of him. The stretch of her flesh. Her back arched, and he kept pushing. There was an extra tightness, an extra resistance. Her breath suspended at the feel of it. He was not stopping. Slow, steady pressure, and then finally the resistance gave way. Her body opened fully and he moved all the way inside.

She looked at him. The cords of his neck were pulled tight and his lips were bared in a fierce growl. But his eyes were locked on hers, and he said one word: "Mine."

"Yes."

She saw his eyes mist with tears. She saw gratitude and awe flash through his expression. And then she watched as his mouth opened slowly. Lower down, he was withdrawing from inside her. A pull that had his eyes fluttering but not closing. She whimpered. She did not want him to leave. She had just gotten used to the fullness. She tightened her thighs around him. She reached forward to touch him. She could only reach his chest. His head was too far above her, so she stroked his chest. She touched his moon-shaped scar. And he pushed into her again.

His movement was faster this time, not so controlled. His breath was becoming more ragged, as was hers. She had been so close before with his fingers inside her. Now she felt the steady build again each time he seated himself fully.

Then he paused. She nearly cried out in frustration. She didn't want him to stop. She didn't want—

His thumb pushed between them. He wasn't careful, but she didn't care. It was thick and hard and pressed exactly where she wanted. He pushed his thumb where she wanted, and he pulled it upward just enough to set her body to quivering. Once more—

Yes! Oh yes!

Sensations exploded through her body. Waves of pleasure drenched her and she willingly surrender all to them. To him.

She felt him enter her again, harder. Faster. Again!

The waves crashed higher at his impacts. Once more.

Once more! Yes! He was shuddering inside her. Finally, he had surrendered.

He was hers!

CHAPTER 25

She made him talk. That was a marvel in itself, Kit thought, hours later. Once, long ago, it had not been so hard. Pleasant chitchat had flowed easily from his tongue. Polite nonsense, sweet nothings. He spoke glibly about anything of no consequence. But even then, his private thoughts were harder to access, and his pain—what little pain he knew in his life—was never discussed. He had been a man that spoke only nice things.

She got him to speak of pain. Of horror and death. Of imprisonment and, most surprising of all, the sweet moments beneath the pain. In seven years, there had been good moments. He had laughed in that time. And she got him to remember that as well.

He rolled over on his back, dislodging her from tracing the scars on his lower back. He was thick with lust for her again, but not so hard that he could not think. And as he looked up at her beautiful face, he became lost in her presence. Not her beauty. Taken inch by inch, she was lovely but not stunning. What stunned him was her quiet strength, her simple smile, and the awe-inspiring truth that she loved him.

She. Loved. Him. His scars, his pain, and his moods.

And everything he said now did not shake her.

"Why aren't you running from me? You should be frightened."

"Why do you keep trying to get me to leave?" she countered. "First you run from me for six weeks, and now that you are back, you want me to leave. Why, Kit? What is so terrifying about me?"

"I have killed, Maddy."

"Yes, and you have been beaten and seen horrible things. So why am I so terrifying?"

The answer trembled on the edge of his awareness. It was there, but he could not voice it. He could not even think it. "I don't know," he lied. The truth was that he was afraid to know. Afraid to look at his fears directly.

She smiled and snuggled down into the bed, resting her head on his shoulder. He wrapped his arm around her and held her close. He wanted to sink into her again, to seek the mindless oblivion of sex that was so much more with her. But she had been a virgin. It was too soon to take her again, and so he held off. And besides, it would soon grow light outside. He had to get her home.

"Don't fall asleep, angel," he said as he pressed a kiss to her forehead. "We need to get you to your bed."

She lifted her head to stare at him. "But why?"

He laughed, the sound rough and painful in his throat. "To save your reputation."

"But why? My virginity is gone. Uncle Frank is a day or so away from throwing me out on the street. Why bother saving something that will be lost in a few days time?"

He shifted, the mention of her uncle making him tense in ways that infuriated him. For the first time in seven years, he had felt at peace, and now one mention of that bastard was enough to push him upright on the bed.

"A lot can happen in a few days, Maddy. Your whole life can change." As he spoke, he touched her face, wishing he had the words to explain what she had done for him. This one night of love and talk had made him feel whole again.

She rose to face him. They were both naked, but she had been covered by the sheet. Now it slid to her waist and her glorious breasts bobbed freely in front of him.

"I don't want to go home. Though..." She sighed. "I do worry about what happened to Rose. I shouldn't have just abandoned her."

"She wasn't abandoned. My brother would see that she got home safely."

Her expression softened with gratitude. "Truly? Oh thank—"

Thump, thump! Her words were cut off by a loud banging at his door. "Open the door, you bastard!"

There was no mistaking that voice. "Uncle Frank!" Maddy cried, her eyes widening with horror.

Kit was on his feet in a second, a long knife in his fist. "Get dressed," he ordered as he moved out of the bedroom, shutting the door behind him. Then he was at his front door, standing just to the side as the bastard continued to bang.

"Open up or—"

In one fluid motion, Kit lurched open the door, hauled the man through, and then slammed him up against the wall. He pressed his blade directly to the bastard's throat and waited in absolute silence to see whether he would kill the man now or wait until after Maddy had left.

The earl was larger than Kit, fully clothed, and he reeked of smoke and brandy. His eyes narrowed and he wanted to shove Kit away, but every time he twitched, Kit pushed the knife deeper against his neck.

"Get off me, you bastard! How dare y-y—" He sputtered to a halt as the knife drew blood.

"I would advise you to be very, very still, my lord," Kit whispered against his ear. "I do not like middle-of-the-night callers, and my hand is none too steady."

But the earl proved that he was made of stern stuff. Or he was too inebriated to realize how much danger he was in. Either way, he glowered at Kit and spoke very softly.

"You have debauched my niece," he hissed. "I will see you hang."

"Really?" asked Maddy as she stepped out from the bedroom.

Inside, Kit flinched. He had meant to keep her a secret in there. At best, all he could do now was use his spare hand to quietly shut the main door. Meanwhile, Maddy was walking forward, her tone excruciatingly dry.

"And how would you have him hanged, Uncle? By your own words, you have been debauching me for the last year or more. He cannot sully what you have already destroyed."

"I have not touched you!" spat her uncle.

"No, you merely ruined my reputation so quietly and so thoroughly that no decent man would have me." She came to stand directly before her uncle, and her hand lightly skimmed along Kit's back. "No one, that is, but Mr. Frazier."

Kit felt his muscles ripple beneath her caress. He was the only one standing naked here, but he was the one with the weapon and the skill to use it. Then her fingers slid along his arm to the back of his hand where he gripped the knife.

"Perhaps I should hold this while you get dressed," she suggested.

"It is the only thing keeping him from hauling you away by your hair and raping you as you scream your innocence. He is an earl, Maddy. And he is much larger than you."

"Hmmm," she returned, pretending to think, and Kit marveled at how calm she appeared. Most gently reared women would be having hysterics. "Uncle, I have twice before stopped Mr. Frazier from killing you. This time will make it a third. I trust you understand that even were you to drag me out by my hair, he would find you. And nothing on Earth will stop him then."

The earl's eyes widened at her words, but the man's arrogance knew no bounds. A moment later, he pressed his lips together in a sneer. "He would not dare."

Now it was Kit's turn to speak. He leaned in, whispering so Maddy would not hear. The memories were so close already, it was a simple thing to start relaying—in graphic detail—the ways he had learned to kill a man. And when the earl was sweating, he finally pulled back and spoke loud enough for Maddy to hear.

"I dare, my lord. I am already a savage with so much blood on my hands. In service to her, I would kill the prince regent himself."

"Kit!" exclaimed Maddy from behind him. He continued as if she hadn't spoken.

"But you, my lord, would be a pleasure to gut. Slowly. Do you know that a man can live for hours while his skin is carefully stripped off his body?" For emphasis, he tilted the knife and allowed it to draw downward. It was as easy as peeling the skin from an apple, and the coppery tang of blood filled the air.

The earl let out a high-pitched squeal of horror, and he immediately shoved Kit back. But he had no leverage, and Kit was planted firmly. As soon as the man moved, Kit used his free hand to shove the bastard's head backward, slamming it against the wall. The earl gasped and his knees when out from under him, but he did not lose consciousness.

Kit stepped back with a curse, allowing the man to fall to the floor. "You should go home now, Maddy," he said. "He probably brought the carriage, but if he did not, there are coins in my pants. Take a hansom—"

"Certainly not! This was my choice, Kit. I will not run away from it just because—"

"Maddy!" Kit spun on her, his knife at the ready. Not against her, but in case her uncle chose to attack while Kit's back was turned. "You will go home!" he snapped. Then he abruptly spun her around so that he could finish buttoning her gown. She had done her best, but there were a great many of the damned buttons. Meanwhile, Maddy was voicing her objections as only a woman could.

"I am not a child to be packed away. I created this situation, and I will not leave it. Besides, you have already threatened his life. You cannot expect me to leave when I know damn well you would do it. You would kill him, Kit, and then what would happen? You would be forced to leave for the Continent, and I will be stuck without a business, without a place to live, and without you!"

Her voice had raised to a higher register. She was not hysterical yet, but her agitation showed. Oddly, it pleased him enormously that she would be terrified at the thought of losing him. And that pleasure moderated the savage within him enough that when she paused for breath, he could speak to her rationally.

He began with a task he knew she wouldn't refuse. "Would you mind bringing my clothes here from the bedroom? I will not leave him alone."

She cast him an anxious look but agreed. She returned within a moment with his new trousers that he had worn earlier. He sighed internally. He would be sad to lose these to the blood that was sure to flow soon, but he had little choice. He would not leave this man alone, not now when he was beginning to realize how very desperate the situation was.

"Thank you, angel," he said as he pulled on his pants.

"You look very savage with that knife in your teeth," she said. It was clearly an attempt to lighten the atmosphere, and he gave her the appropriate smile. But his mouth was behind the weapon, so it had little effect. Then his pants were on and he could once again hold the hilt in his hand.

"It is time for you to go now, angel."

"No!"

"Listen to me. You have been very strong and I revere you for it. But there are some things that must be handled between men."

"Poppycock!" she said as she folded her hands across her chest.

He did smile at that. "Angel, do not argue with me when you know it is true. Unfair as it is, men handle the money."

"And what has that to do with anything?"

"Men handle estates and wills and the protection of women." She opened her mouth to argue, but he cut her off. "I know you are beyond capable, but in this, you will be ruled by me. I need to talk to your uncle, and it cannot be done in front of you."

She frowned. "Why not?"

"Because I am going to expose his sins, angel. Sins that you would rather not know."

That caught her attention. He knew she still harbored some tender feelings for the man. He was, after all, her only living family except for Rose. He had taken her in when she was destitute. He had been kind, in a limited fashion. She would not want to have him irredeemably ruined in her eyes.

He could see those very thoughts flitting through her expression. But then they slowly faded. She tightened her jaw and lifted her chin. "I will stay. I will hear these sins."

Kit sighed. "Angel, have some pity on him and on me. It is hard enough talking about these things. Do not force us to do it in front of a woman. Certainly not in front of his niece."

The resolve in her eyes weakened and she looked to her uncle. He was still on the floor, watching everything with narrowed eyes. His neck had stopped bleeding. The cut was not deep. And Kit could see that the man was already plotting his revenge. The earl would not bow to the inevitable easily. Maddy had to leave.

Meanwhile, his angel released her breath on a sigh. "Is it truly as bad as that?"

Kit huffed, his patience nearing an end. "Madeline. Go! I swear I will not kill him, and I will come to you later today to tell you everything. But for now, save your breath and your reputation—"

"But—"

"Go!"

She didn't want to, but she knew he was right. So with a soft curse, she crossed to the door. "I shall expect you this afternoon promptly!" she said.

He smiled. "I will not fail you."

She nodded, cast one last anxious look at her uncle, then left. She shut the door quietly behind her and Kit sat in silence listening as her steps retreated down the hallway. A minute later, he heard the sound of a carriage pulling down the street. Only after those noises faded did he finally turn his attention to the earl. And only because the man could not hold his tongue.

"I will break you," he hissed.

Kit smiled. "Do you know what my job was among the slaves, my lord? Do you know what I was in charge of?" He twirled his knife as he spoke. And when he grew bored of that, he found his whetstone and began to sharpen the already lethal blade. "I was put in charge of breaking new slaves. It wasn't hard. Most had already seen their lives destroyed, their loved ones murdered, but there were always a few who refused to see the truth. Who were too arrogant to understand their changed circumstances."

The earl arched his brow and pushed himself to a sitting position against the wall. Even from that lowered place, he could still project perfect aristocratic hauteur.

"We are not on a Barbary boat, and you have no power over me."

"Power comes from many places, many tools. In the end, all one has to do to break a man is to find out what he most wants in the world, then destroy it before his very eyes. His daughter sold into slavery, his son castrated, his own strength whipped out of him. I was broken by the death of a boy I promised to protect. It was not until I met your niece that I found something I wanted more than his life."

"A woman?" the man sneered.

"Forgiveness. Understanding. A chance to build a life again."

The earl pushed to his feet. "You'll have none of that now. You've threatened an earl and debauched his niece."

Kit smiled but didn't move from where he leaned against a table. "What you value, my lord, is your position in society. The *ton* looks at you and they see a wealthy earl with a beautiful daughter and a charitable nature. Just look how he took in his destitute niece."

"Exactly!" the earl gloated as he pulled down his waistcoat. "You are nothing but a savage compared to me."

Kit nodded. "True, true, but the thing about reputations is that they are hard to maintain and easy to destroy. Just look at how easily you destroyed Maddy's. A whisper here, a knowing look there, and suddenly you have destroyed the one thing she wants most of all: a husband and a good, respectable life." He lifted his chin and stared hard at the bastard. "You broke Maddy, my lord, you took what she most wanted and destroyed it before her very eyes. And for that you should die."

"I was not the one who rutted with her tonight."

Guilt was a sour burn in his stomach. One day, perhaps, he would forgive himself for the things he had done. But tonight was for the earl.

"She offered herself to me, and I was too weak to refuse. But if she has taught me anything, it is that broken men can be healed. And broken women too, if I have anything to say about it."

"You bore me, sirrah." The earl turned to leave, but Kit was faster. Before the man could do more than turn, Kit threw his knife such that it embedded in the wall right before his nose. And then lest the man have any other ideas, Kit retrieved two other blades from a nearby drawer. In truth, he had seven different weapons spaced throughout his tiny two rooms. He did not need to move more than a step to put his hands on a gun.

Kit breathed deep as he pushed to his feet. It was time to end the banter and get on with the punishment. "I have let it be known that you stole all of your niece's money. She never was your whore, but you let it out that she was so that she would never marry and no one would learn what you had done."

"It's a lie!" bellowed the earl. "She had nothing when she came to me."

"Yes, it is a lie, but one that is well founded. I have paid a young man very well to make noise about his investigation into those allegations. Eventually he will find nothing, but he will take a great deal of time to find nothing. And he will be quite noisy about his suspicions."

"The devil you say!" the man exploded. "I will be ruined in the financial circles!"

"Just as you ruined Maddy in the Marriage Mart."

The earl rubbed a hand over his fleshy face. "I am well known. No one will believe it!"

"Ah, but you have a penchant for gambling, don't you? The earldom is not so well seated as you would have people believe. I am sure that could come to light. And the fact that you had your wife killed because she discovered you had wasted all your money. She was going to tell everyone of your crime."

"That's a lie! I never touched Susan!"

And there, Kit saw the real brokenness in the man. His voice shook with rage at the mention of his wife. There had been true love there, he guessed, and perhaps her death is what had turned the man into a villain. If Kit were still a slave, he would push the advantage. He would pull up the haunting specter of Susan's death and find a way to make everyone believe that the man had murdered his beloved wife.

But Kit was no longer a slave, and so he had enough mercy to bow his head. "No one will hear that rumor, my lord, and all the whispers of an investigation will fade to silence if you do one thing."

The earl narrowed his eyes. "I could have you killed. Taken by footpads in the middle of the night. Have your guts spilled in the London streets for the dogs to piss on."

As threats go, that would probably have most London men shaking in their boots. But such a threat had little impact on a man who had once been a pirate slave.

"You could try," Kit returned, "but even if you succeed, it would not silence any rumors. Quite the opposite, in fact, for I have already given instructions should I suffer an untimely demise."

The earl swallowed. His pasty skin was slick with sweat. "What do you want?"

"Gift Maddy with a showy dowry. Something that would prove to one and all that you have not embezzled anything. Ten thousand pounds should do it, I believe."

"Ten thousand pounds! You're mad!"

"You have the money, my lord. You might have to stop gambling for a while, forego the investment in that mining venture up north, and perhaps economize at home for a time."

"But I never touched her!"

"You said you did. You ruined her, and now you will pay. Eleven thousand, I believe. More if you argue further."

"You bastard!"

Kit merely raised his eyebrows. He saw no point in trading insults with the man. The punishment was already given. All that was left was to make sure the lesson stuck.

Kit slowly pushed to his feet. The earl was still huffing and spitting, but it was a losing battle. He had no other recourse, and so he would bow to the inevitable.

"Fine, you bloody thief! I will gift her with six thousand pounds, and not a groat more."

"It will be twelve thousand now or I shall begin to spread rumors regarding your lovely wife. Where there other reasons to kill her? Was she cheating on you? Did she find you so disgusting that she turned to a lover half her age?"

He expected the earl to attack then. The man was not subtle, and his fury burned the air between them. But the man was also not stupid. He would lose a fight and lose badly. There was more bluster, more dickering, but the end was inevitable. An hour later, a bargain was struck.

"Twelve thousand pounds. Agreed."

CHAPTER 26

It was an hour before dawn by the time Maddy made it home. Questions and worries piled up in her brain until she was numb. What did the men have to discuss? What would she do now as a mistress instead of a miss in search of a man? How would she tell Rose? And how had Uncle Frank found her anyway?

The house was silent when she entered, but there was a candle still burning for her. She took it with her, her hands shaking so bad she spilled wax on her dress. Would she have money to buy a new one? As a mistress, would Kit pay for her gowns? Or would he keep her naked and in his bed every day?

The thought had some appeal, especially given how wonderful this night had been. She was immersed in memories of all that had happened when she pushed opened her bedroom door and squeaked in alarm. There was a dark shape on her bed that momentarily terrified her. But it quickly resolved itself into a girl with a spill of golden blond curls. Rose. Asleep in her bed.

"Rose, honey, what are you doing here?" Maddy gasped.

Rose came grudgingly awake, rubbing her eyes and rolling onto her back in a twist of blankets. "You're home. I was so worried," she mumbled.

"Yes, sweetheart, I'm home. I'm sorry I upset you."

Rose pushed herself upright. "Did he hurt you?" she asked before a huge yawn distorted her features.

"Who?"

Rose grimaced. "Mr. Frazier, of course. I saw him carry you off. His brother said it was nothing. That he would make sure you were all right, but when you didn't come home..." Rose shrugged. "I had to tell Father."

Now she knew how Uncle Frank had found them. "Well, it's over now," she lied. "You can go back to your bed."

Rose pushed her hair out of her face. "I don't think so," she said slowly. "Father said he had to throw you out now. I told him Mr. Frazier had a fit and abducted you, but he said it didn't matter."

Maddy nodded. "I know. But we can talk about this tomorrow—"

"No!" Rose cried. "I don't want you to leave! And I don't want him abducting *you*. Not when he loves *me*."

Maddy froze halfway through pulling off her shoes. In all the commotion, she had forgotten that Rose believed herself destined to be married to Kit. "Sweetheart, you know that Mr. Frazier's mind isn't strong enough to marry. Not yet. What did you think of his brother?"

Rose smiled, and her cheeks colored prettily. "He was very nice, but not very helpful. I knew more about his brother than he did."

"Ah. So you grilled him about Kit."

"I *asked* him about his brother. It's only natural if I'm going to marry him."

"But—"

"Oh, never mind!" she huffed as she suddenly scrambled out of bed. "You don't understand!"

"Rose," Maddy said, trying to make sense of her mercurial cousin. "Wait—"

But the girl was already at the door, releasing a long-suffering sigh before she spoke. "Don't worry, Maddy. And don't pack! I have it all worked out."

Maddy pushed to her feet. "What do you mean? What have you worked out?"

"It will all be settled tomorrow. I have a plan. You'll see."

"Rose—"

"No! This time I am not telling you. My plans go awry when I let you do all the work. It's time for me to take matters in my own hands."

"But—"

"No," Rose said, looking more seriously and more determined than ever before. "I won't let you live on the street. I won't!" And with that she left, firmly shutting the door behind her.

Maddy stared at the closed door, her mind whirling. Obviously Rose had some fool notion in her head, but whatever the plan, it wouldn't happen until tomorrow. Right now, she had plenty to sort through, first and foremost being how to face Uncle Frank when he returned home. But no matter how she tried, she couldn't decide on anything.

In disgust, she fell backward on her bed and flopped her arm across her eyes. Moments later, her mind surrendered and she fell asleep.

She woke hours later, stiff and embarrassed. One look out the window told her it was abominably late.

Possibly after noon! How could she have slept so long? Kit would be here any minute!

She bolted upright and rang for the maid while trying to strip out of yesterday's clothing and comb out her rat's nest hair. Gilly, the upstairs maid, came quickly enough, her eyes alight with curiosity.

Maddy began with the easiest question. "Why wasn't I woken earlier?"

"Lady Rose left absolute instructions to not wake you. Said you were mighty ill."

"That was very kind of her," she said, fully aware that "kind" was not a word she often used for Rose. "But I'm doing better now. Is anyone waiting downstairs?"

"No, miss."

"Well, thank heaven for that." She said as she studied the maid's face. Gilly's eyes were lively and she was biting her lip as if she had something desperately important she wanted to say. "Is there something I should know?" she asked.

"No, miss," the girl answered as she pulled out a fresh gown from the wardrobe. "It's just that we're all right worried, is all, with you sick and Rose gone and the earl not home yet."

Maddy froze. "The earl never returned home last night?"

"No, miss. Sammy heard him come home last night and speak with Rose, but then he left again right afterward."

Maddy nearly groaned. The gossip belowstairs was likely flying! "Well," she lied, "that certainly is a mystery. Do you think you could ask Rose to come up here while I brush out my hair?"

"Oh, no, miss. Lady Rose got up early this morning

and declared that she would go shopping in Mayfair. Didn't want me to come along," she said with a sniff, "but took the little scullery girl Tessa."

Maddy frowned. Her mind was too slow. "Why would Rose want Tessa? The girl is barely ten years old."

"I wouldn't know, miss," Gilly answered with yet another sniff.

It made no sense at all. None of it did. Where was Uncle Frank? And Kit? She grimaced in the mirror. She would get no answers staring at herself in half dress. "Very well," she said, as she ruthlessly pulled her brush through the knots in her hair. "Help me dress quickly and I shall see what I can discover."

Except, of course, there was nothing to discover. No one else had any more information. Uncle Frank was gone. Rose was in Mayfair for whatever reason. And Kit had not yet called. Maddy had no choice but to drink tepid tea and toy with her breakfast. A breakfast eaten at ten past noon, no less. Certainly most of the *ton* lived like that, sleeping in until one or two, but not Maddy. She always had tasks to do, a menu to plan, shopping to organize. Yet even those mundane tasks eluded her today. All she was good for was drawing wet circles from the tea she'd spilled on the table.

And then—thank heaven—the knocker sounded. She rushed to the door, even though it was unseemly. Kit stood in the doorway, looking relaxed and confident as she hadn't seen...ever! She barely restrained herself from throwing herself into his arms.

"Mr. Frazier!" she said warmly. "How wonderful of you to call. Please, would you care to step inside the front salon?"

He nodded politely, but his eyes were hungry as they

roved over her features. She blushed at his look. Had he been thinking of her as much—and as graphically—as she had been thinking of him?

She led him into the parlor, keeping the door open out of habit. It was, after all, the proper thing to do when she had no chaperone. It wasn't until after he bowed over her hand and began murmuring things that she realized just how silly an open door was.

"I have been thinking of you every second," he said against her skin. Then he straightened slowly. "I have been dreaming of kissing your breasts, of pulling your tight nipples into my mouth and sucking on them as I spread your legs and—"

"Kit!" she gasped.

"Yes, Miss Wilson?" His face was the picture of innocence.

She swallowed. Her mind suffused with images of exactly what he'd described. "I think I shall like being your mistress," she said.

Oddly enough, his smile faded at that. She had thought he would be pleased. "Kit?"

"I should tell you what has occurred," he said as he led her to a settee.

She nodded. "Yes, please. Uncle Frank came back only briefly last night. He's been out all morning."

Kit nodded. "I know. He has decided to repair to his family seat as the Season is now over."

She blinked. "But he hasn't gotten any of his things. And he hates—"

"I'm sure he will send for them."

"But—"

"He is gone, Maddy. You need never worry about him touching you again."

It took a moment for his words to penetrate. But when they did, a huge weight slid from her shoulders. She hadn't even realized how much strain she carried until it magically disappeared. She exhaled a long sigh of relief. "He never actually touched me, Kit," she said softly. "He just—"

"He did enough. He ruined your reputation and was cornering you into a life you did not want."

She nodded, but her eyes lifted slowly to his. "But I do want it," she said. "With you."

He smiled, his expression moving from urbane to passionate in a blink of an eye. But then it was quickly shuttered, and he did not allow her to touch him.

"There is more," he said softly. "You need to hear it all."

She nodded, encouraging him to go on.

"I would have come earlier, but I was with your uncle and his solicitor."

She blinked. "His solicitor? Whatever for?"

"The earl has decided to gift you with a dowry, Maddy. Twelve thousand pounds."

"What!" She was so shocked she straightened bolt upright. "No! It's not possible," she said, shaking her head. "He wouldn't."

"He did, Maddy. He has."

Maddy tried to imagine it, but she couldn't. It just didn't fit. "No, Kit, he wouldn't. What did you do?"

"I pointed out his sins, that is all. Told him he has to make up for what he did to you."

"But—"

"He was the one who made it that amount, Maddy. Twelve thousand pounds. The documents were signed this morning." Then he pressed her hands between his.

"Think on it for a moment. You are an heiress, now. You can have another Season, pay for your own clothes, look as high as you want for your husband."

She shook her head. "No, no. I don't want someone else."

"Think on it!" he said, his voice harsh. "You can have anything you want. Even..." He swallowed. "Even virginity can be faked," he said softly. "Women have been doing it for centuries."

She didn't know what to say. What she wanted was so clear in her mind. She wanted to stay in society, selling Kit's jewelry and being his lover. She wanted a husband and children and a respectable life. But apparently those weren't possible all together. Kit had done everything he could to give her what she wanted...except for himself.

"What about you?" she whispered. It wasn't a clear question. She wasn't sure if she meant would he offer for her? Or would he disappear to the country again?

"I know what I want, Maddy. Thanks to you, I am temporarily employed with Sysselmann Shipping, teaching them how to protect against pirates. Brandon and Scher's money is repairing my ship, and Alex— sweet young Alex—has worked a miracle as well. He and his father have found a cargo for me. I shall have income and purpose again. And there is always the sale of the jewelry."

"You won't stop that?"

He shook his head. "You are too good a saleswoman for me to walk away from that much money."

She smiled, but it was only a halfhearted smile as it was only half her desires. "Kit..." she began, not even knowing what she wanted to say. Then the door suddenly burst wide as Gilly rushed forward, a tiny

Tessa stumbling after.

"Miss! Miss, you must hear this!"

Both Maddy and Kit jumped to their feet. The poor scullery girl Tessa was shaking in terror, tears streaking down her cheeks. In her fist was a crumpled piece of paper.

"Easy, easy," murmured Kit as he smiled at the girl.

"Really, Gilly!" said Maddy with a voice that struggled to be calm. "You're scaring us and the girl."

"Lady Rose has been stolen!" Gilly cried. "Tell her!" She shoved Tessa forward.

"Don't be ridiculous!" Maddy snapped, much too used to Rose's flights of fancy to tolerate it in the servants. But neither girl appeared to be exaggerating.

"What's this you have in your hand?" asked Kit gently as he went to touch the crumpled paper. The girl jerked it away from him, her eyes huge, but then she did extend it to Maddy.

"They took 'er right off the street!" said Gilly. "That's what she said. Right off the street!"

"Hush!" admonished Maddy, though confusion warred with fear in her heart. How could a person be stolen? Meanwhile, she had finally gotten the linen out of Tessa's hand. She didn't even look at it, but kept her eyes on the girl while passing the page to Kit. He would read it for her while she focused on the girl. "Now let's start from the beginning," she said. "You went to Mayfair with Lady Rose?"

Tessa nodded, her eyes huge, but at least she wasn't crying so hard now.

"Then what happened?"

It took three tries before the girl would speak, but eventually she got the words out. "She t-told me to wwait. Said I was to stand on the c-corner and watch."

"Which corner?" Kit asked.

The girl started, shying away from his curt tone. Maddy didn't have to look to know that his face had gone dark and cold. So she interspersed her body between his and Tessa's, going down on her knees so that she could be eye-to-eye with young girl.

"Don't look at him. Look at me," she said gently. "Where were you?"

"Outside the milliner. She t-told m-me to stand on the corner. Two stores away! I couldn't help her, mum. I t-tried, but I couldn't! She were gone afore I could do anything!"

"Of course you tried, Tessa, but let's go back a moment. You were standing on the corner. What happened next?"

"She went into the shop. Then she came out. Then s-she went back in. Then she came out again."

"She went in and out twice?"

"Yes, miss."

Maddy frowned. None of this made any sense. Why would Rose go in and out of a shop? And why would she direct the girl to wait on the corner so far away? "Was she meeting someone, do you think?"

The girl shrugged. "I don't know, miss."

"Very well. Go on."

Tessa took a moment. She was still obviously shaken and was trying to catch her breath.

"Aw, go on," snapped Gilly. "Tell 'er about the men!"

Maddy threw the maid an irritated look, but it was Kit who silenced the woman. He simply took the maid's arm and steered her out the door, speaking in charming accents.

"I'm going to need to write a letter," he said to her. "Would you please fetch me the implements? Paper, ink—"

"But—"

"Right now, please. It's most urgent."

"Yes, sir. Right away, sir."

That took care of Gilly, thankfully, which left Maddy free to focus on calming Tessa. "Come now, Tessa," she said gently. "Rose went in and out of the shop twice. And then…"

"These men just up and grabbed 'er! Three of 'em on horses. Right off the street! She screamed, miss. She screamed right loud, but it happened so fast."

"Three men snatched her off the street?" But how could that be? And why? Meanwhile, Kit returned to Maddy's side, placing a gentle hand on her shoulder. It was the lightest of touches, but it felt like a single source of heat against her very cold body.

"What did they look like, Tessa?" asked Kit in a soft voice.

"Dock rats. Smelled like dock rats."

Maddy bit her lip and glanced up at Kit. She didn't know what to ask. She couldn't make sense of it all. He didn't say anything but extended the crumpled piece of paper for her to read. It was mashed and smeared with tears, but mostly legible. And it was written in Rose's own hand.

I have been kidnapped by pirates!!!! They want gold and rubies! Help me else I will surely die!! Oh, what will happen to me?

Rose

Maddy read the missive three times before she looked up. A horrible picture was forming in her mind, one that was as ridiculous as it was completely plausible. Meanwhile, Kit spoke with Tessa, his voice as gentle as possible.

"How did you get that letter?"

"One of 'em. The men. He threw it at me as they were riding away."

"He threw it at you," Maddy said, knowing that Kit already guessed what had happened. "So he already had the letter when he grabbed Lady Rose?"

The girl nodded, but her eyes went to the crumpled missive. "What does it say?"

Maddy sighed, as she straightened to her feet. "It says that Rose is a bloody idiot."

She would have said more, but at that moment the door burst open again as Gilly came in with a tray with paper, ink, and quill. She set it down in a rush, her gaze hopping from Tessa to Kit to Maddy.

"Excellent timing, Gilly. Tessa here has been most helpful and deserves a treat. Would you please take her to the kitchen? See that she gets whatever she wants?"

The woman nodded, then sternly took hold of Tessa's hand. The two disappeared a moment later, and Maddy was quick to close the door behind her. But she couldn't turn around and face Kit. How did she tell a man that Rose had just had herself abducted so that she could get her hands on his gold? It was beyond idiotic, but she was absolutely certain that Rose had done just that.

Then she felt his hand on her shoulder. He applied gentle pressure to pull her back against him. She fought at first. She was about to impose dreadfully on him, but he insisted. Within a moment, she surrendered and allowed herself to fall backward into his embrace.

His chest was solid and his arms were warm as they

enfolded her. Then he pressed his cheek against the side of her head and just held her. For two wonderful breaths, neither one of them said a word. But after that, Maddy had to speak.

"I'm so sorry, Kit."

"Did you know of this scheme ahead of time?"

She twisted abruptly in his arms. "Of course not!"

He smiled at her, and she saw a gentleness in his eyes despite the hard cut to his jaw. "Then it is not your fault. But you must tell me what you think has happened."

Maddy threw up her hands in disgust. "I think Rose was upset because her father insisted on throwing me out of the house. So she hatched a plan."

Kit nodded. "She needs money, so she had herself abducted? So her father would pay the ransom?"

Maddy put her face into her hands. How did she explain that it was so much worse than that? "No," she said. "That's not her plan at all." She focused on Kit's face, on his mouth and then the kindness in his eyes. "Rose believes that you and she are destined to be wed, and I think she was rather upset that you kidnapped me last night rather than her."

Kit huffed out a disgusted breath. "I have never given her any encouragement."

"I know. Rose doesn't need any encouragement to spin her own romantic view. Though I believe what you did sparked her idea. She told me last night that she had a plan, but I was so tired and confused—"

"You couldn't have expected this." He shook his head. "So Rose thinks it's romantic to be abducted by pirates?"

"No, no," murmured Maddy, thinking hard. "That

wouldn't be it at all." Then she knew. "That's why she said pirate gold! She wants *pirate* gold! And you're the pirate!"

Kit stared at her, a brow lifted in question.

"It's the not kidnapping that is romantic, Kit, it's the rescue. She wants you to rescue her, and she thinks once you do, you'll fall instantly in love with her."

"What about the gold and rubies? Does she really believe I have such things?"

Maddy nodded. "Of course she does. She thinks you'll rescue her, marry her, and then I can come live with you two as your housekeeper so I won't have to be a governess somewhere."

Kit took a moment to process what she'd just said. Then he grimaced. "Do you think she mentioned the gold and rubies to the men who abducted her?"

Maddy frowned, not understanding.

"She had to hire someone to abduct her, right? Dock rats."

"Yes. Yes, she'd have to."

"Do you think she told them—"

"Oh! Of course! She doesn't have any pin money of her own. She would have hired them on the promise of payment afterward."

"And those men will be expecting gold…"

"And rubies. Oh, bloody hell." Her gaze connected with Kit's. "What will these men do if things don't go as she predicts? If she's not a cooperative captive?"

Kit stroked her arm in a long caress. "It won't come to that."

Maddy gripped his other hand. "Of course it will! Do you know how whiny she can get when one of her plans goes awry? Good God, I love the girl, but I often want to—" She abruptly cut off her words. She was about to say she often wanted to strangle Rose just to silence her. "Oh my God," she whispered.

Kit wrapped her in his arms, tucking her tight against him. "Don't worry. I'm going to write a quick note to Alex. He's a good man in a crisis, young as he is. With his help, we can find Rose. We'll save her. And then we'll beat some sense into her."

CHAPTER 27

Alex came quickly enough and with the rope that Kit had requested. Kit met him at the door and explained the situation, including the fact that the earl had retired just this morning to the family estate and would not be able to help. True to form, Alex asked one thing.

"Just how stupid is this girl?"

Kit simply shrugged, but he glanced significantly at Maddy, who was pacing the parlor with increasing agitation. He needn't have worried that she would be upset by Alex's characterization.

"She's silly and romantic and young. Very, very young." Her gaze sought out Kit's. "And we need to find her."

"We will," he returned gently as he crossed back to her side. "They need the ransom. They will contact us—" He hadn't even finished speaking when Gilly hauled a dirty boy into the room. This time she was accompanied by the butler as well.

"Miss! Miss!" the woman gasped. "He came to the kitchen door."

Maddy came forward quickly, but she didn't speak. She simply folded her arms across her chest and arched her brows in query. It was a pose designed to intimidate, and she did it very well. So well in fact, that the boy's angry glare at the maid settled into a sullen pout in front of Maddy.

And then they stood there, Maddy arching her brow in query and the boy shoving his hands in his pockets and looking at the floor with a mulish expression. The child appeared to be about twelve years old, small for his age, but already hard. He would not be the one to break first.

Maddy must have realized it too because she opened her mouth to speak, but no words came out. She was that upset and yet trying to be strong. She glanced up at Kit, silently begging him to help, so he wrapped his arm around her shoulder and tucked her close. From that position, he spoke to the boy.

"What's your name?"

The child lifted his chin. "Ain't gonna say."

"Fair enough," Kit returned. "I wouldn't speak either if I was about to hang for kidnapping the daughter of an earl. Nothing you say will save you anyway."

He felt Maddy tighten in shock at his words, but the boy's face rushed through a cycle of emotions starting with shock, horror, but ending in fury.

"It weren't no kidnapping!" he snapped. "She's sitting pretty enough and complaining about the ale."

That sounded like Rose, but he needn't tell the boy that. "You would expect us to believe that an earl's daughter asked to be kidnapped off the street in Mayfair?"

"I ain't got nothing to do with that!" the boy bellowed.

"But you are involved, boy. You're here demanding the ransom, aren't you?"

He shook his head, his jaw tight with fury. "I'm to tell you where to go after you gives me the gold."

Kit smiled, allowing his slave's face to shine through. In seven years, he had seen hundreds of men have their spirits killed, their will broken. Did this boy think he could withstand a man hardened beneath a pirate sail?

The boy looked up, and his expression faltered but didn't break. It would take a bit more convincing. Kit didn't even have to look behind him to Alex. Twisting his hand behind his back, he flicked his wrist at the young man. He knew exactly what to do. After all, it had once been a favorite game of Venboer's. Nice to turn it to their own advantage for once.

Alex shifted silently into position, then neatly slipped a noose over the boy's head. "Ey!" squealed the boy, but it was too late. His throat was already constricted tight enough to cut off his words and nearly all his breath. And the more he struggled, the tighter the noose became. Meanwhile, Kit gently disentangled himself from Maddy to bend down close to the boy's face.

"I care nothing for you, boy, or Lady Rose. She is mad and deserves to rot in Bedlam. So you decide. Do I kill you now? Or do you tell me where she is so we can pretend none of this ever happened?"

The boy's eyes bulged, but Kit could tell he wasn't convinced. The child simply didn't believe that Kit would carry through on his threat.

"You know," Kit said in a conversational tone to Alex, "Rose was only kept at home out of pride. I'll bet the earl will thank me if she dies. No one wants a madwoman on the family tree."

Alex nodded, obviously picking up the thread. "But, sir, we can't count on the street rat keeping silent. He'd tell the earl that we purposely let her die."

Kit sighed and pulled out a knife from his boot. It was long and thin and perfect for what he was about to describe. "I'll do it," he said. "You've never gutted a boy before. Sad to say what I've learned among the pirates. First thing they taught me was the fastest way to make a child bleed out silently."

Alex nodded and pulled the child around by the noose. "Yes, sir. But where do we take him? There will be a lot of blood."

"Not so much. A regular tub will catch it. Then we throw it and the body into the stream. There's one not so far away."

"Excellent idea, sir," Alex returned. Then he looked up at the maid, who was standing there slack-jawed with shock. "Be so good as to inform the cook that we shall be needing the large pot. And then have them all take a holiday, will you? Best they not know what for."

The maid's mouth opened and closed, opened and closed. It took Maddy to snap her out of her daze.

"Gilly! Do as they say! Good God, girl, don't you understand that they're *pirates*!"

The maid started then quickly bobbed a curtsey. "Yes, miss. Right away, miss." Then she dashed away.

That was all that was needed for the boy. It was one thing for the peerage to be calmly talking about killing him. It was quite another to see the maid rush off to carry out the orders that would lead to one's demise. The boy started waving his arms frantically, trying to get Kit's attention.

"I'll tell! I'll tell!"

Kit sighed and shook his head even though Alex was already loosening the noose enough so that the child could speak. "I'm sorry, boy. It's too late. I've decided it's easier to kill you than rescue one mad daughter."

"No! No! I'll tell you everything!"

Kit tilted his head. "But I don't want to hear it."

"You do! You do! They're in an old warehouse. Near the docks! They ain't touched her."

"I don't care."

"She do! She do!" the boy cried pointing at Maddy.

Kit turned to Maddy. Her face was pale, her expression composed. He prayed she understood that he was only pretending. He would never truly hurt the boy. Then he watched her expression shift from frightened to exquisitely sad. She understood, then. Thank heaven! Meanwhile, she folded her arms across her chest and looked out the window.

"I don't like all this killing in my house," she groused. "And Rose is my cousin. She has her charms."

"She *is* beautiful," inserted Alex.

Kit nodded as if thinking. "She is that. But they've probably spoiled her looks by now."

"No! No, they ain't!" The boy tried to take a step forward, but he was pulled up short by the noose. "I'll take you to 'er. I swear it! I'll make them give 'er to you, all nice and tight. Paps'll listen to me. I swear!"

Kit shook his head. "I don't trust him."

And then, with perfect timing, the maid chose that moment to reappear with a hurried bob. "Everything's ready in the kitchen, miss. Ain't nobody there t' see nothing."

"Well?" asked Alex as he tightened the noose as tight as it would go without killing the boy. "Do we trust him? Or do we let the pirate out to play with his knife?"

Kit turned eagerly to Maddy, his voice wheedling. "The staff is already on holiday, Maddy. He's a small boy. There won't be anything for you to clean up."

"No, no!" Maddy cried as she threw up her hands.

"Enough of the knives and the blood." She stomped over to grab the noose out of Alex's hand, then she glared at the child. "You will take us to where they are holding Rose. You will tell them to surrender her without a fight or I will allow him to play." Then she lowered her voice. "He spent years as a slave to the Barbary pirates, boy. And then he *escaped*. He is capable of killing you and every one of your friends. He already did it to the pirates. You and your Paps will be as nothing to him."

The boy was shaking so hard he could barely nod his agreement. So Maddy reached forward to remove the noose, but she was stopped by Alex.

"Leave it on him. It will make him easier to catch if he tries to run."

She frowned. "One good catch will jerk his neck and snap his spine in two."

"Exactly," returned Alex with a dark grin as he took the rope back from her.

Meanwhile, Maddy shrugged and looked down at the boy. "Do you know what happened to our last houseboy?"

The child shook his head.

"He thought he was faster than a Barbary pirate."

The words hit the child broadside enough that he paled to a ghostly white.

"We'll take the carriage," Maddy said.

Maddy had to physically restrain herself from climbing into Kit's lap. They were in the carriage heading God knew where according to the boy's instruction, ready to face God knew what, and all Maddy could think about was that Kit sat beside her and she wanted him to hold her.

It wasn't just that she was grateful for his help. God knew, she wouldn't have a clue how to handle this without him. Between him and Alex, she had no doubt that Rose would come out mostly unharmed. And the relief she felt at that made her knees go weak.

But what really made her want to crawl into his arms was the way he let her lead. He hadn't put himself forward until after she came up empty. She hadn't known what to say to the boy, how best to approach the child, or even what to do with the ransom demand. Her mind had been so blank that she'd just gaped at the child like a dying fish. And yet Kit hadn't taken over until she looked up at him for help.

And then he had been masterful.

Later, she would smile at the way he had tricked the boy. At the noose and the nearly bored way he had talked about killing the child. She ought to be horrified, but she really thought the whole thing funny. Kit would no more kill the child than he would a kitten. Thankfully, the boy didn't know that.

She exhaled slowly, closing her eyes as she tried to release her worry for Rose. Beside her, Kit tightened his grip on her hand, squeezing her gently as reassurance. She felt her lips curve but didn't open her eyes. If she looked at him, she would likely kiss him, and she didn't want to do that in front of Alex and the boy. Still, her heart swelled at his gentle grip, and she tightened her own fingers in response.

So this is what being in love felt like. She had expected the joy when they were together, the despair when they were not. She was startled to discover that this was equally precious: the moments of simple reassurance, the shared problems, and her absolute faith that he would see her through.

All her lingering doubts about becoming his mistress disappeared in a breath. All her worries about tomorrow faded as well. For as long as he wanted her, she would be with him. And though the thought that he might someday tire of her cut her to the bone, she focused on what she was feeling now. On the fact that she finally, completely, and wholly loved a man.

"We'll get her back safe and sound," Kit said softly.

"I know," she answered, her gaze going back to his face. It took an act of will for her not to simply stare calf-eyed at him.

"I want you to stay in the carriage when we get there."

"Absolutely not." The words were out of her mouth without her even thinking it. Apparently being in love didn't mean she had to agree to everything he said. "I will grab Rose while you deal with…with…"

"With the kidnapping criminals?" supplied Alex from the opposite seat.

"Ey!" snapped the boy. "She came t' us! Offered gold!" He tugged at the cravat noose. "Daft bitch."

Alex thunked him on the head for his language, but nobody argued with the characterization.

"I will stay out of danger," said Maddy.

"No—"

"Unless you'd rather deal with Rose's romantic hysterics. I promise you that she has quite a scene built up in her head. After hours of cooling her heels, she'll be ready to throw her all into her performance."

She actually smiled when Kit paled. Alex tried to cover his laugh with a cough, but failed miserably.

"There will be no dramatics," Kit finally snapped. "You will see to that!" he ordered as he pointed at the street boy. "I'm still open to just killing you and forgetting the whole bloody mess." That last was clearly added for the child's benefit. It wouldn't do to have him relax and stop thinking of them as murderers.

The boy nodded with alacrity, and they all subsided into a brooding kind of silence. And in that state, they finally arrived at the warehouse.

CHAPTER 28

Kit felt like he was about to jump out of his skin. He had just climbed out of the carriage, a knife in each hand and another smaller one in his boot. It was a throwing knife, and he wasn't as accurate with it as he'd like. He'd learned close-quarter killing, not long-distance throwing. But it was what he had, even though it was woefully inadequate to protect the woman he loved.

He smiled grimly at that thought. He'd come to accept that he loved his angel. He no longer started at the thought, but allowed it to permeate his entire being. His love for her was as much a part of him now as his need to breathe. Which made it even worse that she was walking into danger with him.

No more sentimentality, he told himself. It was time to act. The knives felt steady in his hands, the slave inside him comfortable with war. He's just spent the last two months quieting the beast inside him, and now it appeared he had only silenced it for a time. With knives in his hands, the slave was back at full strength. His lips curled in disdain and he glared at the boy. "How many inside?" he snapped.

"Don't know. Six. Mebbe eight."

Kit's eyes narrowed. The child was probably inflating the number, pretending to a strength that wasn't there. But even four or five armed men were dangerous. Especially since he was only one, plus Alex, who was good with knots but not with knives or guns. And then there were the two women.

But there was nothing to do now to change it. "Let the boy go," he grumbled. "But leave the noose. So he will remember."

Alex nodded and let go of the rope. Meanwhile, the boy did his own bit of nodding. "Nice and easy," he said, his voice quavering only a little bit. "No blood."

Kit jerked his chin. "Go."

The boy did, moving quickly to the warehouse door and bypassing it completely. Instead, the boy lifted a broken board in the wall and slipped inside.

Worse and worse. Who knew what waited on the other side of that narrow space? He glanced at Alex. "Circle round. See if you can find another way in. And hurry."

Alex nodded and took off at a lope. It was full afternoon, so he was easy to see, as were the workers in the other buildings. But this warehouse was smaller than the others, obviously abandoned and falling to ruin. Even the men hired to watch the nearest other building didn't give them more than a cursory glance.

"Maddy…" he began, but she waved him to silence.

"Do I go first or you?"

He grimaced. "Me," he snapped. "And stay back. Far back. Until I know what waits on the other side."

She nodded, her face pale. He felt his heart lurch within him. He did not want her to be here. He did not want her to see him like this, with knives out and more than ready to kill.

"You are in control, Kit," she said. "You need not kill anyone if you do not wish to."

He blinked. How did she always know just what to say to him, just when he needed to hear it? He was in control. Two months ago, he would not have been so sanguine about this. But now and with her beside him? He was in control. He had to be.

Swooping down, he pressed a swift kiss to her lips. Then before he distracted himself too much, he spun on his heel. A moment later, he was lifting the board and slipping into the darkness inside.

He waited to allow his eyes to adjust. Instead of afternoon sun, the area was lit by two weak lanterns in a cavernous space. He was partially hidden behind a haphazard stack of crates, but only partially. Anyone watching would see him well before he could respond. And clearly, someone was watching.

Within seconds of entering the building, a feminine wail began. It was loud and piercing, a howl like he had sometimes heard from cats. And it was completely staged. He knew because he had heard real screams of terror, real hysterics. There was no mind-numbing horror in her scream, but something more gleeful. Which meant it was Rose, and suddenly he was very glad that Maddy was here. Let her handle the dramatic idiot. He was looking at the men.

There were four of them, plus the boy, all scattered strategically about the room. Rose, naturally, was in the center, gripped in the arms of one of the thugs. Except she wasn't exactly *gripped*. As far as Kit could tell, the man was barely keeping his balance as Rose jerked her body left and right in a pretense of a struggle.

"Oh, my love!" she wailed. "You have come to save

me!"

"Shut up!" he snapped, hoping she could hear him over all that screeching. It helped that the leader of the band of thieves said the exact same thing at the same time.

Rose gasped in shock for a moment, then subsided into noisy fake sobs.

"You got the gold?" asked the man, presumably Paps.

"No," answered Kit calmly as he stepped into the center of the room.

"She said you'd have gold," growled one of the men.

Kit didn't look to the side, but he knew that he was being slowly surrounded. Meanwhile, Maddy crept in behind him.

"I have nothing. She is daft. And you best hand her over before she gets you the noose, and not a toy one like on your boy." Then he spun his knife for effect before sheathing it at his waist. "She's an earl's daughter, you know, and set for Bedlam."

"I am not!" she cried, indignation lacing her tone.

"Well, you should be!" he snapped back, not even bothering to look at her.

"How dare you—"

"Oh, shut up, Rose," interrupted Maddy from behind. "Let go of that man and step over here. Your father has left town and it is the devil to manage all the details. I have need of your help."

That at least penetrated the girl's dramatic scene. She stopped her pretend tears and straightened in confusion. "Father left? Whatever for?"

Kit let disgust infest his tone. "He decided that blackmailing your cousin into becoming his mistress was not in the interest of his health." He allowed his remaining knife to flicker in the lamplight. "It was a cuttingly quick decision."

That's when the boy inserted himself, ripping off the noose with an impatient curse. "They're all daft, Paps. All of them. Cuts earls, boils children in pots—"

Kit huffed loudly, easily playing into the insane image. "Not boil, boy. The pot was for drainage. Even a child your size bleeds an awful lot."

"See!" pleaded the boy. "Murdering bedlamites, the lot of them. Ain't no good to be messing with them."

Kit held his breath a moment, hoping the boy's cries would be heard. They weren't. Paps simply folded his massive arms across his chest and glared. "Daft or not, I were promised gold. Seems to me, we're four against one."

"Three actually. Him, Rose, and me," inserted Maddy rather cheerfully. Kit twisted enough to see that she hefted a board in her hands. Kit frowned. Where had she gotten that board? It was too large and too clumsy by half. "And really, you cannot imagine how much of a problem Rose will be if you dare harm her love. She's quite the fearsome warrior when her man is threatened."

Right on cue, Rose shoved away from her "captor" and ran forward to stand protectively between the men she'd hired and Kit. With a sigh of disgust, Maddy stepped forward enough to grab the girl's torn skirt and drag her backward out of the way. "Here," she said when the girl started to protest. "Hold this and try not to hit me."

"But—"

"*Shut it!*" bellowed Paps. It was a very loud sound that boomed in the space. Surprisingly, Rose quieted on a gasp. "I want the gold."

"I have none," Kit answered calmly. "How much did she promise you?"

"Nothing, nothing!" whimpered Rose. "They kidnapped me for your pirate gold. Didn't you bring any gold?"

"How much, Rose?" inserted Maddy. "How much did you promise them?"

"Gold!" boomed Paps. "She promised—"

"Five pounds," said Kit as he tossed a purse on the floor. "Five pounds for a day's work and I'll not tell the earl of this idiocy. That's a pound for each of you, even the boy."

Paps appeared to be considering it, but two of his henchmen weren't pleased. "If he's got five pounds, he's got more. We done lost a day's wage already."

Kit moved as fast as he knew how. The only way to quell a rebellion was to silence the first voice—swift and hard. So he slammed the man in the jaw with the hilt of his knife. He followed it with brutal strikes to the ribs and when the man doubled over, another blow to the back had him on the ground. He had done this move hundreds of times before. It was practiced and smooth, and usually ended with his knife plunged into the man's back.

He nearly did it. He only caught himself in time. As it was, he pulled back the killing strike just in time. The knife point cut into the man's flesh, but barely deep enough to draw blood.

And then Kit looked up, snarling at the other three men who were just now realizing what had happened. "Dare me," he growled. "Dare to fight me and I won't stop next time."

The other men met his growl with a snarl of their

own, but it was Paps who held up his hands. "Five pounds," he said quickly. "Fair pay for an honest kidnapping." He slowly stepped forward and picked the purse off the ground. "We won't trouble you no more."

Kit straightened slowly, giving a sharp look at Maddy. She nodded and started pulling Rose back they way they had come. Kit followed more slowly, keeping his eyes on everyone else. No one dared move. No one, that is, but a shadow that suddenly appeared from behind another pile of crates.

Kit tensed, ready to throw, but then the shadow resolved itself into Alex. The other men started but didn't attack as Alex used his slow lanky steps to cross into the center of the room beside Kit.

"And don't be thinking to cause any more trouble, boys," he drawled. "You're much too easy to kill. Isn't that right, Paps Turner?" he said as he named the ringleader. "I believe this is yours." He pulled a knife out of his pocket and dropped it on the ground before him. "Oh and this." A purse followed that.

Papas gasped and felt in his pocket. "Bloody hell! That's me money!"

"And this is yours, Sam Heads." Alex dropped another knife and another purse. "Bull Smithee," he added. "Odd name that. I think you look more like a pug than a bull." Another purse hit the ground, and yet another man gasped and felt about his hips for his purse. "And we mustn't forget you, Tommy Peters." Another purse fell.

It was a bold move and one Kit couldn't help but admire. He'd forgotten how good Alex was as a pickpocket. But he could see that they had pushed the thugs to the edge of their endurance. Getting paid five pounds was one thing. Getting humiliated by a lanky, pale-faced young man was something else.

"Alex…" he began.

"Yes, sir."

Then the two spun around and ran.

CHAPTER 29

"Don't bring that in the carriage!" Maddy gasped as she hauled the heavy board out of Rose's hands.

"Oh! Yes!" the girl gasped as she dropped the thing. Then she spent some time wiping off her hands, while Maddy tugged on her elbow. "In the carriage, Rose. Get in—"

"Let's go!" bellowed Kit from where he was running toward the carriage. Alex was barely a step behind, his lanky stride easily covering the distance.

"In! In!" Maddy said, pushing Rose as the coachman also leaped onto his perch. The men scrambled in a breath later, slamming the door shut behind them. Alex was grinning as the carriage leaped forward.

"That was great fun!" Alex laughed as he dropped into his seat beside Rose.

Kit grimaced at the boy. "That was quite a risk you took. One slip and they would have had you."

"But I didn't slip."

Maddy shook her head. "What did you do? I didn't see you at all!"

"He picked their bloody pockets," growled Kit, but his expression was lightening. "How did you know their names?"

Alex grinned. "Talked to the guard of the warehouse on the other side. Nice man. Bored to death and curious about the screeching that was going on inside there." At that he canted a curious look at Rose, who realized that she now had everyone's attention.

"Oh, my love!" she cried as she tried to throw herself diagonally across the carriage into Kit's arms. "I was so afraid!"

He caught her easily and just as quickly threw her back into her seat. "Then you shouldn't go about hiring thugs to have yourself kidnapped."

Rose's eyes widened in horror, then her lip began to tremble. "Oh! How could you think such a thing?"

Maddy leaned forward, touching Rose's hand in the hopes of forestalling the full dramatic force of Rose's acting ability. "We know you did, sweetheart, and I think we know why." She took a breath. "Were you doing it for me?"

"What?" gasped Kit from the side. "She did it because she's a bloody—"

"Hush!" Maddy snapped, then she turned back to her cousin. "You did it so I would have someplace to live, didn't you? You wanted Kit to rescue you, fall madly in love, and then—after you married—I would be able to live with you and not on the street."

"I thought we'd go to Gretna Green," whispered Rose. Then she shot a hopeful glance at Kit. "You were quite dashing when came in. Very—"

"Stubble it, Rose!" he snapped, and Maddy gasped in shock as the full force of his fury descended onto the girl. "Listen well, Lady Rose, beauty or not, I do not love you. I will never love you, and I will never marry you!"

"Oh!" gasped Rose, her hand pressed hard to her mouth. The tears would begin soon, but Maddy could do nothing to stop that. And the girl really did need to hear it.

"In fact," continued Kit, "I'm not sure I can forgive you for doing this. Not only did you put yourself at risk, but Maddy as well. And that"—he shook his head, his words dropping into a low rumble—"that is unforgivable."

Across from him, Alex shifted uncomfortably. "Sir. She's just a silly child who made a mistake—"

"With armed criminals!" Kit nearly spat the words. Then he slammed his head backward against the squab and shut his eyes. It was clear he was trying to calm himself.

Maddy reached over, touching his arm gently. "Everyone is fine, Kit. You saved us all."

He rolled head toward her, his eyes opening, and inside them she saw such despair. "I didn't want you to see me like that."

"I saw a hero. I saw a man who saved my cousin from her own silliness." She didn't glance over at Rose, but she knew the girl heard.

"What if you had been hurt, angel? What if—"

"Hush!" she said, lifting her hand to his mouth. "Nothing will ever happen to me. You wouldn't let it."

He gripped her hand to his mouth, pressing his lips against it. Then he closed his eyes. When he spoke, his words came out as a harsh rasp against her fingers. She ended up feeling the words more than hearing them, but what she felt was so much more.

"I can't have you hurt, angel. I'd die."

"Don't be silly—"

His eyes shot open and he pulled her hand away from his mouth. "I'd die, angel. I love you that much."

She blinked, her eyes tearing. She never thought to hear those words from him. She never—

"Oh!" murmured Rose from the opposite side. "He loves *her*."

Maddy barely heard. Instead, she leaned forward to kiss him. He was there before she could move more than an inch. His mouth was swift and thorough. She opened willingly beneath his onslaught, and within moments she was meeting his fervor with a heat all her own. His hand slid to the back of her neck, and hers grasped his shirt. If Rose or Alex said anything, she did not hear it. But in time, Kit managed to provide some measure of control. He broke the kiss but did not slacken his hold. In fact, he tucked her closer into his arms, where she was quite willing to settle. And then, finally, she dared meet her cousin's wide eyes.

"You see, Rose," she said. "Last night—"

"Angel," Kit interrupted, "angel, wait."

She looked at him, her brows arched in surprise. She needed to make things clear to Rose, but he was fumbling in his jacket pocket, finally pulling out a jeweler's pouch.

"This is the real reason I was late this morning. I had to pick this up, and it wasn't done right. So I stood over the blasted man while he reset it." He opened the bag and poured out a ring into hand. It was a ruby ring, cut in the shape of a heart.

"Oh!" she gasped. "Oh!"

"I knew it would work," Rose said. "Danger and a rescue *always* works."

No one else said anything, least of all Maddy. She

could barely breathe, she was shaking so hard. So Kit gently pulled the ring from her palm and held it out before her.

"Please, angel, Madeline Wilson, will you please marry me? You already have me, heart and soul, no matter what you say. I understand if I'm too frightening. You have other options now, you know. A dowry. A place in society. But if you say yes, I swear I will spend every moment of every day trying to make you happy."

Maddy's heart was beating almost painfully in her throat. Her eyes were wet with tears and her entire body quivered. She reached out to touch his hand, and without even knowing it, she helped him slide the ring on her finger. It was beautiful there, a red heart on her left ring finger. But she didn't look at it. Instead, she looked in Kit's eyes and saw the truth of his words there.

He loved her. He wanted to marry her. She took a deep breath, feeling the honesty of what he said settle into her bones. It felt as true to her as anything ever had, and for the first time since her father died, she felt as if she had come home. She was loved, and she loved in return. This man was her home.

"Yes," she whispered. "Oh yes."

They were kissing again. And this time, she did hear Rose's cheers and Alex's clapping.

"I did it!" crowed Rose. "I found a place for Maddy to live. I knew I could do it!"

THE
REGENCY HEARTS REDEEMED
SERIES

Her Wicked Surrender
His Wicked Seduction

ALSO BY JADE LEE

<u>The Regency Rags to Riches Series</u>
No Place for a Lady
Devil's Bargain
Almost an Angel
The Dragon Earl

<u>A Lady's Lessons Series</u>
Rules for a Lady
Major Wyclyff's campaign
Miss Woodley's Kissing Experiment

Turn the page for an

excerpt from

No Place

for a

Lady

The Regency Rags to Riches Series
Book One

Jade Lee
USA Today Bestselling Author

London, England, February 1807

"'Ey, Fanny! 'Ow bout a diddle wi' me?"

Fantine Delarive winked as she swiveled her hips past a group of leering men, her smile friendly as she focused on the biggest of them all. "Ye ain't got enough t' diddle wi', Tommy boy. Talk t' me when ye grow a mite more."

She tweaked his cheek as she served him his ale. Then she passed on through the dingy pub, trading insults and affectionate pats with the customers.

They all knew her here, recognized her face, called her Fanny, but not a one knew the truth. They would never guess she had played maid to a princess or caught a French spy. They would never believe she could speak Spanish or cook a goose fit for the king. Nor would they credit that she planned to do such things again and again until she was too old to blow a kiss at an aged lord.

They would never believe what she had done, and she could never tell. So she teased the clientele like a two-bit tart, playing her role with consummate skill, because deep inside she did not truly credit it herself.

"Fanny!" called the keep, his gravelly voice carrying easily over the din. "'E wants ye. Tomorrow. Tea."

Fantine hitched her hip up to the edge of a bar stool, allowing a near-blind old man to feel the curve of her knee, but no more. "Tomorrow, tea," she echoed. "Guess I better put on me fancy togs. Not that I keep 'em on fer long!"

Then she laughed as loudly as the rest at her crude joke.

"Good morning, my lord. I trust you slept well."

Marcus Kane, Lord Chadwick, looked up, a single bite of egg poised precisely on his silver spoon. "Whom would you trust with such information, Bentley?" he asked dryly.

"Not even my sainted mother," the dough-faced man replied with a bland expression.

"Just so long as it is not *my* sainted mother," Marcus responded. "I trust that you have seen Paolina safely transferred from my bed to her own."

"Safely settled in, my lord."

A dozen possible responses came to mind, but Marcus washed them down with a sip of tea. His secretary would not understand a one of them, and so he did not waste his breath. Instead, he opened the morning paper knowing he could easily divide his attention between the news and Bentley's itemized list of the coming day.

He was wrong.

"I have canceled your appointment for tea with your sister, citing urgent matters with the Scottish estate."

Marcus's eye caught on a column detailing William Wilberforce's latest speech to the House of Commons, but at his secretary's news, he lifted his gaze.

"Do I have urgent matters at the Scottish estate?"

"No, my lord. But you do have an invitation to Lord

Penworthy's home. The tone appeared somewhat urgent."

Marcus arched his eyebrows. He had not spoken with Penworthy since Geoffrey's funeral nearly three years ago. They had, of course, corresponded over political matters and seen one another in the House of Lords, but this was something else entirely. To be invited to his former mentor's house, and so abruptly, indicated something of supreme import.

Marcus set his napkin aside and rose from his chair.

"Thank you, Bentley. I now recall why I pay you so exorbitantly."

NO PLACE FOR A LADY

available in print and ebook

A USA Today Bestseller, JADE LEE has been scripting love stories since she first picked up a set of paper dolls. Ball gowns and rakish lords caught her attention early (thank you Georgette Heyer), and her fascination with the Regency began. An author of more than 50 romance novels and winner of dozens of industry awards, she loves  writing unusual women who find the perfect man for them. And since they're all rakes and rogues, you know it's going to be hot! Look for Fifty Ways to Ruin a Rake available now.

And don't forget KATHY LYONS. She's Jade's lighter, contemporary half. Her newest hot love story is The Player Next Door. What happens when a basketball celebrity moves in next door to an academic with a unique decorating flair? Fun and games, that's what!

To find out all the latest news on Jade or Kathy, visit them on the web at

www.jadeleeauthor.com

www.kathylyons.com

www.facebook.com/JadeLeeBooks

www.twitter.com/JadeLeeAuthor